JANISHA BOSWELL

Janisha Boswell is an eighteen-year-old author who loves romance and sickly-sweet stories that make her feel welcomed and comforted. She was first published in a poetry anthology at just thirteen years old and has now expanded her capabilities into novel writing. Her first published novel, All the Stars and You, was self published in January 2023. Books hold a special place in her life, and they always will.

FAKE DATES

& ICE SKATES

BY JANISHA BOSWELL

This one is for my friends.
You can make anywhere feel like a home by simply
being around you.

WREN AND MILES SOUNDTRACK

Delicate...........Taylor Swift
Hell N Back.............Bakar
Everyone Adores You (quiet)..........Matt Maltese
Jump Then Fall (Taylor's Version).........Taylor Swift
Glitter......... BENNE
Sparks........Coldplay
Pink + White........Frank Ocean
Reckless Driving........ Lizzy McAlpine
Lost.......Frank Ocean
Sex on Fire.......Kings of Leon
Video Games.......Lana Del Rey
Gravity......John Mayer
Christmas Tree Farm......Taylor Swift
Cocktails for two.......Betty Carter
At Last.......Etta James
Movement.......Hozier
New Year's Day.........Taylor Swift
Save Your Tears........The Weeknd
This is me trying......Taylor Swift
So it Goes........Taylor Swift
You Should Know Where I'm Coming From........BANKS
When The Party's Over.........Billie Eilish
Gilded Lily......Cults
Flying........Cody Fry
The Feels.........Labrinth
We Are Young...........fun.
Glue Song (feat. Clairo)..........beabadoobee
Matilda.......Harry Styles
Ivy...... Frank Ocean
Golden Hour......JVKE
Lover - First Dance Remix.....Taylor Swift
Fine Line......Harry Styles
You Are in Love......Taylor Swift

CHAPTER 1
WREN

"**S**orry, could you repeat that?" I ask again in a small voice, hoping that pretending I can't hear them means that this isn't happening. This can't be happening, right?

When I was told I had a meeting with the dean and Coach Darcy, I thought maybe I was getting an award. A *well done for not losing your shit at your stupid ex-boyfriend / partner for fucking up your routine,* handed to me with an oversized trophy and a bouquet of flowers. "Oh, you shouldn't have," I'd respond coyly with a dashing smile. I would love to see that on a trophy. Or something along those lines. But no. Instead, I'm getting some really sucky news.

"Wren, that's the third time you've said that today. Are you okay?" Coach asks in her thick French accent. Her words almost fly right over my head. I can see sympathy taking over her expression as her deep-set brown eyes flicker with worry. She probably thinks I'm insane. Honestly, it feels like I'm slowly getting there.

"Yes, I'm fine. Just…adjusting," I reply, looking around the office at the ugly brown furniture that I have grown to loathe. I always get chills when I come in here. It has an unwelcoming ambience, and it is always too cold. Something unnerving lingers in the air as I try not to focus on it.

"You won't need to adjust to anything if you find a plan to work around this. It's just a misstep. That's all," Coach explains with a warm smile. I return the smile, but I can feel mine wobble.

The 'misstep' that she's referring to is the fact that I might not be able to skate anymore after our Winter Showcase in December. North University in Salt Lake City, comically located in the south, is famously known for its hockey team and figure skaters. Naturally, being a winter city, people gravitated towards our winter sports more than anything. We enter the championships every year like all the other colleges, but we also host seasonal events for the students and wider community. Although we have a rink each for the hockey and the skaters, people have taken much more of an interest in the hockey team than us.

We only have five skaters left on our team after most of them dropped skating to do a full major or just left all together. Last year, each competition and each event were met with enthusiasm from the students and the community but after Augustus and I got into the regional championships and lost horrifically, no one has batted an eye at us since. I was shunned and embarrassed, not ready to brave another competition or performance. The school run the events and the team purely on ticket prices and charitable donations since it's been loved for so many generations but if no one turns up then we're out of funds; meaning our rink can easily be handed over to the

13

hockey team. The other skaters have lost their passion and as much as I'd hate to admit it, I am too.

I double major with Creative Writing but dropping skating would mean admitting defeat to my mom, NU alma mater and previous figure skater, which is the *last* thing I can do.

"How are you expecting *me* to fix this? It shouldn't be my responsibility to keep the courses that you teach afloat," I snap, not sure how my tone climbed up so fiercely. I take in a deep breath, trying to regain my cool. I want to skate again, *not* get kicked out.

"It's a joint effort," the dean says.

I turn to look at her but her dense expression makes my stomach turn. Even when she looks defeated and angry, she still looks beautiful. Irritatingly so. Her bone structures are strong; telling stories that you want to hear so badly, constantly drawing people in. "We're doing everything we can on our end, you need to do the same. You will need to create some sort of buzz around it and people will start turning up again. It should be easy if you really care about skating."

That's just the thing. I don't.

Not as much as I used to.

My mom has loved figure skating her whole life because her mom forced her into it. After she got pregnant with Austin, she tried to get back into skating, but she was injured in a minor car accident and her knee has not been the same since. She was on the road to recovery just before I was born and threw that idea out of the window. Austin was supposed to skate too, but she never got used to dancing on the ice, so she has been training her whole life to be a professional ballet dancer. The next best thing. It has always been skating and nothing else. School was always seen as a secondary importance. "*Your ability to dance on ice is the best gift you could give to the world*," she would often say. I've never been given any opportunity to do anything else so it's always had to be skating.

I don't hate the way it feels on the ice. I love the adrenaline. The rush. But it's so easy to put up with it now instead of majoring in something I'm not sure I'm actually good at. That's the annoying thing about me — if I know I'm not perfect at it, I'm not going to try.

"Fine. I'll figure out some magical way to make everyone turn up to our performances," I say, sarcasm dripping my tone. Coach claps her hands, a large grin spreading across her heart-shaped face as she beams at me.

"I knew you'd figure it out," Coach replies, winking at me, matching my sarcasm. She hates these meetings as much as I do.

We had a feeling this would happen, but we'd hoped the dean would pull through at the last minute and change the way our program is run. I flash a smile to the dean before waltzing out the room with a headache and no clue what I'm going to do.

My headache intensifies when I see my two best friends rushing towards me from their seats in the waiting area. I look behind them to see a guy sitting next to where they were, his head springing up at their shrill voices. Judging by his jersey I can tell he's a hockey player. Strangely, I feel bad that he had to sit next to those two for the last twenty minutes who no doubt talked the entire time.

"Oh my God! What happened?" Kennedy exclaims the second our eyes connect.

She brings her long arms around me as her wild brown hair bounces off her shoulders. Scarlett, on the other hand, comes

15

next to my other side, her hands planted firmly at her sides, her silky black hair tucked neatly behind her ears. I know she's not going to embrace me as affectionally as Kennedy, but she gives me an encouraging smile. I wait until we're outside in the courtyard before speaking. I explain the situation to them which is naturally met with sighs of "What the fuck?" and "Shit."

"They can't do that. That's such bullshit!" Kennedy shouts, her arms still tight around my shoulder as if she's my emotional support animal. Scarlett doesn't say much but I can tell she's working over plans in her head.

This is how we work. How we've always worked since high school. I have the problems; Kennedy screams about it and throws out arbitrary solutions while Scarlett thinks of a plausible plan which we usually stick to. When I'm not the one with problems, I usually take a middle ground and try to centre the two different approaches they take.

"Well apparently they can," I mumble, kicking the crunchy leaves beneath me as we walk towards our apartment off campus.

Living together has given us the opportunity to get to know each other the way we didn't in school. Scarlett and I have known each other our entire lives as our parents have but Kennedy moved up from South Carolina in high school and we've been inseparable ever since. The second we set eyes on each other in English class, it was a cliché waiting to happen. The blonde, the raven, and the curly haired brunette. It just made sense. We just made sense. Other than our other best friend Gigi who has lived across from my childhood home my whole life, these girls have kept me sane over the past nineteen years.

Our majors are so different, but it only makes our dynamic stronger. Scarlett is a business and fashion major while Ken studies art and photography. We all knew we were going to NU as soon as Austin told us about all the hot guys that she met here while we were in high school. Still, being here over a year and we are yet to meet these hot guys.

"So, what are you going to do?" Scarlett asks, her voice calmer and more levelled than Kennedy's frantic one. Our walk slows as we get closer home, the chilly air urging us forward. We trudge up the steps to our floor since the elevator takes way to long.

"I've got no fucking clue. I'll start a petition or something," I say lazily, waving my hands vaguely in the air when we reach the top. Kennedy nods, her face becoming red as she smiles. She unlocks the door and I slip into it moving out of the way for Scarlett to pass but she doesn't move.

She stands in the doorway, arms planted by her side, her neat hair still a mess from the September breeze. Her eyebrows furrowed and her jaw clenched, she pins me with a strange look.

"What have you done to her?" Kennedy asks from behind me, her tone bored and used to her daily antics. Scarlett might be rational and insanely smart, but she is so dramatic sometimes.

"Nothing," I say, turning back to a puffy faced Kennedy as she removes her layers. "What's wrong, Scar?"

"You can't do a petition. I'm refusing to let you do that. Take it from the girl who wasted her whole final project last year on a petition which landed her a B. A fucking *B* for getting 18,000 signatures," Scarlett groans, finally starting to walk inside. I close the door behind her as we make walk further in, shutting out the cold.

17

'A B isn't bad, Scar," Kennedy says shrugging. I shoot her a look to shut it down, not having the mental capacity or emotional stability to get into the argument. Again.

Scarlett is the youngest and only daughter of three sons, so competition was always high in her household. She's constantly trying her hardest to prove she was as good as them. You wouldn't need to look at her twice to realise that she's smarter than all of them combined. I just wish she could get that in her head. She's confident around us until she's around her family and shrinks in their presence.

"It's bad for me," Scarlett retorts shuddering as she walks into the open living room and kitchen. "A B is like asking for ketchup but getting homemade mayonnaise instead. Both disgusting and disappointing *and* most likely will land you a few hours in the bathroom."

"That literally makes no sense," Kennedy concedes unconvinced. Scarlett and I take off our outside clothes and adjust to the warmth of the apartment. Autumn and winter here are hell but there is no better feeling than coming in from the cold. Once I'm free of my layers, I plunge down on the couch, defeated.

"I need to think of something, like, yesterday. If I can't skate, I can't do anything else," I sigh into the air as the girls walk around me, probably looking for food.

"Why don't you just do your creative writing course? Then you can actually get some feedback on the work you do outside of class. Instead of getting totally biased opinions from us and Gigi," Kennedy suggests, flopping on the beanbag across from me. She tucks her legs beneath her, a box of Cheerio's in her hand.

18

Her suggestion makes me feel sick. It does anytime anyone mentions dropping skating and actually having to do real schoolwork. The thought of being brave enough to do something I have always enjoyed but never really knowing if I was good at it makes my stomach turn.

Growing up, on my way to competitions or practice, I would always have a paperback in my hands, or I'd make up stories of my own. Creating a completely fictional and magical world while my parents went through their divorce was the best escape I could ask for. Their divorce was messier than their marriage, but I wasn't the only thirteen-year-old who had divorced parents. So, I spent the time that wasn't on the ice, nose deep in my own world. I've uploaded embarrassing stories onto Wattpad and other sites but even growing a little fandom, it has never felt like it would stick. I could snap out of inspiration at any moment and that dream could easily die That thought terrifies me. Whether I like it or not, I can always skate.

"Doing that would mean I would need to be a good writer. And that also means admitting defeat to my mother of all people," I say with a shiver.

"Oh shit, I forgot. How did she take the news or was she in on it too?" Kennedy bursts out. I shift uncomfortably in my seat, not really wanting to talk about her. My mom's 'encouragement' amounts to the same force of tiny rats pulling at my hair, forcing me into doing things I don't want to do.

"Well, the dean said that if I care enough about skating, I should be able to figure it out. But my mom said nothing, as always. She's probably on the deans' side," I say, knowing it'll get a reaction out of one of them.

"Ugh, Wren. You're so annoying. Why do you talk about them as if they're two separate people? It's confusing," Scarlett groans with a huff as she drops next to me on the couch. Bingo. I ignore her pouty face and look at Kennedy innocently.

In some ways, my mom has always been my own personal dean. Constantly on my case, pushing me and Austin to do better, giving me strict curfews and just breathing down my neck twenty-four seven. Since joining NU, there has been no difference other than now other students have to face her wrath as well. If it wasn't for the responsibility, I would gain by moving out, I'm sure she would have made me stay closer to home somehow. Seeing her at school almost every day is enough mom-ness for me.

"Ken, are *you* confused?" I ask condescendingly. She shakes her head, her mouth stuffed with Cheerio's. I turn back to Scarlett who has the expression of a miserable child. "See, it's only confusing you, my darling."

Scarlett sticks her tongue out at me as I throw my head back onto the headrest, trying to centre all of the thoughts that are whirling around my brain and tugging on my lungs. I focus on breathing properly as I take in deep breaths thinking about how the hell I'm going to fix this.

I must have dozed off because before I know it, Kennedy is wheeling in The Whiteboard into the living room, taking up nearly all of her short stature. The Whiteboard - always with a capital T and W - has been a saviour in times like these. Surprisingly, whiteboards are popular gifts for business students like Scarlett who, last Christmas, was gifted two mega whiteboards. Naturally, we decided that we could make use of one of them. Since then, we've used it for our iconic pros and cons lists for dates, breakups, changing shampoos or trying to find out a place to eat that isn't Nero's Pizzeria. No one has seen the contents of what we write on here as it's something so sacred to us. Some people think it's sweet but others thing it's completely insane. If we didn't have The Whiteboard our lives would have been derailed by now.

"Scarlett, would you take the honours of being our scribe?" Kennedy announces, holding out the oversized whiteboard pen as if it's the holy grail. Scarlett's face lights up, her green eyes squinting as her sharp cheekbones rise up.

"I would love nothing more," she replies, jumping up and retrieving the pen. "Operation 'Save Wren from dropping out of skating even though she secretly hates it' is underway."

I throw her a sarcastic smile, thinking twice before lobbing a cushion at her which she dodges.

"Maybe we should just paraphrase?" Kennedy suggests, unimpressed as she returns to her seat in the beanbag. Scarlett continues writing out the name on the whiteboard regardless.

"Or *maybe* we should just not assume how much I absolutely love skating all together," I counter, earning me unconvinced glances from the two of them.

I can tell it's going to be a long day and it's only four in the evening.

CHAPTER 2
MILES

"**S**orry, what? Could you say that again?" I ask the

dean, shaking my head to get my eyes to refocus from the brown walls in the office to her disappointed face.

Maybe taking shots before I came was not the best idea. I was convinced that I was about to get kicked out anyway so I thought one or ten wouldn't hurt. That's the same thing I've been telling myself for the last three months anyway and nothing bad has happened. Yet. I would rather be kicked out than hear whatever Dean Hackerly is saying right now.

"What is wrong with you kids today? Are there some intoxicating fumes radiating off the ice that's effecting your hearing? You are the fourth person today to ask me to repeat myself," the dean snaps.

Jesus. What's her problem? I heard once that if you don't know how to answer something, asking the person to repeat themselves is a good way to buy yourself some time. Judging on my first try of this so-called genius tip, I make a mental note not to do it again.

"Maybe you should talk louder," I whisper, not fully registering why. I know I shouldn't have said it when Coach Tucker glares from his seat next to me.

For reasons I can't explain, all I can do is stare at the photos dotted around the office. The muddy brown colour of the walls is sickly but the family pictures she has in her frames are doing weird things to my chest. Not in a Mommy Issues kind of way — well, sort of — but more in a curious way. There's one girl in nearly all her photos, around my age, blonde and fucking gorgeous. Everywhere I look I feel like her green eyes are following me. Drinking only makes me forgetful and terribly horny. I can only blame myself for that.

"Mr Tucker and I were saying that we think it's best for you to stay off the ice for a while." The deans voice brings me back to reality. This is probably the third time she has said it, but it still doesn't feel real. "We've noticed a slip in your grades and in your performance since…" She hesitates but the three people in this room know what she is about to say so she doesn't.

I don't know what I would do if I heard someone else say his name again, soaked with remorse. Yet, I can't tell which is worse — actually saying it or being too afraid to. I think I prefer the latter. I shift in my seat uncomfortably, my jersey suddenly feeling like it's suffocating me. I force myself to breathe but it only makes the gnawing feeling worse.

"I know. I said I would get back into it when we last spoke. I really am trying," I say, trying my best to explain myself which is only half a lie.

I did say I would work better on myself but the part of actually doing it hasn't been working out so well. I quit my job at Nero's so I could focus on school and hockey, but I've not done either of those things. It's easy to say you'll stop drinking

23

after having one more. Just one. It's also just as easy to delay and delay assignments that were due months before everything happened. I know it's sick to use the grief card but at times I feel like I can't get anything done without thinking of him. Even then, when the memories come back, everything else is discarded and I allow myself to cry and rage.

"Listen, Miles, we know you miss him. We all do, but you've had a few weeks off the ice and out of class. We hoped that you'd back into playing but it's been three weeks since the semester started and I've not seen you down at the rink once," Coach says, flashing me the same sympathetic grin everyone has been since it happened.

I don't protest because it's true. The last time I was on that rink, I had just finished playing one of my best games with my favourite people. Since then, I've not been fully *there* on the ice, constantly spacing out until I get put on the bench then I stopped going all together. The thought of going out there again, without him, felt like going to sleep knowing you will have a nightmare. Like knowingly bringing a knife to a gun fight.

I'm not going to put myself in that position, freak about and embarrass myself, because I could never show my face again. Instead, I've spent the better half of three months holed up in my bedroom with a mini fridge stocked with beer. I know it's pathetic and as Evan says, 'It's not cute anymore.' He's right but what else can I do? I'm sure that if I get back on the ice, my legs will become languid, and I'll have to crawl off.

"It's just hard, Coach. I am trying," I say again, a lot quieter and less ballsy than I started out.

"I know you are, Davis, but I need committed and healthy players on my team. When you're ready to come back, there will be a spot waiting for you."

"I understand." I try to keep my head up as high as I can.

I can do this right? An extended vacation is what this is. The guys would kill to have some more time off instead of battling it out in the rink. I'll spend a little more time drinking and *then* I'll get back to training and studying. As soon as I can get him out of my head. People do this all the time. They lose someone, grieve, and they get over it. Somehow.

My chair whines against the floor as I get up out of my seat, taking a last glance at the girl in the photo. Hackerly winces when the uncomfortable sound reaches her.

"Oh, and Miles, in the meantime please take up some extra studying and make sure you're attending all your classes. You can attend hockey practice if you would like but it is not mandatory. You will notice that you have plenty of time to spend on the other half of your course."

I smile through gritted teeth and nod, knowing it's better to hold my tongue. There go my plans.

*

I get home to a chaotic house, but I was expecting nothing less.

My housemates, Xavier and Evan could not be more opposite. I am too but I'm more accustomed to Xavier's lifestyle more than Evan's. In the way that Xavier enjoys hockey and is one of our best players on our team and that Evan despises hockey and would rather sit naked on a hot grill than hear us talk about it. Which is what he probably feels like every day in this house. Unfortunately for him, Evan transferred from Drayton a few weeks into the first semester last year and Carter, Xavier and I's bubble was burst after thinking we had the whole house to ourselves. Evan is only majoring in one subject which is Business and Fashion. According to his first rant of many when he got here, it is the most competitive course to get into at NU. What he failed to mention is that he probably used his daddy's money to get him in on such late notice. He had to stay with us because his parents are apparently teaching him a lesson about responsibility. Xavier and I were lucky enough to get in on a scholarship to play hockey but unlike Xavier, if I fail my classes and my scholarship is removed, I can't pay my way into staying on. It's hockey and four classes a week or nothing. It doesn't take me long to figure out that the loud noises are coming from them, most likely caught in another stupid argument.

"You can't put this disgusting cheese next to my shakes. It's vile," I hear Xavier yell as I cross the living room into the kitchen.

"Well, where am I supposed to put them with your boiled eggs in every square inch of the fridge!" Evan shouts back.

I suppress my laugh and make my presence known as I come into their view. As expected, Xavier is stood in nothing but his sweatpants with his dreadlocks falling crazily on his shoulders. Evan is casually wearing a suit and tie on a Friday night because he either has nothing to do or is on his way to one of his family's galas.

"Honeys, I'm home!" I announce and when Xavier's eyes meet mine his shoulders relax.

"Oh, thank God. I was about to strangle him," he grits out, making his way over to dap me up.

"Don't let me stop you," I mock. I gesture towards Evan, bowing down to him. "How are you your highness?"

He flips me off before brushing his hand through his blonde hair. If he thought the royalty jokes were over by now, he has another thing coming. He doesn't seem to fit into this house at all. He's always upstaging us with his glamours outfits for ridiculous occasions. I don't mind it, though. He's probably the reason why this house is still on all its legs.

"I'd be fucking perfect if you could tell him to stop putting eggs in the fridge," Evan groans, looking as if this argument has been going on for hours. Sometimes I can't tell if he's being sarcastic or not, but I think better than to question it.

"This might not be my house anymore, so I shouldn't be barking out orders," I reply, trying to make light of my situation as I pluck a beer from behind him. I slide off the cap and take a swig, letting the cooling sensation run through me.

"What do you mean? Is that why you were with Hacks?" Xavier asks. I hate that he was the one to shorten the deans name to that. He always shortens any word that comes out of his mouth. It's almost as if he can't bear to say words that are more than three syllables long.

"Yeah, apparently her and coach decided that I can't play until I'm doing better in my class and doing better overall," I sigh, leaning against the countertop.

"Shit. That sucks," Evan says, dipping crackers into his weird cheese. Xavier and I look at it at the same time and our eyes connect. I put my tongue in my cheek to force myself not to burst out laughing.

"Yeah, we can't lose our best player," Xavier adds. "I was gonna to ask if you wanted to go Ryan's party tonight but if you're bummed out, we can chill here. Which is kinda what we've been doing all summer."

I think about it for a minute. I could go and enjoy myself and stop thinking for once or sit at home and wallow in my own pity and think about him. I know which one will be more fun. And I need to have some sort of interaction with humans that aren't either eating strange cheese or topless before I start to lose my sanity.

CHAPTER 3
MILES

Apparently, Ryan Redmond's parties are yearly events.

According to Evan's 'inside sources' Ryan has been at NU for almost six years and no one really knows why. I bother to ask why more questions and brought a six pack of beers with me to his house. Evan stayed at home to study, which is what I should be doing. One last night out won't hurt. Will it?

Parties like these are where I've been wasting away my nights drinking cheap beer until I can't see straight. There's something so strangely comforting about intoxicated and happy strangers. It makes this whole 'moving on' thing feel less daunting.

I take the beers I brought into the kitchen and grab myself a cold one out of the fridge, trying to get away from the music for a second. I take a long gulp too quickly that I start coughing over the sink. I gasp and splutter as I try to breathe normally again. A soft hand comes to my back, and I shiver at the contact, still finding a way to catch my breath.

"Woah there. Take it easy," the calming voice says from behind me.

I turn and I see her.

The same girl from the photo's blinks up at me. The same blurry face I saw coming out of the dean's office earlier today. And, now in the dimmed lighting, I'm reminded of the hallways between the skating rinks. If my memory isn't that foggy, she's probably the same figure I see passing through the rinks; always practicing until late and getting shouted at a tall skinny dude who's probably her coach. I rack my brain around, but I can't remember what her name is, but she must be Hacks' daughter.

The resemblance between her and the girl in the photo is uncanny. The same blonde that had me mess up one of my games because I was stood watching her for a little too long. Just from watching the way she moved on the ice, she effortlessly trapped me in a trance. I try to swallow as I take her in. She's still a little blurry but I can make out her satin black dress which she must be freezing in, and her hair tied in a large clip behind her head. She throws me a puzzled look, but I don't have the energy to stop staring.

I take my time to memorise the curve of her neck and collarbones before she reaches around me. What? When did she get this close? How long have I been staring? Her face is so close to mine that her vanilla perfume hypnotises me. I don't move as I drink in her fresh smell of soap and lavender. She laughs quietly and the sound is so heavenly I restrain myself from drinking her in even more.

"Sorry. I'm just looking for some water," she says with a nervous chuckle. I snap out of my trance and realise I'm blocking the fridge. I move out of the way and watch as her delicate arms reach for a bottle.

"You're the dean's daughter, right?" I ask, clearing my throat. She freezes, pushing a strand of hair out of her face before flashing a shy smile and coming to face me.

"That's me," she replies with a bored expression. I can tell she doesn't really want to speak to me but that makes me want to talk to her more. I'm not sure why but I hold out my hand. "Miles Davis," I say. She hesitates before slipping her gentle hands into mine. Small electric shocks travel up from where our hands meet to my brain.

"Wren." She pulls back her hand, gripping onto the bottle. She stands gingerly next to the counter, just out of reach. I don't know what to do with my hands, so I fold them across my chest.

"I saw you outside her office today, right?" I ask. She hums in response, opening the bottle and taking a sip. "What did you do to land a meeting with her?"

I can tell she doesn't want to answer my question. She backs up further to the counter, mirroring my position with her arms across her chest, unbeknownst to her, slightly pushing her boobs up. I keep my eyes focused on her eyes; green and brown swirled within them.

"I've had a pretty shitty day and my friends were supposed to help me fix it. Instead, I'm here, so excuse me if I don't want to talk about it," Wren explains, sighing. Her voice is silky and relaxed. Almost tired but fierce. Less strained than I thought it would be. Is it bad that I could listen to her talk forever?

"Does your shitty day have anything to do with your meeting with the dean?" I press, wanting to know more. Something in me can't tear my focus away from her. I need to find some way to keep her talking to me. She lets out a small laugh, shaking her head. The sound reverberates through me, instantly sending goosebumps across my arms.

"Do you always ask strangers this many questions?" Wren retorts, pushing off the counter, her stance defensive. Her face searches mine for something but when she comes to nothing, her shoulders drop.

"Just the ones I'm curious about," I drawl, and I swear I catch her rolling her eyes. "Besides, we're not strangers if we know each other's names. If you tell me about your bad day, I'll tell you about mine. Deal?"

She rolls her eyes again but this time it's followed by a small smile.

"I'm sure you saw what happened with the regional figure skating championship." I shake my head. "Well, to spare the details, it was awful. Augustus dropped me and broke up with me in the same breath. We were disqualified obviously, but since then no one has paid any attention to the other events we've held, and the team will be cut if we don't drum up support for it by the Winter Showcase in December."

Jesus. I only heard whispers about what happen at regionals, but I never knew it was that bad. Maybe it's because I didn't really care. The hockey team never interact much with the skaters because they're so uptight from training so hard and don't take any shit from anyone. We try and steer clear unless absolutely necessary.

"That is pretty shitty," I say, taking a swig of my beer.

"Yep," she says, popping the 'p.' The way her full lips move around her words does something to me and I have to clear my throat. She catches me staring and narrows her eyes, her cheeks turning a light pink. "Your turn."

I take in a breath. I put the rest of the beer down the sink because for once, I didn't want to forget this night. "You know what happened to Carter Reyes, don't you?"

Her face changes. Something in her smooths out, relaxes, but I can see the sympathy in her eyes. "Yeah, I do. And I'm so sorry. I can't imagine..." She trails off and shakes her head lightly.

I nod in appreciation. "I found out something my family had been hiding from me and then just after that Carter got into his accident, and I went down this really dark path. I guess I'm still on it. I don't know. Anyway, coach said I can't play until I'm looking better and doing better in my grades which is really fucking hard to do without the motivation."

What I don't mention is how my mom had been cheating on my dad for half of my life and everyone knew, and no one wanted to tell me. My sister, Clara, who I thought I was close with had been hiding it from me the whole time. I don't mention that it's my fault that Carter was driving so late after I called him, a drunk mess, to pick me up. If I didn't think my problems could be solved by a drink, Carter would not have gone on the road that night and he would not have been hit. He would still be here. I know he's disappointed in me. Of course, he is. I didn't lie when I told Coach Tucker I was trying. I am. Every time I think I'll get back on the ice, I can't do it. He should be here, playing alongside me. In some ways, I suppose he is.

"Well, look at us. Two rising stars, slowly falling down," I say with a flourish, trying to lighten the mood. Wren grimaces, her arms hugging her middle.

"How do you know I'm a rising star? You've never seen me preform. I could be really fucking terrible," she laughs, downing the last of her water. I cock my eyebrow and tilt my head.

"You wouldn't be so worked up about it if you were bad. Plus, I've seen you skate before. I hope it was you anyway or else I have some explaining to do to a poor girl on your team," I say, trying to piece together the images of the skater I usually see and her.

"And what did you think?" she asks, suddenly guarded, afraid that I'll tell her that she isn't any good.

"Are there any other blondes on your team?"

She shakes her head, pulling her lip between her teeth. I can feel my dick twitch at the motion. "Why?"

Suddenly feeling ballsy, I lean into her, my lips mere inches from her ear. "So, then I know it was you that completely mesmerised me. Over and over again."

Her breath hitches and I pull away. I watch as she swallows, not sure what to make of my comment. I don't say anything else. We stand there, neither of us speaking, listening to the music blasting from the stereos around us.

"I should probably get back to my friends," she murmurs after a while, searching aimlessly around the crowded house. I don't want her to leave. Not yet. I know we're not even talking but I enjoy her presence. I feel like a moth and she's the flame.

I reach out my hand and grip hers before she walks away. She turns back to face me, her eyes travelling to our hands and then to my face. She jerks her hand away with a puzzled look.

"I have an idea," I announce, my hand suddenly feeling empty. She folds her arms across her chest. "Why don't we help each other out? You need to get people to see your performance and I need to get back on the ice. I don't know if you know this but

34

I'm pretty popular and if I show interest in your little performances, people might start showing up."

She laughs at my idea. Like, a full shoulder shaking, tears springing to her eyes, kind of laugh. I would be offended if I didn't like the way it sounded so much. The way her head tilts back, giving me a perfect view of her throat. The way her voice rasps when she's come down from the high.

"I don't really know you and I don't particularly like you either. Why would we do that?" she asks when she catches her breath.

"Ouch," I say, clutching my heart dramatically. I already knew that, but I thought we were getting somewhere. Apparently not. "Wait, how can you say you don't like me if you don't know me."

"I know of you, and I know people like you."

"Oh, so you're saying that you know people like me, but you don't?" I play on her words on purpose because I don't hate the way she looks at me like she wants to strangle me. It only makes this more fun.

"What? You're not making any sense." She sighs, closing her eyes for a second. "Look, all I'm trying to say is I'm not your biggest cheerleader. Not every girl that you meet is going to drop down on their knees for you if you whisper sweet nothings into their ear."

"Is that what you think I'm doing? Whispering sweet nothings into your ear?"

She laughs incredulously. "No, I think your trying to get yourself laid and it's not working."

I can't understand how she can see through me so well or am I really just that transparent? It's probably written all over my face that I want to touch her again. In any way. Anywhere. And

35

I don't even know why other than this tight magnetic force drawing me to her.

"Right. I thought that girls had the whole 'don't judge a book by its cover' thing written in the first page of their journal."

"Well, you thought wrong," she relays, throwing her water bottle in the trash. "I should really go and find my friends."

This time I let her leave and watch her as she walks over to two dark haired girls who embrace her as if they haven't seen each other in years. I'm still watching when I feel Xavier stand beside me. I can't figure out why I am so drawn to her. How easy it was to talk about why I'm struggling. Her pretending like she hates me is the hottest thing I've ever seen. Watching her try to fight it was the best part of our conversation. Xavier holds a beer to offer me, but I shake my head.

"Were you just talking to Wren Hackerly?" he asks, taking a long gulp.

"Yeah. Well, I think so?" I reply, only half paying attention as I try to keep my eyes on her in the crowd.

"What do you mean you think?" he asks, nudging me with his shoulder.

"I don't think she likes me, dude. Like, even as a human," I say, trying to fight off a smile. I smother it with my hand and pretend to cough. If Xavier gets a whiff of this, he's never going to let me live it down.

"Don't take it personally. I don't think she likes anyone other than those girls she hangs out with. She's pretty hard core," Xavier explains with ease.

"What do you mean? And how do you know?" I quiz, taking my eyes off her to meet his. He holds his hands up in fake surrender.

"Chill. It's just the gossip I hear from Michelle." He and Michelle have been dating for forever. Since one infamous food fight in high school and some heroic tray shielding, Michelle has not left his side. "Anyway, you know what happened last semester with that Augustus guy?"

I shrug in response.

"Right. Well. She dated him since high school and at regionals he completely ruined their routine, supposedly on purpose, and broke up with her on the ice. If someone fucked up my gameplay, I don't think I'd be that nice. I guess everyone's frightened that she's just gonna go ham on him one day without warning."

I conjure up a picture of Augustus in my head and I instantly hate him. He must have been the tall foreign guy who I always saw shouting at her from across the ice. I always thought he was her personal coach or something.

"Oh yeah, I think she was just telling me about that. I don't think I was fully there. She's, like, fucking mesmerising," I sigh, ignoring every flag that is going off in my brain.

"No, no, no. You can't do that. Not now," Xavier shouts, coming right in front of me, blocking her from my view. I take in his dark expression, his brown eyes pinning me.

"Do what?"

"This," he says, wafting his hand across my face. "Using big words that you don't even use in your essays. You can't go following her around like a lost puppy. You can't get attached. I need you back on the team. We can't have you on the bench all season."

"I don't get attached," I mumble. He laughs again. Louder. As if I just told him the funniest joke ever.

"Yes, you do. If Emily didn't go to Drayton, you would have been attached the hip. If you weren't playing, you were either with her or talking about her."

I don't retort. What could I say to that with how true it is.

Emily Fraser and I met through Carter a few years ago but we never spoke at first. Carter had met her on a holiday in Florida and I was not prepared to do the long-distance thing. He always pushed me to date her but there was always something in the way. When we started at NU, she started at Drayton, only a twenty-minute drive away. We made it work for a few months but there was something still missing that I couldn't place. Before everything happened with my mom and with Carter, we called it quits.

"Fine, I'm not going to argue with that but it's not going to happen. I barely know her. If I'm not playing anymore, I won't see her at the rink," I say, mostly trying to convince myself.

He downs the rest of his beer, flashing me a sceptical look over his glass. "Women are fucking crazy. The second you say shit like that, they end up everywhere. It's, like, manifestation or some shit. I thought the same thing would happen with Michelle but here we are. Don't say I didn't warn you, dude."

CHAPTER 4
WREN

After a week of barely seeing each other, other than a disgruntled grunt in the morning, Scarlett, Kennedy, and I are finally sat watching a movie together. I lock my phone after ordering a pizza from Nero's when the title credits of 'Matilda' flash across the flatscreen. Kennedy pauses the TV and turns around from her seat at the floor, just beneath Scarlett and me. She whips her curly hair into a bun before pointing at the both of us with an accusatory expression.

"Two updates. Go!" she shouts. I give Scarlett a concerned glance and she shakes her head with a laugh.

Our first semester at NU was complete bliss. All of our schedules somehow matched perfectly, and we were able to meet up all the time outside the apartment instead of just in the morning or at night. Unfortunately, there was a miscalculation with mine and Kennedy's schedule so by the second semester we were a mess.

We managed to salvage a steady routine and when we finally had time for the three of us, Ken suggested that we each give three updates on our treacherous lives apart to fill each other in. As workloads piled up, the three updates quickly became two; avoiding having to say the same thing twice.

"Okay, I'll go first," Scarlett starts. We turn to look at her and she's only half smiling, always trying to avoid being either too serious or too immature. "One, I no longer have a UTI and two, I finally beat Evan in the class Kahoot."

We all burst out laughing at the absurdity. "Two, very disconnected but still clap-worthy updates. I wish we could do Kahoot's in art. It's sooo boring," Kennedy says, rolling her eyes.

"What about you, Ken Doll?" Scarlett says with an evil smirk, reaching next to her to pick out all the purple candies out of the jar.

"You know that nickname will never stick, right?" Kennedy frowns.

"I'll make it stick. Don't worry," Scarlett says, hauntingly. Ken throws a weak punch into her arm before clearing her throat. "Okay, so, my updates are...I finished our portraits but before you can ask, no you can't see them until I think they're ready," Kennedy exclaims. She has been working on and off for our group portraits, but she keeps saying she's getting close to finishing it and then completely scrapping the painting. I think I've posed for more photos for Kennedy than I have for myself.

"Which isn't going to be for another year," I whisper under my breath. Scarlett hears me and snickers before thinking.

"I heard that, you impatient bitch. True art takes time," Kennedy states proudly. "And second update is I finished the new season of The Crown."

"What? Oh my God! Without me?" Scarlett exclaims, throwing a pillow in her direction.

"I had to! You take, like, a gazillion bathroom breaks whenever we watch anything."

"You're the one that stopped Matilda. You can't spoil it for me now," Scarlett says.

"I *can't* spoil it. It's literally history, just pick up a book," Kennedy retorts, rolling her eyes. She turns to me, her expression calming down from their short-lived argument. "What about you, Wren? You've been awfully quiet."

"I'm just thinking about my updates. Nothing exciting has happened," I sigh.

As soon as the words leave my mouth, heat begins creeping up my cheeks without permission. The second I have time to think about what has happened in the last week I'm reminded of two things: having my meeting with Coach and his face. Miles' dumb, stupid, ridiculously gorgeous face. He's managed to get his way into my head with his confusing conversations and typical hockey guy personality. Just thinking about the way, he leaned into me at the party, his hot breath on my neck is enough to send shivers down my spine.

But it shouldn't. Because the last thing I want is to be one of his Puck Bunnies.

"Oh my God, spill it. Right now," Kennedy demands, her eyes searching mine.

"Spill what?" I say, reaching my arm behind her to shove whatever food I can find into my mouth to stop me from talking.

"Whatever you're thinking, it's about a boy. I can tell," Kennedy says, wiggling a finger in my face. She has loved doing that for as long as I can remember but I don't know why. Even when I know she's talking to me, she loves to point at me for extra emphasis.

41

"How can you tell?" I get out around a mouthful of pistachios.

"Because your face is red as a tomato right now," Scarlett says.

"This is a judgment free zone. Speak your mind, baby."

I stifle my laugh and take in a deep breath. "Fine. Update one is that I finished a new chapter of Stolen Kingdom."

Kennedy gasps and Scarlett's eyes widen with excitement. "Oh my God," they both scream at the same time.

"See I knew it wasn't about a guy!" Kennedy says, completely contradicting her last comment. Scarlett shakes her head fiercely.

"No, you didn't. And you didn't let her finish," Scarlett explains. "But we need to return back to that. I have been dying to know what happens next."

I started writing Stolen Kingdom, a fantasy series, when I was sixteen. It follows a young princess, Carmen, who finds out her whole life is a lie, and she is not actually the real heir to the throne. She is sent anonymous messages and is stalked around her small kingdom in Estonia, and she is on a quest to find out who knows her real identity and what they're going to do about it. It falls into many different categories and the plot takes ridiculous turns, but Scarlett and Kennedy have managed to keep up thus far. They are the only people I trust to read anything I write outside of class.

"You guys know Miles Davis, don't you?" I ask, not fully meeting either of their eyes.

"Of course. He was friends with Jake and he's Evan's housemate. He never shuts up about how annoying he is. Always hockey this and hockey that," Scarlett mocks.

"It's interesting how you hate Evan so much, yet this is the second time he's made an appearance in today's conversation," Kennedy teases.

42

Evan is two things: filthy rich and blonde. He is a gorgeous man, and no one could deny that, but his personality makes all of us cringe. Scarlett most of all. They're in the same class and since he joined NU, later than everyone else, he has been trying to upstage Scarlett. It's been constant competition between them since day one. Constantly battling for the better grade or the best answers. Scarlett is not afraid of any competition but there is something about Evan that makes her skin crawl.

I look over to a red-faced Scarlett, her expression lying somewhere between a blush and pure anger. "You're getting us off topic," Scarlett hisses at her. She turns back to me, smiling. "Continue."

"We were kind of talking at the party. He is really annoying but in a way that's kind of endearing. Anyway, it turns out he's in a shit situation too. I didn't pay much attention to it last year, being so caught up with Augustus drama, but he was really close with Carter Reyes. He's been drinking and wallowing in self-pity for so long his grades have slipped and he's been benched. Judging on the fact that I could have lit his mouth on fire at the party, I don't think he's going to be getting on the ice anytime soon," I ramble.

A weird sensation washes over me.

I feel for him, I do, but there is a part of me that thinks that steering clear from him is the best thing to do. He's jeopardising his future by drinking and doing anything but practicing. I need to focus on getting my life back on track, not trying to fix the hockey boy who's too far in take anything seriously. If he wanted to play, if he really wanted to make Carter proud in some way, he's doing it the wrong way.

"Jesus, that's awful," Kennedy mumbles, her brown eyes wide with concern.

"I know but the weirdest part is that he suggested that I help him get back on track and he'll magically get people interested in me again. It sounded so ridiculous it reminded me of you guys," I laugh.

They're both quiet for a minute, taking it in until Kennedy's face literally lights up. She jumps up out of her place on the floor.

"No, no, nope," I say before she can even say anything. I straighten and throw a finger in her face and say again, "No."

"Yep," Kennedy replies grinning wide.

"You can't possibly agree with him. I feel bad for him but he's a jerk. All hockey players are," I plead.

"That is very true," Scarlett agrees, nodding.

Austin has told me that for many years, this school has always put hockey guys on a pedestal. They do it at every school ever, but here especially. They're royalty. Always thinking they are better than everybody else. Not just at their sport but in everything. They think it's so easy to get girls to sleep with them just because they were a jersey. Even the basketball, soccer and football players aren't like that. Maybe if Salt Lake wasn't such a wintry place to live, they wouldn't feel like it's their duty to be the only thing people talk about. Austin and Scarlett have had their fair share of horrible dates with hockey players and have encouraged Ken and I to avoid them at all costs. The problem is they're hot and they know they're hot and that everybody wants them.

"But he's not just any guy though. Everyone knows he's the best player they have and he's clearly vulnerable enough to ask you for help. You could help him retrain with all the insane cardio that you do and then he can use his pretty boy powers to help you regain your social status *and* your skating privileges.

It's a genius plan," Kennedy more plans out than suggests. I hate that whenever she says ridiculous things, they just make sense. It's her superpower. With the grin on her face, she knows it too.

"In this completely hypothetical situation, how exactly would that work? The last thing I need right now is a project to try and fix," I warn.

"From a completely hypothetical and third-party perspective, wouldn't it help if you pretended to date? Like, put on a whole show about it. People will be interested in you again instead of feeling sorry for you both," Scarlett says quietly. I turn and glare at her.

"Yes! Oh my God, Scarlett. Why didn't I think of that? Fake dating. It's the best trope. It's perfect," Kennedy sighs like the little evil genius she is.

"No. Definitely not. He's probably a dick like all the other guys on his team," I say.

"Is he a dick or does he just have one?" Kennedy jokes, her eyebrows shooting up and down. I roll my eyes at her remark and turn to Scarlett.

"How are you of all people going to encourage this when you know what happened with Jake?" I say, ignoring Kennedy's comment.

"Jake is an asshole but Miles, surprisingly, isn't. He was the only one I could tolerate at any of their after-game parties. You need something to spicez up your dating life. You've dated like two guys in the whole time we've know each other. Augustus was more like your coach than an actual boyfriend so, he doesn't count," Scarlett admits, shrugging.

I hate how right she is. Augustus (never to be called 'Gus') Holden more or less scouted me in high school. We met at the rink one day and he said he saw something in me. At first it was purely a partnership and then we started getting more serious and I looked at him in a different way. He started to look more like someone I could see myself with romantically. Then things got really ugly, really quickly.

"Scar, Miles is so infuriating. And distracting. He's like a lost puppy," I say, my mind wandering back to that night. I would be stupid if I said I didn't find him attractive but I'm not going to admit that to him. How could I say that his gorgeous brown locks, wicked smile, and dark green eyes drew me in so fast? It was hypnotising. Not in a good way.

"You will never fully know if you don't find out. He can't be so bad if he asked you for help," Kennedy suggests. I take in the silence for a few beats, thinking it over. Why are they suddenly so interested in giving him a chance? We would never look twice at guys like him.

"Wren, I'm just going to say what everyone is thinking. You don't have the guts to just drop skating," Scarlett says, her tone even and steady but her words still feel like daggers.

"Scarlett! What the fuck? You can't say that," Kennedy shouts, staring between us worriedly. I slip back further into the couch, ready for it to swallow me whole.

"What? Am I wrong?" Scarlett asks me, looking into me with her green eyes.

"No, you're right. I don't have the guts. I would get too overwhelmed and drop out all together in weeks. Plus, I don't think my writing is good enough yet," I say truthfully, pushing away my hair from my face.

"I think this might be your only option right now, Wren," Scarlett suggests, her voice quiet and almost motherly. I think it over, letting myself fall into the fantasy of it only for a second.

"Do I really have to date him?" I groan. The thought is both exhilarating at the thrill of something new but also irritating to have to engage in frequent conversations with him.

"*Fake* date him," Kennedy corrects. "And yes. You do. No one will care if he posts you a few times on his Insta."

I nod and take in the idea. This could work. I could have a full house at the Winter Showcase, and he might be able to get back in the rink. It would be a win-win. This could also be a stupid idea and we could end up making our lives worse than they already are.

"The next time you see him, get his number, and see if he's still up for it. You don't have to ask him right away, but he was technically the one who suggested it first," Scarlett mentions.

"Fine. Okay," I sigh, giving in.

The doorbell rings and I jump up to get the pizza we ordered. I grab some paper plates from the kitchen and bring it into the living room. We each take our share of slices of pepperoni and margarita and stare up at the screen from our various positions around our small living room. We mostly eat in silence while the movie plays.

"Can we circle back to the new chapter of Stolen Kingdom? I need to hear what happens to Carmen and Marcus right now," Scarlett says when she returns from throwing away our garbage.

Since I started writing this series, we have made it a tradition that every new chapter I write, I have to read it out to them out loud. Almost as if it's our own private book club. This way, I get pestered into writing more and they get the suspense of having to wait. Between chapters, I don't give them any clues as to what's coming next until we're all huddled up on the couch. At first, reading out loud made me feel stupid but they

47

enjoy when I enunciate the voices. It also helps me fill in anything that's missing when I get to read aloud.

We sit now on the floor of the living room on top of our blankets. Instinctively, Kennedy rests her head in my lap, her frizzy hair tickling my thighs. Scarlett lays across from us, her head propped up in her hands. I pull out my laptop and start reading.

We're halfway through the chapter before Kennedy insists on taking a stress-induced bathroom break. At the same time she leaves, and Scarlett goes to raid the fridge, my phone lights up with a message from one of my favourite people: Gianna (Gigi) Kowalski.

Since we left high school, Gigi has been working from home as a self-published author of a semi-famous fantasy series called The Last Tear. Gigi hated high school and middle school and, like me with Stolen Kingdom, she was able to use writing as an escape. Except she has actually made it big with her series by being brave enough.

Gigi: Hi Emmy. I have an update on TLT. Are you free?
Me: OMG
Me: I'm with Ken and Scar right now and they're freaking out over my last chapter, but I'll call u later
Gigi: That's okay. Just let me know before you call. Mr Dixie is feeling catty today. Also, they have a right to freak out, it was an insane plot twist.
Me: Iconically casual pun. Is he okay?
Gigi: It's just cat stuff. You know how he gets without his medication.
Me: Oohh, okay. Just like how you get without yours.
Gigi: Only I can make jokes like that, Emmy.

48

Me: I'm sorry but I can tell ur laughing behind the screen.

Gigi: I did laugh, you're right. Call me later.

I lock my phone and the girls both come into the room, returning to their previous positions. Scarlett offers me some of my chips, but I shake my head, straightening the laptop on the couch next to me.

"Why are you smiling like that?" Kennedy asks with an amused expression, blinking up from me in my lap. All I have to say is 'Gigi' and they both laugh and sigh at the same time. "What's the update?"

"Not much. I'm going to call her later to talk about The Last Tear," I reply. "Mr D is sick again."

"I think he's constantly poisoning himself so he can get out of her house," Scarlett says matter-of-factly. "He's been sick too many times for it to be a coincidence."

"I agree. When I went for lunch with her last weekend, she told me that he ran away. Again," Kennedy muses.

We all have very different relationships with Gigi but that's why she's such a special friend for us. Even though we've known each other our whole lives, whenever we had petty arguments, Gigi was always the one who kept us together. She always pulled us back to each other. If I could find some way to pull away all of her anxieties and get her to live with us, I would do it in a heartbeat. I know how comfortable she is at home and those anxieties are what make Gigi, Gigi.

"Whatever. Whether Mr. Dixie is an undercover spy or not, Gigi loves him with her whole being. It's not hard being a writer and a cat-mom," I say defensively.

"I can't disagree with that," Scarlett nods. She points to the laptop like an eager child. "Read. Now."

49

CHAPTER 5
MILES

I can't figure out how I ended up here and why I can't move away. I was wondering around, trying to find something to do with myself after finishing class. I know I should probably go home and study but as soon as I heard her skates on the ice and the frustrated grunts coming from the rink, I couldn't look away. Not now. I've fallen too deep.

I stand, completely and utterly captivated, watching her glide and turn. She speeds up her pace, does a fancy spin and then comes down hard on the ice, grunting and curling her hands into little fists. Why does it turn me on when she's angry? She skates towards the end of the rink, holding onto the sides, taking a deep breath before continuing the same routine I've seen her do over three times.

I think back to what Xavier said the other night when Wren and I first spoke. As much as I hate to admit it, he was right. I've seen her around more often than usual, over the past week. I've been dying to speak to her again but each time she's around she's either with those two girls or she doesn't notice me all together. The fact that she's cold and dismissive only makes me want her more. Something about seeing her here now feels more intimate. Watching somebody dance like this is like peeling back layers of them. Exposing them.

"How long have you been standing there, you weirdo?" she asks, still mid spin. I walk out of my not so hidden hiding place and come into view. I move to the edge of the rink, leaning my forearms on the railing.

"How could you tell it was me?" I ask, amused. She continues gliding and turning, not looking at me completely.

"Even when I'm spinning, I can still see, you know." Her voice is strong even though she has been working without a break for what seems like hours. "What are you doing here?"

"I don't know," I admit.

She stops her routine abruptly and drifts towards me in her tight pink leotard. She stops right in front of me, her arms across her chest, her cheeks red and puffy, breathing heavily. Just by looking at her my heartbeat triples in pace. Fuck.

"How come you keep showing up everywhere the second my life turns to shit?" Wren asks without missing a beat.

"I was thinking the same thing about you." I grin. She scoffs, rolling her eyes. If I had no self-control, I would've jumped over the railing that's separating us, taking her in my arms. I just want to be close to her in any way. Luckily for the both of us, I have more composure than that, so I lie. "I've got to go to practice."

She cocks her head to the side. "There isn't a practice on today."

"I didn't know you knew my schedule, Wren. If I didn't know any better, I'd think you're starting to like me," I tease, loving the way her face turns red.

51

"The last thing that should be on your mind is me liking you," she retorts, taking out her hair from its bun. She lets it fall before quickly gathering it up again into a looser one. Fuck me, she's beautiful.

"Right, what should be on my mind then?" I tilt my head to the side.

"I don't know. Maybe start my doing something that doesn't make you stink of beer. Why would come here when you've been drinking? It's like you don't even care about playing again," she snaps. Her tone shocks me.

I've only had maybe three drinks to psych myself up to go into class today. I told myself I wasn't going to have any more for the rest of the day, and I intend on keeping that promise. I kind of like that she cares even when she's acting like she doesn't.

"Well, I'm not playing so there's no reason for me *not* to drink. I'll be fine," I say, waving my hands around vaguely. She drops her arms from her chest, rolling her eyes.

"And you think you'll be able to play quicker if you drink more?"

"Why do you care? I didn't come here for a lecture. If I wanted one, I would've stayed at home."

"Then why are you really here?" she challenges. I wait a beat, not meeting her eyes.

"I just finished class and I could hear you in here, so I thought I'd say hi." I tell the truth this time because I know she will see right through me. She lets out a disbelieving "huh," mostly saying it to herself but I catch it anyway. "What?"

She looks at me, her brown-green eyes boring into me.

"Nothing," she says, shaking her head slightly. I wait, giving her and unconvinced glance, knowing there's more she isn't saying. "This isn't related at all, but can I have your number?"

52

There it is. I knew this was all an act. The one where she plays hard to get. She cold and fierce and harsh but it only makes me more drawn to her. I want to know every thought inside her brain. Why she is the way she is. How she can look through me so easily. I've never met anyone so defiant as her and it just turns me on.

"It's not for me. Well...it is. My friends would kill me if I didn't get it," she rambles, rolling her eyes as she talks with her hands. It's a cute look compared to the death stare she gave me earlier.

"Right, okay," I reply with a funny look, pulling out my phone. "So, which one of your friends is it that want you to get my number so badly? I bet it's Scarlett. She used to date one of my teammates, you know."

Her pink lips fight off a smile when she looks up at me.

"Oh, I know." She laughs softly as if there's a hidden joke that I'm missing. The airdrop notification sounds, showing that she's received the screenshot of my number. "I can assure you that it's not. Thank you, though."

I watch her look at me for what feels like the first time. Like, really look at me. The fluorescent lights make her eyes look completely green and her red cheeks have still not died down. I watch her take a sweep of my face; starting with my brown hair which has grown longer than I'm used to, to the space between my eyes, and then to my lips where she hovers for a beat too long. I lean back off the barrier, putting some space between us as I clear my throat.

"Use it whenever you like. You're a fun one to talk to, Wren," I say, turning around and walking back towards the hallway.

"What does that even mean?" she shouts, clearly frustrated. I laugh and make my way out of the chilly rink. Honestly, I don't

53

even know what I meant or why I said it. I just can't seem to get her out of my head, and I don't want her to have any excuses not to talk to me.

*

After a painful week of not hearing from Wren, other than catching small glimpses in the hallway, I go to my safe place. I've been good-ish this week. I've cut down some of the heavy stuff like Bourbon but I'm still balancing the lighter ones that can soothe the pain for a short period.

Since Carter's death I've visited the rockery that the school put together nearly every week. It's located in the courtyard between the rinks at NU. It's a place where I can talk to him. The school offered me someone to talk to but that doesn't feel the same. I don't want to find new ways to deal with it and find a way to turn all my dark thoughts into something positive. I just want to talk to him.

Even if he can't talk back, just sitting here surrounded by all the things that remind me of him make me feel closer to him. Carter was practically my brother. Growing up, he spent a lot of time at my place when he was in a tough place with his older brother while his parents working. Ethan would use Carter as his punching bag instead of working out his frustrations in a calm way. His parents never caught onto it, but I did. Sometimes, he would stay with us for weeks at a time, basically moving in when he didn't want to be alone with his brother. It felt like an extended summer camp. My parents didn't mind and neither did Clara. They all loved him. He was an easy person to love.

He was funny and smart in a casual way. Always too good for anybody. Always rational but fun. He constantly had this light energy about him that not only drew people towards him but made him light up any room he was in.

We discovered our love for hockey early on. As kids, we would go to the games with our parents who were huge hockey fans and when we got older, we started to enjoy the game more. First it was the ice, then it was the adrenaline rush, then it was the crowd and the support and then before we knew it, it became our lives. We started off in little leagues, slowly getting better and stronger until our high school won the championship. It was always our dream to play for the Grizzlies in the NHL. If that didn't work out, which we were sure it would, we'd become coaches or personal trainers. All we wanted was to play, side by side, and win the Stanley Cup.

Those dreams feel so out of reach now. This was supposed to be our year. We were supposed to train harder than we had ever done, stick to a strict diet and win the championship for NU. We were supposed to be featured in the school newspaper. *Miles Davis and Carter Reyes,* it was supposed to say, *carrying North University to another victory.* Instead, I'm wasting away my days and nights with a bottle in my hand.

"I'm sorry, Carter. It's been another bad week," I say to him, adjusting his large picture frame on the rockery. "I keep telling myself I'm going to try but every time I get near our rink, I freeze up. It doesn't feel right without you. I know I need to try harder. I know I do. It's just so difficult. This was supposed to be our dream. Our year. Not just mine. I can't even put on my full gear without throwing up. I have managed to wear my jersey again but the thought of picking up a stick makes my stomach turn."

I laugh to myself, feeling pathetic. A car drives by and goosebumps rise up my arms rapidly. Although it's often noisy here on campus, talking to him here is better than trying to do it at home. After he died, his parents came to get some things out of his room but other than that it's been untouched. It still feels like him. Still smells like him. Nobody goes near it, and nobody mentions it. We've not held a party there since. His room is in the basement and the thought of someone accidentally walking in there is too frightening to risk.

"Enough of the sad shit. I met someone, sort of. She's a piece of work but, so am I. She tough and so fucking gorgeous. I'm positive that she hates me but that onto makes me like her more. She's funny without trying and I can't help but think that the world is trying to tell me something. The second I get benched, there she is, like an angel or some shit. She's been everywhere and I can't get her out of my head. I'm trying not to fuck it up, but she's had my number for a week, and she hasn't said anything."

Each time I talk to him, I keep thinking that he's going to speak back. That he'll tell me in some way that he's okay. To tell me that I need to get my shit together. Or that one day, he'll just jump out of the closet and say, "I got you!" But it's been three months and nothing. I 'm just stupidly waiting for him to come back.

CHAPTER 6
WREN

I don't know what to do. I've been thinking over different approaches to this for the past week and a half, but I've come up with nothing. It doesn't help that Scarlett is sitting an exam so I can't ask for some rational advice. Instead, I'm sitting in the on-campus café, Florentino's, with Kennedy who is on her break from working behind the counter. She is not helping. At all.

"It's not that hard, Wren," Kennedy sighs, taking a sip of her iced coffee. "Just tell him you want to hang out and then bring up the plan. Easy peasy."

"But then he'll get excited and think I actually like him," I groan.

"Why are you making this hard for yourself? What isn't there to like? He's hot, you're hot, you both... like ice."

"He doesn't take things seriously. The last two times I've had a conversation with him, he reeked of alcohol. And not to mention he's a hockey player. I don't date hockey players. In fact, I don't date anymore, period."

"You're a skater too. It's practically the same thing." Kennedy dismisses with a wave of her hand. I throw her a rude look but instead her eyes widen. "Did you hear about what happened with Millie Trainor and Ty on NoCrumbs?"

NoCrumbs is a notorious gossip page based around colleges and universities in Utah, primarily in Salt Lake. There's a chain of them up and down the country, most likely run by Mason Greer and his little minions.

NoCrumbsSLC posts almost daily updates on the latest scandals our school and nearby schools have had. It's a pathetic waste of time for people who run it, but it gets everyone glued to their phones. I used to be one of those people: refreshing the page to wait for an update, numbly scrolling through the account to read what teacher said what about whoever. It's easy entertainment and a perfect icebreaker for any conversation with people in the area.

"No, Ken, I haven't."

"You're so chronically offline, I swear," she huffs, pushing her brown her over her shoulder. "She basically catfished him for *months* and when she finally told him, he was fine with it. They're still dating now, and it's even become an inside joke for their relationship."

"I don't see how that's relevant to anything we're talking about...."

"It is but it isn't. Look, all I'm saying is you should give him a chance to see how this could work. You know how insane everyone gets around hockey players."

"I want to preform again, that's it. I don't want anything more than that. I *can't* have anything more," I relay. She gives an understanding smile in return, not knowing whether to push it or not.

"A bit of romance wouldn't hurt, y'know? Even if it's fake. You need to loosen up a little," she presses softly. I try and let the idea go down for a second, but it doesn't sit right.

"I don't know anything about him," I protest when it's the first thing to come to mind.

"Like what?"

"Like, where does he stand on basic human rights issues? Does he care about climate change? That sort of thing."

"Wren, do *you* even care about climate change?" Kennedy challenges.

"I do," I say slowly, pushing my plastic coffee cup away from me. She watches the movement, and she shakes her head disbelievingly.

"Well, you're about to find out," she singsongs when something behind me catches her eye.

"What?"

"Mm-" she starts but she doesn't need to finish before I see him.

With lethal timing, just as we're talking about him, Miles is here, looking devastating. To his credit, he is looking for a lot less dishevelled than he has the last few times I've seen him. Maybe he's even showered. He's dressed plainly in dark jeans and a white top, his curly brown hair falling down his neck. Fuck. Why can't I tear my eyes away from him? I need to keep myself in check.

"Hey, Wren," he says with a wicked grin.

"To what do I owe this pleasure?" I ask, bored.

Kennedy shoots me a disappointed look as if I'm a naughty kindergartener. He plucks a seat from an empty table nearby and takes a seat to my right, his long legs coming dangerously close to mine. He looks so out of place. Not only are we at a

59

table for two, but his tallness and roughness doesn't seem to fit into this dainty café.

"Are you not going to introduce me to your friend?" he asks, gesturing to Kennedy. She gives a sheepish smile, practically blushing.

"I hardly know you. There's no point introducing you to someone you'll hopefully not see again," I say. I don't know why that whenever I'm around him I feel the need to be more bratty than usual. I kind of like the way he challenges me.

"Oh, but you're dying to get to know me, right?" Miles whines, leaning towards me. God, why does the noise make my stomach swarm with butterflies? Hearing a man groan is one thing but hearing them whine or plead is another. Unfortunately, my weakness.

"Must have slipped my mind," I say with ease. Kennedy is unimpressed, practically pouting like a child as she crosses her arms across her chest.

"Why do you have to make this so hard, Wrenny?" Kennedy sighs. Before I can retort to her use of my worst nickname, Miles jumps in.

"Yeah. Why do you have to make this so hard, *Wrenny*?" he repeats in a mocking tone. He turns to Kennedy. "God, I love that nickname. Thank you– Sorry what's your name, again?"

Kennedy's face lights up as she extends her hand dramatically. "Kennedy Wynter. Like the season but with a 'Y.' Nice to officially meet you." Miles takes her hand and shakes it before turning to me.

"Officially, huh? You talking about me already, Wren?" Miles asks cheerfully. I roll my eyes and when he catches it, he smirks.

"You're infuriating," I say, holding my hands up to him and then closing them into fists with a sigh, dropping them on the table.

We stare at each other, talking with our eyes. His face puzzled but amused, searching my face for something as the crease between his eyebrow deepens. *What are you doing?* I'm trying to say. *I don't know,* he would say, *But you're staring at me. You looked at me first,* I'd retort until we're in an intense staring contest. He opens his mouth to speak but nothing comes out and he clamps it shut.

"I'm sensing some tension here. I'll see you later, Wren. I need to get back before I get fired," Kennedy says, sliding out of her seat and picking up her coffee. She comes over to my side of the small table and whispers 'Play nice' before flashing a smile to Miles and leaves.

"I'm always nice," I mutter as Miles takes over Kennedy's seat, crossing his arms on his chest, spreading his legs out further so he's manspreading. If I didn't find him so agitating, I would find what he's doing right now to be incredibly attractive. I fiddle with my straw of my nearly empty coffee cup.

"Soo," I drag out, not sure what to say now we're alone. The side of his mouth twitches but he doesn't let it turn into a full smile. It was easy to talk at the party because I could run to Scarlett and Ken and I could skate away at the rink but here, it's like we *have* to speak. I say the dumbest thing that can come to mind. "What'cha doing here?"

"Just doing what everyone else is doing; getting coffee."

"Oh, so your first non-alcoholic drink of the day?" I say, keeping my tone light. He laughs quietly and for some reason I want him to do it again.

61

"What?! Coffee doesn't have alcohol? My day has been ruined!" Miles exclaims melodramatically. I like that he's quick. He's able to keep up with my sarcasm which isn't something that I get a lot. Always keeping me on my toes. I hate that it also makes me smile like an idiot.

What *is* he doing? What's his game plan? Why now? We've never really spoken before this point. Sure, we passed in the hallways between the rinks and in the gym a few times but never anything more than a glance. When I saw him at the party, coughing his lungs up over the sink, this was not how I saw it going. I thought I would save this huge guy from dying and continue begging Kennedy and Scarlett to take me home.

"Is it bad that I enjoy talking to you more than most of my friends? You're, like, hella brutal, but that somehow makes me enjoy it more," he admits, grinning hard as if this is the most fun, he's had in a long time. His rashness catches me off guard.

"I think you're hyper fixating on me to avoid fixing your problems," I respond truthfully. Because that's what this is right? He's going through a tough time, and I just happened to be in the right place at the right time. And now, whenever we're around each other we feel the need to talk. It's natural. And honestly, I think I'm doing it too.

He shrugs, looking out of the window. "I guess so."

His voice sounds so far away. He's quiet for a while, staring out of the window at the autumn trees in the courtyard, deep in thought. Just out of reach. For a minute I think I've upset him or said the wrong thing in the wrong way. Great. This is not awkward at all. It isn't long before he speaks again.

"Why haven't you texted me yet?" he asks, peeling his gaze from the window to my face. The way his mind changes and subject shifts almost gives me whiplash.

"What?"

"It's been, like, two weeks and…nothing. Were you being serious when you said you hate hockey guys?" he asks, his voice suddenly boyish and pained.

"Yes, and no?" He raises his eyebrow, moving his head to the side slightly. "I just don't enjoy the hockey culture, I guess. Especially at NU. The parties, the drinking, the social media, the rituals, and the stupidity that is 'puck bunnies.' Us skaters stay away from you guys. It's an unspoken rule. I've been trying my best to follow that, but here you are."

"I'm just irresistible, Wren. You're going to have to get used to it," he says lazily.

"You're more like a leech but sure," I shrug.

"Well, if it makes you feel any better, I haven't slept with anyone in over four months.," he challenges. "I've never referred to a girl I've hooked up with as a Puck Bunny, and I never will."

"It doesn't make me feel any better. It just means you can keep it in your pants longer than the average Joe. Congratulations," I sigh. "That's beside the point. All of my friends' experiences with hockey guys have not ended well. The last thing I want is to be on someone like Jake Callahan's roster."

Miles laughs, a toothy grin spreading across his face. "Fine, I can admit that Jake is a dick but not everyone is like that. You can't just put us all into the same box. What's the word?"

He taps at the table with his forefinger. I can't help but notice how clean his hands are. They're huge yet they look so delicate. If I wasn't so focused on not liking him, I would say he's getting more brownie points just for letting my fantasise about his hands on me for a split second. The way they would look around my- No. No. *What the fuck is wrong with me?*

63

"Stereotype," I say under my breath when I remember to speak. He grins as if I've helped him solve one of the worlds hardest problems.

"Yeah. You can't stereotype us. I'm not saying I'm perfect but I'm a decent guy. Xavier, Harry, and Grey are too. And Carter...he was way too good for anybody."

I see the way his eyes dim at the mention of his best friend. I didn't know Carter that well, the same way I didn't know most of the hockey guys, but he was always one the ones I could tolerate. When Scarlett was dating Jake, Carter was usually with them, and she would always say how funny he was. Everyone says that he had this light energy about him; everyone was so drawn to him. He wasn't like one of those douchey guys that everyone idolises when they pass on. Carter was always kind. Everyone knew that before and after.

"Anyway, I'm rambling. All I'm saying is you need to give people a chance. Not everyone is out to get you. Xavier warned me about you and look, here I am," Miles says, gesturing to himself, grinning.

I lean forward, looking into his green eyes, trying to figure him out. "Warned you how?"

"Oh, nothing. He just said you were pretty hard core," he says, taking a piece of the scone that I forgot was there. He shoves a chunk into his mouth without asking and I'm too in my head to tell him not to.

Hard core.

Nobody has ever called me that before. I know I'm a little tough because I have to be. I can't skate without being tough on myself and setting myself limits. But, hard core feels like something more. Something *just* tangible. I nod my head, turning over his words. I want to give him a chance. I want to

64

preform, and he needs to stop moping and get back to playing. I can't deal with another pitiful look at school from everyone who saw my last performance and the countless NoCrumbs reposts.

"Can I ask you something? You can totally say no but again, Scarlett and Kennedy would murder me if I don't ask," I say bravely. Taking back my scone which, he somehow has nearly eaten half of.

"Yeah, sure. But first, can I ask what your deal is with them? No offence but I've only seen you hang out with them," he says.

"You keeping tabs on me?" I smirk. He shrugs, not giving me an answer. "They're basically my sisters. I wouldn't be talking to you right now if it wasn't for them."

"I don't know if that's a compliment or not," he says, wearily, a sceptical look overtaking his face. I shrug in response too. "What did you want to ask?"

I've started it now. I have to follow through. I take a deep breath, closing my eyes quickly before opening them again.

"You kind of brought up at the party but I thought it was stupid. You were suggesting a way we can help each other out in a mutually beneficial way. Some way I can help you get back on track with training and you can help me boost my image again and let people fall back in love figure skating," I explain, not fully meeting his eyes, suddenly finding the table more interesting.

"No offence, but how could you help me train? You're like five-three," he says, almost laughing.

"It's a lot harder than hitting a puck on ice all day," I mutter. He nudges me softly under the table. I take in a breath, not letting him get to me. "I go to the gym five, sometimes six,

65

days a week. I'm on a strict food plan, I take Pilates classes when I can and I'm on the ice more than I'm in my bed. I don't have the time or the energy to mess up my plan, but I can make adjustments."

He stares at me, impressed and shocked. "Jesus, I do one of those things maybe twice a week. I used to be a lot better but since Carter... I just haven't."

For some strange reason I want to hold his hand, and squeeze it reassuringly, to tell him it's okay to lose motivation but I tell myself not to. We're not there yet. I know how hard it is to get back on track after losing someone. I saw how hard it was for Kennedy after losing her dad when she was a kid.

"I know and that's why I want to help. I can't stand you a lot of the time, *but* I feel for you, and this might actually work," I say, finally admitting it to myself.

"I think so too. How could I help you, though?"

CHAPTER 7
MILES

"**S**o, you're saying you want to date me?"

She groans, shoving her face into her hands. I hide my laugh by eating more of her scone which she hasn't minded me eating. I knew she would warm up to me at some point. What I didn't know was that she'd be so willing to dive into the plan I suggested at the party.

"Are you listening to *anything* I'm saying?" she pleads.

I lean my head in my hands and shake my head. I know what she's saying because I've made her repeat it twice already. I just like getting under her skin. There's something about the way the hear creeps up her neck when she gets angry that I could get drunk on.

To sum up Wren's very confusing plan, she wants us to fake date in order to create more hype around figure skating.

Everyone at NU is crazy about two things: hockey and whoever the hockey players are dating. The team steer clears from most scandals but every now and then Mason Greer, our generations most notorious gossip reporter, will try and make up something to catch someone out on his account.

Being a hockey player has its perks. It means people would love to see me without my jersey on and they're even more interested in knowing who gets to see me without anything on. Apparently, seeing sweaty guys in gear head to toe, roughing it out on the ice is a real turn on for some girls. Wren has made it *very* clear that she is *not* one of those girls. So, Wren wants us to go out a few times publicly and wants me to express my undying love for figure skating all over my social media in hopes that someone will pick it up and repost it.

I'm not against the idea at all because I wasn't lying when I said I haven't slept with anyone in months. If this means getting to talk to her more and spend more time with her, I'll take it. Oh, and I'll be able to play again soon. Since her hand touched my back at the party, it feels like every thought I had before her doesn't exist anymore. Like every reason I had to exist has restarted and found true meaning.

"Okay, I get it," I say, stopping her in the middle of her third monologue. "So, you want us to *fake* date and we'll train together in the meantime with your insane plan?"

She pulls her lip between her teeth, nodding, just like she did at the party. My breathing deepens before I force it to settle. "It's not insane. It's practical. But this could make or break us."

"I know," I say. "Shouldn't we make a contract or something?"

She laughs, tossing her hair around her shoulder. "Yeah, we should probably lay out some ground rules." Just as the words leave her mouth, her phone rings on the table. I watch the way her face drops as she stares at the caller ID.

"Is it your nightmare ex-boyfriend?" I ask, trying to keep my voice light as I can see she's grown uncomfortable by looking at the name. She lets out a small laugh which sounds more like a sigh.

68

"Worse. It's my mother," she groans, pulling out her chair.
"I've got to go. I'll talk to you later, okay?"

"Sure. Tell Hacks I said hi," I say, beaming, using Xavier's contraction.

"I'm not going to do that," she says sternly but she's smiling.
We exchange goodbyes and she's gone, leaving me slightly dumbfounded.

This could be it. I might finally get myself together in a way where I can stop being useless and actually help somebody out too. Since she's so anti-hockey, I'm surprised Wren even wants to do this. With me especially. She has been hesitant to even look at me since the party but now she's ready to dive into a relationship. Well, a fake one. She must really care about skating and her reputation if she's willing to give me a chance. I finish off the rest of Wren's scone before my phone starts ringing. Pulling it out of my pocket, I see the caller ID. I take in a deep breath and control myself not to throw my phone across the room.

It's Clara.

We haven't spoken properly for the good part of four months. Which I thought was better for the both of us. After finding out what she hid from me, I knew we wouldn't be the same as we were. I knew I wouldn't be able to let it go.

Clara and I, seven years apart, we're still really close growing up. She always let me hang out with her friends when they were over, and she would take me and Carter around the Ski Village when she worked there. We grew up in a normal household.

Well, what I thought was normal. My mom teaches middle schoolers, and my dad runs a small garage just outside of town, so we were never rich by any means. We were comfortable.

Clara and I both had jobs by the time we were sixteen and worked our asses off to go to college. But that wasn't enough for my mom.

I only recently found out that since Clara was eighteen, she knew my mom was having an affair with someone she worked with.

The fucked-up part was my dad knew. Apparently, he always knew, and he never said anything. He loved my mom, more than anything and I thought my mom did too. They still live together now, after going to couples therapy, and everything is supposedly handy dandy. I haven't forgiven my mom yet, and I haven't forgiven Clara either. As much as I'd like to ignore her call and shove my phone into a box, it will only give her leverage to use against me or to continue calling me until I pick up.

"Miles, what the hell are you doing?" is the first thing she asks when she answers the phone. I have to close my eyes and feel my chest rise and fall before speaking.

"Oh, hello to you too, sister," I deadpan, knowing that if I sass her in some way, she might save us both the torture of pretending. "I'm just having coffee in a cute café on campus."

"Don't be smart with me Miles," she spits. "No one has heard from you in months and in case you forgot, I'm your emergency contact. The dean called me. Why aren't you going to your classes? And how the hell did you get benched? Hockey is the only thing keeping you there."

I feel the bile rise in my throat. "Since when do you care? It was easy for you to lie to me half my life. Excuse me if I want some mystery in my life to remain." I know it's a low blow but it's too late now. I hear her huff over the phone, growing more agitated.

"Get your shit together or you'll lose your scholarship. We both know that your savings will barely keep you alive for a month. Just go to your classes and don't fuck this up," she warns.

I don't know how many more people are going to say this to me before it fully sinks in. It's so easy for me to say, 'yes, fine,' but it's the doing that I can't do. I can't even pick up a hockey stick for God's sake. The thought alone makes me shiver.

"I'm going to figure it out," I say after a while. "Bye, Clara."

"I hope you do. And Miles…" She pauses, taking in a breath. "I love you."

My chest suddenly feels tight. Suffocating. This feeling has been happening a lot since Carter died and I can't seem to get rid of it. It makes my breathing quicken, and it feels like something heavy is weighing on my chest, like I can't get up. It shouldn't feel like this. It's supposed to feel normal. I'm not supposed be suffering like this. All consuming.

I can't bring myself to say anything other than 'You too,' as I end the call, my hands slightly shaking.

I need to get my act together. It feels like everything in the universe is telling me to but as much as I believe Wren can help me what if I can't help her? What if this whole fake dating thing blows up in our face and ruins her more than she started out? Or worse; what if the uncomfortable feeling that makes me shift in my seat whenever I'm around her isn't nervous jitters and it's something else. Something that, if I ever put into play, could ruin everything before it even begins.

I pull up my phone to find her Instagram account to DM her, but I an IMessage from an unknown number.

Unknown: Hiii, it's Wren. We should meet up soon to talk.

My heart swells. She read my mind. My fingers fly over the screen. At least she's finally using my number. I change her contact and text her back.

Me: Yeah, sure. You can come over to my place. Does Friday work?
Wren: That's perfect. See u then.

I can't ignore the way her texting style makes my stomach flutter. Fuck. Since when did I start to get butterflies over a girl? That's new for me but I'm not surprised. In the short time that we've known each other, I've felt more and more out of control of my body.

My mind seems to wander when her mouth moves, especially when she's saying something sarcastic. She doesn't just let me get what I want because she must be able to tell that I want her. I want her in any way I can have her. She's like a magnet.

A destructive thought is telling me that what Wren said earlier was true. Maybe I am hyper fixating on her to avoid my problems. I'm supposed to be stronger than this. I'm almost twenty and I can't even deal with the death of my best friend in a healthy way. There will be worse days than the day I lost him, so I need to get over this feeling in my chest. I need to get to the other side.

*

When I get home, no one is there. Xavier is at practice and Evan is probably doing some rich boy shit somewhere. The darkness of the house just makes the gnawing feeling worse. It closes me in, suddenly making the dark thoughts clearer. I try to ignore it.

Although we haven't got a full plan, yet, I know I'm going to stick to it. I'm going to have to. I can't let her dreams die because I'm willing to let my dreams slip. I can't do that to her. If I have one drink tonight, I won't have any until Friday. That way I'll be able to let these feelings simmer and when it comes to talking to her in a few days, I should be fine. That's how these things work, right?

Just one drink.

CHAPTER 8
WREN

Since my parents' divorce, five years ago, Melanie Hackerly has been on the quest to establish herself as a woman that can never be shaken. The woman that can conquer all. She wanted to be the type of person people write articles about, the type of woman that could have hundreds of girls lining up to play her in a biopic. That was her plan for so long that when she was injured and went into teacher training, she's still found some loophole to get her to whatever stage she needs to be on in five years.

As kids, Austin, and I, never really saw anything wrong with my parents' relationship. They seemed happy. Whole. We had weekly family outings; birthdays were always a blast and we had regular vacations. There was nothing that we could see to tell us they weren't in love.

Their love was nothing idolise and aspire to; it just was. They kissed and said goodbye on their way to work, they always tucked us in until we reached our teens until one day they just fell out of love. It was quick and simple. There were no arguments or name-calling, they just stopped. My dad told me it wasn't our fault - because it never is - and they went their separate ways.

Soon after, my mom remarried to another recent divorcee, Mike, who has two kids from his last marriage. My mom moved out of our family home into a Spanish-style house just out Salt Lake in Centreville. My dad still lives in our family home, our childhood bedrooms still covered with the same *One Direction* posters I've had for as long as I could remember.

I know I'm not supposed to take sides in the divorce but if anyone were to ask, I'd say I'm on my dad side. No doubt. It's not like my mom has done anything wrong particularly. She hasn't deceived us in anyway, but it felt like for a lot of my life, she wasn't a mom to me. She was always my coach before ever being a mom.

My dad was the only one who let me be a kid. He let me read instead of working out. He let me eat ice cream after dinner, get dirty at the park and he let me wear my pyjama's all day when mom wasn't there. He didn't parade me around like a show pony, he just let me be. That's all I ever wanted from her.

When they split, Austin was nineteen, so she wasn't living at home anymore while she was at NU. My parents had shared custody of me, so I alternated between staying with mom and staying at dads. I always called dads house 'home.' It's where I felt most comfortable. When I was with mom, it just felt like I was third wheeling. Mike's kids were living on their own since they were older than Austin and me. So, every time I was there, they were all over each other. It felt like I was constantly interrupting their extended honeymoon. Like I was an unnecessary flea floating around them. Like I was watching her new life unfold without me in it. Luckily, as soon as I got into

NU, I was able to move in with Kennedy and Scarlett. Still, pulling into her driveway now, their house feels foreign.

*

"What are you going to do about skating?" my mom asks, pouring me another glass of orange juice. I knew the other shoe would drop. She's been dancing around mentioning it for the last half an hour.

Mom's house is a lot smaller than our old one. Everything fits so neatly together, here. Our old house was a mess of toys and random furniture pieces that my dad wanted to get. It was always chaotic, and I loved it that way. Our refrigerator was filled with pictures that Austin and I drew, things that we made at school and photos from our vacations. But here, everything is so neatly put together that you would never expect anything more than two divorcee's living here. The kitchen and living room are connected, with a large French door leading out to their patio with the pool and hot tub. We're sitting out on the patio, enjoying one of the rare sunny days left of September.

"Well, although it shouldn't be my problem, I'm going to figure something out," I say.

"What do you mean?"

"I just…" I sigh, running my fingers around the edge of the glass. "You're the dean. Shouldn't there be something you can do about it? Like, use the school funding to pay for the rink maintenance and the performances?"

She gasps as if I've insulted her. "It's not that easy, Amelia. North has been running this way since I went there. The buzz was always around skating, so the donations made up for the funding. I can't change it now. It's tradition."

I just nod.

There's nothing I can say that would get her to listen to me. There rarely ever is. I hate it when she calls me Amelia. I was born Amelia Wren Hackerly, but my first name never really fit. It felt like something I could never grow into. As soon as I could talk, I forced everyone into calling me Wren. Still, very few people in my life call me Amelia or Emmy.

"Forget I said anything."

Uncomfortable silence settles over us. I can't remember the last time my mom and I had an actual conversation. About something other than figure skating and the school. Something real. Sometimes it feels like that's all she needs me for; to tell her how I'm practicing my triple Lutz, tell her that I train all day, every week, until my body feels like it can't function normally. Until I'm so exhausted and sore that I forget to eat. "That's my girl," she would say, completely unaware that I have force myself out of bed every day to please her. This is how she has trained me. To only care about skating and to see everything else as an afterthought.

"It's as if no one is dedicated to the sport anymore," she murmurs after a while, sighing loudly. I can feel her eyes on me, but I keep mine focused on the pool in front of me, not braving the intense stare from her. "Was I interrupting your plans when I called you here?"

I turn to her, shocked at her sudden change in topic. "No. Sort of. Kind of," I stumble.

"Well, which one is it?" she asks, her tone sharp.

"I was on a date," I say with instant regret. I'm not sure why I said it, but I guess it's kind of true? Why not get straight to the point? I might as well have thrown up all over her by the way her nose scrunches.

77

"Oh. That's, uh, exciting," she says uncomfortably.

She had loved Augustus, naturally, because he always put skating first. *I* was the commodity. Never the first thing he thought of when he woke up. I was the afterthought, just like my mom would have wanted.

"Can I ask who it is?"

"It's not serious. I'll let you know when it is. You might have a grandchild very soon," I say, shimmying my shoulders, knowing it'll get a rise out of her.

"Wren," she snaps. "Don't make jokes like that, it's not funny. I'm too young to be a grandma already."

"*Right*. Not the fact that your daughter is also too *young* to have a child," I say suppressing a laugh. Her face knits in confusion. Another wave of silence sweeps over us. I'm about to get up and make an excuse to leave before she starts talking again.

"When was the last time you spoke to your sister?" she asks.

I try to shake my brain for an answer. Last time I heard, Austin was in Russia, still working on joining The Paris Opera Ballet living with her boyfriend, Zion. The second she finished at NU, she enrolled into another program in Russia where she has been for the last four years. We haven't spoken that much because the time difference is insane but I'm not complaining.

Austin was basically a second mother to me in a better way. She always pushed me to do better, train harder and stay sharp. She was basically my mom's echo but in a softer way. She understood how we all worked together.

She never openly addressed our strange dynamic, but it made the whole 'growing up under mom's eye' thing feel less lonely. That's something I don't miss.

As much as she was kind, it felt like I was getting pushed around in every direction. I do miss her cooking though. Mom was never any good and neither was dad, but Austin was spectacular. We often joked about her being a chef, but she knew she had to stick to ballet. She thought she had to set an example.

"I can't remember," I admit.

"Hmm. She's been distant and I'm worried. Check in on her soon for me," mom says. I wonder what gave her the reason to be distant from my darling mother.

"Okay, sure, I'll just get the next available flight to Russia," I joke. She throws me a daring look. "Fine, I'll call her when I can."

"Thank you."

I get up out of my seat, signalling that I'm ready for the conversation to be over. I get to the patio door and slide it open before I hear my mom call my name. I turn back and she's still facing away from me.

"And Wren, please take this skating situation seriously. I know you like to joke instead of facing your reality, but your reality is you might not be skating when the new year comes around. We both know you were never any good at school."

I bite my tongue. I bite it so hard that it makes my head hurt. I walk out the door with my head held high, but my eyes are prickling with tears. The only reason I was 'never any good at school' was because of her. Because she didn't let me do anything other than skate around on the ice. She robbed me of my childhood the second I could walk.

When I'm strapped safely in my car, I allow myself to break down. To cry out all the tears I've held in since this whole situation happened. It feels like I have the weight of the world on my back. If this thing with Miles doesn't work, I could be completely ruined. I will have to dive into something else that

I've only ever done as a side piece. As an escape. Falling into that is scary.

Even though my creative writing is part of my course it's not equal with skating. I skate basically every day of the week and I only take four creative writing classes. It's figure skating eighty percentage of the time. If I had to do a full major, I don't know where I would start.

I let myself cry until I'm back into my old neighbourhood. I ignore the urge to go to my dad's house and breakdown again in front of him like I have a million times before. Instead, I cross the road to Gigi's house and it's instantly as welcoming as it has always been. Walking up her porch feels like second nature. We spent so many summers on her lawn and her backyard, playing with the sprinklers outside and making forts in her bedroom.

"Wren, what a surprise!" Dianne exclaims when she opens the door wider to let me in. I've always wondered if any of Gigi's family age. Her mom is a stunning blonde woman who reminds me so much of a Polish Blake Lively and she's looked the same since I was born. I tried to clear my face while I was in the car to look presentable, so she doesn't blink twice when I shrug off my coat and my shoes. Mr Dixie, an overweight ginger tabby cat runs in between my legs and then saunters down a corridor.

"Gianna! Emmy's here, kiddo!"

I walk further into the hallway, instantly comforted by her cosy bungalow. I don't come here as often as I should. Gigi doesn't like loud environments, like me, so we only have a few safe places for her; her house being one of them.

Each wall is filled with pictures of baby Gigi and all of her replacement Mr Dixie's over the years. At first it was a secret that her mom replaced Mr Dixie after his first disappearance,

80

but Gigi knew. She was way too smart to know that the cat she had since birth had run away from her. More than once.

Their house is filled with all sorts of achievements and awards from Gigi's childhood. Since she's an only child, her mom never misses an opportunity to celebrate her. It's not long before my best friend materialises in the hallway in her Twilight pyjamas with a paperback in her hands. Her dark brown hair is in two low space buns with her navy headphones hung around her neck. When she sees me, she smiles shyly.

"You should have texted before you came over," Gigi sighs.

"I know. I'm sorry to spring this up on you but I was in the neighbourhood, and I wanted to hang out," I reply, twisting my fluffy socks in the carpet.

"You still could have texted."

"I know, Gigi and I'm sorry. Can we hang?" I ask. Dianne nods and ushers me closer to her and the corridor. Gigi huffs and walks closer to her bedroom. We've been doing this song and dance for as long as I can remember. I'll show up, Gigi will tell me to have called first and then we hang out. Even when I do call first, she's still surprised when I turn up, yet she stays in her pyjamas.

"Why were you in the neighbourhood?" she asks when we reach her woman-cave. Her room is filled with Marvel posters and moon lamps. It's probably the safest place I have ever felt. There's something about the dark blue and purple and slight smell of violets that make this place feel like another home. Gigi sits across from me in one of her many beanbags while I sit on her plush mattress. She is the epitome of a warm fuzzy feeling you can only get around certain people at particular times. With her, you're lucky enough to get that feeling all the time.

81

"I was visiting my dad," I lie, not ready to get into another misunderstanding about my relationship with my mom. Even though she's seen the way we operate first-hand, she still believes that we can just make up and move on.

"You're lying. You're dad's not here this week. If I get some pierogies, will you tell me?" Gigi asks, twisting her fingers through the strands of hair that have fallen in her face. I forgot how close my dad still is with her family.

"Deal." She sends a text to her mom who arrives within a few seconds with a comforting plate of pierogies. She watches me eat one first, moaning when I swallow. She smiles before picking one up herself. "I might be kicked off the skating team and I'm freaking out."

"What do you mean you might be kicked off the skating team?"

"No one is interested in it anymore and because NU is so shitty, we can't even afford to pay for it ourselves without the donations," I mumble around chews.

"And you can't do anything about it?" Gigi asks, her words almost sounding like a statement.

"Well, no. I'm *dating* a popular hockey guy to get people interested in me again but-"

"So why are you freaking out if you've got a plan? You should only be freaking out if you don't have a plan," she cuts me off, shoving more food into her mouth.

"Because it's a shitty situation, Gigi," I explain. She chews thoughtfully, not saying much while a few minutes pass.

"How have I dated more people than you?" she asks, and I burst out laughing. The way her mind works is so fascinating.

"I wasn't trying to make a joke. I've managed to get into multiple relationships with both men and women at the same time it has taken you to date two guys."

82

"So, what, G? What are you trying to prove?" I ask when I can talk without laughing.

"I'm not trying to prove anything. I'm just stating a fact," she replies, taking a sip from her water bottle. "Anyway, who is this popular hockey player?"

"Miles Davis." Her face pauses for a second, her dark eyebrows knitting together before softening. Her eyes widen suddenly. "I know him," she whispers, pulling out her phone to scroll through it. She turns her phone to me and there he is. A perfectly ridiculous picture of Miles wearing his jersey in a group photo with the rest of his team. I have to smother the stupid grin pulling across my face.

"How?" I whisper-laugh.

"Just because I don't go to college with you guys, it doesn't mean I don't have a social life. A lot of my readers are from NU, and you know how I get when I fixate on something," she explains flippantly. I don't push her on it anymore. We've always worked like this. "What's he like?"

"He's nice but he…" I draw out, not sure whether or not to tell her. As much as I trust her with my life, maybe it's best for me not to tell her that it's fake. I have a feeling she wouldn't understand. "He's nice."

"You said that twice. So, is he nice or are you just saying that to cover up the fact that he is *not* nice?" Before I can open my mouth to answer she makes up her own one and nods to herself. "Anyway, does he know that you're using him to skate?"

"I'm not using him, Gigi. But – The thing is-" She cuts me off my standing up out of her blanketed corner of the room.

"Okay. As long as he knows that then I'm okay with it. Thank you for coming to tell me that," she says, and I nod, unsure as to how to go about this. "Now can you get out because it's

83

getting closer to my time in the night, and I don't want you here for that."

"Do you have to kick me out every time? You need to update me on your schedule changes, so we don't have to do this ritual every time," I groan, standing up from the bed. She blinks at me. "Okay. I'll speak to you later. We need to hang out with the girls soon."

"Fine. As long as it's not anytime within the next week because I need to work on my book. Strict deadlines and all," Gigi explains, walking me out of her bedroom. A slight pang runs through me at the mention of her dedication to her writing. Even with every other force in the world tries to tell her that a nineteen-year-old can't write, she still preservers. She has the biggest smile on her face while she ushers me out of her house.

After an enlightening talk with Gigi, I trudge towards my locker room on the campus rink and change into a black leotard with tights and fluffy socks. I bring my skates to the rink and luckily no one is here. It's still early, around seven, so most people are on their way home from practicing or hanging out anywhere but here. I do a small warm up around the ice, my legs and my hands feeling shaky from all the crying I did earlier. Talking with Gigi helped. It always does. But even now, hours after seeing my mom, I can't shake what she said out of my head.

I practice through all my spins and turns until my head hurts. I practice my triple Lutz until my hands hurt from falling and squeezing them into fists. I replay 'Cloud of love' until I'm sick of it. I skate and glide until I'm crying again, feeling pathetic and stupid. Weirdly enough, I actually want Miles to be here and say something witty to make me laugh. Friday can't come fast enough. I practice until the darkness settles outside and I know I'm going to get kicked out soon.

When I get home into bed, I close my eyes and I dream of him.

CHAPTER 9
MILES

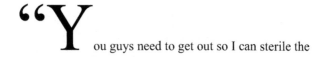

"You guys need to get out so I can sterile the

environment before she comes over," I shout for what feels like the hundredth time.

I knew it was a mistake letting the guys come over tonight. Usually, Friday nights are chill here with me, Xavier, and Evan. But for some reason, Xavier decided to invite Harry and Greyson over too. They've been playing on the PlayStation for the last three hours, none of them ready to tear away from the screen just yet. I clean around them as they make more mess every time I pick something back up.

"So, are you going to tell us who this mystery girl is?" Grey asks through a mouthful of mini pretzels as I pick up an empty chip packet from next to him.

"You'll know soon enough," I say, moving into the kitchen. They continue shouting over the game and at each other. If I wasn't so stressed out, I would join them. There is nothing I love more than playing a heated game of FIFA.

"It's Wren Hackerly," Xavier explains loudly. I shoot him a look through the open kitchen. He shrugs.

I haven't told Xavier about the plan yet because I feel like that's something Wren and I need to talk about first. But it seems like her friends already know so what would be the harm? I know I'm not telling any of the other guys. That's for sure.

"Wait, Ms Hacks' daughter?" Harry asks in his thick Australian accent which I still haven't gotten used to.

He's a year younger than us but he's a ridiculously good player and strangely smart so he was able to get into NU early. It's kind of weird having him on our team but all the girls love him, so we have to put up with his obnoxiousness. I walk back into the living room, inspecting the area before nodding.

"How does everyone know who she is? I feel like I've only *really* seen her recently," I say, trying to make sense of it.

"Because you've been nose deep in bourbon for the past four months," Grey laughs, not looking from the screen. I don't disagree.

After our talk at the café, I haven't had a proper drink since. I've had a few beers throughout the week but nothing heavier than that. The only thing keeping me going is knowing that I'm going to see her later and the idea that I'll get back in the rink soon.

"I don't blame you though, she's hot as fuck. Well, before she got dropped. Since then, she's been acting like she has a cork up her ass," Harry laughs, and my chest tightens. I don't know why I feel so protective over her, but I do, and we aren't even fake dating yet.

"Chill. Don't talk about her like that," I bite out, my voice rough. He turns to me and shrugs.

87

"Sorry, mate," he apologises.

I sit across from them and pull out my phone. I need to speak to her before I lose my mind. I pull up our text chat and fire off my first message.

Me: Hey. Are you on your way yet?

I wait for a while for a response, but ten minutes go by without anything. Slowly, panic begins building in me as I pace around the house, making sure everything looks presentable. She's either bailing on me or something has happened. It's not long before all the guys, including Evan, have gone to whatever party is on tonight. Almost half an hour goes by before she responds.

Wren: Fuck.
Wren: I'm so sorry. Omw now.

*

T en minutes of more panicking later, I'm opening the door to a sweaty and puffy faced Wren.

She's wearing cycling shorts that are way too short and a sports bra, a duffle bag in her hand. Her blond hair is tied back in a messy ponytail and the flyaways stick to her forehead. She looks gorgeous. My smile widens as she walks in, shooting out apologies and waving her hands around frantically.

I stop in front of her, placing my hands on her shoulder and she properly looks at me. Her breathing is still heavy, and it takes her a while to focus on my eyes. She searches my face, not sure where to look but when she moves to my eyes and then to my mouth, she parts her lips.

"I'm so sorry I'm late. I was at the gym, and I lost track of time. And, God, I smell like ass," she rambles, everything merging together into one word. She scrunches her nose at herself, shaking her head. I can't help but laugh.

"It's okay. Just take a deep breath," I instruct and she does.

"Are *you* okay, though? You seem a little…" I add, giving her another once over.

"Tense? On edge?" I nod sympathetically. "Yeah, my mom has been breathing down my neck all week and I can't think straight."

She must have only noticed my hands on her shoulders because she looks at them and then looks at me. I take her in for a few more beats. She gives a sheepish smile and I drop my hands, clearing my throat.

"Do you want to do this another time? We don't have to right now," I suggest, letting her follow me into the kitchen. I try and not dwell on the idea that this is the first time she's been inside of my house and how normal this feels. All the panic and fear that was in my veins earlier has slowly subsided.

"No!" she bursts out dramatically. I raise my eyebrows at her before pouring her a glass of water and hand it to her. She downs it in two gulps and slams it on the countertop. She wipes the back of her hand across her mouth and sighs deeply. It's like she's begging me to fall in love with her.

"Sorry, that was gross. Can I, um, use your shower?"

"It wasn't gross but yes, you can use my shower." I grin. "Do you want a quick tour first?"

She nods her head enthusiastically, blowing her hair out of her face. I take her around the kitchen and the living room to the dining area. I avoid Carter's room and bring her into the den, which I'm lucky I cleaned when I was stressing if she was going to show up at all. I bring her up the stairs and give her a peak into everyone's bedroom. She laughs at how starkly different Xavier's rooms is to Evans. Finally, I bring her to my room.

She audibly gasps as she enters. My room is one of the biggest in the house because I was lucky enough to get first dibs. Each wall is painted dark grey, filled top to bottom with movie and hockey posters. My dresser is stacked with books and sports magazines that I've hoarded over the years. I was smart enough to empty out most of my mini fridge and fill it with age-appropriate drinks.

"Did you clean this just for me?" she whines sarcastically as she walks over to my pile of books. She looks at them for a minute, running her hand across the hardbacks before turning around, leaning against them.

"This is actually the only room I *didn't* clean. Everyone knows that a clean room means a clear mind," I admit truthfully as I stalk closer towards her. Her breath hitches as I tower over her, her green eyes staring into me.

"Hmm," she murmurs, something getting caught in her throat. It dawns on me that this is the first time we've been alone in private, and it turns my thoughts irrational. Impulsive. I brush the hair out of her face, my hand barley contacting her forehead, but she tenses.

"Are you surprised?" I ask, my voice coming out hoarse and scratchy. She backs up a little, making the dresser shake as she braces her hands at both sides of her.

"Actually, yes."

Quickly, she moves from in front of me and slides behind me, so I'm left to stare at the empty space she left. I turn to see her ruffling through her duffle bag, her ass facing me. "Fuck me," she groans. *Believe me, I want to.*

I clear my throat. "What is it?"

She turns to face me, her face scrunched up. "I left my clothes in my locker. You're just going to have to put up with me smelling like sweat."

"You don't smell," I say quietly. She raises her eyebrows, unimpressed. "You can just wear something of mine."

"Are you sure? I don't want to, like, invade your personal space and stuff," she mumbles, looking through her bag again before dropping it. I'm already looking through my drawers before I reply.

"Yes, Wren, it's fine. You can invade my personal space whenever you want as long as you let me invade yours."

She snorts from behind me. "That doesn't seem like a very fair tade," she mumbles.

I return to her with a towel, a white faded tee shirt and some shorts. She picks them up and gives me a smile. I point to the door in the corner of my room. "The bathroom is through there."

She nods and makes her way to the door. I sit down on my bed with a thump, dropping on my back at all the sexual frustration in my body. I drag my hands down my face, sighing.

"I don't usually do this…" she says softly. I sit up to see her with her hand on the handle but her body facing me.

"What? Shower at your fake boyfriend's house?"

"Yes, but I mean I'm usually more put together than this," she laughs, practically grimacing at herself.

91

"It's okay, Wren. You're making me feel better about my own chaotic-ness."

She smiles and slips into the shower.

*

Letting Wren shower here was a bad idea. It was an even worse idea letting her borrow my clothes because she looks so fucking hot right now. She had a clean pair of her own shorts in her bag so she slipped them on along with my shirt which clings to her body in some places which haven't dried properly, and I can see through it. Right through it. She walked out with her arms across her chest, the shirt falling halfway down her thighs and told me not to laugh. I couldn't laugh even if I wanted to with how hard I am. When she sat on the bed next to me and I was smart enough to put a cushion on my lap.

"No one can know that this is fake other than your closest friends," Wren concedes, writing down a rule in her notebook.

"Agreed. I only trust Xavier to keep quiet about it," I reply.

"I'm assuming both Kennedy and Scarlett already know."

"Yep," she beams, popping the 'p.'

We agreed that we'll do the whole fake dating thing until her showcase at the end of December which gives us just under two months. If it doesn't work out, we'll re-evaluate to prepare for my first game. My first real game for the season isn't until January so I have plenty of time to convince Coach to let me back on the team.

"Next thing is family. Do you want to meet each other's parents, or should that be ruled out?"

I feel my body stiffen and I shrug, not sure what to say. "Why don't we come to that when the time comes?"

"Okay, but my mom has asked me a million questions since I accidentally told her. And my dad is going to be very interested. That's just how he is. Are you okay with that?" Wren asks wearily, watching for my reaction.

"That's fine. The last time we spoke she was close to kicking me out so I'm sure she's going to love that I'm dating her daughter," I say sarcastically, pulling her notebook into my lap, adding something next to her second rule. She throws a cushion at me, not finding my joke funny.

"Moving on," she mumbles softly. "We should go out two times a week and have one sleepover, just to show that it's more serious than casual sex. You can come to mine, and I'll come here some weeks. We don't have to stay in the same bed, *obviously*. If we go to parties, we need to attend and leave together to give no one any reason to speculate that something is off."

"Yeah, that's a good one," I reply, not knowing what else to do. She's been taking the handle on this part of the plan, I've just been agreeing to everything, trying not to look at her breasts. It's even worse that she asked for the air con to be put on because I can see how hard they are under the chill.

"What about PDA?" I say, thinking with my dick. She continues typing in her phone, not looking at me. I pull my focus from her legs to her face.

"What about it?"

"Is it going to be a problem?" I ask. She doesn't make a noise or move as if she's even heard me as she continues writing.

"Okay, so I'm just going to assume that making out, hand holding, ass grabbing and anything up to second base is on the table."

93

That gets her attention. Her head shoots up, her cheeks dark red. I can't help but smirk to myself.

"Only if absolutely necessary," she breathes, pulling down the shirt further over her thighs. "And we shouldn't show any displays of affection when we're alone."

I ignore her last addition as she writes it down. "Shouldn't we kiss once before so we know what we're doing?" I ask.

I rest my hand on her bare knee tenderly and I feel her tense beneath me. She closes her eyes and opens them again before placing her hand on mine. She lets out a noise between a groan and a laugh as she takes my hand off her knee.

"Have you ever kissed a girl before?" she asks, mockingly, titling her head to me.

I nod. Adding, "Multiple," with a grin.

She grimaces. "Then we should be fine."

I lay down, throwing my forearms across my face. Well, that plan didn't work out. Which, I'm partly glad for because I don't think I would be able to stop if her lips came anywhere near mine. I hear her shuffle on the bed, I open my eyes slightly and she's sitting next to my head.

Her legs are crossed beside me so I can see the slither of her black shorts. I take a deep breath and close my eyes again, praying my dick isn't as hard as it feels. She continues talking over the plans as I drift in and out of consciousness, *mm hmm*-ing and nodding in response. I feel her soft hand on my forehead, stroking gingerly, and my eyes shoot open at the gentle contact.

"Sorry. I, uh, I thought you were sleeping," she whispers. She bites her bottom lip as I shake my head softly. "Okay, my last and most important rule."

I lean up on my elbows, looking at her under tired eyes. I could get used to this: opening my eyes and seeing her there in my shirt, looking down at me with whatever serious expressions she has now.

"Shoot."

She waits a second, almost afraid to say it. As if speaking her next words have been the only thing holding her back.

"Rule number six: If things get too real for either one of us, we have to tell each other," she explains finally. "I mean real feelings other than attraction. It could mess up the plan."

"Worried you'll fall in love with me, Wren?" I tease. A wicked grin spreads across my face when her cheeks heat up.

"It's you that I'm worried about," she says back without missing a beat. I grumble and she laughs, pushing my head gently so my elbows buckle, and my head hits the pillow.

I hate how right she is. One sultry look from her and I would completely devour her. If she wasn't so committed to keeping our friendship purely a friendship, I would have grabbed her waist and pulled her into me by now and let her straddle me. I shake my head to get out all of the fantasies.

"And what about your side of the deal?" I ask, after staring at her for too long, finding my ceiling more interesting.

"You'll come to the gym with me whenever you have time. Then we'll figure out a good food plan and I'll do some of my own research on hockey training in the meantime," she says.

"Sounds good. It's Sophia Aoki's birthday party next weekend so we could go to that as our first public outing," I suggest but as soon as I said the word 'party,' she groaned. "What? Don't tell me that you hate parties."

"I hate the feeling of being drunk and I hate being around strangers who are," she admits with a shudder.

"Well, if you want this to work, we're going to have to go to a few parties," I challenge.

"Is that all you do, Miles?" she asks, leaning into me from above. I swallow. Hard.

"When I don't have any important games coming up, yes," I admit.

"Why?" she questions, genuinely curious.

"Because... it's fun. You should try it sometime if you even know what fun is."

"Oh, I know what fun is," she bites back.

"Oh, really? What do *you* do in your spare time?"

"Skate. And when I'm not doing that, sleeping," she says, her voice suddenly sounding miles away.

I don't know when we got so close and when she started to touch my hair again but we both haven't made a fuss. She's had this stress in her face since she got here but it's finally seemed to smooth out. It seems like she needs this more than me. Her soft hands graze my forehead and then push into my hair. *What the hell do you use in your hair?* I hear her mumble, almost angrily.

"That doesn't sound very fun," I say quietly when I remember we were just talking.

"It isn't," she says ruefully. We sit like this for a minute or two before she moves her hand. "I should go home. It's getting late."

"Okay," I get out quickly before I ask her to stay. She picks up her duffle bag, but she doesn't move. She just stands, chewing on her bottom lip, looking at me. "I hope you feeling better, soon."

"What?" she says after a while, as if I caught her in a trance.

96

"You said your mom was breathing down your neck. That you were stressed. I just think you should take a break or something."

She shakes her head with a laugh. "There's no rest for the wicked," she says, her smile twitching. "This helped, though. Thank you, Miles."

"Anytime."

CHAPTER 10
WREN

I've been trying to justify what happened with me and Miles for the last few days. Or more of what didn't happen. Who was I to sit there and stroke his hair like his fucking real girlfriend? It was dangerous. Lethal. I had a shit week, skating until my hands and feet were numb and there he was with a warm shower and a shirt that felt too comfortable against my skin. I knew what I was doing when I walked out the shower, basically naked, but I couldn't stop. A huge part of me didn't want to. I didn't leave my clothes on purpose. I was too busy trying to get to his house after I almost broke the treadmill from cranking it up every few seconds. Luckily, I left before I did something I'd regret.

I went back two days ago to help him with his meal plan which was too easy. He was willing to throw out all the junk he had for healthy alternatives. I tried to give him his shirt back, but he refused it. "I don't want it back," he said. "It looks better on you anyway."

I need to figure out a way to control myself before this tension turns into more before we've even publicly announced our relationship.

I'm now running around the house, trying to find my good sports bra to wear to the gym with Miles. I burned through more workout clothes this week than I usually do in a month, and I haven't been on top of the laundry. The only one I have now is a black Nike one which I haven't worn since high school. And not to my benefit now, my boobs have grown a ton since then.

"Did you shave?" Scarlett asks through of a mouthful of toast when I get to the kitchen. She's sat at the island, eating her breakfast while balancing a study video on the back of her cup. She's been pestering me with these kinds of questions all morning.

"No, Scarlett, I didn't. We're going to the gym, I'm not trying to fuck him," I counter but she shrugs. Under very different circumstances I would have. Hell, if I was unstable enough last week, I *definitely* would have. I know it goes against everything I've tried to avoid but there is something so undeniably attractive about him. Something that with one look, I could be completely destroyed. Hockey player and all.

"Can't you do both?" Kennedy asks, walking in the kitchen as she rubs sleep out of her eyes. "He might just trip and fall right between your legs."

"Do you guys both have to be on my case right now?" I sigh frustrated. They both giggle and there's rapid knocking on the door. They exchange glances and pull a stupid face as I run to answer it.

It's Miles. He's in grey shorts and a white tee, a duffle bag slung across his shoulder. He looks devastating. He steps into

99

the apartment and raises a hand to Kennedy and Scarlett who are so obviously ogling. I am too.

"You look hot," he says quickly, gesturing to my tiny sports bra and joggers. I suck in a breath at his forwardness. Swatting him on his shoulder, I try to battle the blush on my cheeks.

"You don't have to pretend to like me. They already know that we're pretending," I say, walking away from him to collect my bag from the couch.

"I know," he whispers. I turn to see him smirking. Scarlett gets out of her seat, standing in front of him. I don't have to see her face that she's either smiling or judging him. They're almost the same height, Miles only a few inches taller.

"Miles. Nice to finally meet you. Again," Scarlett says, her voice humours and light. He shakes her outstretched hand. I walk up towards them, standing at her side.

"Ooh, don't say 'finally.' He'll think that I talk about him all the time," I warn, rolling my eyes. Miles' mouth opens then closes, shaking his head. I smile to myself.

"But you *do* talk about him all the time," Kennedy shouts from whatever corner she's disappeared to. I catch Miles' eyes over Scarlett's head. He raises his eyebrows, but I ignore it.

"You ready to go?" I ask. He nods, exchanges goodbyes with my friends and we head out of the door and catch the elevator down to the bottom floor. He walks past my car in the parking lot and continues walking down towards the main road. "Where are you going?"

He turns around dumbfounded. "To the gym. Why are you taking your car? It's, like, five minutes away." He sighs, throwing his hands up and then dropping them.

"Oh, you sweet, innocent, child. Get in," I demand, and he obliges. He looks so out of place in my car. His larger-than-life shoulders barley fit in the seat, and he has to adjust his chair to give his legs more room. It's comical, really. We barely make it out of the drive before he starts asking me a million questions.

"Where are we going? There's not another gym for miles. Are you going to murder me? Is this a kidnapping? Why aren't you answering my questions?" he asks rapidly.

"If I wanted to kidnap you, why would I ask you to come to *my* apartment?"

"You're right but that still doesn't make me feel any better."

"Can you chill? I said we were going to do *real* training. If there is one perk to my dad owning hotels, it's that I get access to all the private gyms."

He looks at me and laughs. "You're insane."

"That is the second time you've called me that. I'm just being practical. Why would we waste our time in a gym where the equipment is mediocre, at best, when we could go to a luxury one that has just been built."

He doesn't ask any more questions while I drive. He does change the music every two minutes, never letting a full song play. In the last ten minutes I've heard, Taylor Swift, Lana Del Rey, Lil Nas X and Miley Cyrus. I was beginning to think that he's not that bad. That he's not the douche hockey guy I made him out to be. Until he started singing. I almost crashed four times in the thirty-minute drive at his screeching.

"Remind me to never carpool with you again," I say when we walk into the hotel.

"I've got a gorgeous voice, Wren," he whispers in my ear at the reception desk. His breath tickles my neck and I shiver. I ignore him and get our day passes and we walk through the transparent doors into the gym.

Secluded gyms like these, that nobody knows about just yet, are my favourite. They always smell fresh and I'm usually one of the first people to use the equipment. It's like opening the cap of a fresh orange juice bottle. It's so satisfying and calming. We place our bags in the corner of the room and we start a light warm up. It was easy settling into a routine with him. The girls took forever to get into going to the gym with me. After a few painful months for them, they saw it more as an annual thing to come along with me. Apparently, I'm too intense for them. Miles and I quickly get into a smooth rhythm of doing a few miles on the treadmill and the Step Master. We then move to the weights.

"How much can you bench?" I ask when we take a small break. I pull out the lid off my water bottle with my teeth and gulp some while he just stares, catching his breath.

"Isn't that the same as asking a girl what their bra size is?" he asks back. I can't help but laugh.

"That's not the same thing. You don't have to tell me. I was just wondering," I say, getting ready to go on the bench press myself. He stands behind me as I slide in, getting ready to spot me.

"I don't know. Maybe, one-seventy," he concedes, suddenly looking embarrassed. I let out a *huh* in recognition. "What about you?"

"Uh, one-ninety. On a good day," I say, my cheeks turning red. I don't know why I asked, and I don't know why I told him.

"How the fuck can you do that? You're, like, the size of a child. You really are hard core," he sighs. I ignore his child comment and let out a disbelieving chuckle.

"Not really. I've been training since I could walk pretty much. I did a lot of gymnastics growing up, to improve my arm and leg strength," I admit.

The silence stretches between us as we become a mess of heavy breathing and grunting. After alternating on the bench press, we move back to the floor space, changing between weighted squats and sit ups. It brings a strange sense of comfort being her with him. I usually try to work out on my own in these private gyms but knowing someone here is a lot nicer than I thought.

"You're doing it wrong," I groan at Miles for what feels like the thousandth time. I'm a picky eater and I'm a picky person. Watching someone continuously do something wrong is one of my pet peeves.

"I think I know how to do a squat, Wren," he retorts, still standing weirdly in front of the mirror. I go towards him, standing in front of him so he can see me in the mirror.

"Watch what I'm doing," I say, meeting his eye in the mirror. He just blinks at me as I spread my legs to decent position, make sure my back is correct and I squat down low. I didn't think about the proximity until I feel my ass brush against his shorts. I watch him inhale before letting out a shaky breath. I grab his hands from behind me.

"What are you doing?" he asks, his voice hoarse.

"You don't seem like a very visual learner," I murmur as I place one of his giant hands onto my lower back and the other on my stomach. "Can you feel how my back isn't leaning too forward?"

He doesn't say anything. He makes a noise in the back of his throat and nods at me in the mirror. "Just feel that when I go down, okay?" He nods again. Slowly, I lower myself down to the squat position, holding it for a few seconds before coming back up. "See?"

I repeat the motion again before moving away from him. I watch him do it himself until he's got the hang of it.

We mostly work another round in silence until were both on the floor. Miles slides his phone to me before laying down in front of me. I hold onto his feet while he does his first round of sit ups.

"I found some...questions...on BuzzFeed...that we should... know the answers to if we're going to be a fake couple," he breathes. I laugh at his persistence to work out and talk at the same time. I open his phone.

"You should put a password on here, you know?" I say.

"I've got nothing to hide," he challenges. Fair enough.

"They're in my Notes."

I scroll through his phone and open the Notes app. I skim through the questions, not sure what I was expecting. They are all relationship based or weird icebreakers to get to know each other. He sits up from his position because I can no longer hold his feet. We sit facing each other, cross legged, looking sweaty and dishevelled.

"Okay," I draw out. "This will be fun. First question. What was the first thing you thought about me when we met?"

Miles runs a hand through this hair. "Honestly, all I could think about was how hot you are."

"Miles, be serious," I say, poking him with my foot.

"I am!" he replies. I poke him again. "Fine, when we met at the party, I just wanted to keep you talking to me. To keep you interested. I had already recognised you from school and the photos in the dean's office, but I don't know. When we started talking, I guess I just wanted you to like me, and I could tell it wasn't going to be easy."

His honestly catches me off guard. I've always been aware of the way I come across to other people but still hearing him point it out like that makes me feel a little uneasy. I take in a shaky breath, watching his eyes dance across my face. "Thanks for being honest."

"What about you?" he asks, nudging his foot into mine.

"My first thought was: God, I hope he doesn't die right now because that would suck," I start, remembering the night at the party, watching him convulse over the sink. He chuckles lightly. "And then, I thought you were pretty annoying but you're more tolerable now."

"Just tolerable, huh?" he says, plucking the phone out of my hand. I roll my lips between my teeth and nod, trying not to smile. "Okay, I'll take it. Did you go through any phases growing up?"

"Oh my God, *way* too many to count," I say, shoving my hot face into my hands.

"Tell me now. I want to know what little Wren was like," Miles pleads, pulling at my hands. I try to ignore the way the electricity shoots up my arms from his touch.

"Well, my first phase was making everybody call me Wren instead of my first name," I say shuddering. He looks at me, his eyebrows drawn.

"Wait? What?"

"Amelia is my first name, and my middle name is Wren. I hated the way Amelia sounded so I told everyone to call me Wren and it stuck." I shrug my shoulders and he just stares at me in awe.

"*Okay*, so what was little Amelia Wren like?"

"Oh, she was a lot. I went through my One Direction phase; a lot later than I'd like to admit. I once went through a British phase, where I forced everyone in my house to speak with a British accent for a week. I also forced my family to eat my terrible creations that I thought were gourmet meals after watching Master Chef, but they were really just random condiments that I found in the refrigerator. I was just a general nightmare. I thought that I didn't have friends in middle school other than Scarlett, Kennedy, and Gigi because I was skating all the time but it's because I was a little weirdo," I say in one go, surprising myself at how much I just rambled. Miles stares at me with wide eyes and a huge smile.

"I think that's the most you've spoken to me in one sitting," he says through his wide smile. I roll my eyes and he laughs.

"Why do you always talk about skating like you hate it?"

"What do you mean?"

"I don't know. The other day, you were saying how hard you work and how it isn't fun. It sounds like you've quite literally been training all your life. If you don't like it, why don't you just quit?"

No one has downright asked me that in a long time. What can I say?

This has been my mom's dream for her whole life until she was injured.

Her first daughter couldn't handle the ice and I was her only hope. I put the work in, I got good and now it's the only thing I can do. The only thing I'm good for.

"It's complicated," I mutter but he doesn't seem convinced.

"That's a story for another day. What was little Miles like?"

He gives me a sympathetic smile before dropping it. If we got into that now, we'd be here for hours.

106

"I wasn't as crazy as you, that's for sure," he begins. "I don't think I went through any phases exactly. The only thing I can really remember loving as a kid was hockey. Carter and I lived and breathed hockey. It was all we talked about. We could go weeks at a time talking about the same game over and over. I guess I'm still in that phase, though."

I see the way his face changes when he talks about him. It's nostalgic but pained. Something in him smooths out when he talks about him. Remembrance. He looks a little lost. Distant. As if talking about him has made him materialise in front of him.

"Sorry, I don't think that really answered the question," he says after a while.

"No, it's okay," I reply. I've always been a physically affectionate person, so I don't hesitate before I reach out and put my hand over his. He flips over his hand, so his palm is facing up. We both look at our hands before I slip my hand into his. It feels strange but I need to comfort him in some way. "I can tell you really miss him."

"He was my best friend. My brother."

"We don't have to talk about him if you don't want to," I whisper. He shakes his head.

"It's okay. I brought him up." He squeezes my hand before letting go. He stands up, groaning as he stretches. "Come on. We need to get back to work."

"Do we have to?" I moan, falling on my back. Miles stands next to my aching body, towering over me.

"This was your idea. What is it that you say? Beauty is pain," he chants. I reach my arms up and he grabs my hands, pulling me up. When I'm standing upright in front of him, I almost sway over.

"Aw, are you calling me beautiful?" I mock as I shake out my arms and legs.

"You didn't need me to tell you that, Wren," he whispers before tapping me on the shoulder and sprinting to the other side of the gym. Why does this grown man love to play tag?

*

The car journey home is more chaotic than it was on the way there. Miles still sung – horribly –but it was absolute torture when we was stuck in traffic. We're almost outside his house when Miles stops the music abruptly and looks at me. I turn to him for a second before pulling into his driveway.

I look back at his house.

Then back to him.

He's still staring.

"What?" Suddenly I feel uncomfortable under his hot gaze.

"How many guys have you slept with?" he asks without hesitation.

"Is that one of the questions?" I ask back, turning to him. His face is serious but there's something swirling in his eyes. Curiosity? Desperation?

"No."

"Then why do you need to know that?"

"I'm your boyfriend, I think I'm meant to know," he argues. *Fake* boyfriend, I want to say. I shake my head at him. He unclips his seatbelt and opens the door. He gives me a pretend smile and then drops it as he gets out of the door.

He looks adorable and ridiculous at the same time. He walks towards his front door, stomping like a child, before I wind down my window shout after him.

"One and a half," I shout loudly, almost cringing at myself. He turns around, jogging back to me until he's at my door.

"What?" he a, leaning his arms on the hood of the car.

"One and a half. That's how many guys I've slept with," I say quieter this time. His face unknots with confusion as he looks at me intensely.

"A half?" he asks, not hiding the surprise in his tone. "What the fuck does that mean?"

"He couldn't make me come," I murmur. I watch Miles' throat as he swallows audibly, his pupils becoming dilated. I start the car up again and change the gear. "Bye, Miles."

"You... You can't leave like that," he stutters.

"See you later, alligator," I shout as I back out of his drive, leaving his jaw open and hands hanging at his sides.

CHAPTER 11
MILES

Every time I walk into Wren's apartment, it gradually becomes more and more chaotic. It's still the same three girls but with amount of noise and mess they make you'd think that there's at least ten of them. Each time I go, I'm also pestered with more and more questions. Kennedy is always the one asking them while Scarlett murmurs sly comments under her breath. Sometimes I feel like Wren asks me to come early on purpose, while she's still getting ready, just so I can be peppered with more questions.

Now, I'm standing at the kitchen island, with Kennedy sat on the other side, eating dry Cheerio's like that girl from *Monsters Inc*. Scarlett is laying on her back on the couch, just out of view. And Wren… honestly, I don't think I've seen her since she answered the door in her blue leotard before rushing off to change.

"So, what's it like to be fake dating Wren?" Kennedy asks loudly, trying to get Wren's attention wherever she is. "Is it everything you ever dreamed of?"

"Everything and more," I drawl.

"Come on," Ken presses, rolling her eyes. "She's not here. What do you really think about her?"

I raise my eyebrow. "What do you mean? She's great."

"Of course she's great. I know that. I wouldn't be best friends with her if I didn't know that."

I can't lie. Kennedy scares me sometimes. I can't tell what she's trying to get out of me so I decide to tell her the truth.

"She's fun to hang out with even though I feel like she hates me most of the time. She's a lot cooler than me if I'm being completely honest," I admit the second she materialises in the kitchen. Kennedy nods thoughtfully, adding more Cheerios into her mouth. Wren's changed out of her leotard into light washed jeans and a dark green cable knit sweater. Her hair is tied back in a claw clip, two short blonde strands falling in her face.

"You look nice."

She looks at me, walking closer as if she's only just seen me.

"Thanks. You clean up nice yourself." She beams at me before slipping behind me towards the fridge.

"I don't get why you can tell two people about our arrangement, but I can only tell one. Plus, Kennedy and Scarlett ask me a million questions all the time, so they amount to, like, twenty people," I say, turning to face her again. I lean against the countertop, my arms folded across my chest.

"Fine, go and tell Evan. Be my guest," she responds, her head still stuck in the fridge. Within seconds, Scarlett is up from the couch, stood in my face, pointing at me. I look over at Wren for help but she's still searching around the fridge, the door blocking her from view.

"Don't you dare tell that little weasel anything!" Scarlett exclaims, jabbing her finger into my chest. I raise my hands in

111

surrender, but she doesn't move. Finally, Wren comes to my rescue.

"Scarlett, calm down," she says to her friend who backs away slowly, glaring at me. Wren gulps the purple-pink smoothie in her hand before looking at me. "You ready to go?"

I nod enthusiastically and we leave to get in my truck. I scrubbed my truck clean before driving here. We've been taking her precious Honda Civic to the gym most mornings, but I knew I had to do a deep clean before she could ever see my car. I worked at Nero's and saved up for four summers to get my truck; thinking I would use it all the time only to end up moving five minutes away from campus.

We pull up outside of Sophia's miniature mansion and the music is already surrounding us. The lawn is littered with the smokers, talking loudly over clouds of smoke. Cars line up the driveway and onto the block and I turn over to see Wren scanning the surroundings. She hesitates to open the door. I put my hand reassuringly on her knee and she turns to me, her breathing suddenly heavy.

"If you want to leave at any time, just say the word, and we'll go," I whisper, and she waits a beat before nodding. The last thing I want is for her to feel uncomfortable. "I'm going to keep you safe tonight."

We walk up to the house, hand in hand. Well, sort of. She holds onto three of my fingers as if that's all her hand can take and it's fucking up my insides. I can feel Wren's hand squeezing my fingers tightly as we open the door to a party that is in full swing.

Music blasts from speakers in all directions, people stood aimlessly with Solo cups in their hands. Fruity smoke from bongs and vapes infuse my senses and it takes me a second to adjust to the sudden change in scenery. I've spent a lot of time over the past few months at parties like these but this one is something different. It's a million times louder and full that the ones I end up at.

We walk deeper in, trying to find somewhere to get a drink. I'm going to stick to punch today, and Wren was going to stay sober anyway. I need to stay alert in case something happens. I can't have us slipping up on our first public date.

I take my hand out of hers and slip it around her waist, pulling her into me as we go into the kitchen. There are a few people in here but not enough for it to be crowded. Enough that we need to act like we're together.

"Are you okay?" I whisper-shout into her ear. She looks up at me and nods, still looking a little skittish. I pull her further into me, kissing her on the forehead as if it's the most natural thing in the world. She blinks up at me. *Shit.* Should I not have done that? Is it too soon?

My anxieties are relieved when she presses a kiss into my shoulder at the same time that someone taps on my other shoulder. I turn around to a cherry faced Harry. He's soaked head to toe, most likely just coming out of the pool.

"Hey, Miles," he says before registering Wren next to me. "You're Wren, right?"

"Yep," she says, popping the 'p' in the way that makes me shift in my jeans. She blinks up at me as if to silently tell me to say something.

"This is Harry," I introduce, gesturing towards him and Wren. "He talks a lot of shit so don't believe everything he says."

"I don't talk shit. It's just what you don't want to here, Davis," he retorts, laughing. "If you ever want to know any stories about him, just let me know."

"I will take you up on that," Wren smirks. "I've learnt a few things about him myself."

"Oh, yeah? Like what?" Harry asks, throwing me a look. I don't bother to interject as I watch Wren take the lead. I'm glad she's making an effort to talk to my friends after putting up such a fight about wanting to come here.

"He's got an awful singing voice," she says proudly, her gaze drifting from Harry to me and then back to him. I can't hide the grin that's spreading across my face. If taking jabs at me is what makes her comfortable, I'll let her call me every name under the sun.

"Does he? I didn't know that," Harry replies, clearly amused.

"You've got to sing the national anthem at the next game, Davis."

"That's not going to happen," I laugh.

"Oh, but it should," Wren beams. "Have you seen how terrible his music taste is? It's like dating a—"

"*Okay*, that's enough," I say, cutting her off with a laugh. Harry's eyes are wide with curiosity, dying to hear what she has to say. "We're going to go see what's over there."

"I didn't even get to the best part," she whines before turning back to him. "The other day—"

I put my hand over her mouth on instinct and it almost covers her entire face as I slowly walk her backwards out of the kitchen. I turn back to Harry, and he shrugs happily before walking off. Her eyes widen with alarm before softening and staring into me as we continue sidestepping until we're in a corridor.

I can feel her breathing quicken beneath my hand as her green-brown eyes gently pinch together as she looks down at my hand on her mouth. I break my hand away when the realisation sets in on me and I shove it into my pocket. Her mouth opens and closes as she tries to search my face for something.

"What was that?" she asks after a while.

I tilt my head. "What was what?"

"You. Just then. Doing *that* thing with your hand."

"What is that ting?"

"You know what it is, Miles."

"I don't. Why don't you explain it to me?" She shakes her head, trying not to smile. I lean into her and whisper, "You're a little brat."

She snorts. "Oh please. What are you gonna do? Punish me?"

"You would love that, wouldn't you?"

She ignores me, rolling her eyes. Instead of making a comment like I'm expecting she says, "I'm having fun. With you, I mean."

I'm about to agree with her but my voice trails off as I see Greyson, so obviously drunk, waltzing towards us.

I'm dying to know what Wren meant but she shakes off whatever she was going to say.

"Miles," he slurs. "Is this your girlfriend?"

He gestures his cup towards us, his beer almost tipping over the edge. The change from being around Harry to Grey is so obvious on her face. I remember what she said about being around drunk people and I rub her shoulder and nod at him.

"The one and only," I say, and he chuckles with a hiccup. Her face turns pink.

"I'm Greyson but you can call me Grey," he introduces himself.

"Wren," she says her smile tight.

"Let me get you some water, dude. You're already wasted," I say, trying to find Grey's eyes but he's too busy looking around.

He snorts. "Since when were you such a prude?"

Wren stiffens beside me. "I'm not drinking tonight and if you don't want to be benched at the next game, I suggest you get a drink of water."

"Fine, *dad*," Grey mumbles. Wren laughs now. Finally.

I look down at her with adoration, watching her face transform into sunlight as she laughs at my expense. He mumbles something that neither one of us can fully understand. It's weird being sober around drunk people. I don't blame Wren that she doesn't like this feeling very much. She brings her hand across my stomach, nestling into my chest as if we aren't close enough already. The gesture makes my heart constrict when it shouldn't. This is just pretend.

"Well, it was nice to finally meet you, Wren," Grey mumbles when he senses that we want to be left alone. He gives me a messy wink before sauntering off. She bursts out laughing, pulling away from me quickly. Suddenly my whole-body aches for her to be touching me again. Even if it's only lightly. She stands across from me, leaning against the wall.

"Finally, huh?" she says when her laughter dies down. "Do you talk about me to your friends, Miles?"

I shake my head with a laugh. I inch closer to her. "Yes, I do. All the time."

"Really?" she asks, almost sarcastically. I nod my head. "And what do you say?"

"All good things," I say, resting my hands on her hips. She doesn't move or pull away from me. She slowly releases the tension in her body and dissolves in my hands. This is our first public appearance and I'm already getting lost between what's real and what's fake but something about the LED lights is making me hornier than I should. My fingers tug at her jumper, my thumbs barley grazing the skin under her shirt as I lean my face towards her ear. "Let's go to the pool."

Her breath catches before I feel her hands cover mine, slowly guiding my hand from out of her shirt.

"Okay," she rasps in my ear. "You can go in. And I'll watch. Then, I'll drive you to the hospital when you get a disease from whatever is in there."

She tears away from me and starts to walk in the other direction. I drag my hands down my face before catching up with her. When I get to her, I pull her hand into me as we stand, waiting for the people in front of us to move. She leans back into me, her ass melting into me. Too close.

"I was trying to do something cool just then, but I don't *actually* know where I'm going," she shouts over the music. A wide grin splits on my face. I place my hands on her shoulders and turn us around and walk towards the pool. In the right direction.

The pool is just as disappointing as Wren made out to be. Each inch of the rectangular pool is filled with semi-naked bodies, beer cans floating, and beach balls being thrown across it. The water has turned a strange brown colour and I don't want to find out why. We stand next to a wall close to the glass door, our hands unlinked but our shoulders touching.

It's a strange kind of intimacy that I didn't realise I enjoyed so much before tonight. She bumps her arm against mine.

"And you wonder why I don't like parties," she says, looking up at me with her green-brown eyes. I lean my head against door, laughing. I really do get it.

"Yeah, it's not as fun as I remember. But I guess I found them more fun when I *couldn't* remember them," I say. She frowns, her mouth twitching.

"How's that going? The sobriety." she draws out, not fully meeting my eyes. She kicks the stones on the path, her hands behind her back.

"Better. I think. I know I'll never fully be sober, but I have cut down a lot. I remember what happens nowadays and I'm not missing out vital memories," I admit with a sarcastic flare.

It has been hard getting back on track. I always knew the 'one drink' rule would fall through sooner or later. I trust myself enough to have a few beers but never anything stronger. When I'm around her, I want to be able to remember what happens. I don't want to drown out the feelings because I want her to know me. The real me.

"That's good," she says, almost too quietly. We settle into a rhythm of comfortable silence as *'Glitter'* by BENEE blasts out on the speakers, instantly reminding me of a scene from a movie except, we're not screaming and shouting and running around. Instead, we're lingering around like middle schoolers, watching the party in front of us, too afraid and uninterested to join in.

Her right footsteps between my left one, her back still against the wall. She puts her foot back where it was. I do the same until were in a competitive game of footsie.

"What are you doing?" I ask, laughing.

"Trying to win, duh," she replies and carries on nudging my foot. "This is a lot more fun than the party."

When we finally realise what we're doing, we're laughing and stepping on each other's shoes on purpose.

Her head shoots up from her feet and something across the pool catches her eye and she stops laughing.

"What's wrong?" I ask. She looks up at me as if she's seen a ghost. My heart starts beating rapidly against my chest.

"Fuck. Augustus is here," she says, turning to me so she's out of his view. I try and search over her head, but I can't see him. Then again, there are hundreds of skinny tall white guys here. She stands in-between my open legs.

"Put your hands on me," she demands.

"What?" I ask, basically gasping for air. I don't know why I question it after I was just all over her inside. Still, I freeze and blink at her.

She sighs and grabs my hands to rest on her hips as she snakes hers around my neck. I let her turn us around until her back is against the wall instead of mine. She arches slightly, her front flush against me.

Fuck me.

This is not going to end well for me.

Is this supposedto be torturing?

"Can you see him?" I ask before swallowing, her face just inches below mine. She looks behind me and nods before directing her face parallel to mine. My breathing turns shallow when her green eyes drift aimlessly around my face, not knowing where to look.

"Just pretend you're whispering in my ear," she suggests, pulling at the hair on the nape of my neck, playing the doting girlfriend as she looks at me lovingly. She guides my head until I'm breathing raggedly on her neck. I use one arm to brace myself on the wall, so I don't crush her with my weight.

"What do you want me to say?" I ask, quietly. She shivers under my breath.

"I don't know. I don't care. Just do some-" she pleads but her words turn into a sigh when I kiss her neck lightly.

119

It's barely even a kiss. Barley even a touch. My mouth merely skims the soft skin on her neck but when the goosebumps arise across her, I can't help myself.

I kiss her jaw tenderly, careful not to contact her mouth. The feeling instantly makes me feel light and airy as I breathe her in. She smells like Gucci perfume mixed with sweet lavender soap. Her hands move from my neck to my chest, her small hands fisting my shirt, drawing me in closer so I can taste the sweetness of her.

"Is this, okay?" I ask, biting softly against the space just behind her ear. She doesn't respond. Only a soft gasp leaves her mouth. So, I press again, "Wren. Is this okay?"

"Mm hmm. Just keep-" she breathes, not forming correct sentences. "Just keep doing that."

While my mouth explores the side of her neck, my hands go on their own journey. The party around us and the idea of someone watching makes me more ballsy than I should be. Wren guides my hand that has gone limp at my side to her shirt. She slowly lets me slip it under her jumper, my hand hardly splaying across her stomach.

She lets out a low noise of approval when the heat of my hand hits her cold stomach. I don't ignore the way I can feel her abs tensing beneath my hand. I kiss and nibble lightly on her neck and she whimpers.

She fucking whimpers.

Her breathing quickens when I accidentally rock against her, probably feeling how hard I am in these jeans, and she gasps. She's going to be the death of me. But at least I'd die a happy man.

"Is he gone?" I speak into her soft skin, needing to give myself some reason to stop.

"What?" she asks, her voice hoarse.

"Is Augustus still there?" I ask again, taking my hand out of her shirt. I pull my head back to see her with her eyes closed, cheeks redder than I have ever seen them, not even watching if he was there or not. It can't just be me that is feeling the attraction between us. I turn back, and I can't see him anywhere. "Wren. He's gone."

When her eyes open, her pupils are dilated. She searches my face, her chest rising up and down before looking over me. She looks at me for a long time.

Her eyes explore mine before she drops them to my lips. She hovers her gaze there for a second or two before turning around and walking away.

It takes my brain a while to register that she's just disappeared in front of me, and I run after her but she's a lot quicker than I thought. I push through the crowds of people, trying to keep my eyes on the gold claw clip in her hair. I shoot out quick apologies as I almost knock people over as I run past.

I see her sprint towards the bathroom but there's a small queue. She skips it, earning her a few grunts, and runs into it before the next person can even open the door. I get to the front of the queue, and I stand next to the door.

"Hey, what are you doing?" the guy at the front of the queue garbles. He's clearly drunk and too far gone but I apologise anyway.

"Sorry. My girlfriend is in there and I need to check on her. Can you wait a few minutes?" I say, trying to open the door handle. He groans and walks away. The rest of the queue slowly follows after they realise that this might take a while.

"Wren!" I shout through the door. "Can you please open the door? I need to see if you're okay."

121

I don't get a response for a few beats. I lean my head closer to the door, trying to hear better but all I can hear is my heart hammering against my chest.

"Miles," I hear a small sniffle from the other side of the door. "You're just going to laugh at me."

"Wren, are you okay? Why would I laugh at you? Can you open the door? Please," I plead, trying at the knob again. A few seconds go by as I wait by the door, thinking of a way to get closer to her. Would it be insane if I tried to break down the door?

Finally, I hear a click and I push the door open, slowly.

The bathroom is all marble and the bright lighting is startling compared to the dark neon lights on the other side of the door. The music is almost completely muted this far into the house so I can hear the trickle of the tap and the sharp breaths Wren takes in. She's stood, her back to me, her arms tight around her middle, looking out the window as if she's completely immobile.

I walk towards her cautiously.

"Wren. Are you okay?" I ask quietly. I put my hand on her shoulders and they drop with a shaky breath. "What happened?"

She turns around, her eyes filled with tears that haven't fallen yet. She blinks up at me, tears slowly falling down her face. Instinctively, I swipe my thumb across her cheek, a futile attempts to help ease her pain, resting my hand on her face for a second before dropping it.

"I think… I think I'm having a panic attack," she says over ragged breaths. Her head drops to her shoes as I place both my hands on her shoulders, steadying her. "This is, like, my third or fourth one this week. My second one today."

Her hands shake when she brings them to her face, rubbing at her cheeks. How can she still look so beautiful even when she's crying? I try to bring my hands to her face, but she backs away again, moving her hands frantically. She walks away from me until she's sat on the toilet seat, shoving her face into her hands. I sit down on the edge of the bathtub, looking at her with sincerity.

"Wren. Talk to me," I plead, trying to peel her hands away from her face but she doesn't budge. "I've got you. Can you take a deep breath?" I watch as her shoulders rise up, her voice shaky when she exhales. "That's it." I breathe in again with her and back out. I lower my voice and whisper, "What do you need from me? How can I help?"

She takes a few more breaths in, still covering her face before saying, "I don't know yet. It usually depends on who I'm with that makes it better or worse."

"What do you think? Do I make this better or worse."

"Better." She takes another deep breath. "The breathing is helping."

"Good. Keep doing that, Wren." I continue to breathe with her, doing what she needs to relax.

"What is wrong with me?" she says with a sigh, her voice muffled by her hands. I don't know if she wants me to answer that or not, so I wait to see if she'll continue. "I can't see my ex without panicking. How am I supposed to compete in the championships? How am I supposed to do *anything* normal?" She lets me take her hands away from her face and I hold them in my hands. She doesn't look at me, just staring at the way our hands mould together. Her hands are a lot softer and smaller than mine, so I turn them in my hands.

"There is nothing wrong with you. Everybody panics and has anxiety, but people just deal with it in different ways," I begin. She looks up at me now and a part of my wishes she didn't. I've never seen her like this before and it breaks my heart. "I used drink until the tightness in my cheat went away. Which I've learnt isn't very healthy."

"You have anxiety?" she hiccups. I nod.

She turns over my hand in hers, tracing her fingers across the lines in my palm. It's a new sensation I've never felt before. She runs her slender fingers through each line, focusing on the way my hand opens more to let her do whatever she needs to do to relax. Her delicate fingers against my rough ones send a pang of belonging through me.

"Since Carter, I've had this heavy feeling in my chest. I only recently braved it to Google it and I found out it is really common," I admit for the first time aloud.

"I never would have guessed with how extroverted you are," she says, her voice barely above a whisper. I just nod, not knowing what else to say. "How am I supposed to deal with it?"

"Do you know what triggered it? Was it seeing Augustus? Being here? Being with me?" I ask, almost afraid to hear the answer. I just want her to be okay. I want all of her pain to go away.

"I don't know. Maybe it was everything. Seeing him, the party, the people," she trails off, her eyes darting around the room. "Us." She waits a beat before swallowing. "Everything is just overwhelming. I thought that this part of the plan would be easy."

"I can take you home. Is that what you want? Will that make you more comfortable?"

124

"No. If I go home, they won't let me live this down. They'll think I'm not trying hard enough to make this work," she says.

"I think you are. Doesn't that count for something?"

"It does to me but not to them. They think I've been trying to avoid any social interaction since regionals. They already think you make me a better person. Happier. That's why they're being so pushy about it," she explains quietly.

"Do *you* think I make you a happier person?" I ask, a grin widening across my face. She smiles weakly, blinking back the last of her tears.

"Yes," she says through a sigh. She clears her throat. "I mean, my life sucks a little less when you're around."

I don't think I've ever had a feeling like this before. Usually, with the few girls I've been with, we hook up, talk for a few days and then it's over. We never get into this stuff. We never get to be vulnerable. But with Wren, it feels so easy. So natural. Even if our other relationship is fake.

"Come on," I say, standing up. "Let's get some food."

CHAPTER 12
WREN

I've been feeling on edge all week, so I wasn't surprised when I freaked out when I saw Augustus. My mom has been on my case more than ever, pushing me to train harder, to make sure the winter showcase goes ahead as planned.

I've been spamming my social media, trying to get more people to show some sort of interest. Miles posted a picture of us in the gym which earned me a couple followers but it's more of a waiting game to see if they show their support by turning up to the showcase. It doesn't help that Austin is completely AWOL, so my mom has no one else to project on. I was surprised that I broke down crying in the party bathroom and Miles had to save me.

I can't do that again. I've had panic attacks before, but I have never been told how to deal with them. I pushed them down as far as I could, and I ignored them. That's what I taught myself to do. They were seen as inconveniences more than anything. This one was worse because I already had other things weighing on me and seeing Augustus topped it off.

I've always hated parties, so I was expecting the nervousness, the skittishness. I wanted to do it for Miles. He has been training with me all week and he's not complained about it once. The least I could do for him is go to a stupid party for a couple of hours, but I couldn't even do that.

We didn't stay at the party for long after my breakdown. We took a few intimate photos, not showing my face after I ruined it by crying. Miles got a good shot of us in the car, my face buried into his neck as I tried my hardest not to breathe in his scent. The pictures are *all* very intimate, meaning we had to be very close to each other to take them.

After having his mouth on me at the party, I haven't been able stop thinking about it. I'm blaming my horniness on the fact that I haven't slept with anyone in over six months. That's why when we start driving to find somewhere to eat, I tell him stop at the first one we see to get this over with as quick as possible. We end up in a secluded diner, called *Fries*. Where, according to the very short menu, they only sell fries or fries (exploded). We sit across from each other in a back booth after ordering our fries and drinks. I ordered regular fries and Miles ordered the exploded version which I'm terrified to find out what that means. I take a long sip of my Coke, fiddling with my paper straw.

"I'm sorry," I whisper after our small talk dies down. He looks up at me, his eyebrows knitted in confusion as he drinks his strawberry milkshake.

"Sorry for what?" he asks, titling his head to the side.

"I don't know. Everything," I sigh, leaning back in my chair as I talk with my hands. "I just feel so useless. This is the part of the deal where I'm supposed to try my hardest. This is the part that should keep me on the team. I just feel like I keep messing it up. My mom has already got in my head."

"You're not messing anything up. We're still getting to know each other and it's good that we know now what *not* to do. If college parties aren't your thing, we'll find something else to show everyone what a strong couple we are," Miles says cheerfully. At least he's being optimistic and understanding. The anxiety in my chest deflates slowly like a balloon.

Our fries arrive and sure enough, his exploded ones look disgusting. It's even worse that he has the biggest grin on his face while I grimace at them. They're covered in melted cheese, bacon bits, mustard, and hash brown bites. If I wasn't so hungry to eat my own food I would have thrown up by now. We dive into our fries, our conversation becoming drawn out by pauses while we chew.

I make the mistake of locking eyes with Miles the second I begin to lick the salt and ketchup that dripped down my fingers. He watches me, his eyes dark and fierce as I pull out my fingers slowly, not knowing where to look. He stares at my mouth for a long second before looking down at his food.

"Sorry. That was gross," I groan, picking up a napkin.

"Stop apologising." I nod, biting my tongue not to apologise again. "I'm assuming you don't get to do this often." He gestures to my fries that I doused in ketchup. I laugh as I swallow.

"Yeah. I can't remember the last time I had food this greasy. If my mom found out she would have a heart attack," I laugh shallowly.

"Does she, like, monitor what you eat?" he asks, playing with his straw.

"Uh, I wouldn't say 'monitor.' But she does ask when we speak, just to make sure that I'm staying healthy enough to skate. It was worse when I was younger, but I think because I got so used to it, I don't really think about it that much," I say shrugging, poking around at my fries.

He nods in understanding, not pushing it any further. He eats more of his fries before pulling out his phone from his back pocket. "Question time," he announces.

"My absolute favourite time of the day," I say, sarcastically. These questions have opened up a lot about us, especially while we take breaks at the gym. Going into this, I never thought I would be that interested in getting to know him, but it turns out he's really fun to talk to. He knows how to keep things light and where to draw the line.

He scrolls through his phone before landing on one.

"This is a good one. Do you have a flaw that you think I might not be okay with?"

I think it over for a minute while I chew. "I think this will work better if we say what each other's flaws are. It's harder to point out your own flaw."

"So, we're just going to be telling each other what we *don't* like about each other?" Miles asks, titling his head to the side.

"Don't think of it like that. You asked the question. I'm just trying to make it easier," I suggest. "Do you want me to go first?"

"Sure," he says, slurping his milkshake.

"It's not really a *flaw* but just something I've noticed," I start tentatively. "You get very attached to things." His face doesn't move, as if he's already been told this before. "I mean, you literally had a full-on meltdown when we switched to a different gym."

He throws his head back laughing and god, I hate how much I love the sound of it - It's masculine and airy and you just want to melt into it. I can't help laughing too.

"What is it that you said? That I was hyper-fixating on you instead of dealing with my problems?" he mocks. I nod my head, suppressing my laugh. "I don't disagree. It's just something I do but if it wasn't for that, we wouldn't be doing this right now."

"That's very true," I say, raising my glass. He clinks his milkshake carton with my glass. "What about me? What's my fatal flaw?"

"Woah, it's not fatal. Like you said, just something I've noticed," he says, leaving a dramatic pause. "You are a very stubborn person, Wren Hackerly."

I gasp in fake shock. I have been told this my whole life; that I can't let things happen without putting up a fight no matter how ridiculous it seems. I've always stuck to routines, traditions, order. I've never felt the need to branch out of that. To get out of my comfort zone. Everything has always seemed so black and white.

Until him.

"You refused to do this in the beginning, but it wasn't until your friends pushed you that you realised how irresistible I am. And now look at us," he grins, moving his hands between us.

"And how well is that working out for us so far?" I raise my eyebrows. He shakes his head, a serious expression taking over his face.

"Wren," he presses. "We had one set back. We've been out one time. It's going to take a while for us to get used to each other."

"I know," I murmur. "I just really want this to work."

"I know. And it will," he says certainly before digging back into his fries. I pick up his phone off the table, looking for a question.

"Which of my qualities do you like the most?" I ask when I land on one. He chews thoughtfully before clearing his throat. "I like that you are what you get, you know?" he says. I draw my face into a puzzled expression, not fully understanding him. "Like, I knew from day one that you were brutal. I knew that I had to earn it, to deserve it, for you talk to me. You weren't going to let me have you so easily."

"I'm glad you think it's a good quality," I say softly.

"What do you mean?"

I take in a deep breath, my chest shaking on the exhale. "For as long as I could remember, I've kept my card to my chest. Never letting anyone get too close to avoid getting hurt but that was always such a dealbreaker. That's why Augustus left."

"Why do you think you do that?" he asks. "Push people away, I mean."

"Hey," I laugh. "This isn't a therapy session."

He shakes his head. "It's just a question, Wren. You don't have to answer it if you don't want to. I'm just trying to get to know you better."

I sigh. I want him to know me. The real me. If we're going to pretend to date, the least I can know is make it seem like he knows me. I can deal with us being friends at least.

"I think I'm just always trying to be good enough. To keep people interested. Then I started to realise that if I act the same all the time, no one will expect anything different from me."

"You don't seem to be like that with me," he says after a while.

"That's because I know you're not going to break my heart. And you're easier to talk to than most people."

"Why do you think that?"

"I don't know. I just do," I lie.

131

I do know. It's because he's one of the first people to treat me like an equal. To seem genuinely interested in getting to know me. To see me as a normal person and not just someone who can skate on ice. Someone who trains all day every day. He sees me as me even when I don't like who that is.

"What's your favourite quality about me, Wrenny?" he drawls.

"Definitely *not* that nickname," I mutter. He nudges my knee under the table. I nudge him back. "I like how quick you are. I would not have admitted this the first time we met but you keep me on my toes. You're funny in a way that can be seen as annoying, but I don't meet many people like you so to me it's just — sort of endearing. I think?"

His smile doubles as he beams at me. "And to think you didn't even like me a few weeks ago," he says bashfully, shaking his head.

"You're growing on me."

*

W e fire out more questions on the drive home, each question getting more ridiculous. *The stupider the better,* he said. His house and my apartment are actually a lot closer together than I thought. Realistically, I could jog from my house to his and back in fifteen minutes. I just don't know how I didn't pay more attention it before.

It's like he's been hiding in plain sight.

He insists on walking me to my door after parking. I've found myself warming up to him a lot more after tonight. It finally feels like we're actual friends. Not just fake dates. Especially after he helped me. Most guys would have run the other way if they saw their girl having a full-blown meltdown in a party bathroom. But he didn't. Yes, it's the bare minimum but he stayed.

"I hope this is your last question," he groans when we get out of the elevator to my apartment door. I lean my back against my door, and he towers over me, his dark eyes boring into mine.

"It is, I promise." I pause. "What is your love language?"

"Isn't it obvious?"

"Okay," I whistle at his expected answer. "So, physical touch? Got it."

He nods. "Anyone who says anything else is either a virgin or a liar. Or both," he drawls, a wicked grin spreading across his face. "What's yours?"

"The same. And words of affirmation," I say, my voice suddenly quiet, remembering the way his hand felt on my stomach at the party. His breath on my neck. He raises his eyebrows while brushing away one of my stands of hair from my face. He shakes his head a little. "What? Are you surprised?"

He brings his head close to my ear.

Too close.

His hot breath tickles my throat. His thumb traces small ovals from the sensitive part of my collarbone to the side of my neck where I'm sure he can hear my pulse hammering. I take in a shaky breath, my legs suddenly ready to give out beneath me.

"No, I'm not surprised, baby. I heard the noise you made when I touched you earlier," he murmurs, each syllable reverberating through my body. I close my eyes quickly before placing my hands on his chest, gently pushing some space between us.

133

"You just called me 'baby.' Unironically, might I add," I say defensively, blinking up at him, trying to ignore the rest of the sentence.

Miles grins. "Sure did, baby."

I shudder and pretend to gag. "I think I just threw up in my mouth a little." He laughs as if it's the funniest thing he's heard all day and I can't help but join in.

"If you call me 'baby,' I'm going to call you Milesy."

"Call me whatever you want, baby. 'Daddy' is also acceptable," he replies, smirking. I laugh at him and shove him in the arm, and he laughs too.

When we calm down, I say, "I had a good time today. Shitty food and all."

"Me too, but I don't think the food was *that* bad."

"This is why we changed your diet," I laugh as I open the door from behind me. "Good night, Milesy."

"Good night, baby," he whispers before turning on his heels. When I slip into bed later that night, I feel lighter.

I'm trying to convince myself that these sorts of panicking feelings just happen. They aren't going to determine my life and this fake relationship. I tried to shake off all those feelings in the shower, but my hands still shake a little when I reach for my phone.

When I unlock it, it's instantly flooded with followers and tags. I knew Miles was popular, but I didn't know the extent of it until now. I've got follows on Instagram from people that I've never spoken to before and likes from the people that shunned me after regionals. A strange sensation runs through my body when I click onto Miles' profile and there it is.

The most recent post in his grid is a picture of me in the diner we went to a candid of me nudging around my fries as I look down at them, my hair almost covering my face, but you can tell it's me. I don't know how I missed him taking the photo. I look over it again, take note of what I can see before my eyes wander down to the caption.

Eating bad fries in the middle

of nowhere with my girl ❤ ☐.

My heart bottoms out.

Jesus Christ. *My girl?* Why do those two words make my heart constrict and breathing stop? They shouldn't. He doesn't mean it, obviously, but I don't hate the feeling of pretending he did. I wander down to the comments which are a mixture of *You guys are so cute*, *When did this happen?* and *Who is she?* From this picture alone I've gained a shit ton of followers. I check my DM's and I scroll to find any names that I can recognise. I pull up Gigi's chat.

Gigi: I thought you were lying at first.
Gigi: Were you guys really in the middle of nowhere?
Gigi: Also, why are you covering your face? You seem happy.
Me: I don't know exactly where it was, so I guess so. It was a candid and I'm glad to have tour approval, G.
Gigi: You don't need my approval but it's good to know that you care about what people think.

I know Gigi enough to laugh it off and shut off my phone. When sleep pulls me under, I have the biggest and most ridiculous smile on my face.

135

CHAPTER 13
MILES

Since Sophia's, I've been trying my best to find a way for

me and Wren to really get a handle on this fake dating thing.
Parties aren't really her thing which is understandable. I mean,
who really wants to be around a bunch of sweaty teenagers who
are high as fuck? She has a point there but it's very limited to
go anywhere that will create some sort of excitement around
our relationship. I don't want to push her into going to parties if
it's going to freak her out. I also don't think that me being
around alcohol is a good idea when I need to get my head on
straight.

I've spent the last few days moping around, feeling pathetic as I
throw a ball at my wall from my bed, watching it bounce back.
Is this how it usually feels when I haven't had a drink? I've
never realised how lonely I was until I've seen what it's like to
be around Wren. Now, I feel like smashing my head against the
wall out of boredom.

I finally put myself out of my misery and throw on jeans and a
hoodie and jump into my car. I connect my phone to the
bluetooth and put on the playlist that I've started to put together
for Wren. Okay, it's not *for* her but it's also…for her. It's just

songs that not only remind me of her but songs that I know she likes from going to the gym and hearing them on repeat. When I'm not on the ice, I love to discover new music. Carter and I would have a pre-game pump up playlist that we would listen to before every game. Now, just hovering over that playlist makes my stomach turn. Instead, I put on 'Jump Then Fall,' by Taylor Swift and it immediately puts me in a good mood as I drive around my side of town, desperately trying not to go straight to Wren's apartment.

I mean, technically I should be able to go and see her when I want since she's my girlfriend. Fake girlfriend but still. She must be stalking me or something because the second the song finishes my phone lights up with a text from her.

Wren: Campus library. Study sesh. Now.
Me: Damn. Not even a 'please.'
Wren: I'm asking you to come study with me. You should be the one saying 'please' since I'm such a great person to be around.
Me: Who said I want to study with you?

The bubbles appear, suggesting that she's typing but they disappear again and I laugh to myself for getting under her skin. I can't help it sometimes. She's just too easy to wind up and lucky for her, I like it when she gets mad at me.

Wren: Miles, would you please come study with me so I don't fail my test. Not to be dramatic but you're my last hope.
Me: That's my girl.
Me: Wait. What is that supposed to mean? I'm supposed to be your first choice.
Wren: Just get to the library.
Me: I'm on my way.

I can count on one hand how many times I've been to the campus library. It's a large Adam-style building that contrasts the other modern architecture around the rest of the school, right across from Florentino's. Me and books don't mix well, which is why I chose a course where I could do minimal reading. I can read a banging biography but textbooks are a no-go.

I walk through the large doors, scanning my NU card onto the machine to go through the security gates and I'm in the middle of unknown territory. There are floor-to-ceiling bookshelves, filled with deep brown paperbacks and textbooks. I know it's a library, but it's *too* quiet here. So quiet that the second I accidentally step on the wrong piece of wood, the few people that are in here snap out of their study focus and give a death glare. But it also draws my attention to the one person I wanted to see.

Wren is sitting at a table tucked in the back of the study zones, the only person in her section. She has a pile of books on the right side of her, her laptop displayed in front of her. She looks different in this setting. She's not sweaty and panting from skating or working out. Instead, she's got owl frame glasses on, her hair is tied into a high ponytail and she's wearing a white tank top and shorts, her knee pulled up to her chin.

I walk over to her with the biggest grin on my face and I step on another wrong plank of wood. You'd think that they'd try to make the floors as soundless as possible but no. Wren shakes her head at me, pulling up her glasses to rest on the top of her head.

"Could you be any louder?" she whisper-shouts when I sit across from her.

"Hello to you too, girlfriend," I say sarcastically, leaning on my elbows, looking at her adoringly. Maybe the cute puppy look gets a lot of girls going but Wren could not look more turned off if she tried. I reach over to tap her glasses and pull them onto her face. "These are cute."

Her nose crinkles as she rolls her eyes. "Thanks," she murmurs, looking down onto her laptop and then back to me. "I need you to test me with these questions." I raise me eyebrows and she whispers, "Please."

She turns the laptop towards me and I see the list of questions she has in her Word Doc about a book called 'Atonement.' I have no idea what that is but the questions seem interesting. Well, interesting if you're into literature. Is this my pathetic way of admitting that anything that Wren's into, means I am into it too by proxy.

"Is this all you need me for?" I ask, scrolling through the endless list. She nods, scribbling something down onto a notebook. "Couldn't Kennedy and Scarlett do this? As much as I know I'm going to enjoy asking these questions, I know I wasn't your first choice."

"Do you have any volume control?" she whispers, pinning me a scary look. I didn't think I was talking that loud but fine.

"Scarlett has an exam today and Kennedy's working."

"And you don't have any friends from your class?"

She shrugs before shaking her head. "Just ask me the damn questions, Milesy."

And I do.

I learn all about the cultural and social setting of the novel and a bunch of other random shit that I don't need to know. I don't know how she's worried about passing this exam when she answers every question immediately and exactly with the answers that she's written down. I have no idea what most of the stuff she's talking about means, but it seems like she has a handle on it.

When I finally get to the last question, I turn the laptop back around to her. "What's next?"

She scrolls through it, picking up her very annotated copy of the novel before typing something down. "I need to write down some last minute notes and then I'm going to do a timed essay."

"And you need me here for that, why?"

"So you can confiscate my devices. I'll get too distracted if I have them in front of me. It's what me and the girls usually do," she explains. That makes sense. I can barely study when I've got anything in front of me. Maybe I should come to the library more often but if she's here…maybe that's not a good idea.

"Do you have that little self-control?" I tease, making sure to keep my voice quiet.

"I have a lot more self-control than you do," she challenges. "I'm just gonna make these notes and then do the essay. You should go and explore while I write."

"And risk getting death-stared by every person in here? No thanks," I say, leaning back in my chair, crossing my arms. "I can just watch you study."

"Fine, you perv," she murmurs before getting back into the zone.

Watching her study is slightly motivating me. I know I should have brought some of my own stuff with me, to study for exams that aren't for months, but I would have just got distracted anyway. Have I mentioned how beautiful this woman is? How is she managing to read, write and listen to a podcast all at once? I can't figure it out for the life of me but her dedication to studying as well as skating is one of the most attractive things I've ever seen. I've been making paper boats with her spare paper for almost an hour. She's still not ready to write her essay yet so I'm this close to dying of boredom. I tap her pen with the fluffy end next to the laptop as she types away.

"Wren. Wren. Wren. Wren," I press and I know it's about to irritate the fuck out of her. "Wrenny, Wren, Wren."

She stops typing, slamming the laptop shut dramatically. "What!?"

I smile wide, popping my dimple out and everything. "Hi."

Her face almost breaks for a second but she sticks her tongue in her cheek before opening her laptop again. She starts typing as she says, "Don't do that."

"Do what?" I ask innocently.

"Annoy me like a puppy."

"Isn't that what boyfriends are for?"

"*Real* boyfriends," she clarifies. "*Real* boyfriends can annoy me. *Real* boyfriends carry my books for me. *Real* boyfriends don't rest until they've given me the best orgasm of my life. But you, Miles Davis, are my fake boyfriend."

Because I have no self-control, I say, "Are you trying to hint something, Wren?"

"No," she snaps, blushing. "All I'm saying is, it's empty in here so you don't need to do that. Rule number three."

Fucking rule number three.

*

When Wren finally finishes her essay, she picks up all of her shit and we walk across to Florentino's. It's busy here, as

140

always. This shop is rivalling Starbucks with the special menu the school has created. If there is one good thing about NU besides hockey, it's this cafe. We walk up to the counter, my arm around her shoulder, Wren's books clutched to her test, and I'm sure we look like every cliched couple in a teen drama. "What's your usual order?" I ask when we join the line. She tilts her head to the side, thinking for a second.

"It depends what the special is. Ken is always whipping something up in there," she says, nodding to her best friend who is working frantically behind the counter. "Her mango smoothies are fantastic."

"In this climate? It's fucking freezing outside and you want a mango smoothie?" I ask, clearly shocked by her poor choice of drink.

"Okay, fine. What would you suggest?"

"Deluxe hot chocolate, obviously," I say flippantly. "It's fucking expensive here but it's good."

"That's not the most expensive thing on the menu," she whispers, shifting from one foot to the other as we move further down the line.

"Really? What is?"

"The caramel crunch cappuccino," she concedes, avoiding eye contact with me.

"Let me guess. That's your usual order," I say, laughing. She nods.

"Even with Kennedy's discount, it's still ridiculous," Wren replies. "It is the best drink though."

"I'm a nineteen year old student. What makes you think I can afford a seven dollar coffee?" I spit out and she laughs, shrugging. "You're lucky, darling. You are the only exception."

"Oh my God, you're quoting Paramore to me right now," she gasps. She fans herself dramatically. "I think I'm falling for you, Miles."

I laugh with her and nudge her in the shoulder to move forward since we're next in the line. When Kennedy sees us she smiles wide, clearly our biggest fan. She's dressed in her pink Florentino's uniform and her apron that is covered in small pins, showing off all the groups she supports.

"There is my favourite couple," she exclaims. "What can I get for you?"

"The most expensive drink you have," Wren chimes in, smiling at me. I'm going to be fourteen dollars more broke than I was this morning but if it makes her smile like that, I'd do it again in a heartbeat.

"Coming right up," Ken says, rushing off to serve the next person after I pay.

We walk out of Florentino's sipping our drinks walking towards Radnor Hall where Wren's classes take place. I'm holding both of our drinks in my hand while Wren hooks one arm into mine, holding her books with the other. It would probably be super cringe if I was feeding Wren her drink if it was anyone but her. I swear every time we walk past someone, they do a double take. I don't think I'm ever going to get used to this. The stares. The whispers. The looks.

We've kept mostly quiet as we drink our cappuccinos. I can't lie. This drink is amazing and unfortunately worth the money.

"Wren! Oh my god. I was just looking for you," a girl with dark brown hair rushes towards us when we're walking past the library. The girl I've never seen before in my life hooks Wren's arm into hers, taking her away from me.

"You were?" Wren asks, looking back to me as her friend walks them in front of me.

"Yes! I was trying to find you to talk about the essay we had to do for Atonement," she explains. "Aren't you going to introduce me to your boyfriend?"

Wren turns around, looking at me sceptically, her eyes suddenly wide and unsure. "This is Miles Davis. I'm sure you know him. Miles, this is Katie Buxbaum from my creative writing class."

"So you guys really are dating?" Katie asks, looking between the both of us. We nod. Her eyes narrow for a second before she nods again, slowly. "Cool. So will you guys come to my party tonight, then? It's a lowkey thing but most people from class are going."

I'm about to respond but Wren awkwardly unlink her arms with Katie's and picks up her drink from my hand and throws it into

142

the trash.She slips her fingers into mine instead, signalling to me that she doesn't want to talk to her.

"Thanks for the offer but we're busy tonight. We're like newly weds. Just can't be apart from each other," Wren says, her voice an octave higher than usual as she snuggles into my side. "I'll see you in class." Wren practically runs down the corridor, pulling me along with her, turning the sharp corner until we're away from her and panting.

"What the hell was all that about?" I ask when Katie is out of sight. "That could have been a perfect opportunity."

"I didn't want to go, okay?" Wren pants, her big green eyes boring into me. "My social battery has already run out and I swear I've never spoken to Katie before today. The thing is, she's really nice but I don't want to build our friendship around the basis that I'm sort-of popular now. I'm sure she's great but I just-"

I cut her off, placing my arms on her shoulders as she clutches the books to her chest. "Hey. Can you chill? I just wanted to know why you didn't want to go and now I do. You don't have to explain everything to me. I'm not going to push you. Okay?"

"Okay."

"Okay. Now give me your books," I demand.

Her eyebrows crease. "What?"

"Let me hold your books for you, woman," I say, plucking the books from her. "Oh, and your bag too." I sling her tote bag over my shoulder, feeling ridiculous and proud all at the same time. She shakes her head at me, laughing.

She hooks her arm through mine again, walking us down the corridor towards her class. "These are the kind of fake-boyfriend perks I need."

"You know…" I start. "I can give you all the perks if you want."

"I'm good," she replies, scrunching her nose. Her phone rings and because her hands are finally free, she reaches into her back pocket and pulls it out. "I've got to take this. It's my dad. My class is jsut there. I'll see you later."

She starts to collect her books and her bag from my shoulder. She starts to walk, leaving me behind but I call after her. "I think your forgetting something."

"What? I have all my books," she concedes.

"My kiss." I grin.

"Right. How could I possibly forget?" she mimics, walking back up to me and presses the softest kiss to my cheek.

This is going to be perfect.

I get to watch her study. I carry her books. I walk her to class and then I get a kiss on the cheek. Fake dating Wren Hackerly might be the best thing to ever happen to me.

CHAPTER 14
WREN

What was I doing and why couldn't I make myself stop? Even though I've kept up with my gym and skating routine, the little free time that I have has been spent with Miles. Miles Fucking Davis has taken over my life and the worst part is – I don't mind.

I knew the girls were right when they said he made me a happier person because he does. He doesn't pester me about skating, about my diet, about school. We just talk. A lot of it is nonsense but we talk. And it feels good.

He's been pushing the line lately but so have I. There is no denying that there is constant sexual tension between us but we're both working hard on not acting on it. Sure, we've both said a flirty comment here or there but in private we've never done anything that we *should* be doing in public. I am still sticking to my main rule: if this get too real, in whatever way, we have to let each other know. I can't risk this becoming too powerful.

It wasn't easy helping Miles get back to his position that he was in before everything happened. We've been to the gym nearly every day over the past two weeks, gradually getting more difficult but he's stayed on top.

Being seen around campus with Miles definitely has its perks. I never used to wander around other than when I was on my way to class, but it turns out there is a life outside of the rink.

We went to the campus library, Miles' arm over my shoulder and I could have sworn there was paparazzi. Okay, maybe not but it felt like it. We were constantly interrupted by other people who were calling him 'bro' as if they spoke before that interaction. The guys want to be him. I get it. He's hot and he's popular but by the way some of these guys are up his ass, you'd think he's Brad Pitt or some shit.

And the girls — they are even worse. They come over and say "Hi" as if they weren't the same people who mocked me after regionals. As if they weren't the ones who dropped out of figure skating, leaving the rest of us to somehow salvage the little hope our team has. I guess people are just glad to see us happy again.

I've spent most of this morning at the rink, spinning and gliding until my head starts to throb. I'm trying to add the finishing touches to my routine for the showcase but filming it has been a nightmare.

Scarlett doesn't have the patience to stand and film it for me, even though she says that she *loves* to watch me skate. And Kennedy is just a lost cause who claims that her arms ache too much to be able to film a five-minute performance. I go through my routine full out for the millionth time and I don't even need to strain my eyes to see that he's here.

"You've got to stop sneaking up on me like this," I say as I land my Lutz on a wobbly leg, groaning at myself.

"Do you have eyes at the back of your head or something?" Miles asks as I see his blurry figure walking down the last set of stairs. He stands at the end of the rink, his forearms dangling on the railing, a lazy smile hanging on his mouth.

"No, you just breathe *really* loud," I say sarcastically. He rolls his eyes. "What do you want?"

"Do I have to want something to speak to my *girlfriend*?"

I still haven't gotten used to those words on his mouth, no matter how fake they are and how many times he says it. Only two people have ever called me their girlfriend: Augustus and my two-week boyfriend in middle school, Ryan. To hear anyone say it, it'd be insane, but coming from him it's even more strange.

"My bad. What's the matter, *honey*?" I amend. He shudders at the pet-name which makes me equally as uncomfortable.

"Okay, chill. We're nineteen not ninety," he says shaking his head. "Our first game is coming up, it's only a friendly but I can't play yet. So, I was thinking that we could go together, to watch. Everyone will go insane when they see me on the bench."

I can't help but laugh at his confidence. "How are you so sure everyone will go '*insane*'?"

"Because women love to scream my name," he whispers. I fight off the heat on my face as I push away from him, skating backwards.

"You're disgusting, you know," I shout, even though we're not that far away.

"You can stop acting like you don't like me. It's not cute anymore, Wrenny," he whines.

147

"Who said I was pretending?" I grin. He opens his mouth before closing it again, shaking off whatever he was going to say. "And you calling me Wrenny isn't cute either." I groan at his insistent use of the nickname Kennedy introduced him to. "Watching you act like you hate it is the best part of my day," he says proudly, grinning at me with that ridiculous face of his. I roll my eyes, but he can't see because I'm in the middle of turning. Then a thought pops into my head, reminding me why I was thinking of him in the first place.

"Oh shit," I say, tumbling towards him.

"What? Are you okay?"

"Yeah, I'm fine. I just forgot to ask you something and it's kind of late notice," I explain, frustrated with myself for not asking earlier. "Can you pass me my guards? They're in my bag." Miles turns to look in my gym bag and pulls out my white guards for my skates. I glide to exit the rink, holding onto the railing as I slip them on before sitting down on the bench, finally being able to breathe. He slides next to me, wonder and curiosity dancing in his eyes.

"What's up?" Miles questions.

"My dad invited us to this gala event at one of his hotels. He said he wants to meet you, but I know we said we'd discuss the whole family thing, but it slipped my mind. It's in three days. No one from NU should be there but my dad knows we're 'dating.' You can totally say no if you're not comfortable and I can just make an excuse," I ramble, my hands doing most of the talking.

"I'll come," he replies quickly. "Should be fun, right? Evan goes to galas all the time. Isn't it like the Oscars for people who have boring jobs?"

"Yeah, sort of," I laugh.

"Do you think he'll like me? Your dad," he asks, wearily.

"Definitely. He likes everybody," I say truthfully. He draws back a little, clearly hesitant. Without thinking about it, I touch his knee reassuringly. "I'm not just saying that, either. He's a very nice guy and he's probably my favourite person to ever walk the Earth. He'll probably call you 'son' the second you meet."

That makes him smile. I really am not just saying it. My dad is one of the friendliest people I've met. Sometimes, he's a little too friendly which is why I often question how he's managed to stay in the hotel business for so long. He's nice and he's kind but he won't let people walk all over him, that's for sure.

"Another thing…." I draw out when the thought comes to my head. "Usually with these events, my dad books me a suite to stay for the night to save me travelling back home late. When I told him about you, he got us a room. Obviously, you don't have to stay the night but just so you know."

His face lights up. "You think I'm going to pass on going to another fancy hotel with you after seeing that gym?"

"I feel like there was a *sliver* of a compliment in there for me," I say, squinting my eyes.

"There was, Wrenny. There was."

I roll my eyes, again, at his use of that name. I grab my bag and stand up before slinging it over my shoulder. "Wear something nice and I'll pick you up at three."

"You got it, Wrenny Rainbow," he says with a commander's salute.

"Hey, you've already got 'baby' *and* 'Wrenny,' so please don't tell me that's going to be a thing too."

"Oh, it already is."

*

149

"**I**'m never going to forgive you for this, Wren. I have so many emotions inside of me I think I might explode. Actually, I'm moving out," Kennedy groans, dropping onto the floor dramatically.

"I'll be moving out with her," Scarlett adds, falling to floor on top of Kennedy.

I have just read them the latest chapter to Stolen Kingdom and I killed off one of the main love interests, Erik. He was a personal favourite of the both of them. I kind of loved him too. He was the kind of book boyfriend that all my friends obsessed with. Dark features, too tall for anyone, dominant and completely lacking any sorts of self-awareness. I poke them with my feet from the couch as they squirm.

"You guys are so dramatic. He's not even real," I say, joining them on the floor.

"He was real to me!" Kennedy sobs, throwing her hand across her face melodramatically. Scarlett sits up, tutting at her as if she wasn't on the floor a few second ago. "I already fan-cast Austin Butler to play him in the movie."

"It's not going to be a movie," I mutter under my breath. Kennedy pretends to sulk with a pout.

"Speaking of things that aren't real... How are you and Loverboy?" Scarlett asks with a shoulder shimmy. Over the past few weeks, I've gotten used to Scarlett's variations of nicknames for Miles. I've heard, Hockey Freak, Milesy Cyrus, Loverboy, Miles a Million, and Miley. Honestly, I don't hate them.

"Things are good. He's getting better with training, and I got a ton of Instagram followers. Oh, and Gigi approves. Things are looking up," I say proudly.

"Cool but how are…you know…*things*?" Scarlett repeats with more emphasis, gesturing suggestively towards my private areas. Kennedy shoots up now, looking at us with expectant eyes, mischief dancing in them.

"What she's trying to say is: have you fucked him yet?" Ken asks without batting an eye.

"I wasn't going to say 'fucked,'" Scarlett drawls with an eye roll. Her face suddenly turns serious. "But yes, have you?"

"No, I haven't. And I don't think I'm going to anytime soon," I sigh. "But the sexual frustration is slowly eating away at me. I've burned through two sets of batteries for my vibrator in the past week."

I hate to admit it but it's true. Seeing him nearly every day has *not* helped the throbbing between my legs. He's an attractive guy and we have to go to the gym together. Listening to him grunt and groan is not making this any easier. Not because I want him but because I haven't slept with anyone in months. We're both attracted to each other, that much is clear, but the second we act on it outside of the contract, it could be messy. It also means that every time I close my eyes he's right fucking there.

"You dirty bitch," Scarlett mocks, her face wide in a smile. I shove my face between my hands. "You need to sleep with someone and quick. It doesn't even have to be with Miles. It isn't in your little contract, is it?"

I lift my face up to them. "*Technically* it's not but I don't want to do that. It feels too close to cheating, and I'd feel disgusting afterwards."

"Because that's so much better than a vibrator," Kennedy retorts sarcastically.

"Well, at least it can make me finish," I say, getting up from the floor.

We all burst out laughing until our stomachs hurt. Kennedy is the slapper, hitting us until we're basically bruised while she laughs hard. I'm the one with the wheeze and Scarlett just sounds like an evil baby genius.

"Poor Augustus," Scarlett says between her hysterical laughter. My phone starts to ring beside me and I see my Dad's caller ID and I pick it up.

"Hi, dad," I say when I answer it.

"Emmy! I thought I wouldn't be able to get you with how busy you were the last time you called," my dad replies, being the drama queen he is.

I laugh. "I had to go to class, dad. I'm not busy now. What's up?"

"Is your boyfriend coming to my opening gala?" he asks, leaving no room for small talk. Before I can respond he adds, "I've sorted out the room and everything so I hope he can. If not, it's totally fine. I understand how you kids are these days."

"Yes, he said he can come," I say and the girls try and hold in their laughs.

"Perfect. I can't wait to meet who has been making my daughter so happy," he replies. I wish he could see me rolling my eyes. "I got you a luxury suite so you don't have to worry about sleeping in different beds."

"Yeah. Dad. About that. We don't need to share a bed because-"

"Wren," he presses. "I want you to know that I trust you. And I know that you and your mom don't have the best relationship

152

but I don't want that for us. If you and your boyfriend want to cuddle, who am I to stop you?"

"But dad-" I try again but he cuts me off.

"Wren. It's settled."

"Mom would never do this," I murmur, laughing at my dad's persistence.

"Good job I'm not your mom. Isn't it, kiddo?" dad adds before cutting the call on me.

CHAPTER 15
MILES

I had no fucking clue what to wear to this thing and all

Wren said was to "wear something nice." Because that was so
much help. I raided my closet, and it turns out that I have
nothing nice to wear. Not even anything decent. I can't show
up to a fancy event with my fake girlfriend's dad looking like
an orphan.

Luckily, I knew just the person to ask.

Evan got me a link to a good tailor who wasn't crazy
expensive, and I dug into my savings to buy myself a suit and
bow tie. It's nothing too flashy but it should be enough for the
occasion and considering the price, maybe even my wedding.

I thought I would be more nervous but I'm mostly just excited
to get a weekend away with her. Although our 'contract' says
we should have sleepovers once a week, we've really only done
that a few times. We were both too awkward over the whole
ordeal so whenever it got late, we slipped out of each other's
houses without making a fuss. I don't know if I could trust
myself with her in my room after what happened the last time.

Maybe I need to get laid. Not by her. But by someone. And soon.

"Please tell me you brought your outfit in your bag," Wren pleads the second I slip into her car in my dark jeans and faded tee. I throw my bag into the backseat before putting on my seatbelt.

"No, Wren, I'm going to wear this to the event," I reply sarcastically, gesturing towards my outfit. "Obviously it's in my bag."

"Did you get something nice to wear?" she asks as she checks her mirrors while backing out of my drive.

"Define what you mean by nice..." I tease, leaning over to play with the radio until a station I don't hate comes on. Listening to Wren's Taylor Swift playlist while we work out has had its effects on me. Now, I can't do anything active without some *1989* or *Reputation* action. Her music cures the soul. It has to be magic or some shit.

"I don't know. Something charming, smart, dazzling," she lists, staring out at the traffic we quickly merged into. I watch her dark blue nails tap onto the steering while and I'm hypnotised for a second.

"Aren't I all those things anyway?" She gives me an unimpressed glance. Maybe it's too early for my bullshit. "Yes, I brought something nice."

"Okay, good," she says softly. She murmurs something under her breath as she taps her fingers impatiently. The car in front of us remains stationary when the light turns green and her face heats up as she pounds the steering wheel with her tiny fists without hitting the horn. "God! Can you drive your fucking car!?"

155

I've never seen her road rage before, and I don't hate the way her cheeks flare up and her chest rises and falls. I can't stop staring at the way she puffs air through her nose and rolls her eyes.

Is it bad that I like it even more when she does it to me? I decide not to say that and instead try and tread on something lighter.

She starts to angrily hum to Frank Ocean's *Pink and White* and it's a little terrifying.

"You seem...tense," I mention quietly, turning down the song. She turns to me for a split second before focusing on the road. She looks back at me for a beat longer as if she's trying to see straight through my brain before returning back to the road.

"I haven't slept properly in almost two weeks," she grits out, her knuckles gripping the steering wheel.

"Why? What's keeping you up?"

"Oh, nothing," she says cheerfully. I can tell she's about to go on a sarcastic tangent. Luckily for her, it's my favourite thing ever. "Just, having a quarter life crisis over my career in figure skating. Oh, and my sister has been off the grid for almost two months and my mom is starting to project all of her frustrations onto me. The usual."

"Wait, you have a sister? You've never mentioned her before," I say, surprised at he casual revelation of her sister which I never knew about until just now.

"I'm sure I have," she murmurs, giving me a sideways glance but I shake my head with a shrug. "Her name's Austin. Just think of my mom but twenty-five and a ballet dancer."

"Ah," I nod. "You guys aren't close?"

"We are. Sort of. She was like my mom's test run before I was born so if I thought I had Mommy Issues, Austin has it worse.

156

She's been in Russia for the last four years at this ballet program. We haven't heard from her in a while and everyone's a bit worried," she explains.

"Are you worried about her? Is that why you're stressed?"

She groans a little, shrugging. "I am but I'm not. Austin is tough. A lot tougher than me. She's always been independent so I'm sure that whatever she's going through she'll get through it. It only stresses me out because when my mom doesn't have two kids to fuss over and all the weight lands on me. That's why she's been so hard on me about getting the skating stuff sorted as soon as possible."

My mind instantly drifts to Clara. How I've been pushing her away over something she was trying to protect me from. Maybe I should reach out to her. Carter would have told me to. *She's your sister, you big dummy,* he would say. Each time we would fight as kids, that was always his comeback. It didn't take me long to notice that he wanted me to have a good relationship with my sister because he never had one with his brother.

"She'll come around. Family is hard. Believe me, I know," I say as reassuringly as I can.

"You never talk about your family, and you talk about *everything*." She laughs softly. "But just so you know, you can talk to me about them. When you want to, that is."

"I know," I reply. "You've already got a lot on your plate and I don't want to burden you."

She smirks, glancing at me. "See. You can be thoughtful sometimes."

"I never said I wasn't."

"I know. I just said it in my head."

As we drive over, I try and remember the countless stories she has told me about her dad. From what I've heard he's probably the only person that Wren truly loves apart from her friends. When she talks about him, she doesn't hold back anything like she does with her mom. She doesn't talk about him as if he's simply just the person responsible for creating her.

She told me about how much she adores him; how grateful she is to have him as a dad while her mom was hard on her. Over the last three days she's been quizzing me on the things that her dad likes and what he doesn't. She drops another ambiguous message as we merge into more traffic.

"Cream cheese," she mentions flippantly, keeping her eyes focused on the road. I never found women driving so attractive until her. She just looks so in control and fuck me if it doesn't turn me on.

"Like or dislike?" I ask.

"Loathe," she growls, slowly turning to me, her eyebrows knitted together. I widen my eyes and slouch back in my seat, trying to suppress my laugh.

"Okay," I whistle. 'No cream cheese."

"*Never* any cream cheese."

*

T he hotel looks a lot fancier than I imagined. I have to crane my head back to take in all the storeys of sleek black glass from top to bottom. The inside has gold accents across most major centrepieces and along the railings, giving it a regal touch as a grand piano sits in the foyer. Her dad *owns* this? It's insane.

Wren navigates us around as if she works here. She seems so natural at this, as she links her arm in mine, walking us around. So comfortable. She talks to the staff as if they are old friends that she needs to catch up with. Honestly, I wouldn't be surprised if they are. There is still so much that I feel like I don't know about her. So much that I'm dying to know.

We make our way through the glass elevator to our suite which seems to take up most of the top floor. There are three main rooms: the master bedroom with a California king sized bed, a huge bathroom, and a living room space with a mini bar. Obviously, we're not legally allowed to drink so everything is empty, but it's still cool regardless.

"So, I guess I'm sleeping on the couch," I say when I return the bedroom. Wren has begun unpacking her things onto the hangers neatly, walking back and forth from her suitcase on the bed to the closet. I don't understand why she insisted on bringing so many clothes for such a short trip.

"Miles. I had to through the troubel of having to explain to my dad that I wanted sperate beds. He's doing the whole 'I trust you' thing. Plus, this bed could fit like three times the size of us on here and there would still be room. We can share it for one night, right?" Wren explains, turning around to me. "You probably won't even notice I'm there."

"Okay but no funny business," I relay, mainly reminding myself to keep it in my pants. I could never *not* notice her. She laughs and walks towards me.

"It's you, you should be worried about, not me," she says into my ear quietly, her hand on my bicep. She brushes past me gently as I swallow. Hard.

This is going to be a great fucking weekend.

After an hour of dilly dallying, we're finally getting ready for the gala. I'm stood in front of the wide full-length mirror, watching a YouTube video on how to tie my bow tie. I don't

159

know I let Evan talk me out of getting a clip on one. He said something about making a good impression. I'm grunting with frustration when I see a glimpse of her in the mirror behind me. Her eyes lock with mine and I don't bother to hide my libido. She looks devastating.

She's dressed in a dark blue evening gown, her tits looking perfect, stuck in the thin straps. Her blonde hair is tied back into a neat bun with a small silver clip. Her silver earrings dangle almost to her shoulders which match with her heels. She walks towards me, painfully slowly and my hands fumble around my tie.

"Need help with that?" she asks gently, gesturing towards my bow tie. I nod, basically foaming at the mouth. When did I forget how to speak?

Her delicate hands come towards my neck as she unties the knot I made. Very slowly. I watch as her hands work at the mess I made, and I try and swallow. She looks up at me, smirking, before looking back down to my tie. I can't ignore the breathiness in her voice as she asks, "What?"

"Promise me you'll come back here with me tonight," I get out when I find my voice. Her eyebrows furrow. She looks up at me, but I watch her in the mirror.

"What do you mean?"

"You look…fucking stunning, Wren," I whisper, and I make the mistake of looking at her properly. Her wide green-brown eyes stare into mine, her lips slightly parted. "I'm just saying I won't be surprised if someone tried to take you home with them."

"The only person taking me home tonight is you," she murmurs. My heart skips multiple beats as I almost topple over.

I know it shouldn't take this long for her to tie my tie, but her hands are still on me, even when I can see it's done.

"Are you sure your dad will like me?"

"Yes, I'm sure." She looks up at me as she takes a little step back. Her heel almost catches with the carpet, but I pull my hand around her waist to steady her. As if on instinct, her hands come to lapels of my blazer, pulling herself up into me. "Now stop worrying."

"What if I bring up cream cheese?"

"Why would you *ever* bring up cream cheese?" she asks, the lines of a dimple battling her cheeks.

"I don't know. I might get nervous and say something about it."

"If you do, I *will* go home with someone else tonight right after I murder you."

With my shitty timing and my even shittier luck, it seems as if I've managed to will my worries into existence. From the short time we've been in here, there has been this one guy with his eyes on Wren the entire time.

He's dressed like all the other men in this joint accept he's one of the few who look our age. Even when we're sitting my hand tightly around her waist and her head nestled in my shoulder, he still doesn't stop trying to fuck her with his eyes. Not that she notices.

It turns out these things are pretty boring when you can't drink. All the people around us are drunk, laughing loudly and finding everything funny. Wren and I are sitting, eating pistachios out of a bowl, waiting for something to happen. Anything.

Wren looks more energised than me, clearly used to these sorts of environments as she looks around with a happy expression on her face.

161

"Is this what it's usually like?" I ask after another round of silence.

She sighs, slouching back in her chair. "Pretty much. It was better when the girls would come. We'd make up silly games to pass time. It was more of an excuse for us to dress up."

I tilt my head at her in curiosity. "Oh yeah? Like what?"

"Just people watching, making up lives for strangers that we see. Wanna play?"

I'll do about anything to pass the time at this point. "Show me how it's done, baby." I smirk as she shudders.

"Okay. You see that guy over there?" she asks, her gaze setting on a group of men, but one guy in pants and a button down stands out as he's the only one without a blazer. I nod. "Middle class. Divorced his wife because she watched a movie he introduced her to without him. He likes it soft and timid, you know...In bed. But, she was an animal. He couldn't admit it to his buddies so he lied and said *she* was the one who couldn't take his sword of thunder."

I roar out a laugh at the randomness and she does too, smiling at me. "Your brain is brilliant."

"Why , thank you," she mimics coyly. She nudges me in the shoulder. "Now, your turn."

"Okay...the guy next to your guy. He lives a very happy life. Wife, kids, the whole shebang really. But, he has a secret. He probably has a porn collection or something from the way he's fidgeting like that."

"Not bad, Davis. Not bad at all," she says, shaking her head with a grin.

"I learnt from the best."

She gives me one last smile before turning back to the crowd. "Okay, that woman over there with the pixie-cut definitely has twins. I can just tell from the lines in her face. They give her hell but she loves them. She has an older son though, who looks like Schmidt from New Girl and he is for sure robbing her without her knowing. But she'd let him get away with it. Freud and all that."

"How am I supposed to beat that?" I ask, gaping at her but she shrugs. I scan the rom for somebody and then my eyes connect with the creep that has been staring at her all night. "The guy, our age, he's obsessed with you."

"What?" Wren chokes out, almost laughing.

"I'm being serious. He's been eye-fucking you all night."

"Now you're really not understanding the game," she mutters, shaking her head at me like I'm a disappointing kid.

"I'm telling the truth," I challenge, turning to her. Her green eyes narrow at me, trying to figure me out. "It's like he's begging me to strangle him."

The words are out of my mouth before I can stop them and Wren looks at me with that sexy, evil grin of hers as she tilts her head playfully.

"Jealousy looks good on you, Davis," she murmurs before she turns away from me, leaving us in another round of silence.

"Dad!" Wren exclaims suddenly, pulling my attention away from the pile of pistachio dust we've created. She jumps up to embrace a kind looking man in his early fifties. He's in a dark blue suit and white shirt, not that much taller than me. When she pulls out the hug, she turns to me with the biggest smile I've seen on her lips. "This is Miles Davis. My boyfriend."

Boyfriend. I don't fight the smile that splits across my face as I stand up, filled with pride. I stretch out my hand for him to shake it but instead he pulls me into a huge hug.

"It's a pleasure to meet you, Mr Hackerly," I muffle.

163

My face is squashed against his chest, and I see Wren giggle. "The pleasure is all mine, son."

He pats me on the back hard. Wren stands at my side, with a smile, giving me a double thumbs up. *Well, that was easy.* He sits down across from us, his deep brown eyes flickering between the two of us as Wren moves her chair closer to mine, so her shoulder nestles in my chest.

"So, what do you do at NU, Miles?" Wren's dad asks, folding and unfolding his hands at the table.

"I play hockey. I'm currently on the bench but I'm getting back up there," I reply with a shrug. All of my focus turns onto my thigh where Wren squeezes it reassuringly. I look down at her but she's staring ahead like she hasn't just set every nerve in my body on fire.

"Ah, that's good. I used to play back in my day, but I wasn't any good," he replies with a vague waft in the air.

"I've seen the videos, dad. You were insanely good," Wren challenges with an easy laugh.

"Eh, I guess so," he shrugs shyly. "How are you your finding second year at NU?"

"It's going okay. It's better than first year but the content is getting harder," I admit.

Wren's dad nods. "That's good. This one over here thinks her classes are too easy." He nods over to Wren and she rolls her eyes. Her dad turns back to me. "Would you fancy having a few rounds on the ice sometime?"

"Yeah." I respond too quickly and Wren backs away from me to look up to me, her eyes glistening. "That would be great." Wren's dad only stays for a few more minutes before he has to go back and forth speaking to more people. I notice how comfortable she is around her dad in this environment. The

164

same way she is around me. She doesn't tense or freeze up when she's talking to him. She talks animatedly with her hands, expressing her excitement in a childlike way.

She doesn't need to be anyone other than Wren. Not Wren the Future Olympian. Just her. The person I can see myself liking more and more each day. The person whose whole face lights up like sunlight as she talks about the things she loves with her dad. When she leaves to go to the bathroom while I get us drinks from the bar, her dad appears beside me. He studies me for a minute and I feel suddenly uncomfortable under his gaze.

"You making her happy?" he asks, the playful conversation from earlier becoming serious.

I nod. "I'm trying to," I say, and it doesn't feel like much of a lie.

"Everyday?"

"Everyday."

He nods at me and pats me on the shoulder. Is this what all dad's do? "Good," he concedes before disappearing again.

I also didn't realise how big the world of hoteliers was until tonight. It looks like people from up and down the country — and across the world — come to these events.

Weirdly enough, it reminds me a lot of my family and how loud and chaotic we are. Birthdays in the Davis family are always insane. Thoughts and feelings are always at full volume. They look a lot like this but with more drinking, more cheesy music, and more burnt food.

"So, Mr Hackerly, I have a very important question to ask," I begin when her dad returns to the table, feeling a little mischievous. Wren must know exactly what I'm up to because she glares at me.

Wren's dad finishes his Scotch and looks at me. "Please, call me David," he pleads, waving his hand around. Wren laughs a little, still glaring at me. Honestly, it's a little creepy.

"What do you think about cheese? Just in general. Like? Dislike?" I ask, feigning curiosity. Wren elbows me in the rib and I smirk at her. "Oh, or *loathe* as your daughter likes to say."

Mr Hacke- *David* laughs. "You know what, Miles? I cannot stand cream cheese. Everyone thinks-"

I can tell he's about to go on a rant but Wren cuts in. "Miles hates cream cheese too." She blinks up at me, her eyes silently screaming at me. "Don't you, *Milesy*?"

I can see the disgust on her face at using the nickname but I fucking love it. I'm a sucker for a pet name.

"Yep, sure do," I bite out, turning back to Wren's dad, leaning on the table. "Now, tell me, David, what is it exactly that-"

"Dad!" Wren basically shouts. She's a first one. She must really not want her dad to talk about cream cheese. "Why don't you tell Milesy about how you almost made it pro?"

"You're too kind, Wren. I was nowhere near making it pro," Mr Hackerly replies, shaking his head.

I almost choke on air as I spit out, "Kind? I'm sorry to tell you this, Sir, but your daughter is everything *but* kind."

Wren glares at me as her dad laughs. "I *am* kind. People are delighted to meet me."

"Delighted? No. Frightened, maybe." I shrug, hiding my smirk. She pokes me in my rib and returns her attention back to her dad, asking him about his hockey career again.

Of course, Wren gets what she wants, and her dad forgets about the cream cheese debacle and tells me all about his days as a

166

young athlete in nearly every sport. It's no wonder Wren likes working out so much.

I laugh at his terrible jokes and ask him follow up questions. You know, playing the part. Wren eats up every second of it, smiling at me like she wants to hug me and kill me at the same time.

Mr Hackerly disappears again, speaking to some reporters.

"So, what do you think to my dad?" Wren asks, her head resting in her hand on the table. She looks at me with dreamy eyes and I can tell she's exhausted.

"He's nice. Kind. *Very* different to your mom," I admit.

"Yeah, she can be pretty intense," she replies. "It's nice to have a balance."

"I can see where you get it from — both sides of your personality. You're brutal and really fucking hard core but you're a little softie on the inside," I coo, scrunching my nose up at her. She rolls her eyes before smothering her smile in her hand, trying to hide it. "See?"

We melt into my favourite kind of conversation: the one where we get to learn more about each other. She talks more about her sister and what a good cook she is. She over-explains her dynamic with Kennedy and Scarlett, telling me what their sun, moon, and risings are. *Whatever the fuck that means.*

In return, I tell her about me and Carter as kids and how we created our own annual Olympic tournament called the Reyes-Davis Games. I avoid talking about my parents for obvious reasons and instead tell her about how I peed myself at my first hockey game as a kid. She listens intently, slowly leaning into me as I speak. Until the dark-haired boy comes into my view again.

167

I give him, what I hope to be, a look to back away, but he stalks closer, his face twisting into an evil grin. He's just seconds away from our table, his eyes completely focused on Wren's exposed back. I have to do something.

Instinctively, I hook my finger into her chair and pull her closer into me, our legs basically intertwined. She yelps as I interrupt her rant on what my zodiac sign means about me. I put my hand onto the exposed skin on her shoulder and she looks at my hand and then back at me.

"What are you doing?" she asks softly, her wide eyes searching mine. He's practically here at this point.

Fuck it.

I grab her face between my hands, and I kiss her.

CHAPTER 16
WREN

I can feel myself melting into him. His large hands slip
around my neck, his fingers curling in my hair as he dips my
head back, deepening the kiss. Our mouths move against each
other in sync. Like we were made to do this. For each other.
Miles Davis is kissing me and I'm kissing him back. What is
this life?

I hear myself whimper softly when he slips his tongue into my
mouth, but I don't act like I didn't. Instead, I hold onto the
lapels of his blazer and pull him into me until he can't move
any further.

I'm sure this is more than just pretending to kiss. More than
putting on a show for whoever is watching. But for some
reason, I don't seem to care. I don't care that I'm enjoying it.
The only thing I can focus on his how he feels against my
mouth for the first time. It's not like anyone can see what the
inside of our mouths looks like. I don't know what it looks like
either, but it feels like heaven. It feels safe and exhilarating at
the same time. I knew we would have to do this one day, but I
didn't expect it to feel so good. I feel him laugh and smile

against my mouth when another sound leaves my mouth without permission when his hand dives deeper into my hair. When did I get so over my head over a kiss?

I pull apart from him.

"What was that for?" I breathe when I'm able to catch my breath. I 'm panting like a dog. He blinks back at me, his mouth parted, and his pupils dilated.

"It was that guy. He was staring at you again and he was about to come over here. I had to give him a reason not to. And would look at that? He's gone. Sorry, I should have asked first," he rambles. I can feel the heat rushing up my neck again in waves as I watch his mouth move. That mouth that was just on mine.

"No. It's okay," I say, our faces still too close. I push further away so our noses aren't basically touching anymore. "You sure you didn't make that up just so you could kiss me?"

"I wouldn't need to make anything up to get you to kiss me," he mutters before looking away.

*

After an excruciating evening of small talk and fake laughs, I lean against the gold railing to take off my heels on the elevator on the way back to our room, desperate to get rid of the throbbing in my feet. When my feet hit the cool ground, I wince slightly before sighing deeply. I can feel Miles' eyes on me, something along the lines of a smirk on his lips.

"What?" I ask, flashing him a daring glance.

"Nothing." He shakes his head, trying and failing to suppress his smile. He gives me a long look before facing towards the door.

170

When we get back to our room, we're both defeated from eating terrible food and laughing at my dad's jokes that were so *not* funny that they were funny. Miles carried our conversations with ease, flowing from each group of people to the next. He was a natural. At all of it. Pretending to like me more than friends, knowing the right way to make my dad laugh, knowing what kind of jokes to make to the hoteliers. And that kiss? That speaks for itself.

The second we reach the living room, I drop onto the couch, lying on my back, my head on the arm rest. It's the kind of couch that I could easily I could fall asleep on right now. I consider for a second to let Miles stay in the gigantic bed while I let sleep pull me under right here.

"Can you just chop off my feet?" I sigh loudly. Miles stands behind me on the other side of the couch laughing. He's taken off his blazer, his bow tie hanging loose around his neck.

"I don't have my amputation equipment with me, but I can give you a massage?" he suggests, looking down at me. His brown hair drops a little in his eyes and I tell myself not to reach out and push it away. It should be illegal for anyone to look this good right now after such an exhausting day. Especially him.

"I would *die* for a massage right now. I'm sure there's a masseuse around here somewhere. I'll find one in the morning before we leave," I say, making a mental note to do so.

"No, I mean, now. For your feet," he responds calmly, gesturing towards them.

The lack of alcohol has made him more attentive; less sarcastic and more focused and sensitive. It's a weird combination mixed with how much he oozes sex right now. Before I can protest, he's sat next to me, sweeping my feet into his hands on his lap. My feet immediately feel like butter under the touch of his rough but gentle hands. I instinctively sit up on my elbows as I stare at him in awe.

"Miles," I get out, but my breath catches when his fingers run smoothly over the inside of my foot. "My feet are gross. You don't have to do that."

"I don't mind," he says without hesitation. His voice is hoarse when he growls, "And no part of you is gross so *stop* saying that."

I slip in and out of a haze as his fingers work magic around my ankle and my sole, relieving more and more of the pain. Involuntary sounds leave my mouth, and his grip tightens on me. He lets out a sharp breath before continuing softly.

"When did you learn how to do this?" I ask quietly.

"I kind of taught myself. My feet would get so sore after practice sometimes, so I just googled stuff. You should learn, then I won't have to do this for you all the time," he laughs.

I wiggle out of his grip and I nudge him in his hard stomach, but he grabs my foot again and continues rubbing small circles around the pad of my foot with both hands.

"Hey, I told you that you didn't have to do this," I protest but he doesn't respond.

Silence washes over us for a few beats. I let myself fall into the rhythm of his hands working over me. It's not long before I start to think about other places where his hands could be. On my thigh. On my stomach. On my- *Nope.* Not going there.

It's not him.

It can't be him. I'm just a pathetically horny teenage girl. That's all.

Instead, I stare up at the ceiling, deciding that it's more interesting.

"I think I might take the whole beauty is pain thing too seriously. My mom always said that if it's not hurting then it's not working," I say after a while, trying to laugh but it comes out more like a sigh.

"That doesn't sound good, Wren," Miles whispers. I laugh again but this time the sound comes out clearer, but he isn't laughing when I look at him. He stares down at my feet, shaking his head lightly. "Don't you feel like you're too hard on yourself?"

"Sometimes… Sometimes, I think I'm not tough enough on myself. I don't know if you've noticed but skating is, like, the *only* thing I'm good at. So, I might as well be really good while I'm at it," I admit.

My stomach twists when the realisation of saying this for the first-time washes over me. I've always known that skating is my life but saying it aloud makes it more final.

Indefinite.

"Not that it matters what I think, but I think you're plenty tough, Wren. A lot tougher than me," he says after a few seconds. I look up at him but he's already looking at me, his green eyes hooded and relaxed. "For whatever reason you feel like you need to prove yourself, I just want you to know that you don't need to do that with me. I like you the way you are."

My heart practically doubles in size. "You're not so bad yourself, Milesy," I say through a smile. He looks at me. Something dangerous in his eyes as our gazes burn. His eyes dip to my mouth for a second and I exaggerate a sigh. "I think that's me done for the sappy shit tonight. Come and help me with my dress."

I get up from the couch, carrying my shoes with me to the bedroom where I find my sleeping shorts and tank top. I drop

173

my shoes on the floor and walk into the gigantic bathroom where I'm surrounded by mirrors and bright lights. I take out my jewellery and place it into the boxes I brought with me and start to wipe off my makeup. I rinse and dry my face before taking out my hair out of its clip and brush it out, leaving it to fall to my shoulders.

Finally, I catch a glimpse of Miles in the doorway in grey joggers and a white tee. Maybe he's been stood there the entire time and I haven't noticed. Maybe I've been too caught up in getting ready for bed so I can sleep off all these feelings that are sifting through my body.

"Finally," I murmur "Can you zip this down for me?"

He walks towards me slowly, his eyes connected with mine in the mirror. This isn't the first time I've seen him like this — relaxed, tried and effortlessly sexy — but something else lingers when he comes up behind me. The proximity of him sends goosebumps up my arms rapidly.

"Did you have a good time tonight?" he asks me, his voice rough as if it was hard for him today. He still hasn't touched my zipper; he's just looking at me passionately in the mirror. He slowly brings his hands around my hips, his fingers connecting at my stomach and then pulling back to rest on my hips. *God, why does this feel better than that kiss?* He's not even doing anything other than his hands on my hot body. I close my eyes at the contact, ready for him to do anything to me. "Wren?"

My eyes snap open and I realise I was almost arching into him. "Mm hmm," I say after I've cleared my throat trying to shake off whatever that feeling was. My voice still sounds hoarse and shaky when I say, "I just want to get out of this dress."

174

He nods and pushes my hair to one side of my shoulder and starts to zip down my dress, painfully slowly. Like, so slow that I could run down from the thirtieth floor to the bottom at the same time it takes him to move it down a few inches.

He keeps one hand on the top of the zipper, his fingers barley grazing my neck, but it makes me shiver regardless. His eyes are focused on zipping me down but when he gets further down, he realises there's nothing underneath but bare skin, his breath hitches.

Maybe this is a dumb idea because I don't every worry aout how my back looks too him. I've always been self conscious about the deep bruises and scars that I've acquired from training as a kid at different sports and stupid rituals that the girls roped me into.

Even when he's finally done, he still keeps his hands on me, not ready to let go. I don't tell him not to. There is something wildly comforting about his hands on my body. Something that feels just right. I don't move when he gently starts to bring one side over my shoulder, his eyes locked with mine in the mirror. The first strap falls, almost exposing my chest. I watch my face flame up, the heat rushing to my cheeks like a tidal wave. He brings his face to my neck, his breath ragged and desperate, his mouth barely touching my skin. My pulse quickens so rapidly that I'm sure he can feel it under his mouth. He moves his hand to the other strap.

"Miles, you should stop," I whisper, my voice shaking.

"Why?" he murmurs into my skin as he bites onto my shoulder softly. My stomach summersaults. Every single nerve in my body focuses on that small spot on my shoulder and my brain almost flatlines. "You just smell so good," he whispers and I shiver again.

Ignore him and say, "You know why."

He groans, dropping his head to my shoulder, but he listens. He tears away from me leaving me in the bathroom.

I would have let myself slip. I would have easily let him kiss me right there, but I didn't. It doesn't help that I can feel the wetness building between my thighs. I take a quick shower, using the shower head to force all the throbbing feelings away. I don't bother to put my shorts on because it's so hot in the bedroom and I'd end up taking them off anyway. I slip into a pair of panties and put on my tank top, a reckless part of me hoping that he'll still be awake. But, when I go into the room, he's snoring already on one side of the bed.

I sigh and slip into the other end, putting as much space between us as possible.

CHAPTER 17
MILES

Sleeping on the edge of the bed that night in the hotel was fucking torture. As soon as she told me to stop, I went back to the room, and I was knocked out: part exhaustion and part frustration. I knew that offering to massage her feet was a bad idea. And I knew what I was doing in the bathroom also wasn't smart, but I needed to touch her. After hearing her moan into my mouth, I wanted to do it again. I knew she wouldn't let me until it was necessary.

It got worse when she got out of bed in the middle of the night, accidentally waking me. She went out of the room to get some water, half asleep, in nothing but pink underwear and a white tank top. I didn't even notice that I was sleeping next to her, half naked, the whole night. Yep.

Pure.

Unadulterated.

Fucking.

Torture.

I thought she would be willing to break the rules just once, but she didn't, and we didn't talk about it the next morning. We slept and woke up, got ready and headed home as if nothing happened. As if I wasn't willing to eat her out on the bathroom counter.

Since this is our second year at NU, we were invited to the Sophomore-Only Drive-In that the school organises. We got to take part in voting for the movie and this year's theme was thriller. 'Us' by Jordan Peele definitely wasn't my first option but it gives Wren and I a perfect opportunity to showcase our relationship before the hockey game next week. The only problem: Wren's been avoiding me like the plague since what happened at the hotel.

Nothing even happened. I'm a teenage boy and she's a beautiful fucking woman who told me to zip her dress down. That's it. Okay, so I might have kept my hands on her longer than I needed to but how could I resist? That dress was perfect and I've not felt the touch of a woman in way too long. I need to get myself in check because I can't have Wren looking at me like she hates me all night.

I drive to her apartment to pick her and the girls up. One thing I wish I knew about Wren before we agreed to do this is how long it takes her to get ready. She texted me nearly three hours ago saying that she's starting to get dressed after being at the rink all day. Still, I've been sitting in the parking lot for almost twenty minutes before she finally materialises through the doors of the apartment complex.

She's dressed in blue denim shorts and a blue NU sweatshirt; a brave choice in this Utah climate. Regardless, she looks insanely hot. The shorts are giving me a great view of the long expanse of her legs. Her hair is down which is rare but it's my favourite look on her. I barely even register that she's in the car until her seatbelt clicks in and she turns to me.

178

"Are Kennedy and Scarlett not coming?" I ask, looking past her into the darkness of the parking lot.

She shakes her head. "They'll meet us there."

I nod and put the car into drive, leading us out onto the main road which leads us to the secluded field where the Drive-In is being held. Wren's doing that freaky thing where she's humming along to the song I put on while still managing to look and sound angry at the same time. I turn down 'Freakin' Out On the interstate' by Briston Maroney slightly when we get to stop light, turning to her.

"What's wrong?" I ask while she stares straight ahead.

She turns the song back up. "Nothing."

I turn it down. "Something's clearly wrong. We don't have to go if you don't want to."

She turns it up. "I didn't say I don't want to go."

I turn it back down. "Well, you're acting like it."

She turns is up again. Louder. "I'm turning it up so you don't hear how pathetic I sound," she says over the music. I don't tell her that I can hear what she's saying perfectly fine if this makes her more comfortable. "Me and the girls had a fight and we hardly ever fight. It was about you." Immediately, I smile, turning to her as the traffic starts to move along. "Okay, it wasn't about you. It was more about us. They don't think I'm trying hard enough to make this work and the fact that we have a deadline on this thing only makes it worse. And I'm worried that we're not doing enough for people to actually take an interest in skating again."

I sigh, my shoulders dropping. "Wren. We just started with this whole thing. You need to be patient because if you keep trying to force something to happen, it's not going to happen. We'll

179

take a few pics tonight and the game next week will surely get more people on board."

She turns to me and I'm trying my best not to crash the car so I can't even look at her gorgeous face. "You promise?"

"Yes, I promise," I reply. "Now turn down this fucking music before I burst an eardrum."

*

As expected, the field is absolutely packed with cars. I've only been to a Drive-In once and it was where I had my first kiss in high school. I don't remember much from that day, other than being so fucking nervous. Thank God I've learned a few moves since then. When we get closer to where all the cars have lined up, I park my truck next to Xaiver's as he and his girlfriend Michelle sit on the hood of the car with a bag of popcorn between them.

I watch Wren scan the surroundings, the same nervousness she showed at the party. "Are you ready to do some extremely painful socialising?" I ask, keeping my tone light as I shut off the car and unclip my seatbelt.

"I'm as ready as I'll ever be," she murmurs, opening her door. I quickly round the truck, wanting to tug her into my side as we walk towards Xaiver's car. She lets out a noise between a grunt and a sigh when I put my arm around her shoulders. *Well, this is going swimmingly.*

"Davis, finally! The movie is about to start," Xavier says through a mouthful of popcorn when he spots me and Wren. Michelle shakes her head at him. I honestly don't know how she's put up with him for so long. He shifts his vision to Wren and his face breaks out into a smile. "And you must be the famous girlfriend."

Wren laughs and the sound soothes me. "And you must be the famous best friend. It's really nice to meet you."

"You too," he says. He nudges Michelle in the shoulder. "This is Mitch, my girl."

Michelle laughs. "Literally nobody calls me Mitch other than these two dorks. 'Michelle' is also fine."

Wren joins in on the laughter, shaking her head at me. We started calling her Mitch as a joke in middle school and then it just stuck. "It's nice to meet you, Michelle."

"Well, we better set up our camp before the movie actually starts," I say to them, looking down at Wren. Michelle and Xaiver nod, digging back into their food. I turn us around, leading us both to the car.

I set down the back of my truck, opening up the space for us to get seated comfortably. I could be perfect at this boyfriend shit if this was a real relationship. I brought blankets, cushions and our own snacks because the food here is scarily expensive.

Wren seems to be impressed too because when we're climbing into the truck she doesn't make any snarky comments. If I didn't know any better, I'd say I'm earning some brownie points.

We sit at the edge of the truck, our legs dangling off the edge and our snacks on either side of us. When I notice Wren shivering, I push myself closer to her, desperate to give her some of my warmth.

"Are you cold?" I ask.

"I'm fine," she says. I swear she is the most stubborn person I have ever met.

"You're shivering," I say and I place my hand on her thigh as the goosebumps arrive across her skin and she gasps. I lean back into the truck, plucking one of the blankets and draping it

181

over both of our legs. "There," I murmur, almost to myself as I spread it out over us. The last thing I expect her to do is to latch onto my hand.

I look at our interlocked fingers; her small hand in my big one. She does that thing girls do that drives me fucking insane as she circles her thumb on my hand, pulling both of her hands into her lap. Under the blanket. The thumb thing and the fact that my warm skin is touching her bare thighs is driving me equal parts angry and horny.

Fucking hell.

I need to get laid.

"Are you going to do that all night?" I ask when I'm struggling to even breathe properly.

"Do what?" she asks innocently, turning her head to the side as the glow from the large screen glitters in her brown eyes.

"You know exactly what you're doing, Wren." She still hasn't stopped moving her thumb over my hand and she tortures me more by hooking her right leg over my left one, letting our hands rest on the inside of her thigh.

Then I look back up at her but she's trying to seem focused on the screen as she whispers out the side of my mouth, "Michelle is staring at us and I'm pretty sure half of NU's population is here. The least we can do is look cosy."

"Yeah," I say, "Right."

Because this is fake. Everything about this is pretend. It's hard to feel like it's pretend when she's this fucking close to me and every nerve in my body is being set on fire one by one. She doesn't even flinch when the first jumpscare appears. She must be superhuman because I'm latching onto her like a baby. This movie has no business being this terrifying. She does flinch when Kennedy and Scarlett appear out of nowhere.

They both stand in front of us, blocking our view from the screen. Scarlett looks pissed and Kennedy seems like she's more interested in wanting to watch the movie than she is about confronting Wren on whatever they've argued about. I think this is my signal to leave.

"I'm going to get us some food with Z," I say, detangling myself from her grip and the covers. "I'll let you guys...chat."

Wren gives me one of her death stares but I don't want to be caught in the middle of a cat fight so I can make up for that later. Instead, I rush over to Xaiver's car and haul him from his seat, needing someone to talk to while I get out of whatever Wren has got herself into. We get into the long queue for refreshments and Zaiver nudges my shoulder.

"You two are looking cosy. How are things going?" he asks.

"Cosy. That's exactly what we need to look like," I reply, kicking the stones beneath my feet.

"You sound pissed, dude," Xaiver laughs. "Which is saying something because you're not actually dating her so you shouldn't be pissed. Do you like her for real?"

"No. God. I just didn't realise how hard it would be to fake date someone like *her*," I admit, sighing as I look up at the pitch black sky, littered with stars.

"What does that mean?"

I turn around and look for our car and I spot her. She must have made up with Kennedy and Scarlett because I can see them in the back of my truck too, talking animatedly to each other. Girls are weird in that way. One minute they can't stand each other and the next, they're best friends again. Xavier turns around too. Wren's laughing with them, double tucking her hair back behind her ear like it's a movie.

"I mean, fucking look at her, Z. I knew that she was pretty. I knew that the second I laid eyes on her but actually getting to know her - you know, for the contract - has changed every single thing about her. And I swear, if she touches me one more time tonight, I don't know what I'm going to do."

Getting that out feels good. I know I shouldn't act out on any of the impulses I have but the attraction that I have to her and her brain is driving me insane.

"You're already in too deep, man. Just get through the next few weeks and if her show goes well, you don't have to keep doing it anymore, right?" Z asks. I nod. "Then, you can get laid and not have to worry about it messing up your plan."

I nod again, taking in that idea. I can do that. I need to be able to do that. "Yeah. You're right."

We turn back around and move further down the queue. When we finally get to ordering, Xavier buys a drink for him and Michelle and I order some M&M's. When we get back to our cars, even more people have gathered around my truck. Grey and Harry are both there and Michelle has moved from Z's car into the back of mine, talking away with the girls.

This is great.

"Miles! Fancy seeing you here," Grey drawls, holding his hands out wide as if we didn't all text in the team group chat before arriving. He said he was going to try his luck with one of the netball girls. What he didn't say was how he was going to take up all the space in my car. "We thought you abandoned your girl, here."

I look down to Wren and she's laughing, clearly warmed up to my friends. "Yeah, babe. What took you so long?" she asks, painting on that innocently adorable face of hers as she snuggles between Kennedy and Scarlett.

"Well, I wouldn't have taken so long if I knew you guys were all ready to take over my car," I reply sarcastically, seriously looking for a place to sit. "I swear I saw Kennedy's car over there."

I look out into the space where Ken's parked."The vibes are better over here," she says cheerfully, dismissing me with a shrug.

I turn to Grey and Harry who are taking up the edge of the truck. "And what's your excuse?"

"The vibes are better over here," Harry mocks and Kennedy shoots him a look. "Oh, so it works for her but not for us?" This time *I* shoot him a look. "We got an Uber here."

"Great. Now I've got nowhere to sit," I murmur, trying to figure out how they've all managed to fit in the car.

"Don't get your panties in a bunch, Milesy," Wren says, standing up to step over everyone until she's beside me looking at the truck. "A little rearranging and we should be fine.

After everyone steps out the back of the truck, we try to get everyone into a comfortable position. Michelle and Zaiver take the far back of the truck, snuggled up into the far corner. Kennedy sits in front of them with Scarlett in front of her, her legs dangling out of the back. Grey sits next to Scarlett on the front with Harry behind him, in front of me and Wren. Of course Wren and I are in the worst position ever. Not because we barely see the movie but because Wren is sitting right in my lap.

"You've got to be shitting me," I murmur when Wren tries to make herself comfortable in my lap which means she's brushing her ass all over my dick.

"What?" she asks, turning to look at me.

185

"I said you look so pretty," I bite out and she narrows her eyes at me before turning around.

I can't even focus on the movie. It's not even scary at this point. Because what's scarier is the fact that when Wren goes to speak to Kennedy and Scarlett, she leans forward a little, making me wrap my arms around her stomach so she doesn't fall as her ass grinds into mine. No one else seems to notice the amount of pain I'm in as they all shield themselves from the movie.

"Can you keep still? You're making it worse," I whisper just for her to hear. I can tell my breath is hot against her neck because she shivers, her back slightly arching into my front.

"This isn't comfortable for me either, Davis," she murmurs, turning around so our faces millimetres apart. Her dark eyes pin mine as she says, "Especially with your dick jabbing into my ass."

Right. So it is that obvious.

I do what I do best.

Deny, deny, deny.

"It's a biological reaction, Wren. Don't get too excited."

"Right," she says with a mocking tone. And then - because she's a fucking sadist - she grinds herself against me on purpose and I groan. "This is all just biological, right? That's why your heart is racing and you're gripping onto my stomach like it's the only thing keeping you alive. Biology."

"It's a scary movie."

She laughs quietly. "You can think of all the excuses that you want, Davis. But that doesn't change the fact that you're hard and I'm turning you on without doing anything."

Yeah….no.

I'm not doing this.

186

I'm not letting my fake girlfriend make me feel like my balls are about to fall off if she doesn't do anything about it. Because she *can't* do anything about it. We're meant to be friends, first and foremost. And from what I've seen in other relationships with my friends, friends don't almost bring the other to orgasm in the back of a truck simply by grinding their ass against the other.

I stand up abruptly and everyone's heads turn around and they all sigh when they realise it's me and not one of the tethered from the movie.

"What are you doing?" Wren whisper-shouts. I start to step over them as I try to get out.

"I need to pee."

Am I really running away from my problems like a child? Yes. But it's better than sitting there and letting her torture me. Still, I can't seem to get away from her because I barely make it more than twenty steps away from the car before she's behind me.

"Miles," she presses but I keep on walking. "Miles," she says again. "What the hell is wrong with you?"

That makes me stop in my tracks and I turn around. Her hands are out at her sides, clearly annoyed at me. "What's wrong with *me*?" I snap. "What's wrong with *you*, Wren? You say you want this to work because you're scared of running out of time then you pull shit like that when you know you don't need to and then you have the nerve to ask what's wrong with me? It makes no fucking sense."

"I wasn't doing it on purpose," she challenges, her tone biting.

"Oh, so you weren't purposefully moving against me like that just then?"

187

"Okay, the last time I was doing it on purpose but it was a joke."

I step closer to her. "But it's not a joke, Wren. This is our future you're playing with here. You're the one who is so worried about messing this up and you can't do shit like *that*. You can't ask me to zip down your dresses or grind against my lap. You can't wear shorts and you can't wear your hair down because-"

"You're *not* telling me what to wear, Davis," she says, defensively. "Fake boyfriend or not. You're not controlling how I look."

"You're right. I'm sorry. That's a me problem and it's unfair of me but-" I get cut off by the strange smile that has formed against her mouth. "Why are you smiling?"

"Because all of your friends are staring at us and they probably think we're fighting," she says through a toothy smile.

Honestly, this woman scares me. She steps closer to me, tugging on my sweatshirt.

"So we're not fighting…?"

She shakes her head. "Just shut up and kiss me."

"What?" I breathe out.

She grins. "You heard me. Pucker up, big boy."

"You're insane," I say, laughing. "Are they really there or do you just want to kiss me that badly, Hacks?"

"I dont think I'm the one who wants this badly, Milesy," she says, making a very suggestive nod to my hard-on. "It's concerning how you're turned on even when we're fighting."

Fuck it.

I don't need any other reason to kiss her.

I let her pull me in, letting her take the lead on this one since I was the one who initiated the kiss at the gala. She slowly rises to her tiptoes, her sweet perfume slowly reaching my brain as she gently brushes her nose against mine. I'm practically panting, waiting for her to turn her head and reach my mouth. Of course she does the unimaginable and kisses my bottom lip before pulling on it with her teeth. My eyes flutter closed for a second but I force them to stay open and I catch the smug smile that has spread across her face.

She finally does what I've been waiting for but the moment is all too fleeting as the kiss is just that; a kiss. It lasts maybe three seconds before she pulls back, leaving me wanting more and more and more.

"Now that we've kissed and made up, turn your frown upside down and look like that was the best kiss of your life," she demands, linking her fingers within mine, turning us towards the car again.

*

We manage to make through the rest of the movie with no more slip ups. She keeps still on my lap and when she holds my hand again, she doesn't do that thumb thing that makes me want to kiss her again.

I touched her for too long at the gala and she got payback. That's all it is. Now we're even and we can make sure this stays pretend.

Rule. Number. Three.

When I drive her back to her apartment, we barely say anything as this strange energy crackles between us and I can't bear the tension anymore so I grab her arm before she tries to leave. She turns to me, a funny look on her face and I loosen my grip.

"We're going to be fine. You know that, right?"

"If you say so, Davis," she says sarcastically.

189

"Can you drop the act for one fucking minute and be real with me," I say, trying not be frustrated. "When you stress out, you stress me out. So please, know that it's going to be okay. I need you to know that I've got you. That you can trust me."

I watch the exact second that her face relaxes. She needed to hear this as much as I needed to say it. "I trust you. I do. But it's just scary. You know, if this doesn't work."

"But it will. If you let me try for you, it's going to work."

"Okay," she sighs.

"Okay?"

"Okay," she says again, rolling her eyes. "Thank you for today. I'll remember not to wear shorts next time. Oh, or leave my hair down. Or do anything that could possibly drive you crazy."

"That will be the last time I ever tell you anything, Wrenny," I say, laughing. She flips me off before hopping out of the car and walking up to her apartment.

I take it back.

I don't think dating Wren Hackerly is the best thing to happen to me.

It's going to be the thing that destroys me.

CHAPTER 18
MILES

After having to snuggle up next to Wren at the Drive-in and our kiss, I'm praying that in some way, this hockey game will give me more reasons to touch her in public. I know it's pathetic but touching her is like a drug. Once I've had one hit, I just want more. And more. And more. Until I can't anymore. I'm putting on my jacket, ready to leave when my phone lights up with a text. It's Wren.

Wren: What do I wear?

I roll my eyes with a laugh and shoot back a message.

Me: Literally anything.
Me: I'm coming to get u in five mins.

She's been freaking out over this for the last week, obsessing over an outfit. Hockey games at NU are the highlight of the week. We always get a full house even when the games are just friendly. Everyone loves the atmosphere, the rush and the energy that radiates off the players. I can't wait to get myself

191

back out there. As Coach doesn't forget to remind us 'It's what you do before the season starts that makes a champion.'

Coach has been checking in to see how I'm doing, and he told me that he'll let me know as soon as he thinks I'm ready to play again. Wren has been easing me into getting back on the ice in my full gear but it's a lot harder than I thought. Each time I step out there and I see the nets, I freeze up. I'm going to have to get there eventually. I'm going to need to put in Wren's dad's advice about playing when I finally get back onto the ice.

I need to.

For carter.

I drive the distance from my house to Wren's apartment in a few minutes, trying not to miss the start of the game. I can only hope that if I drive, it can give us an excuse to go somewhere afterwards instead of driving straight home. I get to her door and knock twice before Kennedy opens it. A wide grin splits on her face and she lets me in.

"She's through there," she says pointing down the hallway. I look down the hall and then back to her. "When you hear frustrated groans, you'll know which one it is."

I wait for a second before following her directions. I don't know why I'm so anxious to go to her room. I've spent a few nights here, as part of our contract to take late night photos but I've only ventured in the living room, the kitchen, and the bathroom. I usually come over late, after she's finished practice and we hang out for a bit and take a few photos. I pull out the couch and I go to bed. It's that easy. Most times, she's gone to practice before I wake up. Sure enough, I hear frustrated grunts coming from one of the rooms and I knock on the door.

"Wren?" I ask wearily. "It's me. Miles."

"Yes, I know what your voice sounds like *Milesy*," she sighs sarcastically. "Open the door."

Entering her room is like looking straight into her brain. A chaotic, beautiful mess.

The white walls are covered in music posters, figure skating posters and pictures of her and her friends. A shelf is covered from top to bottom in trophies, medals, and certificates. I don't know why I'm surprised because I knew she was good but fuck. There is almost not room for anything else on the shelves. A dressing table in the corner holds a vinyl player and a stack of Taylor Swift records next to it. And best of all, Wren is sat in the middle of the floor, surrounded by thousands of clothes in a sports bra and leggings. She looks up at me and her face drops in exhaustion.

"You're going to have to leave me here. I'm not going," she groans melodramatically. I crouch down in front of her and tilt my head to the side.

"Yeah, you are. I got you a present," I say cheerfully, holding out my cap and my NU Bear's hockey number seven jersey. She looks at them and then at me.

"Do you know how tacky it is for me to wear your jersey?"

"Well, who else's jersey would you wear? If you're gonna wear a jersey it needs to have my name and number on it. I'm not let anyone else thinking you're someone else's," I challenge.

Okay, maybe I do have a jealous side. Her mouth tilts into a grin, probably considering teasing me on it but I speak before she can. "Plus, it makes you look like you care and that we're in a committed relationship."

She groans before grabbing my shirt out of my hand and standing up out of her heap. She pulls she shirt over her head and looks in her full-length mirror. Naturally, the jersey hangs

193

loose on her and falls halfway down her thighs. I stand behind her and put my hands on her shoulders. Wren looks at herself in the mirror, slightly unimpressed.

I love that she has my name written on her back. Believe it or not, I have never given another girl my jersey. Emily was never bothered but with other people I've dated, they get so territorial about it but I don't have to worry about it with her.

"See, you look fabulous," I gush, smiling. She shakes her head and turns to me, my hands still on her shoulders.

"I look like I'm dating a hockey player," she says before a horrified expression takes over her face. "Oh my God. I'm *dating* a hockey player."

I laugh hard while her jaw hangs open. I put my cap on her head and tap it. Her nose scrunches as I put two fingers under her jaw and close her mouth. "Yep, but we're going to be late."

"Why are you so worried about being late? You're not even playing."

"I know but it's not the worst thing to be on time," I retort.

"You're the one who likes to take hours to get ready."

She huffs and we walk out of her room. Before we get to the door, we're stopped by Kennedy and Scarlett, both with their mouths on the floor. Kennedy — like always — is dressed in denim dungarees with embroidered flowers on it as if she's a preschool teacher. Scarlett is in black jeans and a pink tank top, cautiously walking closer to Wren.

"Amelia Wren Hackerly. Respectfully - what the fuck is this?" Scarlett says dramatically, motioning to Wren's outfit.

"I am speechless. Like, no words," Kennedy exclaims.

"I know. Desperate times call for desperate measures," Wren sulks, grabbing my hand, pulling us past them. "We better go before someone gets grumpy."

194

W e get to the stadium and as I expected, it's completely packed. There's a certain buzz that radiates from each wall as we make our way through the crowds of people. We walk up to our seats, people's heads turning as they see I'm not down on the ice. It's weird having this many people care about what we do.

Unlike Zaiver's dad, my dad doesn't fund the team in anyway so it's not like anyone *needs* me on the team.

I keep my arm around her shoulder until we're sitting comfortably in our seats with a perfect view.

I've just finished explaining to Wren how the game works for the third time when Sophia Aoki sits down on the seat below us. She does a double take when she sees Wren and me.

"Hi, Miles. Long-time no see," she says, pushing her dark hair behind her shoulder, getting a better look at me. "I thought you'd be on the ice today."

"Nah, not yet. I'm still working on my training," I say with a shrug.

"Yeah, I get that," she replies understandingly.

Sophia, Carter, and I became close in high school through Greyson who had grown up with her. She quickly became one of our favourite people when we found out how much effort she puts into her own studies but how she shows genuine interest in everyone else's lives. She became a good balance for us when we were starting out here and she's kept most of the team sane since high school and I'll always be grateful for that.

She turns to look at Wren.

"You're Wren, right? I don't think we've met."

195

"Hi," Wren replies smiling, snuggling further into me. "It's nice to meet you."

"You too," Sophia grins before turning to me. "I thought you two were coming to my party, but I didn't see you there."

I feel Wren stiffen beneath me as she looks up at me and then flashes a shy smile. I run my hand down her arm quickly before resting it back on her shoulder.

"Yeah, we went for a little while, but we didn't stay for long. Sorry we didn't get to say 'Hi' then," I explain.

"No, it's cool. Can I say that you guys are so cute together!" she exclaims. Wren's face turns red with heat when I slip my hand down to her waist, squeezing gently. "And Wren, you're a figure skater, right?"

"Yeah, I am," Wren replies. Sophia's face lights up, quite literally. Her smile always reaches her eyes as lined dimples form on her cheekbones in a childlike way.

"That's so cool! I always wished I could skate but I'm *soooo* clumsy So I like to live vicariously through them by watching the team play," she laughs. Which is very true. She fell into a Koi pond outside the venue of our High School prom and whenever I see her around, she walks like she has two left feet. "I'd love to see you skate sometime. Do you have any competitions coming up?"

"Yeah, actually. We're doing a winter showcase in December. I'd love to see you there," Wren says, and I can't help but smile. That's my girl. As introverted as she seems, seeing her interact with other people makes my chest swell. She gets herself worked up about it but when she realises that my friends are not out to get her, she relaxes a little and lets herself enjoy talking to people that aren't Kennedy and Scarlett.

196

"Great. I'll be there. I'll ask some of my friends to come and I'll bring Brie." Her smile widens at the mention of her girlfriend. "Are you going to be there too?"

"Of course. I wouldn't miss it for the world."

Sophia smiles and then she pulls her bottom lip between her teeth, a nervous tick I've noticed she's had over the years. "Miles, can I ask you something?"

I sigh, knowing what's coming next. "Soph, we do this every time." Wren looks up at me in confusion. "Sophia, here, is a little photographer. You've probably seen her photos all over the school and on the school Instagram account. She still looks confused so I add, "She wants to take a photo of us."

Wren smiles shyly but before she can say anything, Sophia cuts in. "I'm planning on making a mockumentary of some sorts for this seson and I need some more pictures of NU's star player. I need to schedule in an interview with you soon."

"That sounds really cool," Wren starts. "But do I have to be in it? I'm not on the team."

"Yeah, but you're on my team," I murmur and she rolls her eyes. "Come on, baby. Just one photo."

She groans. "Fine. Just one."

Sophia squeals happily and whips out the camera that she takes with her everywhere and instructs Wren and I to sit closer together until she's basically in my lap. As I keep my arm around her shoulder, she uses one of her hands to wrap around my middle, snuggling her face into my shoulder.

She feels too good like this. Too much.

"Say, 'Hockey!'" We do as she asks, no matter how cringe it is. The camera clicks and Wren doesn't pull apart from me. Sophia holds up the back camera to her face and squints at it. "It's perfect."

"Can we see it?" Wren asks.

Sophia laughs. "You'll see it once the video is done."

I wipe the confusion off Wren's face with a kiss to her cheek as Sophia turns back around.

We keep quiet most of the game as I watch Xavier and Grey with concentration as they shuffle on the ice. We're in the lead during the first period against Fraser College, one of our more friendly opponents. We usually play against each other before the season starts just to get warmed up. It almost always ends with a fight – like all hockey games – but not any hard feelings. Most of the guys on my team went to high school with people on their team so we're all familiar with each other.

During the first intermission, Wren peppers me with more hockey questions before another one of my friends turn up behind me in the queue for the vending machine. Charlie Jacobs is one of those guys that I don't see often enough to call him one of my close friends, but I have seen him at nearly all the parties I went to over the past few months. He's a cool guy but he doesn't exactly fit in with my friendship group.

"Davis! I wasn't expecting to see you today," Charlie exclaims, running a hand through his blonde hair in disbelief. "It's good to see you in daylight, man."

I laugh nervously as Wren blinks up at me, twisting open the bottle of water. She moves closer to me as I watch her watch him. My friends are not at all like hers, so I wrap my arm around her shoulder, tugging her close to my side.

"Yeah, it's good to see you too," I reply finally. I look down to Wren fiddling with the plastic around the bottle. "This is my girlfriend, Wren. She skates. You should come to one of her performances sometime."

198

"Jesus, I can talk y'know," Wren murmurs as she looks up at me before turning back to Charlie, a smile playing on her lips. "But, yeah, I do skate. Don't let Milesy bully you into coming." "No, I definitely will go." Charlie laughs with a huge grin. Right answer. "You probably wouldn't believe it, but I used to skate as a kid. I wasn't very good, but I appreciate the sport." "You're right. I wouldn't have guessed," Wren says. I can't tell if she's being sarcastic or not as she takes a sweep of his thrifted cream jeans and white knitted sweater. Charlie smiles at her and turns to me.

"Funny question, actually," Charlie starts, rubbing the back of his neck. "If you're dating Wren does that mean Em is single?" "She's been single for months, Charlie," I huff. Wren does flinch at the mention of my ex. There's not much of a story there to be told other than every guy on the team wanted her even when she was with me. "If you're asking for my permission to date her then sure. I really couldn't care less." "Okay, cool. It's just - You looked like you would kill anyone that even looked at her when you were dating so I wanted to make sure." Wren looks up at me with an evil smile and I can tell she's going to make fun of me later.

"Yeah, well, I don't care anymore. If you want to date her, go ahead," I say finally. I know that Emily would eat him alive, but I don't say that. "The game is starting up again. We better get back to our seats."

I don't let him say bye before I turn around with my arm still around Wren. She doesn't say anything while walk up to the seats. She just sits with a happy expression on her face before I pick up her water and throw it in the trash. When I sit down, she places her hand on my thigh and my breathing stops. For someone who loves physical touch so much, whenever she

199

touches me, it feels different. It feels like every nerve in my body is set on fire one by one.

It feels like a slow, torturing, perfect way to die.

"Jealous *and* protective. Wow, Davis. You really are something," she whispers into my ear. As she draws back, the smell of her clouds my thoughts and I don't respond.

It would be too risky to tell her that I would protect her with my life. I would never let anything, or anyone hurt her. The game starts up again and I push away those feelings to focus on the players.

When we score another goal, Wren, and I both get out of our seats and cheer, the excitement completely taking over us. Chaos erupts around us as the stadium grows loud with chants and cheers. She jumps into my arm and hugs me tight. Her arms around my neck and my hands on my waist don't feel strange or unnatural. They feel welcoming. Without thinking about it, I kiss her on the lips quickly before pulling away. I make sure to not make it any deeper than that. Only a peck. Her eyes widen in shock for a moment before she returns her celebratory smile to the rest of the team.

See.

This is easy.

We can do this.

*

The locker room is loud and chaotic when I walk in. Most of the guys are still in their jerseys, spraying water around as they whoop and yell. There is no better feeling than winning a game alongside your best friends. When they see me, they start cheering even louder.

"Look who decided to show up," Harry announces, gesturing towards me, looking out of place in my jeans and hoodie.

"You guys did good. Could have been better if I was there though," I laugh. Tyler Vaughan stalks towards me, patting me on the back.

"No need to get cocky, dude. You need to get back out there. This season is going to be a nightmare without you," they say, rolling their eyes at the rest of the team before slipping away into the showers.

"It's up to Coach. I'm still training and getting my head back in the game. Coach just needs to give me the all-clear," I reply shrugging. All of the team nod in agreement, understanding why I haven't been in the best shape.

Then Jake starts laughing hysterically from the corner of the room. Who the fuck does he think this is? Is he a villain in a kid's movie? Everyone's heads to turn to him as he makes himself the centre of attention. Like always.

Jake and I were good friends in first year. We both got onto the team and like all my other teammates, we bonded instantly. Carter was never really a fan of him. He always thought Jake was too much for the team. Too much chaotic energy and not in a good way. He always took things a step too far, especially during prank week. Then he started dating anyone he could get his hands on. He dated Scarlett which didn't last very long when he cheated on her. Considering who her family are, he's lucky he got away without a scratch. He's a good player which is the only reason anyone on this team tolerates him.

"Are you, Davis? Because I haven't seen you on the ice in over four months," he drawls, coming closer to me. I swallow, suddenly feeling rage and nausea at the same time.

"Dude, calm down. No one has been feeling it since Carter died, especially Miles. They were practically brothers. Give it a rest," Xavier cuts in, coming to my rescue.

"Don't give me that dead friend bullshit. If Davis wanted to play, he would have by now. Instead, he's too busy flaunting around with his girlfriend," he says, moving closer in my face. I take a breath in, trying to calm myself down. "What's her name? Wren? Hacks' kid?"

"Keep her name out of your mouth, Callahan," I bite out, my fists clenching and unclenching at my sides. I feel bile rising in my throat, but I swallow it. I've never felt this kind of anger and exhaustion all at the same time. I hate the way it makes my pulse quicken and my jaw clench.

"Or what? You going to go crying to Coach about it? Grow the fuck up, Miles. If you ever want to play in the NHL, you're going to have to stop moping over Carter and stop drooling over that whore. If you're not careful, she might follow in her friend's footsteps."

I get closer to him, our faces inches apart.

"Talk about her, or her friends, again and see what happens." I growl. An evil smile spreads across his face slowly. "I swear to God, Callahan, if you so much as breathe near her, I'll crack your fucking head open."

"Oh, shit," he laughs. "Does she really fuck that good, Davis?" I bite my tongue so hard that it almost bleeds. I take a deep breath in before turning around. I can do this. I can take the high road. I can walk out of here and leave him to crawl back into whatever hole he came from. If I mess up now, I could be off the team for good. I walk close to the door before I hear him again behind me.

"Yeah, go home and cry to your little slut," Jake shouts.

I turn back around.

Fuck this.

CHAPTER 19
WREN

I'm standing outside in the cold, practically shivering as I

wait for Miles to come back from doing whatever he was
doing. I've tried calling him, but he hasn't picked up. I could
walk home from here, it's only ten minutes away but I don't
want to leave him. He drove us the short distance here and if
somethings happened, I don't want to leave him alone. So, the
least I can do is be here when he comes out. I sit down on the
curb outside the sports centre, and I wait for him.

"Wren," I hear a quiet voice from behind me. I stand up quickly
and I see him. Miles walks towards me gingerly, as if his legs
don't work properly. "You waited."

"Of course, I did." He comes closer to me, and the bright
streetlight shines on his face. That's when I see the bruises. His
right eye is shut while marks and bruises cover his face and
neck. I reach out to touch his face, but he pulls his head back.

"Jesus, Miles, what happened?"

"Can you drive? My eye hurts," he murmurs, holding out his
keys to me. I nod and get into the driver's seat of his truck. I've

never been in this kind of situation before. I've never had to take care of someone like this. Me and the girls take care of ourselves pretty fine but when we do need each other it's not because we've been punched in the face. Miles and I drive in silence.

"Are you going to tell me what happened?" I ask quietly. He shrugs and looks out of his window, not meeting my eyes as if he's embarrassed.

When we get to his house, no one is there. It's eerily silent as we trudge up the stairs. We go into his bedroom, and he sits down on his bed, resting his head against the headboard, his legs stretched out straight. He's barely said a word since we left campus. Which is worrying since he talks a LOT.

I run down into the kitchen, feeling helpless as I put some ice into a Ziplock. When I get into his room again, he's still sitting there, his eyes closed. I put my knees on both sides of his legs, straddling him but not sitting down as I press the ice to his face gently. He winces at the sensation but relaxes after a few seconds.

"What happened, Milesy?" I whisper as I put the ice down, touching and examining his face carefully.

"It doesn't hurt that bad. You should see the other guy. I'm fine," he says, trying to be cheerful as his lip twitches. I tut and shake my head.

"Oh, you're fine?" I ask sarcastically as I gently prod my finger on his cheek, and he hisses. "This looks really bad. We should get it checked out."

"I'm fine, really," he retorts more convincingly this time. My chest pinches as I look at him, opening and closing my mouth, trying to tell my brain to say something. Miles beats me to it.

"Can you stay tonight? I need you."

205

The whine in his voice undoes me. After what happened at the hotel, I told myself to be more cautious around him but then things like this happen. Where he says that he needs me in that whiny voice of his. Or he says 'please' and bashes his eyelashes at me. Or when he convinces me to do things that I said I wouldn't. Like wearing his jersey and straddling him as I tend to his face.

"Fine," I breathe out and he smiles wide. "But no funny business."

"What*ever* do you mean?" he drawls, innocently, blinking up at me.

"You know what I mean."

I inspect his eye, trying to do my best to see what could help. It's gone down a little since we've been here but it's still fierce. I put the packet down again to give his eye a rest from the cold. It's not swollen, just badly bruised underneath. He'll probably have a black eye in the morning, though.

I start to climb off him, to put some much needed space between us when his strong hands come onto my hips. He runs his rough hands from my above my knees to the top of my thighs.

"I want you so badly, Wren. Me and you for real," he says, throwing his head back with a groan. This is exactly what I meant by funny business.

"You're delirious," I laugh, trying again to move but he keeps me there, hovering over him. His hands rest on my thighs as his thumb strokes the inside and I almost buckle beneath him.

"No, I'm not."

"You are."

"Ask me again in the morning," he challenges, "and see what I'll say."

206

"Fine. I will."

I try and move *again* but his hands on my ass dig into me, and I suck in a breath. "I'm not going to be able to sleep tonight if I don't even try."

"You did try, and you failed," I tease. His face doesn't move.

"Just kiss me. Just one time. If you hate it, we can stop and we can pretend it never happened. I'm hard as a fucking rock right now," Miles groans as if being in a bit of pain has made him more bold than usual.

Before I can argue, he pushes me down onto him and I gasp. He wasn't lying. I can feel him through the thin material of my leggings. The throbbing that I have myself isn't making this any easier. My voice sounds scratchy when I speak.

"Miles, if we do this once we'll just think of another excuse to do it again."

"I can control myself, baby. Can you?"

He looks up at me with passion and intensity and I shake my head. From this position, the pet name doesn't sound so bad.

"This is a really fucking bad idea," I pant. Every rational thought I had is thrown out the window as I crash my mouth into his.

It's more frantic and exhilarating than the first time we kissed at the gala. Hell, it's a lot more chaotic than the peck he gave me earlier. My hands instinctively dive into the curls at the back of his neck, pulling and gripping, as his hands explore my ass before venturing up my shirt. I can do this, can't I? A stupid kiss with my stupid fake boyfriend. Easy.

Only, this kiss is anything but stupid. There is something so insane about the way his mouth tastes like sweetness and fall. Addicting.

I press featherlight kisses onto his bruises before sliding down him slightly to get better access to the column of his throat. I kiss and suck frantically like he did to me at the party and he groans. Like I've been starving for him. I didn't know this could feel so good. A low noise comes from the back of his throat when I nip at his collarbone.

He moves his hands out from under my shirt to my ass, grabbing and slapping before pulling me back up into a sitting position. I make the mistake of rolling against him, feeling the friction between us and I whimper. He brings his hot mouth to my neck, kissing the space under my ear, making my shiver.

"Can I take this off?" he breathes hoarsely, tugging at his jersey.

"Are you sure? I thought it was boosting your ego," I say into his skin, and he laughs. "Yes, you can take it off but we're not going anywhere past second base."

"Why not?" he whines. He pulls his jersey over my head and when it's free, he dives back into me, kissing my exposed chest.

"Because..." I pant. "If we do, I won't want to stop."

He replies by slipping his hand up the material of my sports bra, his fingers splaying out across my breasts. *Jesus H. Christ.* My head lolls back when he brings his fingers to my nipples, teasing gently.

"You feel so soft," he whispers, "so good."

I don't know how I'm going to get this to end. I don't know if I ever want it to. The roughness of his hands isn't like Augustus'. They're purposeful and masculine like they know what they want.

I roll over him again and he groans, taking his hand out and squeezing my ass. He moves me over him. Fast.

"*Fuck*, Miles," I cry out. We're basically dry humping but I still feel like I could finish just like this. He kisses across my neck again as he murmurs into my skin, '*You feel so fucking good.*' I moan loudly as the words leave his mouth while he bites me softly and he laughs, helping me ride over him. He fucking laughs.

"We need to stop," I say between pants. He continues kissing across my chest. "Miles."

"Mm," he murmurs into my skin.

"Miles, we need to stop. Like, now," I say again as the intensity builds in my abdomen and between my legs. I push myself away from him, holding onto his shoulders at arms length. His lips red and parted and his eyes wide. I don't need a mirror to see that mine are too. I could easily dive back into a messy kiss right now – because holy shit, he looks so good – but I force myself not to.

"Yeah…Yeah. You're right," he replies, dragging his hands down his face. He waits a beat before continuing as I watch him. "There are some shorts in my drawer for you to change into if you want and a clean shirt."

I get out of the bed on wobbly legs and grab a clean shirt from his drawer and some shorts. I go into the bathroom to change. I pull off my sports bra which has gotten sweaty and slip on his black shirt and shorts.

I hear Miles say something through the door and I freeze.
"What?" I ask.

"We both wanted that, right?" he asks and my stomach drops.

"Yeah," I reply after a pause. "But that shouldn't happen again. Not when we're alone."

I hear Miles move through the door and he sighs. "Yeah. Rule number three and all that."

"Exactly," I say, remembering the reason we made the list in the first place. "Rule number three." He doesn't say anything else for a while so I add, "It was a moment of weakness."

He clears his throat. "Of course."

When I look in the mirror, my face is red, and my pupils look huge. Thank God, I had some sort of self-control. I knew we would get carried away, but I can't. I can't afford to mess this up now. Not so close to the showcase.

We don't say anything when I slide into the bed next to him, turning away from him so I don't do anything I regret. His breathing slows and for a second, I think he's gone to sleep.

"I'm not a violent person, Wren," he whispers into the silence. I don't have to think about my response.

"I know."

"One of the guys were saying some really fucked up stuff about you and Carter and I just lost it. I'm sorry," he murmurs.

My heart sinks through my ribs as I turn over to face him. Knowing guys at NU, I know better than to ask what they said about me. Especially since they're hockey players. His eyelids are heavy as he avoids my eyes.

"Why are you sorry? You didn't do anything wrong," I reassure him. The way his mood has shifted so intensely shocks me. I've never seen him so torn up. So upset at himself.

"If Coach finds out, I won't be able to play but with what they were saying, I'd do it again in a heartbeat. I'll ruin everything," he explains, his voice cracking. I brush my hand over his cheek, and he melts into it, closing his eyes.

"That's not going to happen, Miles," I whisper.

"It might."

I brush his hair out of his face gently until he falls asleep. Even after his breathing has settled and he's deep in sleep, I keep my hand there. Deep into the night and I stay there, watching him. I can't ruin this for him by acting on impulses because that's all they are. They are just parts of this that we have to ignore. He needs to play again more than I need to skate. He deserves it. He needs this.

CHAPTER 20
MILES

I wake up to an empty bed, a throbbing headache and a hard on. I had a feeling she'd be gone when I woke up but a part of me was hoping that she'd be downstairs making breakfast or something. She kept me warm last night. Safe. Anchored. The only thing left of her is my jersey folded neatly at the bottom of my bed. I turn to my bedside table and there's a note in her handwriting, a bottle of painkillers and a glass of water.

> *Take these.*
> *I have to go to practice.*
> *XO*
> *Wren*

I take out two of the painkillers and down the glass of water before wandering in the bathroom. I take a look in the mirror and my bruise isn't look as bad as it was last night but it's still pretty angry looking. I know I shouldn't have got in the fight but by the way they were talking about Wren and Carter made my stomach turn.

After Carter passed, everyone on the team was broken up. It was the first and last time I saw any of them cry. We talked about him regularly, keeping his memory alive until one day they all moved but I stayed there.

I stayed waiting for him, looking through photos and trying to will him back into existence. Sometimes, when we're all drunk and emotional we'll bring him up and toast to him but on a regular day everyone seems to have forgotten about him. But I can't.

Every time I got up, it felt like I was dragging my feet through quicksand, trying and failing to get better. Just sinking back in right where I started. All the guys have probably had their fair share of sad moments but sometimes I feel like the only person who's actively trying to remember him. But what good is that when I can't honour him too? Our first match of the season is in January and if I'm not ready to play by then, I might as well give up.

Most of the morning goes by in a blur. All I can think about is her. Her hands in my hair, my hands on her ass and her moaning my name when we were barley moving against each other. I don't think I've been that turned on in my life. I knew I was straining between my jeans, and I needed to deal with it, but I sucked it up and focused on making her feel good.

I haven't heard from her since she left this morning, but I know she's probably skating until her feet are sore. Or maybe she's avoiding me? We didn't speak about what almost happened after the gala so should I be expecting some sort of response from her after last night?

Sure, we kissed, and it felt fucking amazing but maybe to her that's all it was. I was the one who asked her, and she said yes. That's it.

I don't have time to overthink it before I hear rapid knocks at my front door. I rush downstairs to open it and instantly, I wish I hadn't.

With long brown curly hair and a sheepish smile, my sister stands in the doorway with her arms across her chest. I blink at her, hoping that she'll disappear when I open my eyes but the doors already open and she's pushing past me.

"What are you doing here?" I ask, shutting the door behind her. I remind myself to check through the peephole before answering the door again.

"Miles, me and you need to talk," she says sternly, shrugging off her coat and holding in her hands.

"I thought we already did that."

"No, like, really talk. You can't keep running away from me. You're nineteen. You're too young to be running away from your problems already." She walks further into the house, looking around.

"Fine. Let's talk," I grunt. I lead us into the kitchen, and she takes a seat at the breakfast bar, swinging around to face me as I stand at the other end, my back against the counter. "Do you want a drink or something?"

She shakes her head. "You should sit down for this."

I take in a deep breath and sit down next to her. I know I've been running away from her, from my family, because it's too much deal with on top of everything. How was I just supposed to move on like everyone else? The same way everyone moved after Carter died. It's just not that easy for me.

"I didn't tell you about mom because I was trying to protect you," she begins. *Okay, so we're going straight into this. Great.* "And don't roll your eyes before you let me explain."

214

"Go ahead," I say. A huge part of me has wanted to know why. Why I was the only one who didn't know. Why everybody was so okay with it.

"I found out about the affair in the worst way possible," Clara starts, her fingers tapping on the table. "I was going into the school to surprise mom for her birthday, like we planned to the week before. I had just started college and you were still in middle school. I had flowers and chocolates, and I went in, and she was kissing him. At first, I thought maybe dad had a new haircut or something but as I got closer, I realised it wasn't him."

"So, what did you do?" I ask, my voice sounding smaller than I thought. I thought the surprise idea we had worked out perfectly. I wouldn't have expected it to be that moment that she found out. Mom got home from work like normal and we had dinner together like we always do. Nothing felt off.

"I did what any eighteen-year-old who had just caught their mom cheating would do. I burst through the door, screaming, crying, and shouting at her. She told the guy to leave, and she sat me down. She apologised and told me that it wasn't dad's fault, and it wasn't any of our faults either."

"That still doesn't explain why you didn't tell me."

"I didn't want to, Miles. She told me to. She said that I could tell you if I wanted and she wouldn't hold it against me, but I chose not to. I know how you are, and I couldn't let it crush you and set you back. You were only a kid, and I didn't want you to spend the rest of your life hating her. Not like I did."

That makes sense.

I don't argue.

I don't make a snarky comment. I just let it sink in. If I found out then, I *would* have hated her. I would have held onto it, used it against her in any way I could, and I still wouldn't be over it.

When I know something, it consumes me. It becomes all I can think about and there's no way of telling when I'd get over it.

"How did you do it? How did you forgive her?"

"Well, it helped that I was at college. If I saw her every day, I don't think I would have done it so easily. I just had to *let go*. I had to move on with my life. I had goals that were bigger than this setback in my life. At the beginning I was angry, and I wasn't sure when I'd stop thinking about it, but I had to push forward."

"I don't know how to do that. How to just let it all go." I sigh and run my hands through my hair, defeated.

"I know you don't, that's why I couldn't tell you. Do you remember that action figure you had? The army one with the interchangeable outfits?" I nod and she continues. "You had that with you all the time. You had in your hand in the stroller, you held onto it while you were potty training, and you brought with you to your first day of kindergarten. It was old and mouldy by the time you were eight and do you remember what happened when dad tried to throw it away?"

"I screamed at him and said I'd run away if he didn't give it me back," I say, laughing at the memory. I had almost forgot about that. I was such a dramatic child. Maybe I still am.

"Because you couldn't let it go, Miles. You thought it was this precious thing that you couldn't live without but when you got a new pair of skates you forgot about it, and you moved on. That's why I thought that if I waited to tell you, you'd be more open to forgiving her. I thought you'd find it easier to move on," Clara admits, looking at me sympathetically. I don't say anything for a while.

216

"Do you think that's why I'm still thinking about Carter? Why I can't move on. I feel like everyone has moved on and I can't," I ask, my voice wavering. I only ask to try to make sense of it myself.

"I think... I think that's a different thing, Miles. Loosing someone is a very difficult thing and everybody deals with it in different ways. I don't think you need to worry about how long it takes you. It's not something you can just wake up and move on from."

"Everyone else has. Clara, I can't even put on my helmet without feeling like I'm suffocating," I say truthfully.

I don't know when I started crying but I did. Hot tears run down my face. I don't bother to hide it. I've got used to crying now. At first, I thought it was something to be embarrassed about. Something that shouldn't be happening but then it starting to feel relieving. Cathartic.

"Oh, Miles. I know we haven't spoken but please tell me you've been talking to someone about this." She brings her hand to my back, rubbing reassuringly. I sniffle and try to blink back the tears.

"I have Wren," I say, mostly as a reminder. Because I do, right? Even though I haven't heard from her since our kiss, I still have her. I have to.

"That's good. I'm glad to hear that but who's Wren?" she asks, her nose scrunched up.

"She's my girlfriend. She's just..." I laugh. How could I even begin to describe her? How could I tell her that she's completely taken over every single thought in my brain. That's she's the only thing I can think about. Her stubbornness and all. "She's everything."

Clara nods in understanding. "We've got a lot to catch up on."

217

CHAPTER 21
WREN

I shouldn't have kissed him. I shouldn't have done a lot of

things. I shouldn't have stayed the night either because I knew how badly I would want him. I knew that I get impulsive when I'm around him. I couldn't even sleep last night because I was so turned on. I got up when he was asleep and locked myself in his bathroom to deal with it.

It was worse when I slipped back into bed, trying to keep as much distance between us and his hand slipped around my stomach, pulling my ass right into him. Luckily, we made it through the night and in the morning, I focused on the real task at hand and left him the painkillers. I only have two weeks before the showcase and I can't mess that up now.

After a long day practicing and trying to get Miles out of my head, I'm sat with the girls in the living room while they ask me more and more ridiculous questions. I've been dodging them for the most part as I lie down with ice packs on my sore knees.

"*So*, what was it like?" Kennedy asks with a huge smile.

"What was what like?" I sit up further on the couch, so I can see them both properly. Kennedy is sitting in the beanbag and Scarlett is on the floor, lying on her back.

"The kiss. You can't just be like 'yeah me and Miles made out for real' and ignore it," Kennedy explains.

"That's exactly what I'm trying to do. If I think about it too much, I'll do it again and this whole thing will be over. I can't do that. Not so close to the show and so close to the hockey season," I say, turning over my ice packs before resting my head back on the head rest.

"Fine, don't tell us. But, judging by the look on your face, it was better than the kisses you write about in Stolen Kingdom," Kennedy mentions, looking at me innocently. I don't have the energy to argue with that. It's true. It was probably the best kiss of my life. Scarlett frowns at her and turns back to me.

"Have you spoken to him since you ran off this morning?" Scarlett asks and my stomach drops.

"I didn't run off. I just didn't want to be there when he woke up. It would have been too hard," I admit. "It was the best thing to do."

"Was it or was it just easier?" Scarlett asks. If my knees didn't hurt so bad, I would have smothered her with my pillow, but I know she's right. She always is.

I don't let my mind wander to what would have happened if I stayed for any longer than I did. We're both so strangely attached to each other. Like there's something, intangible, which is constantly tying us together. Even when we know we shouldn't. When we can't. Not for real, anyway.

Rule number three.

I'm about to say something but my phone chimes and vibrates next to me. I reach into the pocket of my shorts and retrieve it. I smile wide when I see a message from Gigi.

Gigi: Why haven't you posted any pictures with your boyfriend? Did you guys break up?
Me: We didn't break up G. It's been twenty-four hours since I posted.
Me: Any updates on TLT?
Gigi: If you keep up with my posts, then you would know. But, no, there are no updates yet.
I saw the pictures at the hockey game, how was that?
Me: It was actually fun. I think you would have enjoyed it.
Gigi: I'm sure I would have. There is nothing I love more than crowded spaces.
Me: Ha-ha. So...
Me: That means that you're not coming to my show?
Gigi: No, Emmy, I can't. I'm trying to get better with crowds, I promise.
Me: I know you are, G. Love you more than Marcus loves Carmen.
Gigi: I don't think that's possible. You wrote their love to be extremely powerful. Also, you couldn't love me the same way because they're in a romantic relationship.
Me: Would it kill you to say that you love me too?
Gigi: It wouldn't kill me; I just don't want to say it.

I laugh at Gigi's last message and throw it next to me. The second it hits the cushion it starts to ring again. When I reach for it, I see the unknown caller ID, my pulse instinctively quickening. I swipe the answer button and bring the phone to my ear.

"Hello?"

"Wren? It's Austin. Are you alone?"

My chest tightens at the sound of her voice. It's been so long that I almost forgot what she sounds like. We've had a few calls over the last few years but nothing anything to remember. She's always busy so it's always a quick 'Hi, how are you?' on her way into the studio. I've always wanted a better relationship with my sister. She does her thing and I do mine. It's that simple.

Goosebumps immediately spread over my skin as my heart races.

"Is it your lover boy calling for phone sex?" Kennedy coos.

"No. It's Austin," I say, the words sounding foreign coming out of my mouth.

They both turn to me in horror as I pick up my ice packs and limp into my bedroom, closing the door. My hands shake as I sit down on the edge of the bed. "I'm alone. What's wrong? No one has heard from you in months. Are you okay?"

"My life is over. My career is over. I won't be able to dance anymore," Austin says quickly.

"What? Are you hurt? What happened?"

"Worse," she replies.

"Austin, what could be worse than that?" A huge part of me doesn't even want to know the answer. Austin is a lot less dramatic than my mom. She's always been the rational one but with the complete terror in her voice, I don't think I want to know.

"I'm pregnant."

The line goes strangely silent. Austin has never wanted kids. It's not that she doesn't like them. How can you hate a baby? But Austin's life plans were very simple. Ballet. Get married.

221

Ballet. Even as kids when asked what she wanted to do it was always 'ballet' with certainty and 'marriage' with a question mark.

She has done everything in her power to make sure that one plan stays consistent and that it actually follows through. In a way, I have a very similar to plan. Although, if I ever got pregnant it would be more of a miracle not to skate than a drawback.

She's been dating Zion for as long as I can remember, and they've made it work between her schedule and his job as a book editor. I knew they were serious when he moved away with her to Russia a few years ago but *this* was clearly not in their five-year plan.

"How far along are you?" I ask when I get my voice back.

"Too far. Maybe four months?" I don't say anything. What am I supposed to say to this? "Emmy, I *can't* do this right now. This was supposed to be my last month here and then I was meant to move to France in the new year with just Zion - not him *and* a baby."

"Wait, you got into the company?"

"Why are you so surprised? I worked hard and I got in," she says bluntly. Right. I forgot how uptight she was. "They won't want me anymore if they find out that I can't dance for at least a year."

"What are you going to do?"

"I'm going to figure that out. I was calling for a favour mostly," Austin says cautiously.

"Sure. What is it?" I ask, half of me afraid for the answer.

"Can you tell mom for me? I won't be able to stomach the disappointment. I've told dad already, but you know what he's like. He was just happy that there's a possibility he could get a grandson," she laughs quietly.

"Austin, I don't know if I can do that," I stutter. "I don't want all that pressure on me right now. I've got a show coming up."

"Great. That's perfect," she says, and I wait, not knowing where she's going with this. "Just tell her right after the show, when you've done your best performance and she'll be so proud she probably won't even care."

I wait a minute, not saying anything. My future in figure skating at NU is riding on the back of this showcase. Not only do I need people to turn up, but my mom needs to enjoy it. She needs to see that I've put my blood, sweat and tears into my practicing. And now, she needs to be prouder than ever so Austin's pregnancy can fly right over her head. If not, this could end badly for the both of us.

"Thank you, Wren. I owe you for this one," she says quickly without my reply before ending the call. I sit on my bed for what feels like hours, dumbfounded and my body suddenly feeling heavy.

When the anxieties creep up into me, I rush into my bathroom, and I throw up. When I'm scared and anxious this happens. A lot more than I'd like to admit. When the retching doesn't stop, both of the girls run into my bathroom. Kennedy holds my hair back while Scarlett rubs my back, not saying much. After I feel like it's all out of me, I go to my sink and brush my teeth, the both of them still in my bathroom, looking concerned.

"I'm, uh, I'm going to the rink," I say, when I turn around to them, my voice suddenly not sounding like my own.

Scarlett inches towards me.

"Wren, it's past nine o'clock. I don't think the one on campus is open," she says.

223

I brush past her and go into my bedroom. They follow behind me.

"And not to mention you've been there all day. Take a break," Kennedy suggests as I pack my duffel bag with my leotard and essentials.

"I'll find one that's open," I bite out and I walk out of my room into the kitchen. They follow behind me again as I grab a couple bottles of water and I shove them into my bag, avoiding their eyes.

"Wren," Scarlett says, carefully, shifting from one foot to the other. "I don't think this is a good idea. You need to take a breather. You just threw your stomach up. You were like this before regionals."

"Yeah and look where that fucking got me. I didn't take it seriously enough. I put being with Augustus over skating and I didn't practice enough. I could have prevented that. If I fuck this one up, I'm over. I'm done," I shout.

They both take a step back, neither one of them knowing what to say. Kennedy's eyes soften as she looks at me. Scarlett looks irritated and a little disappointed. She's had to put up with side of me for the longest time. She's seen me after losing a comp as a kid, she's seen me after winning and still needing to do better. Constantly trying to do my absolute best. To be flawless.

"Look," I sigh, my voice quieter. "I'm sorry for shouting but I'm in a really difficult situation right now and I need to clear my head."

"Then talk to us. That's what we're here for," Kennedy whispers, her voice weighty with emotion. "You don't run away when things get hard. We don't do that."

I want to grab them both into a hug. I want to tell them everything. I want to tell them how it feels like I'm constantly

224

being held down by a giant, cutting off my blood circulation. How I'm constantly hearing the words *You're not good enough* over and over.

"I can't. I'm sorry. I can't," I stammer as I slip out of the door.

CHAPTER 22
MILES

Since the night of the game, I've hardly seen Wren.

We've been to the gym like usual and hanging out on campus but she's not fully there. Even while we're together, I do most of the taking while she nods and mm hmm's. It's like only a part of her is there. The part that was there in the beginning but without the sarcastic comments. Instead, I get concentrated looks and two-word answers. I thought we grew out of that. Even when I make my hilarious gym jokes, she just ignores them.

"Why did the cheese go to the gym?" I said once while I caught my breath, stood over her while she did sit ups.

"Why?" she asked with a bored expression, not even a waver in her voice even after doing fifty sit ups.

"Because he wanted to *cheddar* a couple pounds," I replied. She just blinked up at me, not even a crack of a smile on her face. I remember when these kinds of jokes would earn me a toothy grin and a kick in the stomach. Now, she doesn't even care. Or even pretend to care. She stood up and looked at me.

"Can you spot me on the bench press?" she asked. She barley looked at me for the rest of the day.

I'm beginning to think that the kiss was a bad idea. Sure, in the moment we both wanted it. Badly. She was really fucking enthusiastic about it when she was moaning my name. Since then, in all the posts we've put online, she's asked me to cover her face because she looks too tired. Even when we walk around campus between classes, she keeps a baseball cap over her head. Even though to me, she still looks beautiful. I know she's probably stressed about the showcase, but I didn't expect her to be this distant with me.

I just want her to talk to me. To let me in.

She told me that this is what she does. That she always holds people at arm's length. I believed that when I first met her. I knew she was going to be closed off and I knew I had to work for her to let me in. But I thought that after a while, after we got so comfortable with each other, that wall would crumble. It turns out that wall just been put up stronger than before.

After speaking with Clara, I've felt lighter. I still haven't made the brave decision of calling my mom yet but I'm getting there. I've gotten used to watching videos of Carter and hearing his voice without feeling my stomach turn. I've also been out in the hockey rink with my gear on. Getting used to being on the ice again has been a difficult adjustment but I'm slowly getting there. And I can't remember the last time I've had anything stronger than a Stella.

I got a phone call yesterday from Coach, asking me to meet him this morning. He knows about the fight. He has to. Someone must have told him, and this could be the start of the end. I could lose my scholarship and I'd have to move back home and start community college and get my old job back.

227

I walk the distance from my house to the sports centre to clear my head. I hear the grunts and groans from the figure skating rink, but I tell myself not to look. If I look now, I'll go to her and mess up her practice and send myself into a procrastination spiral which is the last thing either of us need right now.

I get to Coach Tuckers office and the door's already open. His office is more like a closet filled top to bottom with sports equipment. There are tons of equipment for sports that he doesn't even coach and certificates and medals hung on the walls. His desk is piled high with paperwork and folders but when they're cleared it's easy to see the pictures that he has on his desk. His most famous photo of him, his husband and their three Corgi's which he tells us was the day he found out he got the job at North.

When I go in, I'm greeted with a smile, and he gestures towards the seat in front of him. I can't read his face just yet. I can't tell if that's a good thing or not.

"Miles, I'm sure you know why you're here," begins, strangely cheerfully. He leans his forearms on the table, his eyebrows knitted together in a serious expression.

"Uh, I think so," I reply cautiously. He lets his expression drop and he sighs deeply.

"I heard about what happened after the game. More like, I *saw* what happened. Harry showed me a video and I heard about Jake said to you. I'd like to say that I'm sorry he said that," Coach says, and I shrug, not wanting to relive that moment. "I understand *why* you did it but I'm still disappointed."

"If you're going to kick me off the team for good, can you just say it?" He laughs, shaking his head.

"Miles, I'm not kicking you off the team. You think I haven't seen you throw a few punches at other players during the

228

games? These things happen and neither of you reported it or were badly injured. As long as you and Jake are cool with each other, I want you to play our first game of the season. You've proved that you're in a better place apart from that mishap and your grades have improved a too."

"Really?" I exclaim, not able to contain the excitement in my voice. Coach smiles wide, nodding. "You're not going to regret this, Coach. Thank you."

"It's fine, Davis. I still want you to practice over the holidays to prepare. If you need someone to talk to, you know, about Carter... I'm here."

"I know," I say before pulling back my chair and thanking him again.

I have the biggest smile on my face when I walk around to the rink Wren is skating on. I know I shouldn't but I'm too excited to not tell her right now. Sure enough, she's in the middle of spinning with her foot high above her head in a black leotard. She skates forwards before doing a triple turn in the air and landing wobbly.

"Fuck me," she groans loudly, and she begins again.

"I've got good news," I announce. She stops abruptly and stares at me for a long second before floating over to me. She stands at the railing, her face red and puffy. "I got back on the team." Wren's face lights up and her smile widens. "That's great, Miles. That's really good, honestly. That's great."

"Yeah, you said that twice," I laugh, shifting from one foot to the other. "But it's all thanks to you. So, thank you."

"You don't have to thank me. You're the one who put the work in."

I shrug, grinning and we stay silent for a while. She looks at my face in a curious way as if this is the first time and she's trying to figure me out. Her eyes land on my lips, and they hover there for a beat. Her tongue runs against her bottom lip before shaking her head softly.

"How's practicing going?" I ask, trying to cut out the tension.

"It's good. Could be better," she replies, waving her hands in defeat. "I do need to get back to it, though." She nods her head towards the empty rink.

"Sure," I say. "Also, I'm doing that interview with Sophia soon and I'd love for you to come. It could drum up some support for us. Plus, you deserve a break."

She sighs, chewing her bottom lip. "Fine."

My face cracks into a smie. "That's my girl."

*

I try not to take what she said personally when I get home but there's a feeling in my chest that I can't ignore. I know she needs to practice, especially with all the pressure that her mom puts on her, but something feels off.

Maybe it's because I've never seen her like this before and I'm slowly getting attached to her. This is the first time I've been around another person who plays a sport that they've dedicated their lives to. This showcase is so important to her. If this goes badly then she might not be able to skate again.

I've told her before that it would be fine if she did. If she did something else. But she pushed the idea away. She pushed me away. "It's all or nothing, Miles," she said once. I believe that she puts her all into everything she does even just in practices, but she can't see it. She only notices the tiny flaws and the unnoticeable mistakes.

Sometimes, people think she's mean or insane. I think she's fucking brilliant.

I just wish she could see herself the way I see her.

CHAPTER 23
MILES

I'm trying my best to convince myself that Wren and I are fine. I'm back on the team, even though I haven't played my first game yet, and Wren's showcase is coming up. She's been training like an insane person so that's why it took a lot of convincing for her to come along to this interview at Sophia's house.

I've been friends with Sophia for as long as I can remember and she has been in her, what she calls, 'influencer era' for years. Becoming the leader of the NU Press has given her the perfect opportunity to make her dreams real. She gets to interview students from different subjects and by the end of our fourth year, she's aiming to create a huge graduation video to show everyone. Since the hockey season is about to start, she's coming around our team to interview everyone. The only thing about Sophia and this project is that she's kept it very secret. We've had mini interviews before that she posts on Instagram and TikTok but since this is her big project, we're interviewed and won't get to see it until it's completed.

She sets up her house into a comfortable interviewing space and the team and usually their other friends and partners join us so we can hang out afterwards. I know Wren's not going to enjoy the whole socialising aspect of today so I try and get us there early.

We're now driving towards Sophia's house and Wren isn't doing that angry humming thing. Instead, she's silent, no doubt in her head about the showcase. Which is even more concerning because Taylor Swift is playing. I turn up *'New Romantics'* and her face doesn't even crack.

"Hey, can I ask you a question?" I ask.

"If I say no, are you going to ask me anyway?" she retorts. I glance at her and catch her playing with one of her french braids.

"Yes," I say. "What would be the first thing you'd do if you won the lottery?"

She laughs a little, the sound rushing through me like a gentle wave. "These questions are getting more and more random," she says, but I shoot her a glance to continue. "I'd buy me and the girls a house where we could each have our own wing and then order as much pizza as possible."

I grin. "Not even a salad? Wren, you animal."

She laughs agai. "If I've won the lottery then I wouldn't skate professionally. Just for fun. So I wouldn't need to watch what I eat."

"Do you *want* to skate professionally? Like, the Olympics and all that."

She sighs a little. "I don't see that as my end goal. I don't know… It's hard to explain."

We get to Sophia's house and I park on the sidewalk, not wanting to end this conversation just yet. I turn to her as she stares straight ahead. I can't have her pushing me away again. I need to let her know that she can open up to me and we can actually have real conversations. "Can you try?"

She turns to me now, propping her leg up on the seat to get more comfortable. "I know everybody who skates at college dreams of competing on Team USA but I can't see myself doing that. I can see myself skating and when it stops being fun, I'm going to stop. If that's five years from now or in five days, I'm not going to force myself to skate. I know it sounds stupid and it seems like I have no direction but really I'm fine with just-"

"Seeing where life takes you?" I say, finishing her sentence and she nods, allowing herself to be vulnerable with me. "I get that

233

and you don't need to be afraid of admitting that. Not everyone has a five year plan like Xaiver does about the NHL."

She nods again, glancing over to the house and then back to me. "Thank you for understanding that. And I just want to say that I am trying. With this, I mean. I've just got a lot going on right now and it's hard to get out of my head sometimes."

"You can let me into your brain, Wren. I'm never going to judge you."

"I know that but this is something I need to work on on my own."

She's clearly keeping something from me and it's not just stress about the showcase. It's something more that she isn't telling me but I don't push her on it and scare her away.

"Do you remember what I said at the Drive-In?" I ask. "When you stress out about this, you stress me out. So please, can you relax for me? Soph will be able to tell something is wrong and your show is coming up."

She unbuckles her seatbelt. "Thanks for the reminder," she murmurs and I roll my eyes at her.

Sophia's house looks even bigger in the daylight. I used to spend most of my days here when I was nose deep in bourbon. She's one of the lucky kids who have always had a close relationship with their parents and have a childhood home near campus so she never had to move out.

When I get out of my side of the car, I grab Wren's hand in mine and she melts into me. We've finally got over the first awkwardness of holding hands in public and after *that* kiss, we've become more comfortable around each other's bodies. We step up onto the porch and I pause for a second, knowing that inside is going to be a hell of hockey players.

"Why are *you* preparing for this? It's bound to be a lot worse for me than it is for you. This is your safe space. The last time I came here I had a panic attack," Wren murmurs, tugging on my hand and looking up at me. Does she have to look so good all the time? Those french braids are doing absolutely nothing for me and rule number three. "Come on, Milesy. You're a big boy, you can handle it."

I smile and I don't tell her how difficult it's going to be to see the whole team together after the last interview we did all

234

together we did with Carter. I don't tell her that it's going to take everything in me not to rip Jake's head off the second I lay eyes on him. Instead, I squeeze her hand tighter in mine and step up to the door.

With that, the door swings open and the room erupts into cheers and music blasts from the speakers, no doubt with Grey's playlist playing. The entire hockey team is here, crammed into the living room and the hallway along with a bunch of other random people I've never seen before. I know that the interviews take place in the basement that has been soundproofed so there's no wonder why it's so loud up here. I pull Wren with me through the crowd until we get to the kitchen, standing on opposite sounds of the island.

"Is it just me or are you getting really vivid deja vu?" I ask, remembering the night of the party. Wren laughs a little, picking up one of the waters that are on the island.

"If only you were choking over the sink again," she drawls, shaking her head at me. I'm about to make a snarky comment but Xaiver appears, his arm around Michelle as they sport matching NU Bear's jerseys. Michelle writhes out of his grip and pulls Wren into a tight hug. "Michelle! How are you?"

"I'm fabulous," Michelle replies, pulling out of the hug and holding Wren at arms length. "I *love* your hair like this, Wren. Isn't it so cute, Miles?"

"The cutest," I say, no word of a lie as I watch her face turn a bright pink. It's so easy to make her blush and I want to do it all the time. Xavier stands beside me, smiling, as we watch our girls gush over each other's outfits. Well, my *fake* girl. Because that's all we are. The more I tell myself that, the more I start to believe it.

"Those two are going to be best friends. No matter how you guys end things, you can't make my girl upset about losing Wren. She's, like, obsessed with her," he says, low enough for only me to hear. Yeah, she's not the only one.

"Can I be honest with you guys?" Michelle says, turning towards me and Xaiver. Wren watches her, clearly unsure about what's going to come out of her mouth. "Wren is the best person you've dated, Miles."

Wren laughs, throwing her head back. "You can stop with all the compliments, Michelle. You don't have to try and flatter me," she says, twisting the end of her braid between her fingers.

Mitch shakes her head. "No. I'm being serious. You bring out the best in him. I've seen him through many stages in his life and this is by far the happiest. Losing Carter has been hard for all of us but you've managed to make him somewhat happier."

Wren stands there, frozen. This is what we want. We need people to be invested in us but this feels like we're crossing a line somehow. I know she's made me a happier person. Even if this is pretend, the way she makes me feel is so real that it scares me. Not the way that she turns me on or drives me crazy but the way that she talks to me, listens to me and even when she's trying to push me away, she still tries to make an effort. Before I can respond to try and save this somehow, Sophia's voice echoes off the walls. Because she's one of the most extra people I've ever met, she's managed to connect a microphone to the speakers in the house. Now, this is an upgrade from last year.

We can't see her from the kitchen but there's no doubt that she's standing on the table in the living room, making this into a performance.

"Hello, everybody," Sophia's voice booms. "I'm so glad so many of you could make it. If you've just arrived, refreshments are everywhere and so is the food. We're going to get straight into it and I'm inviting the first five people into the basement where the group interview will take place. Afterwards, individual interviews will take place. If your name is not called, sit tight and you will be down next. First can I have Xavier Dawson, Harry Butler, Jake Callahan, Greyson Aoki-Park, and Miles Davis downstairs. Please, and thank you!"

Xavier and I look at each other and then back to the girls. "I guess that's our que," I say, nodding at Wren to come over to me and she does. "Do you want to stay up here or come down?"

"If Michelle is going then I am too," she replies, beaming at her new best friend. We start to make our way through the crowds as I hold onto Wren's hand as we go down the stairs to the basement. It shouldn't be this nerve-racking. It's just a stupid interview with my stupid friends. That's it. "Miles?"

"Mm hm."

"You're squeezing my hand," she whispers. "It hurts."

"Shit. I'm sorry," I say, releasing her hand and allowing her to curl her hand over three of my fingers. I bring her hand to my mouth and kiss it as she blinks up at me with those killer green eyes. "Better?"

She nods. "Much better."

When we get down to the basement, it looks a lot more professional than I thought. On one side of the room, there's a white wall with a neon light that reads 'Sophia's Corner' behind a couch that's big enough to fit ten of us on there. On the seats on the couch, there is a sheet of paper with our names on them, which I'm assuming is the order Sophia wants us to sit in. I'm on one end next to Harry, Xavier, Grey and then Jake on the other end. I've not even bothered to look in his direction since we got down here, knowing that chaos would erupt if I did.

On the other side of the room there are brown chairs and tables filled with drinks and snacks for the people that have agreed to stand silently and watch the interview up close. Sophia's director's chair also makes this whole thing feel more official. You'd think we're about to go live on air not for a graduation video with the amount of effort that she's put into this.

We all take our seats and Wren and Michelle stand on the other side of the room, lingering around a table near where Sophia's chair is. I try to get my heartbeat to settle when I notice the team photo that Sophia has hung up on the wall. She has one of all the major sports teams at NU, including the skating team which she probably took for the yearbook. In our picture, it's the one where we're celebrating our season win last year, Carter being held up by all of us with the trophy in his hands. I shake off the uncomfortable feeling and try to settle down. I look over at Wren and she does the dorkiest most adorable thing ever, smiling wide as she gives me a double thumbs up. I can do this.

"Are you guys ready?" Sophia asks, setting up her camera on her tripod and pressing record before mouthing a countdown.

"So, we are here with the first interview of the day with some of my favourite players from the North University Bear's hockey team. We have Miles Davis on your right, followed by Harry Butler, Xavier Dawson, Greyson Aoki-Park and Jake Callahan. What a dream team, I must say."

"When you've known each other as long as we have, it's hard not to work together so well," Xavier says, looking up and down the line. Everyone nods in agreement. "Of course, it was different for Haz over here, since he's only just joined the team in first year."

Harry groans at the nickname we've all got for him and we all laugh. "Just because I didn't play with you guys in middle school or high school, doesn't make me *that* new to the team," he retorts.

"How does it feel being the baby of the team, Harry? It must be a lot different to playing hockey in Australia," Sophia says, crossing her legs and getting into her serious position.

"It feels good. I mean, in my town, ice hockey was pretty uncommon so when my dad said we were moving here, it gave me the best opportunity to try out for a team," Harry explains.

"And how have you been settling in?" Sophia asks curiously. She gets cut off by a loud groan coming from Grey. "Got something you want to say, Greyson?"

"Yes," he concedes. "You're asking all the boring questions, cuz. No one wants to know about how Harry enjoys the team."

"First names only, Greyson Phillip Aoki-Park," Sophia relays, pinning him with a death stare. "Moving on. How are you, as a team, planning on tackling the opposition in the new year? I hear you've got a very competitive season ahead of you."

"Out hustle, out work, out think, out play and out last," Xavier says, repeating our mantra that we have been using our whole lives. Obviously, Jake snorts at that.

"Come on with the BS, Dawson," Jake laughs. "What we're really going to do is beat the competition with whatever force we have. Hockey isn't just a mind game, it's a physical one too."

"Great. Thank you for that insight, Callahan," Sophia mutters, scribbling down notes on her notebook. I look over to Wren and she is not trying at all to hide the disgust on her face.

"You're welcome," Jake replies proudly.

"Okay, so, you all agreed to talk about this before coming so here is just a small warning before we get into it," Sophia begins, not breaking eye contact with me and I know exactly where this is going. "You all lost a vital team member at the beginning of summer and I know it has not been easy for any of you. Some more than others. I grew up with Carter as well, and we all knew he was going to do amazing things. My next question is, how are you planning on honouring him during this season? Xaiver, would you like to go first?"

Xavier nods, looking at me before facing the camera. "Unlike some of the tactics Jake likes to use, Carter was the calmest one on the team. I don't know how we managed to win every game with him even though he seemed to be the most chilled out and relaxed on the ice. While the rest of us were pushing into people, knocking them over, Carter kept a levelled head. That's how I'm planning on honouring him, by keeping calm and spending as much time out of the penalty box as possible."

We all nod, agreeing with the perfect answer. "It'll be easier for some more than others, I assume," Sophia starts, "Ahem. Greyson."

"Yeah, yeah. Whatever. I'm only in the sin bin because I like to play dirty for the win," Greyson says easily.

We seamlessly float into a conversation of Sophia asking rapid fire questions before going back into the deeper ones. I don't think I could do this if it was anyone else but because I've known her forever, talking to her feels easy. Fun, even.

I can't decide if having Wren here is making it better or worse. She's still standing with Michelle, watching me intently. I can tell that she's listening to every word that I'm saying and I hope that it's taking her mind off skating for once and allowing her to be with us in the moment.

Sophia asks us about how we balance hockey and school, where we see ourselves in five years and more hockey related questions. I stay quiet for the most part, only answering questions that everyone else gets stuck on. But Sophia's next question catches me a little off guard.

"We all know that hockey is a team sport but what people really want to know is how you stay focused in the game. How

239

do you ensure that you are on the right track and are going to perform your best as well as making sure it's a team effort?" she asks.

I look down the line, hoping that someone is going to pipe up. "I think that this is Davis' question," Grey says, looking at me suggestively. Sophia nods and I feel everyone's eyes on me in the room.

I take a deep breath and just let out absolutely everything. "As everybody knows, Carter is my best friend. We grew up together and we were inseparable. I took his death hard and I didn't let anybody in. I was drinking a lot – sorry mom," I admit, remembering that if my mom comes to graduation, she's going to know I've been underage drinking. Everyone in the room laughs quietly. "I lost motivation to train and I hardly ever went to the rink. But then I met Wren." The smile that was on her face drops as I connect my eyes with hers across the room. "She turned my life around and she really *saw* me. She became the storm to the calm, quiet loneliness that I was in in the best way possible. She thought that I was hyperfixating on her instead of dealing with my problems but I managed to kill two birds with one stone and I got though some of my problems while also getting a gorgeous, smart, talented and just fucking brillaint girlfriend."

"No cursing, Davis," Sophia warns.

"Shit. Sorry," I say and Sophia gives me an evil glare. "Wait, no. Fuck. Can you take that bit out?" Sophia shakes her head at me, disappointed. "All I'm trying to say is that having someone who cares about you by your side is what helps me stay focused because I know that I'm doing it for myself and so I can be the best version of myself for her."

The room is eerily silent as I look at Wren, watching the way her features soften. Her eyes aren't wide and panicked like they were when she first came here. Instead, her eyes haven't left mine since I started speaking and her mouth is pinned into a warm smile, no doubt trying to decipher if what I said was true or not. Hell, I don't even know half of the words that just came out of my mouth and where the truth lies within them.

I break eye contact with her, unable to bear the look on her face and focus back on the interview. Sophia asks the group a few more questions before letting us branch off before our individual interviews. I go over to Wren and she's now alone as Xaiver has pulled Michelle away.

"You good?" I ask, standing in front of her. She nods. "Is what I said okay? You know, for the sake of the interview."

"Yeah, it was perfect. I don't know how you managed to make all that up on the spot," she replies, almost laughing.

"It wasn't hard to talk about how much I enjoy spending time with you. Even when you give me a hard time," I say, stepping in closer to her. I watch her audibly swallow as she blinks up at me. I tug on her braid, forcing her to tilt her head up to me and she looks way too good from this position. I lean down to whisper in her ear, "They're watching."

She lets out a shaky exhale. "Of course." She pulls back, trying not to make it obvious that she wants to move out of my grip. Wren clears her throat, looking down at the floor. "I need to go to practice. Will you be able to drop me off?"

"Seriously, right now? Can't you stay for a little longer?" I ask, shifting my weight on one foot to the other.

"I need to go. I've already missed out of a lot of time just being here," she says, looking up at me. "If you've got to stay to do your individual interview, I can just walk."

"I can do it really quickly and then I can take you. I'll just ask Sophia-"

She cuts me off by rising on her tiptoes and pressing a kiss to my cheek. "It's okay. You stay. I'll see you soon."

She doesn't wait for me to respond before she's already climbing up the stairs out of the basement.

CHAPTER 24
WREN

I know that running out of the basement was a bad idea but I can't tell Miles about Austin right now. I haven't told anyone about Austin yet. He said it himself that I stress him out when I'm stressed, so me leaving that night was the best thing to do. For the both of us. I even managed to get in a few hours of practice before the school rink closed. Still, I basically dragged myself to the rink this morning so I could get in a few hours of practice.

I've been avoiding my mom like a fucking disease but I can't deal with seeing her right now. As much as I love my sister, I hate that she's put this kind of pressure on me, especially right before I have my show. I know my mom is hard to please but I'm sure she would come around if Austin could just own up and tell her. Having a baby is such a huge thing, I'm confident that my mom could find it somewhere in her black heart to accept it. Instead, I'm greeted with four feet of flowers every time I walk into my apartment as some sick way of my mom showing that she still cares that I exist without actually trying to speak to me.

I make my way back home after a long day at the rink, ready to avoid the girls and take a long bath before snuggling in my bed with a paperback in my hands. Most nights, Scarlett and Kennedy watch a movie like we used to before I had the weight of the world on my back. But now, I'm so used to walking past them, mumbling a 'good night' that I don't even realise that they've spoken to me.

"What?" I say in the near darkness, tugging my duffel bag higher up my shoulder. I step closer into the living room, looking at their makeshift fort that they've huddled in. They both pop their heads out of the fort, pulling the blanket around them.

"We're going out tonight and you're coming with us," Scarlett demands.

"I want to stay home. I'm exhausted," I say.

"You're always exhausted. A night out will wake you up," Kennedy adds with a shimmy.

"The showcase is in less than three weeks," I say, sighing. As much as their friendship means the absolute world to me, sometimes I just want to be alone, needing to find a way to figure out how the hell I'm going to figure out the situation with Austin.

"No, Wren. You're going to speak to us because that's what friends are for. You're not going to shut us out because you're stressed. Let your stress become *our* stress," Kennedy relays.

"You guys really don't want to know what's been going on," I whisper, everything that has happened in the last few weeks coming rushing back to me.

"Try us," Scarlett challenges.

*

"What the fuck? Are you serious?" Scarlett exclaims once I've finished explaining everything to them. Everything from the Drive-In, to kissing Miles, to finding out about Austin to whatever the hell it was at Sophia's house. It feels good to vent even though most of what I'm saying doesn't make much sense to me anymore.

We're at a secluded bar that Scarlett managed to get us into because of her family's access to getting away with drinking without getting asked for ID. I don't usually drink but being around these two, I feel safe enough and hell, I'm going to need it.

243

"Unfortunately, I'm being very serious," I say, sipping more of my cocktail.

"No wonder you've been so distant," Kennedy says quietly, shaking her head. "Does she really just expect you to tell your mom for her?" I nod. "Jesus. If Mia ever asked me to do something like that, I'd tell her to suck it up and do it herself."

"I tried but she cut me off and isn't answering any of my calls," I admit, feeling helpless

"So what are you going to do?" Scarlett asks.

"I don't know. I'm going to wait it out and see if she'll tell her herself. I just know that this whole thing is going to come crashing down on me, no matter who tells her."

As if they both planned it, they both trap me in a hug from both sides and I melt into them. We have always done group hugs like this; the person who needs it the most is almost suffocating in the middle with the others acting as the anchor, keeping us together. When we pull apart, I can still feel them around me, making anywhere become a home with them in my arms.

"Tell you what you need, Wrenny?" Scarlett asks.

"For you to stop calling me that nickname?" I ask hopefully.

"Shots!" she shouts.

And we do.

We drink so fucking much.

I don't think I've ever consumed this much alcohol in my life but it's making me feel alive. As if all my problems can be dealt with tomorrow and all that matters is being in this moment with my friends. My friends that are screaming Taylor Swift lyrics at the top of their lungs. I try to make a mental note to apologise to the bar staff who have had to put up with our atrocious singing for the last two hours.

"I love you guys so fucking much," I scream when *'Blank Space'* finishes. They pull me into a tight hug again, their microphones jabbing into my stomach. "Like, so, so, much."

"Oh no," Kennedy shouts.

"What is it? Have I had something in my teeth this whole time?" Scarlett asks, frantically searching for her mirror in her purse .

"No. Your teeth are perfect, babe. I just realised that Wren is an emotional drunk," Kennedy says, pouting at me.

"I'm not emotional and I'm not a drink," I slur, waving her off.
"*Drunk*, babe. You mean you're not *drunk*," Scarlett says, patting me on the back. Thank god she knows how to speak. "And you are. Watch."

She pulls her phone out of her back pocket and clicks on her home screen and it's a picture of the two of us at our kindergarten graduation. We look so tiny and small and so cute. We've got the biggest grins on our toothless faces with our graduation caps and gowns on. Then she clicks the screen and the worst thing happens. It changes to a picture of all of us, Kennedy now included, at our high school graduation, smiling as we hold our diplomas.

"See, that's just cruel," I say, the sob ripping through me unexpectedly. "I miss you guys."

"We're right here, Wrenny. And we always will be if you let us," Kennedy says, looking at me with her gorgeous brown doe eyes. Then the waterworks are really flowing. God, I can't get myself to stop. "More drinks!"

Then we drink more as the last few weeks I've had fade into a blur. Then my mind goes into a no-go zone. The Miles Zone. Suddenly all I can think about are his green eyes and his kind words and the fact that I've pushed him away since the interview and that I've tried to avoid thinking about him.

I do the stupid thing and pull out my phone which opens up to a picture of the two of us. It's a selfie he took while he was confiscating my phone as I studied. He's got the cheesiest grin on his face and is holding the camera high so you can see me in the background, my head buried deep in books. By the time he gave me my phone back, this was the picture he changed the home screen to and I haven't had the energy to change it back.

I do an even stupider thing and I call him.

He picks up on the second ring.

"Milesy, baby. I miss you," I say, the words unable to stop coming out of my mouth as they come out garbled. The girls look at me with a sceptical look and I turn away from them, walking towards the bar to sit down. "What are you doing? Who are you with? You're not cheating on me, are you?"

Apparently I'm a jealous drunk too. I hear him laugh low over the phone. "I'm on a Costco run with Evan. What are *you* doing?"

"Drinking at a bar with Kenny and Scarlett," I say through a yawn. I whisper as if it's a secret, "I think I'm drunk."

"Really? I couldn't tell," he replies, also whispering before returning back to his normal voice. "Are you okay, though? What bar are you at?"

"Shhhh. Stop shouting at me or I'm going to kiss you."

He laughs but I don't see what's funny. "You're going to kiss me? Do you mean kill, Wren?"

Oh. "Stupid autocorrect."

"You can't autocorrect with your voice, baby."

"Stop calling me baby or I *will* kiss you," I murmur but I don't think he hears me. All I hear is a sharp inhale so I continue. "Can you come and get us, please. I need you."

"Can you turn on your location for me?" he asks gently and I fumble to change the screen so I can send him my location. "I'm on my way."

Less than twenty minutes later, we're still all very drunk, a little less sad than before and the boys have turned up. Maybe I should have given Scarlett a trigger warning about Evan showing up because she almost throws up when she sees him. Which I can't tell is because of the alcohol or because of the disgust she has for him. Evan is casually in pants, a crisp white shirt and a black tie hanging loose on his neck while Miles is wearing grey sweatpants and a white shirt.

Scarlett comes beside me as we stand in a line, staring at the boys as if they've interrupted something. "Why is *he* here? You promised no blondes," she tries to whisper but she's basically shouting in my ear.

"I promised no such thing. Plus, he was already with Miles in his fancy car," I say back, singing the last few words. *Yes, he has a driver. What is this life?*

"I can't help it if I'm blonde," Evan retorts, running a hand through his hair.

"You can dye your hair," Kennedy suggests.

Evan nods. "Done."

"No! Don't do that," Scarlett says, stumbling towards him as if he's about to dye his hair this minute. Evan laughs, holding her as she almost falls into him.

"You *just* said how much you hate my blondeness."

"That doesn't mean I want you to dye it, you idiot" she mumbles, trying to get herself out of his grip but he keeps his hands on her forearms. "Would you really do it if I told you to?"

"If it annoys you that much, of course I would, Angel."

What the hell?

When did this happen? Has he always called her Angel? And has she always let him? I'm not going to remember this in the morning so I will start to erase it from my memory now. They both stare at each other and it's hard to tell which one of them is drunk at this point.

Until Scarlett finally says, "I'm drunk I don't know what I'm saying." *I'm drunk and I don't know what I'm saying; title of your sex tape,* I want to say but maybe right now is not the time to bring up my Brooklyn Nine-Nine obsession.

"Drunk thoughts are sober words," I say, trying my absolute best to wink at Scarlett.

"That's not how the saying goes. But good job, baby," Miles says smiling down at me as he wraps his arm around my waist. "Can you walk okay?"

"I think you might need to carry me"

"Really?" I nod, smiling up at him. "Fine."

He picks me up in a fireman's carry, hauling me over his shoulder and I'm lucky I'm not wearing the skirt that the girls begged me to wear. Luckily, all Miles can see is my fully clothed ass in my favourite pair of jeans. He carries me all the way to the car as Evan has Kennedy and Scarlett on each side of him and they slip into the back with us. We drive home mostly in silence and Miles insists on walking us up to the door.

After the girls have gone to their rooms, Miles follows me into mine. I'm still a little tipsy, on the verge of falling asleep but the second that Miles comes into my room, I'm fully awake. It's pitch black outside and Miles Davis is in my bedroom and he's looking at me, waiting for me to do or say something. Anything.

He steps closer towards me and the back of my knees hit the bed and I sit down. My heartbeat is racing a thousand miles per hour as he kneels down in front of me and- Pushes me down? Obviously he wasn't about to go down on me because that would be insane and not to mention, extremely stupid. Instead, he urges me to get inside my covers and he wraps them around me.

He passes me the glass of water that I hadn't realised was there and I take a few gulps. He places it back on the nightstand and gets into the bed with me. I'm laying down, tucked neatly under the covers as Miles sits beside me on top of them, looking down at me.

I turn to the ceiling and say, "I'm sorry about that."

"I'm just glad you're having fun. You deserve a break sometimes, you know," he says, sliding down onto the bed next to me, our shoulders brushing against each other. He looks up at the ceiling too as I turn to him before facing upwards again.

"I don't deserve anything. I don't deserve you and I especially don't deserve a break," I say into the air. I don't know what's going on with me? I know how pathetic I sound but I can't tell my mouth to stop. He turns to me now, one arm resting beneath his face and the other wrapping a finger around my hair and it distracts me for a second that I almost miss what he asks next. "What do you mean?"

"I don't think I try hard enough. If I tried hard enough my mom would actually like me and I wouldn't be constantly trying to win her approval."

His face is so close to mine now, the light touch of his hand centring me as his words reverberate through me. "You have no idea do you?"

"What?" I breathe.

"You have no idea how special you are, Wren, and it breaks my heart everytime I hear you speak like that. Because I would give up everything in this world for you to realise that you're perfect in every way that counts."

I suddenly feel like all the alcohol has left my body as the words leave his mouth and puncture me right in the heart. This is exactly what it feels like for my inner child to be healed.

I do what I've been needing to do since I saw him today and I wrap my arms around him. It's a little struggle at first since we're both lying down but once we're comfortable, I nuzzle my face into his neck, breathing in his lavender smell. Instinctively, I hook my leg over his. Not in a way to be purposefully sexual, it's just what feels the most comfortable right now and he hold onto me tight.

"Can you stay here tonight? Just hold me," I ask into his skin, not wanting him to leave me just yet. Yeah, I really am an emotional drunk.

"Rule number three, Wren," he says.

"This doesn't count. I'm not asking you to sleep with me. Well I am, just not like that. Can you, please? I need you. Here," I admit, realising that this is the only thing keeping me calm. The only thing that is keeping my heartbeat at a settled pace.

"Anything you want," he says, brushing my hair out of my face.

He gently pushes me to turn around until my back is flush against his front, his arms braced tight around me. I don't tell him about Austin or how stressed I am because it doesn't feel like the right time. All I need is to be held by him and it seems like he needs it too. So, he holds me.

All night.

He's just there.

CHAPTER 25
WREN

I've spent the better half of two weeks practicing non-stop.

Maybe I've started to go delirious since I've not been eating well, and all my days have become on big cluster. Every time I close my eyes, I see myself falling on the ice again and I can't get that image out of my head. I need to get it out my head. I know I've been distant with Miles after that night at the bar, but I had to. After having a few days off to hang out with my friends, I've needed to go back to skating everyday.

Whenever I'm around him, I'm drawn to him, and I want to do things that I know I shouldn't. Things that will distract me. That is the last thing either of us need. He was good for a distraction when everything felt so far away. When the showcase was months away instead of tonight.

These showcases are not graded but they're for fun to lead up to the real competitions. In a way, it's a good practice to have in front of an audience before the holidays. This way, if people turn up here, they're more likely to turn up to the real events. Coach Darcy says it's vital to do things for fun in between comp season and I usually enjoy them. I love the feeling of skating. I like being on the ice and my body just flowing with the music in a practiced motion.

But nothing is ever fun with my mom. If anything, these things give her more of a reason to critique me. "Denise Beillmann was sixteen was she landed her first triple Lutz," she always says, comparing me to one of my idols. With Austin's situation, it means that I have to do my best. Now more than ever.

With all the practice I've been doing, I haven't spoken to either of the girls much either since they convinced me to go out. They know when I get like this: I push everything else aside and I focus on doing better. Since I shouted at them and left, I have been sneaking out early in the morning to avoid talking to them and I sneak back in late at night when I know they've gone to sleep. Even on the few days when they're both watching *New Girl* re-runs late at night and offer me to join them, I decline and lock myself in my room. Since we aired out why I was stressed, they've understood that sometimes I need time for myself.

I've been practicing all morning, doing the most I can to make this routine flawless. There is one other duet on my team and three soloists: Eva, Madelyn, and Augustus. They don't take these showcases as serious as the comps, but I have run into them a few times at the other rink in town. We all have a strange relationship.

Since Augustus and I broke up, we've not spoken, or barley glanced at each other. We were pretty close with the other skaters when we were together but when we broke up, they all took his side. They all think I'm too cold and insecure and that he was right to breakup with me. That I deserved it. They only think that because they don't have the weight of the world on

251

their backs every time they need to skate. They get to do it for fun. They have that choice.

"Good luck today," I hear a voice from behind me as I walk towards the locker rooms. For a second, I think it's Miles but when I turn around, I see him.

Augustus Holden.

He's a few inches taller than me, a typically uptight Russian with dark blond hair and scarily sharp cheekbones. He's attractive in a way he shouldn't be. It's almost unfair. It's just my luck that I see him before my performance.

He stalks towards me in his white body shirt and I freeze.

"What?"

"I *said,* good luck. We both know you're going to need it after regionals," he growls as he towers over me. My back presses against the wall, trying to put some space between us but he moves in closer.

"Don't give me that bullshit," I retort, "We both know that you messed up our routine on purpose."

"Ah, Amelia. That's not what happened, and you know it. I told you I didn't want you anymore and you couldn't take it. It's not my problem you let your feelings get in the away of the performance."

I curl my hands into fists and take a deep breath before shoving him in his chest, but he doesn't move by much. "Go fuck yourself, Augustus."

"Oh, you'd love that wouldn't you," he snarls, leaning further into me as his expensive cologne invades my senses. "I know you like to watch when I get myself off."

I take in another deep breath, and I meet his icy blue eyes and whisper between pushes at his chest, "Fuck. You."

252

I didn't even realise there was someone else in the corridor until I see Miles' tall body next to me, almost towering over Augustus. He's dressed in dark jeans and a white top, but I can only see the large expanse of his back.

"Wanna say that louder, baby? I don't think he heard you," Miles says, turning back to me before blocking Augustus from my view as he pushes him, and he stumbles back.

Is it just me or has the temperature climbed up in this corridor? Augustus laughs incredulously, looking at me from the side of Miles as he points at him. "*This* is your boyfriend?"

I nod.

Fake boyfriend.

Fake.

Fake.

Fake.

Augustus gives him Miles a once-over, snickering like a middle schooler. There must be something that I'm missing because my fake boyfriend is gorgeous in comparison to Augustus. No matter how irritating he is.

"Got a problem with that, *Gus*?" Miles asks and I can literally see the blood drain from Augustus' face. If they were to fight right now, my money would be on Miles. Augustus is tall but he couldn't hold a candle to the burliness of Miles.

"Not at all," he bites out, shaking his head before sauntering off down the corridor. I let out a real breath of relief this time and Miles turns around to me.

I immediately burst out laughing. *This* is why Augustus couldn't take him seriously. Hell, even I can't. Even though this guy oozes sex he also has poor fashion choices. His T-shirt has 'I heart my girlfriend' written across it in bold letters and a red heart. I shake my head at him.

"Come here," he sighs over my hysterical laughter. I do just that. I walk into his open arms and wrap myself around his middle, falling into his lavender smell. His arms feel like coming home after being away for weeks. I can't believe I tried to push this away after what he did for me a few weeks ago. He rubs his hand down my spine reassuringly. "You okay?"

"I'm perfect," I muffle into his shirt. I give him one last squeeze before pulling apart from him as he catches both of my hands, beaming at me. "I'm sorry you had to see that."

"I'm glad I was here. Someone needed to put him in his place," Miles growls. He shifts his weight to his left foot, letting go of my hands and shoving them in my pockets. "The shows starting soon. So, I'll let you get ready."

I nod. "Thank you, Miles. I appreciate it." He smiles at me before nodding to the locker rooms, urging me to go.

I turn around and go into the locker room. *I appreciate you,* I want to say but the words get stuck in my throat. I keep my composure when I get out my black and emerald outfit for tonight. I stay calm when I take off my leggings and sweatshirt. I'm fine when I step into the shower but as soon as the heat hits me, I break down.

I allow myself to cry. I give myself fifteen minutes before I have to suck it up and move on.

I cry out of the pressure, the constant torment of trying to always do my best.

I cry for Austin, knowing that I have to do well in order to tell my mom after the show.

I cry over Augustus' stupid comment and Miles' sweet words. Over his hugs and how I could have had more of them this week. How badly I wished I hadn't shut him out.

I get out of the shower and put on my costume. I look into the mirror as I apply subtle makeup to my inflamed face. I braid my hair into a bun and secure it with some bobby pins before I head out of the door.

When I get back into the small arena, people are already starting to fill the area. A lot more people than I thought would turn up. I search the slow emerging crowd, but I only spot Sophia with a few other girls sat around her. I can't see where Miles has gone to, and I can't see my girls either. Before I can worry about that, my mom starts strutting towards me in her dark blue pantsuit: a black handbag in one hand and her phone in the other.

"Oh, Amelia. I'm glad I could catch you before the show," she says frantically as she places her hands on my face, inspecting it. She tilts my face up to the side as she stares into the space between my eyes and underneath them.

"Hello to you too, mother," I muffle, as her hands squeeze my cheeks before she drops them. "Coming to wish me luck?"

"Yes, and I must speak with you afterwards." My stomach drops. Maybe she already knows. Maybe Austin sucked it up and told her herself, saving me the torture of doing it.

"I need to talk to you too, actually," I say.

She pulls out her phone and scrolls through it, ignoring me as she mumbles to herself. She always gets like this before performances. More jittery and antsy than I am. I call her name to snap her back into reality but she's still scrolling.

"Ah, it's better that we talk afterwards," she says dismissively when she finally looks up at me, her pupils huge. "Remember to stay focused. Stay sharp."

I nod and she rushes off to her seat. I look up into the stands and now even more people are here. It's still not as full as it would be at the hockey games but it's something. It's better. I search the crowds and I see them. Miles is stood up, no doubt, searching for me too still wearing that stupid shirt.

When his eyes connect with mine, he smiles wide. I lift up my hand sheepishly and wave, he waves back before tapping on Kennedy and Scarlett's shoulders and pointing to me. They both get up and wave their hands as if they're trying to flag down a taxi. I laugh to myself before the lights start to dim and Eva Devinsky starts her routine.

She's gorgeous as I watch from the railing, basically drooling. She glides and spins to *'I'd like you for Christmas,'* by Julie London, not missing a step or a beat. It's hypnotising watching her gracefully work around the ice. I could watch her for hours if I could. She finishes with a flourish and the crowd cheers, and I whoop. I move towards the entrance, knowing that I'm next. This is it.

They announce my name on the intercom as I glide onto the ice, getting ready in my starting position as *Video Games* by Lana Del Rey begins.

CHAPTER 26
MILES

I meant it when I said that she was mesmerising. Watching her here, in her full outfit, the music reaching the speakers and the rink almost full of people. She performs her routine flawlessly, not a single misstep. Her face is concentrated but effortlessly beautiful. She glides across the ice gracefully, each spin and turn landing smoothly.

I can't tear my eyes away even if I wanted to. There is something so elegant and satisfying about watching her skate. I watch as she gets lost between the lyrics and the movements. I look around to see everyone else with the same expression: pure hypnosis. Even though playing hockey is similar with the adrenaline and the thrill but this feels so different. When we're on the ice we're fighting, roughing each other up as we try to score a goal. But this?

This is completely magical. Utterly consuming. I could watch her like this for hours and I would never get bored. If she didn't hate it when I watch her practice, I could spend the rest of my life just sitting in this seat while she moves around the ice.

She looks so peaceful while she dances, her body moving seamlessly with the music. I can tell there are so many intricate patterns and details that she puts into this routine. Like the way she rolls her head back slightly, the way her arms right down to her fingers flow. Even when her eyes close for a few seconds, there are no faults.

She looks up at me for a split second and I smile at her, but her smile wanders somewhere else in the crowd, and it drops. Her face turns sour as she turns back around, skating in the other direction. My heartbeat quickens and my stomach twists. I try to find who she is looking at, but I can't see anyone else other than Kennedy and Scarlett who are watching her beside me with adoration.

Her routine comes to an end, and we stand up to clap and whoop. Wren gives a shy smile in her finishing position before skating off the ice. I walk down to her as she's getting off the ice, not able to wait any longer. Even when I get down to her, people are still cheering.

"You did amazing. Like, so fucking good, Wren," I say when she steps off. I slip my hand around her waist and kiss her on the cheek. She doesn't throw me a confused look like she usually does, instead she slips out of my grasp and pushes away from me which is worse.

"Thank you," she replies bluntly as she catches her breath. "I didn't land my Lutz as good as I did in practice but it's fine. I think. Did you meet my mom up there?"

Her words come out in a weird breathy clump. "What? Uh, no. I didn't know she was here." I look around the stands as people watch the duet on the ice.

She makes a *humph* sound as she sits down at the bench outside the rink. She sits there for a long moment, not saying anything until all the performances are over and everyone surges out of the stadium. Even when Kennedy and Scarlett come over to say well done, she gives them a smile before dropping it and turning to face the empty rink. They don't make a fuss and they walk away. I don't know what to do. She's not said a word since they left and she just stares out into the empty space, her eyes fixed on something unknown.

"What's wrong? Is there anything I can do?" I ask when more silence fills the stadium. I put my hand on her back reassuringly. Her mouth opens and then she shuts it. She shakes her head as if to get rid of whatever she was about to say. Heels click behind us, and we both turn around.

"Mother," Wren says curtly as she stands up. She turns and walks towards her mom who is rather dressed up for the occasion "Glad you could join us."

I stand up, brushing myself off as I walk toward her, standing next to Wren. I didn't know I would be meeting the dean as the guy who's dating her daughter. If I did, I would have worn something that isn't jeans and a shirt saying how much I love her daughter.

"Yes, well, I had to take a phone call," Ms Hackerly says with a waft of her hand.

"Yeah, I noticed. It was hard to miss since it was right in the middle of my performance," Wren mutters. It takes me a second to put the pieces together.

That's why she's been so distant.

Why she stopped smiling at me.

"Speak up, darling," she drawls but Wren stays silent, practically shrinking away in her presence. I shift next to her, not knowing what to do with myself. "Is *this* your boyfriend everyone has been telling me about?"

What is it and everyone asking that question like *that* today? Like I'm a disappointment. As if I'm not good enough for her. First Augustus, now her mom.

Wren nods as I swallow the distaste in Ms Hackerly's tone. Her dad might like me but her mom doesn't. I don't think she likes anyone. "Hi, I'm Miles Davis. We had a meeting a few weeks ago. I play hockey here. Sort of," I ramble as I extend my hand. She gives it a weird look before shaking it.

"Yes, I know who you are," she says. *Okay.* She turns to Wren. "Listen, your performance was good. I know I was distracted but it doesn't take a genius to point out your Lutz needs more work."

"Of course, you found space in your busy schedule to critique me. You're unbelievable," Wren scoffs. She hooks her arm into mine. "We're going."

She tugs at my arm, looking up at me with teary eyes before walking in the other direction. I don't say anything because what am I supposed to say? I knew they had a shifty relationship, but I don't think it's my place to step in. She doesn't need me to save her. All I can do just follow after her like the lost puppy I am.

"You said you needed to speak to me about something, Amelia," her mom shouts after us. Wren stops walking and turns around, her cheeks red as if she's been caught. What the hell is going on?

"It's nothing. It's fine. I'll call you," she stutters.

"Okay, fine. If you want to be like that. I was going to go away to Palm Springs after Christmas and into the new year with Mike," her mom begins but Wren interrupts her.

"Great. Have fun."

"*But* he has an important surgery coming up and he doesn't want to disrupt his schedule. That's why he called me. We were going to reschedule but he suggested that we let the two of you go. If you'd like," Ms Hackerly explains, not seeming happy about the idea at all.

"I need to practice," Wren says, her voice somewhere between surprise and anger. I look down at her and her face is hard. Unmovable. I put hand around her waist and pull her into me. "I think we should go. You need to take a break," I whisper into her ear. She tenses at the way my breath tickles her skin as she inhales a shaky breath. "You deserve it, Wren."

"Okay. Okay, fine," she murmurs before turning to her mom, her voice stronger. "Thank you. We'd like that."

*

"**S**o, what are your Christmas plans?" I ask Wren as we eat in her living room, sat on the floor around her coffee table. We ordered Thai food. Well, *I* ordered Thai food, and she took a salad out of her refrigerator.

"Uh, nothing. My mom said that our flight to Palm Springs is on the 26th so I guess I'll spend Christmas Day here with Kennedy and Scarlett. My family aren't very Christmassy people," she mumbles between chews.

"Oh yeah? How come?"

"Since the divorce, it's just felt kind of unnecessary. Especially after my mom remarried because her step kids are, like, ancient, so we've not bothered with it much."

"Do *you* like Christmas though?" I ask, nudging her under the table with my foot. A smile creeps up her face. She's more chilled out than before. I think the whole pressure of the performance got to her but since she's eaten, she's lightened up. Food always solves Wren-related problems.

"I kind of have to when we're covered in snow every year," she mutters, not fully meeting my eyes. "I guess I do like it. I like the seeing my friends and family part the most but the whole gift giving thing was always an afterthought."

"My parents are having Christmas Eve dinner at home this year. They invited us but I wasn't going to go because my mom and I are in a weird place. But if you want to, we can go," I ramble, unable to stop the momentum.

I wasn't going to mention that I was invited because as soon as I got the message from Clara, I was going to decline it but hearing this, I had to ask.

"Of course, I'll go. How could I miss the opportunity to see baby pictures of you," she beams.

"Are you sure? My family is a little…unhinged." I cringe at myself.

"They can't be anymore unhinged than mine."

"Let's test that theory, shall we?"

Wren gives me a wide smile before shoving more salad into her mouth. She chews thoughtfully, looking down at her food and then at me.

"You never talk about your parents. Is there anything I should know before we go?" she asks cautiously. I let my heartbeat pick up before forcing it to settle and get it out.

"My mom had an affair a few years ago and I only just found out," I say quickly, trying to get it all out there at once. "That's why we're in a weird situation."

"Oh, that sucks. I'm sorry," Wren replies, sympathetically. "But your parents are still together, right?"

"Yeah, that's the weird part. My dad somehow found it within himself to forgive her. When I thought they were going on date nights it turns out they were going to couples therapy," I laugh but it sounds forced.

"And you haven't forgiven her?" It sounds more like statement than a question, as if she can already tell. Like she's able to see right through me.

"I'm trying to. I'm just scared that if I see her, I won't know how to act," I admit. "We haven't really spoken since I found out and I don't know what I'm going to say."

"That's something that will come to you when we go. I'm going to be there. If you want to leave at any time, I can pretend I have diarrhoea or something," she suggests, laughing. I laugh with her but shake my head.

"I couldn't let you do that. I don't think Clara would ever let us live it down," I say, and her eyes widen. She scrambles from her side of the table and kneels in front of me, her hands on my shoulders, shaking them slightly.

"Shit, Miles. I forgot you have a sister. She's going to hate me," she concedes frantically. I chuckle and put my arms on her shoulders, like she's doing to me.

"She's going to love you, Wren. You've got nothing to worry about."

"Yeah, but she's a *girl*. She'll know. She'll find something she doesn't like. I know she will."

"There is nothing about you that she wouldn't like. You're perfect."

It's like time stopped when I said that. It's like everything else around us seized to exist and we're left floating outside of this moment. Oblivion. I knew I was cutting it close by saying

263

'love' and 'perfect' in one go. I watch her, almost in slow-motion as she takes in a sharp inhale.

We stare at each other for a long minute, the weight of the day crashing down on us as my words hang in the space between us. All the hurt and anger that was there when she was talking to her mom earlier has vanished. Instead, she looks at me with a smoothed out and relaxed expression. Her eyes drop to my lips, and I wet them on purpose. She hums. The noise ripples through me.

We haven't been this close since the night after the game. I don't move as she brings her hand from my shoulder to my cheek. Her thumb brushes just beneath my eye as her slender fingers reach the back of my ear.

"Miles," she whispers my name like it's something sacred. The word comes out of her mouth like a sigh, as if she's tired, frustrated and fed-up all in one.

I mirror her position, my hands curling around her neck as she inhales again We look at each other, dangerously, ready to risk everything. Then, with the shreds of the self-control I have left, I drop my forehead to hers.

"I should go," I whisper into the space between us.

She lets out a sigh before nodding. I stand up and grab my jacket and I look back at her when I almost reach the door.

"Thank you," she murmurs.

"What?" I ask. She's still in the position that I left her in, kneeling down, staring out of the apartment window.

"I said, thank you. For everything."

My chest tightens at her words. "Anytime."

It takes all that I am not to grab her into my arms and kiss her deeply. To really have her. For real. For once.

Instead, I unlock the door and slip out of it.

CHAPTER 27
WREN

I'm never failed to be amazed by the Christmas decorations in Salt Lake. Although, each year, I feel like they get more and more extravagant. The girls and I like to keep our decorations simple with a small silver tree and decorations to match while the other apartments in our complex do the same. The second we venture out of our part of town; the houses get more glamorous. This year I've seen one house transformed into a giant present and one house with Christmas trees almost bigger than the one in Rockefeller.

When I walk up to Miles' truck, he's blasting Mariah Carey's Christmas songs. I laugh as I open the door and slide in, watching him with adoration. I know I almost slipped up the other night after my performance, when I held his face. Physical touch has always been my love language and it felt like the best way to show my gratitude.

I couldn't bring myself to say it then, but I am so grateful for him. He sat with me for what felt like hours after the show when I waited for my mom to show up.

He still brought me home and ate dinner with me after he saw how bratty I was acting with her. I'm not proud of it but I was really pissed about her missing the end of my performance. She tends to have that nasty effect on me. I am glad that she's letting us go to Palm Springs though, I was lucky that I didn't tell her about Austin.

I do need the break. I know she wanted me to do it after the performance but after everything, I didn't have the energy to. She's going to have to wait.

"Merry Christmas, my love," he drawls as if he has only just noticed I got in the car. I turn down the music and frown at him.

"Hey, what happened to Wrenny Rainbow? It was starting to grow on me," I groan. He laughs as looks at me and then back at the road. Then he gives me another glance.

"You look hot," he says without missing a beat. I give him an unimpressed look.

"Do you have to say that every time?"

"Yes. You need to get used to it," he replies with a smug grin. I ignore him.

"You could have told me to dress down," I say gesturing to his jeans and thick jumper. I put on a short red skater dress and black boots, with a long black puffer coat to keep warm, assuming this would be more of a formal thing.

"What part of 'you look hot' don't you get? If you look better than me, they'll know that you care, and they'll focus on *you* instead of me."

"I don't want them to focus on me," I moan, sulking back in my seat.

"You could be wearing a garbage bag and you'd still be the most gorgeous woman in the room, Wren." He looks at me

266

intensely when he says it, his eyes taking another sweep of my outfit. I'm telling you; this man has no filter. I hold up the bag that I brought in my hand. "I got your mom a necklace and I couldn't find anything for Clara or your dad but I'm sure-"

"It's fine," Miles cuts me off. "Thank you. You really didn't have to do any of that but I'm sure my mom will appreciate it."

"Are you sure?" I ask, turning to him while he drives. "I didn't even ask if she prefers gold or silver. What if-"

He stops the car abruptly and he's lucky we're in the middle of an empty estate. He turns to me with a serious expression.

"Amelia Wren Hackerly. Stop worrying for five minutes and just live in the moment. Can you do that for me?"

I stick my tongue in my cheek at his sudden seriousness. "I can try."

"Good," he replies sternly.

"Fine," I say back.

"Great."

"Perfect."

He holds my stare for a few beats before he smiles, smoothing out the tension and turns back to driving. I pick up Miles' phone from the holder and look through his playlists, trying to put some decent music on. I find one called 'Songs for Wrenny,' and I laugh.

"What's this?" I ask, looking through it.

"Can't really see when I'm driving, baby," he says through a smile.

"Hey, rule number three still stands. Cut out the 'baby' stuff," I warn and he nods. "There's a playlist called 'Songs for Wrenny.'"

He laughs a little, glancing to me and then back to the road. "You weren't supposed to see that yet."

"I mean, it says the songs are *for* me. Why can't I look at it?"

"It's not meant *for* you. More like, songs that you like and songs that remind me *of* you," he says and my cheeks inflame with happiness.

"No one has ever made me a playlist before," I say.

He snorts. "What did I just say? I didn't make it *for* you. It's more of a present for myself."

"Whatever makes you sleep at night, Davis," I say, laughing as I scroll through it. "Can you tell me which one is your favourite that reminds you how amazing I am?"

"The Taylor Swift one. *Christmas Tree Farm*," he says immediately.

"That was quick."

He shrugs. "I add to it a lot," he replies. "Put it on. I wanna hear you sing it."

"I can't sing, Miles," I say, shaking my head. He snatches the phone from me and puts the song on with one hand.

"And neither can I."

When the first verse plays, he doesn't shock me when he starts to sing terribly. He nudges me when the chorus starts and I can't help but joining in on one of my favourite Christmas songs. We're both singing together awfully, laughing between lines as we drive to Miles' hometown. He makes me feel ridiculous in the best way and I love this side of myself.

I see Miles grow more skittish as we get closer to his house when he stops singing. Even when we're pulled up outside, he doesn't try to get out the car. Instead, he taps his hands on the steering wheel, staring at the other houses on the block. I put my hand on his.

"If you don't want to go, we can drive away and never look back," I suggest with a smile. He shakes his head with a weak laugh. "How about this? If you feel irritated, angry, or upset just squeeze my hand and I'll squeeze back. That way you'll know that I'm here. I'm going to be here, Miles."

He nods and squeezes my hand. I squeeze back. We keep our hands together as we walk up the gravel of his childhood home. It's a small bungalow in a quiet suburb in Fruit Heights. It's the kind of house you drive by, knowing a happy family lives here. The house is a gorgeous dark brown colour, and the lawn is covered in light snow. It feels cosy. Safe.

He knocks on the door twice before it opens. Miles' dad is a tall, light skinned man with kind features. He looks a lot less intimidating than the pictures he showed me on the way over. He's at least five heads taller than Miles' mom, a breath-taking woman with dark brown locks flowing long past her shoulders.

"Merry Christmas, you two," Miles' dad says as if we met before, with a huge smile on his face. He pats Miles on the shoulder and nods at me with a smile. "I'm Ben."

"It's so nice to meet you, Wren," his mom exclaims, smiling at me. Miles' hand tightens around me, and I squeeze back. "Thank you for inviting me, Mr and Mrs Davis."

"Oh, just call us Portia and Ben. We don't mind. There's no need for the formalities." She turns to Miles who has been avoiding eye contact with her. "Miles, love. It's good to see you."

He grunts something in response not saying anything other than, "Wren got you a present."

I shoot him a look, knowing that he's trying to avoid talking to his mom while throwing me under the bus. I clear my throat as his mom smiles at me. "It's only something small," I say, handing her the gift bag.

She beams at me, her mouth forming the same dimples as Miles. "Oh, that's so thoughtful. Thank you, Wren."

Im about to respond but before I do, a tall, curly haired woman - I'm assuming is Clara - comes around the corner in a pink tracksuit. Maybe I am too dressed up. Her face lights up when she sees us. She pushes past her parents and pulls Miles into a hug.

"I didn't think you'd show up," she says through a grin when she pulls apart from him. He shrugs and looks over at me, his faces a deep red. "Wren! I've heard a lot about you. I didn't know you'd be as pretty as he said."

I blush and I'm about to speak before Miles's mom interjects, saving me for what would have been an awkward thank you.

"Why don't you take off your outdoor clothes and come into the kitchen with us girls?"

Everyone else slips away into whatever corners of the house they need to be in. I start to unzip my coat, but Miles stops me, zipping it down for me. I watch him work slowly at the zip at my front, his eyes focused on me. It's the kind of intimacy we haven't acknowledged since the kiss. He comes behind me and pulls on the sleeves.

"You don't have to do that," I say, almost laughing at this gesture.

"I want to."

He hangs up my coat with the others and I get a peak of some of the baby pictures hung on the wall. I start to walk in the direction as Clara and Portia before Miles' hand grabs mine. I turn to him.

"Are you going to be okay?" I ask. He nods and shrugs at the same time.

"Are *you* going to be okay in there?" He motions to the direction of the kitchen, and I smile. "Call me if you need saving."

I start to turn in the direction of the kitchen, but he holds onto my hand until the last second, until my arm is almost ripped out of my socket. This whole time, I've been worrying about what's going to happen with Miles instead of worrying about what's going to happen if I'm left alone with his family. He gave me a small run down on the way over, but this is only the second time I've met any of my boyfriend's parents.

The kitchen is small and intimate with cream stone features. Clara is sat on the counter, her legs swinging and her tall stature overcrowding the kitchen, while her mom chops vegetables on the other counter. Her head shoots us when she sees me.

"You and Miles seem very happy together," she says, and it catches me off guard. "I can tell by that way he looks at you." I laugh nervously, not knowing how to go about this. "He's a bit much sometimes but I'm glad you're able to handle him," Clara jokes as she jumps off the counter.

"If I'm honest, he wasn't my cup of tea at first and I definitely made him work for it, but he's grown on me," I admit.

"Atta girl. It's all about the chase," Clara laughs. "Sometimes he needs to be dealt with that way, though. He thinks he can get what he wants without working for it."

"Ay. Miles *is* a hard worker in some respects but sometimes his heart is a little misplaced," his mom mentions.

"What do you mean by that?" I ask, suddenly wanting to know more.

Miles' mom sighs, pausing her vegetable cutting, looking of into the distance. "He loves a lot, and he loves hard. He always

271

has and he always will. Sometimes, he can't let go of things and he latches on. It consumes him." She sighs. "I'm sure that is partly my fault."

"Mom," Clara presses, rolling her eyes as if they've had this conversation before. I stay quiet, letting the new information about Miles settle in.

"Enough talk about him," Portia says, wafting her knife around. "You girls are going to have to help me dish out this food."

*

Eating Christmas Eve dinner with Miles' family was a lot less awkward than I thought it would be. Although Miles doesn't talk to his mom much, everyone else seems to be getting along great. Clara basically carries the table with her work horror stories.

She works on low budget film projects with her friends and enters them into festivals. You wouldn't believe how many of her stories end with getting booked for a job, but it turns out to be some weirdos wanting to film a porno. Even with the inappropriate jokes she makes, neither one of her parents seem to bat an eye at the candour. If something like this was said around my mom, she would have slapped me silly.

"Oh my God, Miles, have you told Wren about Felicity?" Clara exclaims loudly when we're eating dessert. Their parents have gone into the kitchen, leaving us to talk in the dining room.

"Oh, Clar, don't," Miles replies, shaking his head with a blush. I've never seen his face go so red before and it's making my stomach crowd with butterflies.

"I have not heard about this. Who is Felicity?" I say, leaning on my hands at Clara. She takes a long swig of her wine before starting.

"She was Miles's first crush. He was probably around five or six and there was this girl in his kindergarten class who he thought was cute. So, he came to me, asking for my help. And as the hopeless romantic tween I was, I suggested that he write a song for her. I think Miles should tell the rest of the story." She gestures to him. He's still shaking his head but now he's laughing.

"Long story short, I sung her the song at recess, and she started crying. *Not* out of happiness," he admits, shoving his face into his hand.

"I must hear this song immediately," I demand. I look over to Clara who is smiling wide, but Miles' expression is serious. I nudge him with my knee and his face cracks.

"Felicity, will you be with me? Felicity, do you like cream cheese? Felicity, your eyes are so pretty," he opera sings at the top of his lungs.

I start hysterically laughing, tears springing to my eyes. I've always known he was a bad singer but Jesus. That poor girl who had to hear this at recess. I would have cried too. He takes a deep breath as if he's about to continue.

"No, please stop," I scream, and I cover his mouth with my hand. A devilish smile spreads across his face as he nips my hand with his teeth. I pull my hand away, shaking it out as I glare at him.

"I think he's learnt a few moves since then if he's managed to get *you* to date him," Clara comments, tipping her glass towards me. I look up at him and he's already looking at me. I hide the smile on my face my snuggling deeper into his side,

273

letting myself pretend that this is real for two seconds. Which is easy because Miles is great to be around. He doesn't expect anything of me. We just exist. "Do you want to know what he said when he first told me about you?"

"I'm genuinely frightened to find out," I say.

I feel his warm hand slowly move from his thigh to mine, just beneath my dress. He squeezes it gently before leaving his hand there. I cross my legs, trapping his hand between my thighs on purpose and I hear him suck in a breath. I can feel the heat on my face, so I try not look at him.

"He mentioned you for the first time and I was asked who you were. Then he said, 'she's my girlfriend but she's everything.'"

I can feel my heart racing as soon as the words leave her mouth. *Everything*. Why does everything he pretends to say make my heart swell? I can feel the tears prickling at my eyes, but I blink them back and turn to him.

"He said that?" I ask Clara while still looking at him.

I can't tear my eyes away from him. He looks at me passionately, as if we're suddenly existing outside of time. As if there is no one else in this room but us.

"I did," he murmurs.

*

When Miles takes me home, we wait in the car when we're parked outside my apartment. I don't feel like going in just yet and I don't know why. I know my girls are going to be waiting for me, ready to pester me with questions the second I get in there.

Instead, I turn to Miles.

He's taken off his jumper and he's in a short-sleeved black top, his curly hair falling wildly on his forehead as he taps rhythmically onto the steering wheel, letting us sit in comfortable silence.

"You're getting too good at this," I say, the words falling out of my mouth almost accidently.

"At what?" he asks, slowly turning to me.

"The whole boyfriend thing," I say, "Why is it that you weren't dating anyone? Isn't it supposed to be in your culture?"

He laughs, running a hand through his hair before pinning me with a look. "I've had one serious relationship: Emily. But you know about her. We just didn't work out. We had different goals and we weren't committed to make time for each other."

I nod, chewing on my bottom lip. "But it's different with me?"

"Yes, Wren. It's different with you."

My heart trips over itself. "Because we're fake dating?"

He shrugs. "Sure."

"Do you think-" I begin but he cuts me off.

"I had a good time today," he begins and I smile. "I know my family are a bit much to deal with, but you made it bearable. Better."

I don't follow up what I was going to say. Because what *was* I going to say? I've had a good day with a nice boy who turns out to be more than what he lets on. That's the only reason why I feel like I want to stay in the car and sing christmas songs with him forever.

"I had a good time too," I say, breaking eye contact with him as I glance up a the apartment blocks. "I'll see you tomorrow, then."

"Tomorrow, and the day after that, and the day after that and the-"

"Don't make me regret taking this vacation, Milesy," I reply, cutting of his rambling.

"I would never compromise having so much alone time with you," he replies with that smug smile of his and I slip out of the car.

CHAPTER 28
WREN

Deciding to host Friendsmas is probably the best decision I've made all year. Even when we all lived at home, we always spent Christmas day together. After spending the morning with our family opening presents, we'd go all go over to Gigi's house and eat as much shit we could.

The holidays have been hard for Ken because her mom and sister still live in South Carolina while we're here in Utah. It's too expensive for her to fly out and too far for her to drive, so last Christmas it was just us three. I always call my parents on Christmas Day but to them, it's seen as a day off work for my mom more than anything special. I had a long call with my dad, wishing me and my girls a merry christmas, as well as sending me a new pair of skates. My mom's 'merry christmas' came in the form of a four foot bouquet with a generic and impersonal card.

I asked Gigi to come over too but as soon as she heard that Miles and his friends would be here, she declined.

We decided to do Secret Santa which wasn't very secret since there's only three of us. It didn't take long for us to guess who had who, but we still act like we don't know. We sit down on the living room floor, all in our Christmas pyjamas which we intend on wearing all day, each with a present in front of us.

"Okay, I wonder who had me," Kennedy starts with an eye roll, shaking the box in front of her. I look over at Scarlett who's beaming. She opens the box and pulls out two hardback books. "Oh my God! Shut the fuck up. Who had me?"

"Doesn't that take away the whole purpose of secret Santa?" I ask.

"Okay, so it wasn't you…" Kennedy says, giving me an evil side eye before turning to Scarlett. "How did you get these?" She holds up two special editions, signed copies of her favourite author Jasmine James' new novel which she has been obsessed with all year. They've been sold out everywhere but somehow, she managed to snag two.

"I have my sources," Scarlett shrugs as Kennedy drools over them. "Now me."

She picks up her present which is in a small envelope. From me.

I try and hide my smile when she opens it. The anticipation surges through me as she takes out the small handwritten note.

"To Scarlett," she reads aloud. "Here's a present that you can use for the next year, and you don't have to lie about sleeping with the hotel owner.' Wren! You sneaky motherfucker. How did you do this?"

"I have *my* sources. Plus, if you keep pretending to get access to the hotel without a real ID, you're going to get thrown in jail. Now, you can stop lying about it. You can use it for a whole year too," I explain. She jumps into my arms, and I almost topple over as she suffocates me. "Okay, my turn."

I get back up into a sitting position and pick up the gift bag in front of me. I know it's Kennedy who got me this from the process of elimination and the terrible wrapping. I take out the hundreds of tissue papers before digging my hand into the bag and I pull out...

"Batteries?" I ask Ken. She nods her head and gestures towards the bag for me to keep looking through it. Then my hand finally hits a big box. I pull it out and start laughing.

"What is it?" Scarlett asks from across me, her knee bouncing like a child. I turn the box around so she can see the front of it. Scarlett also bursts into hysterical laughter. "This is the most Wren thing I've ever seen. Now I wish that Ken had me."

"I had to do a lot of research for this. And the week when the Wi-Fi was down, I had to go to the library, to search up where I could get a good one. You wouldn't believe how many times my account got blocked for searching 'Where can I buy the best vibrator,'" Kennedy explains.

"Thanks, Ken. You always get the best presents," I say when my laughter dies down.

"Well, I thought if you're not going to sleep with Miles, you might as well get some action elsewhere." She shrugs.

I don't have the energy to make any snide comments because as much as I'd like to joke about it, Miles and I have not slept together. There have been opportunities — many opportunities — but one of us always shut it down. The second we sleep with each other; this whole thing will be over. The fake part and the friendship part.

It's not long before Miles and his friends arrive. His friend, Xavier, a kind black man, comes in with a bottle of champagne.

Evan, rich boy of the century and Scarlett's nemesis, arrives in jeans and a button down.

And Miles looks so fucking sexy.

It's unfair that he can look so good all the time. It doesn't help that he has a sweet gooey heart and a wicked smile. That combination is deadly.

Knowing someone on the inside as well as the outside is a different kind of attraction.

When he walks in, he immediately snakes his hands around my waist and presses a kiss into my neck even though the only person who doesn't know it's fake is Evan. It wouldn't take a genius to know that there are some moments that aren't fake. The things we do for the sake of it — to give in to the pleasure for a second.

"I got something for you," he whispers into my skin and everyone around us groans. My chest pinches as I look up at him but he doesn't say anything as he drags me by the arm into the corridor to my bedroom.

When we get inside, his woody cologne clouds my senses as he towers over me, my back pressed against my closed door.

I finally speak. "What are you doing?"

He smirks. "Close your eyes," he demands.

I raise one eyebrow. "Why...?"

He takes a step back, hiding the small bag that I only just noticed, behind his back. "Do you trust me, Wren?" I nod, because I really, *really*, do trust him. Probably more than I should. And I'm excited to find out what he got me. "Then, close your eyes."

I do as he says, all my other senses heightening as I feel him move closer to me. The fresh lavander smell of his soap crowds my mind and my nose as I feel his hand come to the top of my chest where my collar is opened slightly.

My breathing picks up as the tip of his fingers skim the expanse of skin on my chest. "Miles," I breathe. "What kind present do you have that requires you touch me?"

"Baby, I could think up any excuse to touch you, but this isn't one of those," he whispers, his voice hoarse as his mouth feels so close to my own. I'm betting that if I moved my head a slight inch, our noses would touch.

I feel him starting to button down my Christmas shirt, very slowly. The same torturous way he did at the gala. When I feel the cold air of my room hit my stomach, I know the shirt is unbuttoned. I don't have to open my eyes to see how hard my nipples are. I'm around him all the time in my sports bra but this feels different. It shouldn't be this intimate. Whatever it is he's doing.

I don't know which one of us it is that gasps when his hand barely touches the skin below my belly button.

"Shit, Wren. I didn't think this through," he murmurs.

"Think what through?" I ask. He only responds by catching my wrist in his hands and he pulls at the sleeves of my shirt and it drops it to the floor. I hear the rustling of tissue paper and then I feel a soft fabric stretch around my head and he pull my arms through it gently, tugging it down on my stomach. "Can I open my eyes now?"

"Yeah."

I do. He's grinning at me with that smug face of his, probably loving the way I get flustered so easily. I look down to the shirt he pulled over my head. It's a white shirt, the same one that Miles wore at my showcase with a bright red heart. Instead, it says, 'I heart my boyfriend.' He dusts off my shoulders, holding onto them as he looks down at me. "Now we can be matching." I can't control the laugh that escapes me as I look up at him. "It's perfect. Thank you," I say and I can tell how hard I'm blushing. I shift from one foot to the other, feeling uneasy under his gaze. "I didn't get you anything, Milesy."

He leans down and presses a kiss to my cheek as if it's so normal. It should be normal by now but it doesn't feel like it yet. "You don't need to. I'm spending the next week with you. I think I'll survive."

*

Nobody says anything about the shirt when I go back into the living room, apparently used to Miles' antics. After we finish cooking dinner, we set it out on the kitchen island and do a mini buffet. Everybody lines up, taking a paper plate to save the washing up, and get the food they like. We probably made enough food to feed a whole football team, but I know the girls will live off of this for the next week while I'm in Palm Springs. I stand at the other side of the island, waiting for everyone to get their food first.

"Save some for the rest of us," Evan mutters to Scarlett who's taken one of the last pieces of bacon in the foil tray. She looks over at him, her face plastered into a fake smile.

"You're right, sorry," she says sarcastically before picking up her bacon and shoving it into his face. He doesn't fight back. He lets her shove more into his mouth until he can't take it anymore. "Do you want some syrup with that?"

He shakes his head, vigorously but he smiles behind his full mouth. He smiles? He's one weird guy. "Yeah, I thought so."

We all mostly eat in silence until we're all so stuffed, we spread out in the living room. Everything feels so natural here, like we were all made to be friends in some weird way. Evan and Xavier lay out on the couch while Kennedy sits in her beanbag with Scarlett's head in her lap. Miles sits on the other couch, and I sit next to him, my head on his shoulder.

I knew that moving into this apartment with my girls would make this place feel like a home but now, it feels even better. As if the word 'home' is screaming off the walls at full volume.

"So, what did you guys get for Christmas?" Xavier asks. Evan sits further up, with a smug grin on his face. "Not you, Branson. Nobody wants to hear about what car daddy bought you."

Evan slouches back down and I giggle, suddenly feeling the champagne hit me. I don't ever drink but today feels special and I feel safe enough around these guys. Especially after my first time getting drunk was an emotional mess, I'm trying to be more cautious.

"You guys did secret Santa, right?" Miles asks. I look up at him and nod as he's clearly oblivious to what I got.

"I got these books from Scarlett," Kennedy beams, holding up her new prized possession. I know she's not going to shut up about this until Jasmine's new book comes out.

"I got an all-exclusive access to my favourite hotel from Wren," Scarlett says proudly, flashing a toothy smile at me. "If you're lucky, Miles, maybe she'll sugar momma you too."

Everyone bursts out laughing at her remark and I stick my tongue out at her. I keep quiet, not knowing if saying what I got is the smartest idea.

"What about you, Wren?" Xavier asks when the laughter has died down.

"What about me?"

Evan's eyebrows raise. "What did you get?"

283

"Uh, nothing," I reply, cheerfully.

Xavier and Evan look at me confused. I swallow and look around the room, trying to find something that I can say to change the subject. It's too late to rush off and pretend the food's burning. Miles rubs my shoulder, turning his head down to look at me.

"You're telling me that none of your friends got you a present?" Miles asks, his eyes narrowing at me. I shake my head, biting my lip.

"I got her a vibrator. The *best* one in town," Kennedy shouts, and I shoot her an evil look along with Scarlett. "What? She was too scared to say it. A woman's pleasure should not be an embarrassing topic."

I feel Miles stiffen beneath me, his breathing becoming strangled.

"You two having trouble in the bedroom, Davis?" Evan asks, laughing.

Miles ignores him and the conversation around us moves on. It's better that he didn't say anything. It's better that *I* didn't say anything.

What would he say?

No, she fucks like a God or *Yeah, we've not gone anywhere past second base because she's too scared for this to get real.* I feel him bring his mouth closer to my ear, his breath tickling my neck.

"Are you trying to make me jealous or are you just trying to turn me on even more? Either way, it's working," he whispers, and my breath gets caught in my throat that I end up coughing like a maniac as he smirks at me. I don't need a mirror to be able to tell how red my face is right now.

Luckily, I'm saved by Evan of all people.

"Let's play truth or dare," he suggests. Scarlett scoffs and rolls her eyes.

"What? Are we in middle school?" she laughs.

"I never said it was going to be PG," Evan retorts. She raises her eyebrows at him, sitting up out of Kennedy's lap. "Truth or dare?"

"Truth," Scarlett responds, holding his stare. The energy between them is lethal.

"Where is the weirdest place you've had sex?"

Kennedy and I exchange knowing glances. Kennedy clears her throat, attempting to smother her laugh while Scarlett gives her a wicked grin before turning back to Evan.

"In public or in general? Or both?" Scarlett asks innocently.

"Let's go with both," Evan replies.

"Our business class. A few weeks ago."

Evan practically chokes on air, coughing horrifically while Kennedy and I finally burst out laughing. Miles lets out a 'Jesus Christ' under his breath while Xavier's mouth hangs open.

"I'm afraid to ask but where their people in there?" Xavier asks, grimacing.

"No. Well, I don't think so anyway. It was pretty dark," Scarlett answers with a shrug.

"With who?" Evan asks when he gets his voice back.

His face is unreadable. It's hard to tell whether he's angry, dissatisfied, turned on or all three. You could cut the tension between them with a knife.

"That's for me to know and you to never find out," Scarlett says, tapping her nose.

"Okay, moving on," Evan drags out, turning towards me and Miles. "Wren, truth or dare?"

"Dare."

"I dare you to kiss the hottest guy in the room," Evan says with a dark smile. I'm beginning to think he just enjoys stirring shit up. Before I can retort Kennedy butts in, again.

"God, if you want someone to kiss you so bad, just say it. You're starting to sound desperate," she groans.

"I'm not. I just want her to do when she's been dying to since *I* got in here," Evan drawls. I feel Miles shift beneath me, his grip on my shoulder tightening. Evan's a good-looking guy but there is no way I'm going to kiss him.

"Well, obviously, it's not you, Evan. And sorry, Xavier it's not you either *but* you were close second," I say, and he shrugs happily. I move out of Miles' grip, as I scramble on top of him, straddling him in my new favourite shirt and Christmas shorts.

"Uh, hi?"

"Hi," I whisper back, smiling at him, before my fingers snake into the back of his head, pushing it gently onto the headrest and my mouth covers his.

It's the kind of release I've needed since our last kiss. It's slow at first, patient, our mouths getting used to the sensation again. His hands instinctively come around my hips, pushing me further into him until my front is flush against his hard chest. I let myself drown in him, letting his lips fight over mine. Everything around us blurs when his tongue slips into my mouth, and I whimper as quietly as I can. I know exactly what I'll be thinking about tonight when I use my present.

I'm surprised I don't explode into oblivion when his hands slip under my shirt, wrapping around my back. I bite on his lip gently as I pull away from him, both of us panting.

I stay straddled on him, his hands still under my shirt when I turn back to the rest of them. The girls are trying not to laugh, and the guys do the same but with something else in their eyes.

"God, he said kiss not whatever that was," Xavier says, retching. This is why we work well together. Xavier is the voice of rationality.

"You get what you wanted, Evan?" Miles asks, his voice breathy from behind me. He bites my collarbone gently; his eyes connect with Evan across the room.

"You guys are so boring. You didn't have to choose him just because he's your boyfriend," Evan whines. I climb off Miles, but as I do, I can feel him between his jeans. I try to ignore the throbbing I feel between my legs as I sit beside him, nuzzling my face into his shoulder.

"Even if he wasn't, I still would have," I whisper.

*

T hey continue to play truth or dare while I slip away into the kitchen, cleaning up some of the plates and dishes that we ended up using. Today has been a good day. Our friendship groups are so different that they make so much sense. I'm glad that he has good friends.

Yes, Evan can be a bit much but for the most part he's tolerable. And Xavier is just the sweetest person to level out their energies. He was constantly trying to make sure everyone was okay all night, checking if the girls were drinking too much.

I'm putting dirty dishes into the sink when Miles comes through from the living room. He doesn't say anything, he just stands beside me, waiting for me to wash the plates then he dries them.

"Did you mean what you said earlier?" he asks in the midst of the comfortable silence.

287

"What?"

"Earlier. About you wanting to kiss me even if we weren't together. Or pretending to be together."

I can't think of a reason to deny it anymore. There's nothing that I could say or do that could combat this feeling I've had inside me since I met him at the party. Since he let me into his life and completely changed mine.

"Yeah, I did mean it," I admit. He groans and when I look up at him, he throws his head back dramatically. "What? Are you annoyed?"

"No," he says with a slight edge. "I don't know. I guess I'm a little frustrated because you know how badly I want you. How badly I've wanted you since the beginning. For real. But whenever I try to make a move, you run away. Like you did the morning after the game."

His voice is calm and levelled but his admission still shocks me. I try and ignore the way my stomach crowds with angry butterflies when the words leave his mouth. His eyes look hurt. "That's a different thing."

"Is it?" he asks, slight pain and irritation in his tone.

I open my mouth to speak but I'm interrupted by Xavier, Evan, and Scarlett walking into the kitchen. The boys look absolutely fucked. I don't know when everybody got so drunk, but I was focusing on keeping myself sober enough.

"If you're staying for a bit, Miles, I'm going to drive these two home," Scarlett groans, patting Xavier on the chest. He makes a strange noise from the back of his throat. "You guys gonna be okay?"

"Yeah," I reply. I look up to Miles but he's not looking at me. Panic settles in me.

"Actually, I'm going to go too," Miles says, walking away to get his jacket. Scarlett nods as she opens the door. I walk toward him, trying to reach for his hand but he pulls it away. "Miles," I breathe. He turns around to me, his expression hard. "You're still picking me up tomorrow, right?"

He comes closer towards me and kisses me on the top of my head. "Yeah. I'll be here."

CHAPTER 29
MILES

We only have a week. Seven days. Monday until
Sunday. That's all we get. This is all the time I get with her
until next year and things start to get more serious for the both
of us. That's why when we're on the plane and Wren falls
asleep, I make a plan of what to do to make this a really good
vacation. A much-deserved break for her. I book us in for
massages, hikes, saunas, and I look around for a nice restaurant
to go to.

I'm really cutting deep into my savings for this, but I need to do
something nice. A grand gesture of some sort. There's a bar
having a New Year's Eve party that we can go to too. Maybe
this is all too much. Maybe I'm in way over my head but I want
to do this for her.

On the drive to the airport, on the plane and even when we
drive from the airport to the hotel, she ignores what happened
last night. Her specialty. Although, a part of me is planning on
ignoring it too. I don't want to ruin these next few days because

after this, we could be done. If my first few games go well and she qualifies, we'll have no reason to be doing this anymore. It'll be over.

She'll go back to skating regularly and I'll go back to playing. I know how she was before her performances when she avoided me, so I know the same thing will happen again but even worse when competition season comes around. Even if that happens and we're over, the least I can have are some memories to come back to. Something to hold on to.

By the time we check into the five-star hotel, we're both exhausted. We throw our bags down and settle in. This room is a lot bigger than the one that we stayed in at the gala. Instead of a massive bedroom, the room is smaller sized, but it has two huge bathrooms as each side of it. The kitchen and living room are connected in another room, with the refrigerator filled with drinks and snacks that Ms Hackerly probably asked for before it was cancelled for her and Mike.

We spend the first few days in a haze, going through all the things that I booked for us to do. We go for massages, mostly for Wren. Hearing her moan with pleasure didn't help when I had mine right next to her.

We spend our days out in Palm Springs, visiting the most touristy places we can, and we spend our nights binging bad movies and eating room service, talking about everything and nothing.

I could get used it though.

Both of us sat in robes, eating ice cream, slouching on the couch, watching movies. Sometimes, she talks about whatever book she's reading and I'm only half listening. I just like watching the way her mouth moves. If she's picked up on it, she hasn't made it obvious.

This morning, we decided to go down to the beach to read. Although, I'm doing more staring than I am reading. I'm lying on my back, slightly angled towards Wren who's lying on her stomach, her head propped up on her bag while she reads. The sun has blessed her with small dark freckles along her back and arms and I'm fucking obsessed with every single one of them. She's wearing a lilac bikini with a white knitted cover up. She looks ethereal. Effortlessly so. I don't think I could tear my eyes away even if I wanted to. She looks heavenly. Peaceful. Being with her is like watching the ocean crash against the shore. It's like looking straight into the fucking sun.

Looking at her now, you wouldn't guess the number of snarky comments she said to me in the past four months.

"Can you stop ogling?" she asks without looking up from her book. I pick up mine and pretend to read it. I'm still figuring out how she does that. I can't, for the life of me, decide how she's always able to catch me watching without looking at me.

"I'm not ogling, I'm reading."

"Really?" She turns to me, squinting her eyes, her head resting on her hands. "What are you reading?"

"The McDavid Effect." She snorts, smothering her laugh in her arms. "What's so funny?"

"It's not funny. It's... typical, that's all."

"What's typical about a hockey player reading about hockey?"

"Everything." I roll my eyes and grab the book out of her hands, and she tries to reach for it.

"And what are you reading? *Romance*? Isn't this the book that Kennedy got for Christmas?"

"Yeah, she's letting me borrow it. Give it back." She tries to reach for it again and looking adorable while trying to. I push my hand up higher so she can't see it. I skim the page she was reading, and I gasp loudly.

"Amelia Wren Hackerly, this is straight up porn." Her face turns even redder than it was earlier from the sun.

Every day, I learn something new about her. Like how she insists on wearing panties and a tank top to bed, knowing I can't touch her. And how she loves to read romance novels with very explicit sex scenes.

"It's *not*. Jasmine is a great author. She writes about her own real experiences with love. It's entertaining. You could learn a thing or two," she retorts as she snatches the book out of my hand, putting it into her bag.

"It's filthy is what is," I say, and she shakes her head with a soft laugh. "How about this? Whatever you read now, I'll do to you later."

"Not going to happen, Davis," she murmurs before turning her sun kissed face away from me and resting back on her arms. Well, it was worth a try.

*

"W hy don't we go out tonight?" I suggest one night after we're both tired from hiking on the Araby trail. I stand over her from the back of the couch while she lies down, her eyes closed but she's still awake.

"I'm exhausted, Miles. We've done, like, everything on everyone's bucket list *ever* in the last few days," she says sighing deeply. She opens her eyes, and pushes herself up on her elbows, looking at me.

293

"Don't you want to go out for some real food? We've been living off room service for four days," I whine, as I walk over to her side of the couch, and her eyes follow me.

"Aren't we going out on New Year's Eve? We can wait until then."

"Yeah, but it's going to be packed with people," I groan as I crouch down next to her, batting my eyelashes at her. "Don't you want to go out somewhere nice? Somewhere where we can eat good food. Just us. Just one night, Wren."

"Jesus, you're so fucking dramatic," she groans before standing up.

I'm feeling giddy as I go into one of the large bathrooms to get ready. I'm lucky I packed a nice outfit in case something like this was to happen. Okay, nice might be stretching it but it's decent.

I try to brush out my hair, but it still looks wild. I've never known how to deal with my curly hair, so it just does its own thing. I put on a white button down and black pants, trying to look smart casual. I'm sure Wren is sick of seeing me in jeans and hoodie and honestly, so am I.

I wait in the kitchen for her to finish getting ready because, as always, she takes hours to get ready. I stick my head into the fridge to find something but they're only tiny bottles of tequila which doesn't seem like a smart idea right now. This feels like a night I want to remember.

"Ready to go?" a breathy voice from behind me calls.

I turn and the wind is knocked out of me. Literally. I think I've died and come back to life.

Wren is dressed in a silky black evening gown with tiny straps. She holds a silver purse in her right hand which matches with her stilettos and earrings.

294

Her hair is slicked behind her ear as it falls onto her back. I have to back myself up into the counter for stability, so I don't fall over. I swear fucking music starts playing as she walks towards me, painfully slowly.

Jesus fucking Christ she is incredible.

'Cocktails for two' by Betty Carter instantly comes to mind when she gets closer to me. I blame Wren for her stupid headphones that meant I could hear her jazz playlist on the whole flight.

"You look so beautiful," I whisper, my voice sounding breathy and almost unsure. She blinks up at me and I wrap my arms around her waist, pulling her into me as if it's the most natural thing in the world. My hands feel so at home on her body. As if they just belong.

"So do you," she murmurs. Watching her try to fight herself just makes me want her even more. She stares at me as she takes in my outfit, her eyes roaming all over me. God, I could sit down and let her look at me all day. "Like, really, *really* good."

"You know, for someone who complains about my ego, you sure do feed it a lot," I coo, and she throws me a funny look. She rolls her eyes as she presses a kiss to my cheek before turning around and slipping out of my grasp.

I got us a table at the hotel we're staying at, so we only have to walk down past the lobby, but I still hold her hand even though we don't have to pretend out here.

"What are you doing?" she asks, looking at our linked hands and then at me.

"I just want to hold your hand," I admit, squeezing her small hand in mine. "That a problem?"

"No," she says quietly and doesn't bring it up again, latching onto my fingers.

The restaurant is built to hover just over the LED pool with a cosy cabin vibe. Our seats are on the patio outside, giving us a perfect view of the live band who play smooth blues music. People gather around them, glasses in their hands as they sway to the music under the sunset.

When we sit down, we both order steak and fries and a cherry blossom lemonade. I'm starting to think that my bad eating habits have rubbed off on her. We go through the never-ending list of questions to ask each other as we eat.

"Okay," she says, popping a fry into her mouth before scrolling through my phone. "These are getting a lot deeper than the other ones. Is that okay?"

"Sure. These are my favourite type of questions." I grin at her, but she frowns a little as she locks my phone and slides it over to me.

"What's one thing you would change about your family if you could?" She bites her bottom lip as if she's regretting asking the question. I chew on my steak for a few bites to think it over before answering.

"I wish my family were more upfront with each other. Instead of being too scared to say things, y'know?"

She shakes her head gently. "Hm. What do you mean?"

"Like, I've always been a pretty dramatic kid. I would get really attached to things. To people. And I wasn't afraid to express that, but my family have always been weird about it. My dad ignores things that he can move on from, my mom pretends like they don't exist and Clara... She always finds some way to diminish my problems and to make them seem

296

smaller than they are. I don't know, I think they just feel better hiding things," I admit.

As I said it out loud, my stomach twists as if I've just finished binging McDonalds. I hate how uncomfortable it makes me. I hate how whenever I talk about them, I can feel my chest tightening. That's why at the Christmas dinner, I kept quiet. Even when my dad and I were alone, we stuck to talking about sports and boring things instead of what we were really thinking. I knew that if I tried to say anything, I'd ruin the night. Or they'd back me up into a corner and tell me to calm down. That I was overreacting. Wren's quiet as she waits for me to continue.

"I think they just find it easier to ignore problems. They've been treading on eggshells around me since I found out about mom and since Carter died. You know how much I talk. I can't just do that. I can't move on easily and I can't just ignore things that are clearly there. I know my parents love each other but sometimes that doesn't feel like enough. They're not *happy*. It's worse to be unhappy with somebody and still stay with them."

"I'm sorry," Wren says quietly. I shrug, smiling. "But you know you can always talk to me, right? Even if it's utter nonsense. I like hearing you talk."

"You do know I'm going to use this against you in the future. You can't ever tell me to shut up again," I joke. She smiles wide. "What about you?"

"I don't like the pressure," she says without missing a beat. She tries to laugh but the noise doesn't come out properly as she fiddles with her fork. "Austin's pregnant and she told me to tell my mom for her."

I almost choke on my food. "What?"

"Yeah, she told me a few weeks ago. It was just after we, y'know, made out. Anyway, that's why I was so off with you before the show because I was planning on telling her after. I had to do my absolute best so if I told my mom, it would fly right over her head. Then, I saw her miss my performance and I got angry, so I didn't tell her and now here we are."

I'm quiet for a moment, not knowing what to say. That's really messed up. I can't imagine having that weight on your shoulders. She looks out at the crowds of people, smiling softly at the music playing. Something in her face changes when she speaks next.

"Do you want to know what the worst part is? She didn't even think about my side of it. Austin wanted me to tell her after the showcase because she thought that if I told her then, she'd have all of her focus on me and forget it. It's like me skating trumps her getting pregnant. Like she knows that mom would fixate on me instead of her."

"That really sucks. I'm sorry. Do you know when you're going to tell her?" I ask after a while.

"I don't know," she sighs, falling back into her chair deeper. "I'm hoping that Austin will suck it up and tell her herself. I can't deal with that kind of drama. Not so close to comp season."

"Yeah, that's fair."

We both dig back into our food before it gets cold, neither of us asking any questions before she sits up on her chair, her arms resting on the table, her head in her hands. "Next question."

"They just get worse," I say, picking up my phone to scroll through it.

"I'm a big girl, Milesy. I can handle it." She gives me a wicked grin as she nudges me under the table. I push back, chuckling at her.

"Okay." I close my phone, mirroring her position. "Do you believe in love?"

"That's easy," she laughs, pushing her hair over her shoulder before giving me a dead look. "No."

"What do you mean 'no'? You look like a person who does. Considering the kinds of books, you're always reading."

"Oh, don't get me wrong, I love love. Does it exist? Sure. But do I want it? Definitely not."

Her candour shocks me. This whole time I thought she was a romantic underneath all the stubbornness. A hopeless one at that. I thought that after reading all those romance books, she'd aspire for that. That she would crave it. Hope for it at least. She looks out to the band again, her eyes not braving mine, as they play 'At Last' by Etta James with wicked timing.

"I love the idea of love. The way it's written about in books and in movies. But actually, being in love — it's scary. It's all consuming. Falling in love is so easy but it's just as easy to fall out of it. My parents did. They acted like everything was fine. They went on pretending. And then just one day, it was gone. All the sparks, all the reason they had to stay together just seized to exist. I don't want that. I don't want to be constantly waiting for the day my partner doesn't want me anymore. The torture. The anticipation. I just couldn't live like that."

"Yeah," I say quietly. "I get that, but I don't think you should be scared. It's a powerful thing; being in love. We're young and we're going to feel things that are more than lust and sometimes the only word to describe that is love."

She turns to me now, tears lining her eyes. "Can't there be another word? We use the word love for everything. I *love* my friends. I *love* my shoes. I *love* this food. It doesn't *mean* anything anymore. Can't there be something that has the same meaning, carries the same weight but doesn't feel indefinite. Binding. Something that doesn't have to tie you down to that person and suddenly change everything. When you're in love with a person romantically, you can't go back. But when you change your mind, as humans do, it becomes a big thing. But I guess that's what people want though. Something tangible to change in their relationship. To make it more serious or some shit."

We both look at each other for an extended moment. The way her brain works blows my mind and I'm obsessed with it. I want her brain. Her mind. Her everything. Anything that she's willing to give me. I wait for her to continue. There's something lost in her eyes, something distant as she doesn't break eye contact with me.

"If I ever feel anything remotely close to being in love, I just want to *exist* with that person. I don't want to ruin it by binding us together by a word. An emotion."

I'm shellshocked for a moment, not sure what to say. This girl has flipped around nearly every single thought that I had about her. I finally muster up the courage to ask, "Did that mean you were never in love with Augustus?"

She shakes her head. "Not really. I knew he loved me and I appreciated it. I knew I had some strong feelings for him but I didn't want to let us fall into that."

I nod. "Do you think you feel this way about love because you feel like you don't trust it or because you don't deserve it?"

"Both?"

"Well, that's bullshit, Wren. You're worthy of everything good in this world."

She still holds eye contact with me but I see the way her eyes glimmer. "Even love? Even if it breaks my heart?"

"*Esepecially* love," I say, "even if it breaks your heart."

We're quiet for the rest of the day. Neither one of us wanting to say more than a few words after we just bled out our emotions onto the table. Something shifted. I don't know when or how but something else had changed between us. Like the string that was holding us together has pulled us even closer without us realising. The silence that could be uncomfortable, feels welcoming.

Even after we're back in the hotel room, sat on the couch watching New Girl re-runs, we don't say much. When we get into the bed, practically meters separating us, our backs to each other, she finally breaks the silence.

"Do you think I'm insane?"

"What?" I ask.

"Do you think I'm insane for not believing in love? You always say that - that I'm insane. Don't you think it's weird that I'm scared?"

"No. I think it's smart. Practical."

CHAPTER 30
WREN

"**S**urfing?" Miles asks when we're on opposite ends of the huge couch in the hotel room. He's flicking through a list on his phone while I try to finish reading my book. Which I've been trying to do for the last two hours but he won't stop bothering me.

"No," I say again.

"Yes."

"No."

"Maybe…?" he says, leaning over and pulling my book from my hands, grinning at me. "Come on. You're only in Palm Springs once."

"I could be here next week if I wanted to."

"Right, I forgot. Scarlett said that you'll sugar momma me if I'm good."

"I never said I'd be bringing you along if I came back," I retort, narrowing my eyes at him. I sigh and soften my tone as I say, "Do you really want to go surfing?"

He nods, suddenly excited like a puppy. "More than anything."

"Fine, but I want to be back here before lunch time."

*

We don't make it back before lunch time. In fact, we don't make it back until the surf instructor has had enough of us and the sun starts to set. Miles somehow managed to rope me into surfing with him. We were both terrible at it and it only got worse when the instructor suggested we tried tandem surfing. I can't tell if I'm disgusted or impressed with Miles' determination to actually catch a wave. We were out there for what felt like hours, sweaty, sticky, hot and every other disgusting feeling you get after being out in the sun all day. Instead of going back to our room like I suggested so we could order room service, I'm being dragged down a street to a bar, still in my skirt cover up and bikini top while Miles is shirtless in his swim shorts.

"I need to shower properly. Please don't tell me we're about to eat here," I groan, letting Miles pull my exhausted body into the near-empty bar. I take a look around and it's a nearly deserted space with a few people scattered around and a karaoke machine in the corner. "No," I breathe out.

"Oh yes, Wrenny," Miles says, pulling me into the dance floor. "Is it Opposite Day or something because it feels like you've been ignoring everything I've said no to all day," I say and he pulls me into him. He doesn't say anything as he winks over to someone at the bar. "Miles Middle-Name Davis, what are you doing?"

"Harlan," he says, wrapping one arm around my waist and clasping his other hand in mine.

"What?"

"My middle name is Harlan," he explains and I snort. "Don't ask. I have no idea where my mom got that name from. I think she was expecting me to turn out to be some big CEO or something."

I laugh, throwing my head back. "It's cute. It's giving hardcore grandpa vibes."

"Glad to know it's grandpa names that get you going," he starts, spinning me out and then pulling me back into him. We're not even dancing properly to the kind of fast paced music that is playing but it's too fun to care. "And not my amazing looks."

"You're so full of yourself. You know that?" I say, laughing as he makes me spin again.

303

"You could be full of me too if you"re nicer to me," he retorts and I gag. "I'm kidding. Rule number three and all that."

"Glad to know that it's you putting your dick inside me that will breach rule number three and not this very romantic, very up-close dance we're doing," I say when the song changes to a slow, smooth jazz. He pulls me into him as I rest my head on his chest as he holds my hand with one of his as I wrap my other hand around his back.

"This," he says, gesturing between us, still holding onto my hands, "is only whatever you want to call it, Wren." He continues to sway us, out of beat, to the music.

"That's not confusing at all," I murmur, wrapping my arms loosely around his neck. I almost forget that we're both practically naked, our sweaty skin clinging to each other until my front is flush against his. God, has he always felt and smelt this good? Even after spending all day at the beach. Because right now, I could die in his arms as he holds me like this. "Can I ask you something?"

"Anything."

"And you've got to be honest with me," I warn, listening to the rhythm of his heartbeat.

"Always."

I take in a deep breath. "Would I sound stupid if I said that I want to stay here forever?"

"I think that's the best thing you've said to me all day, Wren," he whispers. "You don't have to follow it up by explaining to me how you mean it in a platonic way or because we're pretending to date because I get what you mean. In whatever way you meant that, I'm right there with you."

"Okay, good."

"Great."

"Perfect."

"Do you have any hobbies other than skating?" he asks and I look up at him, testing my chin on his chest. "I know that was a real one-eighty but I've been thinking about it and I want to know."

I nod, resting my head back down on his chest. "I like to read. A lot."

"And you find that…fun?"

304

"It's the best. Getting lost between pages, finding myself within characters and getting so caught up that you forget to look outside for a second. It's the best type of consuming feeling. Don't you ever feel like that about something that isn't hockey?" I ask

"I feel like that about music. I think," he says. "Maybe not as intensely as you do but I do enjoy listening to music. Sometimes it's the way certain songs sound and how it makes me feel and other times it's the words that are so well written. But most of the time it's both."

It feels like my heart is expanding. Is that possible? Or is that even a real thing? Because when Miles speaks to me it feels like my heart is about to burst out of my chest because not only is it beating so fast, but because it's being talked to, cared for and understood so deeply that it just wants to jolt right out.

"That's why you made that playlist for me that you didn't really make for me," I tease, remembering the amount of adorable songs I found on there.

"Exactly," he concedes through a laugh. "What's your favourite song?"

I think about it for a second. I change my favourite song the same way I change my outfits. It depends on what mood I'm in or where I am. "Right now, it's 'Carry On' by Norah Jones.."

He laughs a little, pulling away from me to hold me at arm's length. "You're going to have to sing it for me because I don't know it."

"I already told you, Davis, I can't sing," I say, shaking my head.

"If you do one, I'll do one," he says, walking over to the karaoke machine. He holds out the microphone to me. "Deal?"

I grab the mic off him. "Fine."

I stand next to the machine, looking at the tiny screen for the lyrics, mentally preparing myself for embarrassment. It's only Miles and a few other strangers in here but it feels like everyone's eyes are on me. Even if there were a hundred people in here, I'd only ever be able to feel him.

He stands across from me, his ankles crossed and his arms folded across his tanned chest, grinning. I start to sing; not my best but it's something. I even do a little dance between the small interludes of piano and Miles dances along with me, clearly enjoying watching me let loose. It's so easy to just be with him like this that it worries me. But also knowing that at the end of the day, it's his bed that I'm going to be crawling into and his arms that are going to wrap around me even when they shouldn't. Because, here, we're untouchable. And whatever we do or say is going to be contained into this tiny bubble we've built.

When my song's over, Miles takes the floor, psyching himself for the song he's chosen. He does a mini warm up, jumping up and down and pretending to crack his neck before the song starts. Immediately, when the song starts, I burst out laughing. Obviously, because Miles is Miles, he chose 'My Shot,' from Hamilton the musical.

He can't fucking sing to save his life, I've known that. But he can sort of rap?

I watch as he has the whole room's eyes on him while he raps every single line of the song. It's not many but it makes this whole thing feel like a real performance. I've never seen him so at home. I never would have pegged him for a theatre kid but from the way he's clearly memorised these lines, I might have been wrong about him. He keeps his eyes on me the entire time, giving an Oscar-worthy performance, pointing at me at any chance he can get until I'm crying-laughing so hard that I need to sit down.

I don't know how I didn't realise it earlier. Maybe weeks ago when he picked me up from that bar and looked after me but I might, actually, have real feelings for this boy. Like, feelings I definitely should have. The kind of feelings that I have not only between my legs but also in my chest. Which is extremely dangerous for so many reasons.

When his five minute rap is done, he stumbles towards me, out of breath and chest heaving. "That was the most tiring workout I've ever done in my life," he says, falling into me.

"Okay. Come on, big boy," I say, pushing his weight off me and onto the bar stool beside me. "I'm hoping that five minutes isn't how long you always last."

He gasps, holding a dramatic hand to his chest. "Are you making a sex joke?"

"No," I say, fiddling with my straw in my lemonade..

He tuts at me, shaking his head. "Didn't want to get me a drink?"

"And miss that toe curling performance? No way," I say, pushing his drink towards him. "You can have mine."

"Wow, Wren. Making sex jokes and letting me drink some of your drink? If I didn't know any better, I'd think you're finally warming up to me."

"You don't know any better," I murmur. "Plus, I warmed up to you a long time ago. It just took a vacation and a day full of surfing for me to show it."

"Nah, I think I figured you like me more than you'd admit when you kissed me," Miles retorts, sipping on my drink.

"Are we talking about the same kiss because I remember you were the one who begged for it," I say, my cheeks flashing at the memory.

"Okay, fine. I'm admitting it because I'm not afraid to deny the fact that I wanted you badly that night and you let me have you," he whispers so low that I can feel it in my stomach.

All I can focus on is *that night* because that is all it was. It was a moment of weakness. We were both turned on and reckless. That's it. It might have driven me insane for weeks but I'm over it now. We've got a more important task at hand.

*

When we get back into the hotel, Miles immediately hogs the bathroom, desperate to get the smell off him. Surprisingly, I've become comfortable in my sticky bikini top over the past few hours and I don't want the smell of the beach - or the smell of him - to come off me just yet. Instead, I sit outside on the balcony, letting the last of the summer breeze flow through my hair.

I pull up my phone and call Kennedy, knowing that she should be with Scarlett right now. They pick up on the second ring, their bright faces filling up the screen.

"Hiiii," Kennedy says. "We miss you!"

"I miss you guys too," I say, smiling at them. "What are you guys doing?"

"We just came back from Miles' house. Apparently hockey players want to party every night. You should know the kind of lifestyle you're getting yourself into," Scarlett warns.

"Well, it depends on how long you're planning on keeping this up for," Kennedy adds, trying to keep her whole face in the tiny screen.

"Yeah. I'm not exactly sure where we're going with this," I say, glancing back into the bedroom to make sure he's still in the shower. When I turn back to the screen, both of the girls are looking at me concerningly.

"What does that mean?" Scarlett asks.

"You guys have to promise not to kill me," I say. They both cross their hearts, holding up their Boy Scout promise.

Before I can speak, Kennedy pipes up. "You're falling in love with him, aren't you?"

My eyes widen and I turn down the volume on my phone. "No! God. What? Don't be ridiculous."

"You totally are," Scarlett adds in.

"I'm not," I say as confidently as I can. "I just like him a lot more than I thought I would, okay? He actually listens to me and makes me feel valued and seen. He forced me to go surfing with him and then we went to a bar to do karaoke and I think I've had one of the best days of my life."

"And your tan is looking gorgeous," Scarlett says, pulling the phone closer to her face. "I bet those freckles are driving him insane."

"I don't know. I haven't-"

"You're getting off topic," Kennedy chimes in. "Are you going to tell him?"

"What are you? Stupid? I'm not going to tell him anything. I don't even know what I would say. It's not like they are even real feelings anyway," I say, trying to convince myself.

"Who said they're not real? Because if your telling yourself that then you're fucking stupid," Scarlett says and I hate how right she is. "Don't tell him if you don't want to but don't you dare invalidate your own feelings. If you don't know what those are yet, that's cool. But that doesn't mean you have to pretend you're not feeling them."

I nod, taking in her advice. "When did you get so wise?"

308

"I always have been, you're just too stupid to realise it," she says with a shrug. "Anyway. We've got to go and binge-watch Love Island. We'll see you in a few days."

I say my goodbyes and end the call, trying my best to listen to what Scarlett says. I hate how she's able to see right through me and understand exactly what it is that I need. I don't need to tell him right now but I do need to figure out my feelings before they start to turn into something bigger. The glass door to the balcony opens and I flinch, turning around to a freshly showered, topless Miles who is leaning against the door frame. "Hey. You okay?" he asks, crossing his arms against his chest. "You seem a bit jumpy so I'm guessing there's going to be no scary movie tonight."

I laugh. "No, because then I'd have to put up with your screeching."

"That was one time," he says. It was more than once but I don't say that. He scratches his stomach, my mouth practically salivating. "Are you hungry?"

"What?" I say, snapping out of my trance.

"I asked if you were hungry," he says, coming closer to me. He places his hand on my forehead. "You sure you're okay? Are you sick?"

I shake my head, letting his hand fall. "I'm perfect, Doc. Just tired. All that singing and surfing has really got to me."

My face splits into a huge yawn and so does his. "Me too. I'll set up the TV in the room and we can have an early night."

He walks back into the room and I'm left with no idea what to do.

CHAPTER 31
WREN

I don't know how we got here. I don't know how I went from wanting to rip his head off at that party a few months ago to be in a bar, in Palm Springs, on New Year's Eve with Miles Davis. The strangest part isn't that I don't know, it's that I don't care.

For some reason, being here, in a crowded bar with Miles' hand on my back doesn't make me scream. It makes me want to melt into him. We don't have to pretend here so is that why it feels so real?

The last week has been heaven. I know I should be training and preparing myself for comp season but I'm sure I can spare a week. I deserve a week. We've spent the past few days, eating, talking, travelling and doing more talking. I learnt a lot about him and myself being here than I have in the last four months of knowing him.

We have still tried to keep up with working out and using the gym in the hotel, but we stay for an hour at most before running back to the room or to the beach. It feels like nothing can touch us here. All the pressure, the stress, the grief. It feels like the world is at our fingertips. Or maybe I'm just starting to feel the shots we took earlier.

It's half an hour until midnight and we're standing at a bar, trying to speak over the loud music that's reverberating off the walls.

"What was that?" Miles basically shouts in my ear, his hand on my waist, leaning his face to mine.

"I said that I'm going to stop with being strict on drinking," I shout back to him. A crooked grin splits across his face.

"Really? *That's* your New Year's resolution?"

"Yeah. I kind of like how it feels now. I feel like I'm floating," I say.

"You've had, like, two shots, Wren. I hate to be the one to break it to you but you're a lightweight."

"I'm not!" I shout, pushing him gently in the chest.

"I put some water in your bag. Drink some, please. Do you want to go somewhere quieter?" Miles asks, moving me with him as we walk around the room. If I could form real thoughts, I would thank him for being so responsible. For taking care of me. He searches around for a way out.

"Does such a place even exist?" I ask.

"There's a small room over there." Miles points down a corridor with brighter lights than the dark ones in the main bar. I stand still, not willing to go down the sketchy hallway. He turns around and looks at me, puzzled.

"I think that's where all the orgies and murders happen," I say, shuddering.

"There's only one way to find out, Wrenny," he smiles. "I got you."

311

But as we start walking someone shouts his name. He looks
back at me, thinking it was me who called him. I shake my
head and shrug.

"Miles!?" the shrill voice from behind us shouts again. We both
turn this time. A dark-haired woman walks towards us in a
bejewelled silver dress, and I instantly recognise her. My
stomach tightens.

Miles has never been closed off about his ex-girlfriend, Emily
Fraser. Mostly because she comes up a lot when he talks about
Carter. She's short-ish woman with dark brown hair that cuts
off at her shoulders. She studies marine biology at Drayton so
she's smart and gorgeous. She's the opposite of me and I can't
figure out of that's a good thing or not. I take a little step back
and Miles' strong hand wraps around my waist, pulling me into
his side.

"Oh my God, it *is* you!" she shrieks and before either of us can
register, she pulls Miles into a hug, his hand slipping off me.
As if I'm not there.

"It's good to see you, Emily," Miles says when she pulls away
from him. His hand returns to me again. "This is Wren. My
girlfriend."

"So, I heard," Emily says as she gives me a once over. Her fake
smile doesn't even reach her eyes. She turns back to Miles,
ignoring my presence. "Are you staying in town for a bit?"

"Yeah, only until Monday. Our flights in the evening," Miles
explains.

"Aw, that's tomorrow. If I had known we could have hung
out," she groans.

She comes closer to him, her hand resting on his chest. *Okay.*
So, we're doing this. Miles doesn't look at her. In fact, he looks

312

straight over her head. It doesn't take a genius to know that she's drunk and he's too nice to tell her to do one.

"I miss you. I miss your body," she whines and that's where I draw the line. I grab her hand and push it off him and push her back gently.

"Hi, I'm sorry but I'm right fucking here. If you wanted to flirt with my boyfriend, you could have *at least* waited until I slipped away for a second," I say, coming into her face.

The darkness of the bar and the LED lights have given me a lot more confidence than I should have. I'm lucky I just about tower over her in my stilettos or else I'd look ridiculous.

"Miles, can you tell your girlfriend to chill?" Emily scoffs. She blinks up at Miles, but he steps back away from her, pulling me into him again.

"No, she's right," Miles says, looking at me and then back to her. "You don't have the right to say shit like that anymore."

"I can say what I want," she retorts, spluttering.

Miles groans, lowering his voice so only we can hear. "And Emily, you're lucky I'm talking to you nicely because the last thing you deserve is nice. I don't want to shout at you and cause a scene because I'm a decent human. So please, step back so me and my girlfriend can leave."

She blinks at us and I want to laugh so badly.

"Happy fucking New Year," I say to Emily before grabbing the cuffs of Miles' shirt and getting us the hell out of there. I know it was a petty thing to say but it made my blood boil. Exes like that are not good for anybody. The kind of ones who want you back when you've moved on. That shit sucks.

We wait outside of the bar for a cab, not saying anything as we sit down on the sidewalk. There is something comforting about being around Miles in this setting, watching cars drive past and

313

drunken strangers howl behind us. He's sitting next to me, sighing loudly as he throws his head back, probably as frustrated as I am.

"Thank you for doing that," I say quietly. I don't know how it came out but it's New Year's Eve and I'm feeling emotional.

"Doing what?" he asks, turning his head to me.

"For not pretending I wasn't there," I reply.

"Why would I do that?" he asks, sounding genuinely confused.

I shrug. "Have people done that to you before?"

"Not on purpose," I admit. "I've always felt like I take up too much space because I do so many things that people find interesting. But, when I was with Augustus, it was like he was trying to compete with me. Like he wanted to make me feel small and insignificant. Sometimes, he'd just pretend I wasn't there."

The words fall out of my mouth at a stupid pace, spilling all my secrets like it's nothing. It's definitely the darkness. I don't like oversharing this much but with Miles, it seems to easy.

What shocks me that he pulls me into a tight side hug, his strong arm tightening around me and I fall into him for a second. "I would never do that to you, Wren. Ever."

Miles and I don't hug. We kiss and we hold hands when people are around. But we never hug. It always feels too intimate. Like were crossing a line.

*

We go back to the hotel mostly in silence, walking past people as they go down to get ready for the countdown in the lounge. We go back to our room, standing outside on the balcony, watching the early fireworks that are being set off down the horizon. It's not long before the new year's about to start.

"That was hot," Miles says nudging me with his shoulder as we lean against the railing, looking out into the darkness. I turn to him and laugh.

"You're like a horny teenager. You think everything is hot," I scoff.

"I am a horny teenager," Miles challenges. *Barely,* I want to retort but instead I snort and he smirks, adding, "Only when you do it."

"Someone needed to get her in line," I murmur. He turns his body to me, his left arm resting on the railing. I mirror his position and I shudder as I say, "I *hate* that it made me so mad."

"Can't you just admit that you wanted to defend me? That *you*, not my fake girlfriend, but *you* wanted to defend me," Miles says. His fiery expression catches me off guard as he closes the space between us.

"What are you talking about?" I breathe. *Are we really doing this right now?*

"Why can't you just admit that you want me — like you said at Christmas? That you want me for real. Just as badly as I want you."

"Miles," I whisper, a half plea.

He steps closer towards me, our noses grazing each other, as his breath hitches. "Tell me, Wren. Does this feel fake to you?" I don't say anything. What could I say? Each day being around him, it gets harder and harder to deny the heavy want building inside me. That I'm low-key annoyed that I didn't bring my Christmas present with me. That the past few days have been the most fun I've had in my life. That being with him makes me better. Happy. Whole.

The countdown to new year's begins outside.

Ten.

"Miles... I *can't* want you. You know that."

Seven.

"I'm not asking what you can and can't do. I'm asking you what you feel. What do you *want*, Wren?"

Two.

"I want *you*," I whisper. *One.* Fireworks explode beside us as he grabs my face and pulls me into him, catching my lips with his.

Something magical and indescribable happens when our lips meet. I gasp at the suddenness of the kiss, and he uses the opportunity to slide his tongue into my mouth. I can feel myself floating. As if we're existing outside of this moment. Maybe it's the alcohol I had earlier or the heat between my legs, but I feel myself slipping away.

He pushes my head back lightly, deepening kiss as I whimper into his mouth at the force of him. He's not rough but it's hard enough that it shocks me a little and makes the intensity in my lower stomach build. He tastes sweet. Like cinnamon.

When I realise my hands have fallen limp at my sides I reach up for the nape of his neck, curling my fingers into his hair. He guides us to the railing and pushes my back against it which is good so he can't see the scars and bruises that I've got n my back over the years. Too many training days gone wrong and too little time to explain that to him.

I come up for air, the wind blowing into my face as I tilt my head back. This time, I go back in gently, my teeth skimming his bottom lip. He smiles into the next kiss, even when his warm mouth touches mine, I can still feel him smiling.

God, we're barley even kissing anymore as we just smile at each other like goofy high school kids and I love it. One of his

316

hand's snakes around my waist, pulling me into him, my dress getting caught in the wind. It's then that I can feel how wet I am. How much it's dripping between my thighs.

"Let's go inside," I pant when I can get a second to breathe. He responds by picking me up from the waist and wrapping my thighs around his middle.

While he carries me into the bedroom, I kiss at his neck, inhaling his cologne. He drops me down onto the edge of the bed, my dress pooling beside me. I quickly reach down and slip off my sandals as he unbuckles his belt. I lay back down, staring at the ceiling, waiting for whatever to happen to happen. This is a good idea, right? We could do this, get it out of our systems and if this plan works, I'll never have to see him again. No matter how bad I want to.

"Are we doing this?" Miles asks, kneeling down in front of me, basically reading my thoughts. I push up on my elbows and nod frantically, panting. "Wren. It's fucking great that you're enthusiastic, but I need you to tell me with your words."

"Yes. Yes. We're doing this, Miles," I say. Only he can make consent sound so hot. He pulls the material of my dress upwards, just exposing my thighs but he hesitates at the foot of the bed. "Do you need some help?"

He laughs, shaking his head before staring at me for a long moment. Without being able to process it, his hot mouth presses a kiss onto my thighs, making me squirm. He presses featherlight kisses along one thigh before moving to the next. It's so slow. Drugging. One of his hands wrap behind the back of my thigh, tugging it around his chest while the other splays across my breast. On top of my dress unfortunately. He kisses up my thigh until he gets to where I want him the most, but he

317

doesn't go all the way. Instead, he makes his journey back down.

"Miles. If you're not going to put your mouth where I want it, I'm going to deal with it myself," I groan after he brings his mouth to the edge of my panties three times without doing anything. I look down to him, but I can only see his hair, his face buried deep into my thighs. That's what I like to see.

"You're very impatient," he mumbles against my skin. "I've been waiting for this since I met you so I'm going to savour it."

"How do you think I feel? My vibrator can only do so much," I whine. He laughs into my thigh again, tickling me. He still doesn't move anywhere near my panties. Finally, I stand up and he falls back onto his heels, looking up at me. "You're taking too long."

I reach behind me, struggling slightly, as I reach for my zip and drop my dress down to my ankles. His mouth falls open when he notices I'm not wearing a bra as I stand there in nothing but my pink panties. The cool chill of the wind hits me, and my nipples go hard. He's still shell-shocked when I bend down and start to unbutton his shirt.

"I can do it myself," he mumbles when he gets his voice back, blinking up at me.

"Can you?" I cock my head to the side with a smug grin and he hums.

He shrugs off his shirt and takes off his jeans, until we're both stood there with nothing but our underwear. I take my time to memorise the curves of his tanned chest with my fingers, feeling him tense beneath me. I'm about to make a snarky comment but he brings his hands around my waist. The skin-to-skin contact makes all my nerves and senses sing. I step backwards slightly until the back of knees hit the bed.

318

"You're so beautiful, Wren," he whispers, and he presses an open mouthed kissed to my chest, just above my breast. I gasp at how light and tender the feeling is. "So, fucking, beautiful. I want to worship you."

"Then do it if you're not all mouth." I smile but my voice turns into a yelp when he pushes me onto the bed. He climbs over me, looking at me with a sexy, evil smile. He kisses me on the lips gently once before slowly making his way down my body. His lips catch onto my nipple and a moan slips out of my mouth. He laughs against my stomach, and I dig my heel into his back as payback. His glorious journey down my body stops at the waistline of my panties.

He looks up at me, dead in the eyes, as he hooks his fingers into the sides and pulls them down. I wiggle slightly as he pulls them over my ankles. I close my eyes, but he doesn't move. For a second, I think he's moved off the bed, but I open my eyes and he's just staring at my bare body in front of him.

"What? Is, uh, something wrong?" I ask, wearily.

It's been a long time since I've had anyone this close to my naked body. Augustus and I had sex before but even the foreplay was nowhere near as good as this. I never finished once with him. Well, to him he thinks I did but it turns out I'm just really good at faking it. Miles looks between my legs and then back up at me as he swallows.

"You're soaking, Wren," he says as if it isn't obvious.

"Are you going to do something about it?"

Before I can even get my words out, his fingers slip inside of me in one quick motion. My words turn into a moan at the sensation. I immediately roll over him to cause more friction as he pumps in and out of me faster.

"*Fuck*, Miles," I scream when his tongue moves over my clit. The sounds that I can hear myself making mixed in with the slick sound of his fingers inside of me are obscene. But exhilarating. His mouth and his fingers move inside me in a practiced motion, as I squirm beneath him.

I grip onto the sheet, turning my head to muffle my cries into the pillow. I had a feeling that feeling him inside me would be insane, but I could never have imagined this. I can't remember the last time I got this tuned on. Actually, I can. It was that night at his house when he asked me to kiss him.

"Such a good girl," Miles murmurs into my skin, "So wet for me."

Is this what dying feels like? I'm willing to let it happen.

"Miles, I'm going to-"

Just as the words leave my mouth, his takes his fingers out of me, leaving me throbbing even more. I look down at him, my chest rising and falling. He keeps his eyes locked with mine as he puts his fingers in his mouth, a low sound coming from the back of his throat as he slowly drags them out. I can feel myself drowning at the sight of him.

He kneels off the bed and I sit up further to see what he's doing. He doesn't take his eyes off me as he slides down his boxers. I gulp when his dick springs free, dripping with pre-cum. *Holy fuck.* I scramble impatiently to the end of the bed at the same time he crawls onto it. I grab onto his shoulders and swing him down so he's underneath me.

"What are you doing?" he laughs when I pin him down with my hands. Slowly, I drag my hands down his stomach until I get to where he's straining. I circle my tongue around his tip before slowly slipping him into my mouth and then back out, staring into his green eyes. "Jesus, Wren."

320

I use my hands to pump up and down his length, gaining more grunts of approval from him as I taste his saltiness. I fit more of him into my mouth, my eyes almost watering. He threads his fingers into my hair, his face pained with pleasure as he looks down at me.

I take him out of my mouth, dragging my tongue along his shaft. "Is this okay? I've not really done this before," I admit. He groans when I lower my mouth onto him again, gaining more of him. The grip he has on my hair tightens when I start to suck faster, feeling him deep in my throat.

"You're perfect. Just like this. Fucking perfect," he pants. He thrusts himself down my throat until I'm gagging on him, loving the way he feels and tastes.

"Fuck. I need to be inside of you."

I don't wait long before taking him out of my mouth and kissing up his abdomen until I reach his face. I kiss tenderly along his jaw, lifting his head slightly so I can whisper into his ear.

"Do you have a condom?" He nods his head and reaches down to get his jeans. "I was kind of hoping you'd say no. Did you plan on doing this before we got here?"

He gives me an evil grin when he sits back up in the bed, condom in hand. "I knew you wouldn't be able to resist me."

I smother his words with a long kiss before sliding down him, taking the condom with me. I straddle his thighs as I open the wrapper. I take it out but and roll it onto him. I'm about to guide him into me but his hand covers mine.

"What's going to happen after?" Miles asks, his voice wavering.

"Nothing is going to happen."

"What do you mean?"

321

"We're going to do this right now. We could do it a million times until our legs are numb but when we get back to Salt Lake we go back to pretending, okay? We need to make sure you're in the season for good and that I can qualify for the championships. If whatever this is spills into what we're pretending, it could end really badly," I say in a hurry, desperate to get him inside of me.

"Would it? Or wouldn't it be better? We wouldn't have to pretend," he asks quietly. I try to let myself think about that idea but it's really fucking hard to think straight when his dick is inches away from me.

"Miles, can we not talk about this *right* now?" I ask, nodding to his erection. He nods and takes his hand off mine, slipping them around my waist. "I just want to..."

My words turn into a disgruntled moan when he slams me onto him in one quick motion as he fills me up. I brace my hands on his chest as I roll over him, my mouth hanging open as I pant. Once the first wave of pain settles down, I melt into him. It's almost as if our bodies were made to be doing this with each other. We move in sync as he guides my hips around him moving in circles and forwards and backwards. His hands dig into my ass, and I gasp. It should be a crime for this to feel so good.

All the pent-up tension, the small touches, the stolen glances all led up to this exhilarating high that I never want to come down from.

He thrusts into me deeper, his pace quickening as he leans forward to fit my breast into his mouth. I moan his name louder than I'd like to admit. I don't even recognise how whiney and desperate I sound. I greedily grab onto his hair, shoving his face deeper in between my breasts as his hips thrust forward into me while he whispers into my skin. *You feel so good, baby. If you keep talking, I'm going to finish right now*, I whisper back. *Good,* he says. The high ripples through us at the same time as I clench around him, his name slipping out of my mouth. His thrusts become sloppier as his orgasm soars through him, and he groans. Stars burst behind my eyes as I collapse on top of his chest.

"I don't think I'm going to be able to skate anymore if my legs don't work," I pant, propping myself up on my forearms on his chest. He laughs a little and kisses me on the forehead, our breathing still heavy.

When we settle down, I slip out of the bed to pee. To think. When I look in the mirror, I see a puffy faced Wren blinking back at me. I almost want to laugh at how insane this feels. I should be more concerned. After resisting him for so long, I finally succumbed.

This could be the start of something dangerous. Something all consuming. Something that we'll both get attached to. A habit I won't be able to kick. The distraction that I can't afford. Before I can splash water on my face, Miles comes behind me in the mirror, his chin resting on my shoulder. I lean into him, smiling in the mirror. He brings his hand around my front, teasing my nipple.

"Round two?" he whispers into my skin.

I nod enthusiastically.

*

I collapse beside him again onto my back for what feels like the hundredth time. Only this time I can actually feel myself

323

falling asleep. It's well into the morning now and small slithers of sunlight are starting to peak through the windows.

I look over at Miles for a second, watching his heavy breathing subside.

That's when the weight of the day comes crashing down onto me. I knew that if we do it once, we wouldn't want to stop. And we've done it at least plenty of times in several different places. When we get back home, everything is going to be different. Everything will change. I roll over onto my side, my back facing him.

"Miles?" I whisper. He responds by wrapping his hand around my stomach, pulling me into him, his head nestled in my shoulder. "We really broke the rule this time. I'm scared."

"I'm here."

That's it. Two words. A statement. A promise. A gift.

CHAPTER 32
MILES

I wake up to the sound of rustling and movements from outside of the bedroom. My head spins when I reach out to hold onto Wren like we have done all night, but she isn't there. My eyes open fully and search the empty bedroom. She's gone. The only thing that lingers is her perfume. I hear a louder clatter outside and sit up. As I check my phone on the nightstand, I realise that it's only just past ten. Although I'm not hungover, it feels like it. Sex drunk.

We spent most of last night doing anything but sleeping and I don't think we got to sleep until after four in the morning. I force myself to climb out of bed and see what the noise is.

I walk into the kitchen, the bright lights peeking through the window. Wrens' back is to me as she rifles through her suitcase that she brought full of books. As I inch closer, the floorboard creaks and her head spins around.

"Sorry, I didn't mean to wake you," she mumbles, tossing her hair over her shoulder.

"What are you doing? It's ten AM," I yawn, rubbing the sleep out of my eyes. "Aren't you tired?"

"Oh extremely," she says cheerfully. "I'm just going to the beach. I need to- I just need to read for a while to clear my head. I'll be back before we have to leave."

Her smile doesn't reach her eyes when she looks at me. Remains of freckles scatter along her nose and cheeks and I'm instantly reminded of where my hands were all night. She seems to have the same thought as she takes a quick sweep of my body while I'm in nothing, but my boxers and her face turns a deep red.

I make my way towards her when she turns her back to me again and I wrap my arms around her waist, kissing on her neck lightly, feeling her warm body mould into mine for a split second. She pulls away from me, kneeling down to look through her mini bookshop. She stands up again to turn to me. Her brown-green eyes don't meet mine when I try to search hers for something. Anything.

"Is something wrong? Are you okay?" I ask cautiously. She stands up to me on her tiptoes and presses a kiss to my cheek. "Everythings fine, Milesy. I just need to get out of here for a little bit. I'll be back." She offers me a small smile before walking out the door.

When she's gone, I lie back down on the empty bed, staring at the ceiling for what feels like hours. Long painful hours without anybody to talk to. Anyone to hold.

Did I do something wrong? Maybe we went too overboard last night. And this morning. It's like every time we tried to go back to sleep, we went back to each other instead. Like it was the first of the last times we would do this. It didn't feel like I was getting it out of my system. It didn't feel like scratching an itch.

326

It felt like I was preparing myself for what's going to be a few weeks of hell. I knew she'd try and block me out after we had sex, but I thought that it would take her longer to freak out than rushing off straight away.

I need to think of some way to make her believe that this was a good idea. That she doesn't need to run away from me. From us. Whether or not either of us are willing to admit it, I'm still the moth and she's the flame. We're tied together in some strange, unshakeable way.

I catch a taxi into town, to a good bar restaurant to let myself think. I knew she'd be close to the hotel, so I didn't want to stay near her in case she didn't want me to interrupt her own thinking time. The best thing I can do is to give her space to figure out what she wants. Whatever the fuck that is.

I knew from day one that I wanted her. That I couldn't think about anything else but her. That she fascinated me and challenged me. A part of me knew that I was hyper-fixating on her because she reminded me of Carter. I know that he would be screaming at me now to not mess this up.

Unsurprisingly, this early in the morning on New Year's Day, the bar is deserted. In a shady bar like this, I knew my fake ID would be accepted so the bartender doesn't look twice when I continuously ask for more shots. I shouldn't be doing this. I've worked too hard to fuck it up now.

All the good reasons I had to come to the bar fall out of the window when I hear the same whiny voice from last night. Emily Fraser.

For a second, I think I can slip away. Maybe if I turn my head, down my drink and walk out she won't notice me. Or maybe if I approach her first, she might just leave me alone to drink until my flight. None of those things happen. Instead, dressed in blue jeans and a white sweater, she slides into the seat next to me at the bar, somehow looking refreshed as if it isn't New Year's Day.

"Hey, Miles. Nice to see you again. Sober. Well, I'm sober this time you're definitely not…" She searches my eyes, but I try to look away. This is the last thing I need right now.

"Pleasure to see you as always. I don't want to do this right now," I groan, swishing around my shot glass before downing it.

"Do what? I'm just saying hi. Your *girlfriend* was the one who had a problem with it," she drawls, leaning against the bar. I look at her for a second before turning back to stare in front of me.

"No, it wasn't just her. I had a problem with it too. You acting like you hate her, isn't cute. You're lucky she didn't say anything else to you last night."

"Yeah, like what? She looks harmless," Emily challenges humorously.

"Wren is anything but harmless. Just keep your distance and everything will be cool," I say, turning to her.

"You're no fun," she grumbles, sulking.

"I'm heartbroken," I whine sarcastically.

She gives me a quick look before sliding off the seat and walking away. I don't know what's gotten into her. She was never like this when we were together, but I knew she was a little protective. I didn't expect her to be jealous too.

I groan at myself when I remember just how protective Wren was last night and everything that happened after. Because fuck me, it was hot when she got angry.

Like the loser I am, I pull out my phone and flick through photos of us over the past few months. My whole camera roll

328

has been consumed by her the same way my brain has. I've always been a picture-taking person.

I love to have these kinds of memories on my phone to look through over the years. Whenever I post any pictures of Wren and I, my followers go insane as if we're the new celebrity couple. Hell, my home screen is a picture of her gorgeous face smirking at me when were at the gala.

One of my first pictures of her is when we went to meet up at the gym one cold morning. I forgot to give her my keys before I told her to go to the car so I could pee quickly. When I walked back out, she was stood at the side of my truck with the most ridiculous look on her face. Her hair was braided into two pigtails, wrapped in a huge puffer jacket, a beanie, and a scarf while she sulked at the camera as I snapped pictures of her. "It's for the memories," I said, and she pushed me almost making me topple over in the snow. I catch myself smiling and don't bother to hide it.

I have tons of candid pictures of her in the library, at the rink, in my room, in her car. And my current favourite picture of us; a candid taken by Kennedy on Christmas Day. In the photo, I'm leaning on the sink drying the dishes while Wren washes them, but the picture is a small moment caught where we both look at each other, smiling as she passes a dish to me. Kennedy sent it to me on Instagram and I didn't get it until I was in bed that night. *To add to the photo album for your kid*s, the message read.

It's moments like those, the ones that we don't always remember but appreciate, are the ones where I can feel myself falling for her even harder. Where being around her makes me feel like all the problems that I thought were huge are able to subside. Even if only for a little while. Being with her this week has stopped this constant orbit that I have been in, trying to get her to pull me into her. To get her to notice. But when that happens, she pushes me back out again and I'm stuck circling around her.

I sit there, scrolling aimlessly through my camera roll, smiling to myself. I'm so caught up in listening to her laugh that could melt in my hands that I don't realise the tall dark-haired guy who sits next to me. He looks around my age, maybe a little younger but definitely not allowed to be drinking,

"Is that your girlfriend?" he asks, nodding towards my phone. Instinctively, I lock my phone and turn it face down on the table.

"Yep. I think," I reply but my voice sounds distant. As if it's not my own. The drinks must be getting to me.

"What do you mean, 'you think?' Is she or not?" He looks at me with kind eyes. His features seem boyish and friendly, a lot like Carters.

"Do you want to hear a story?"

CHAPTER 33
WREN

I am able to see the future. All the goddamn time. I know things are going to happen – bad things – but I still do them anyway. It's like an irritating feeling in my brain that I can't ignore and have no choice but to follow through with. I've seemed to have got used to making bad decisions. I knew sleeping with Miles would be wild and exhilarating but I didn't expect the very low low I would experience afterwards.

This was a good distraction; spending our days going on small adventures and our nights cooped up in the hotel, believing we were untouchable. Believing that we could ignore every red flag but if we tried hard enough, we could make them green. It was fun. And that isn't something I get to feel often. That free liberating feeling of not having to worry about tomorrow, my diet or my training.

But when we slept together, something shifted. Sure, if we made out it would be fine, we could go back to Salt Lake and pretend it didn't happen like we've done before. But this? This is something different. Something substantial. He's seen me naked for God's sake. He has seen and touched nearly every part of my body. This is something that we can't ignore. Well, something we can't ignore any more than I've tried to.

As soon as I opened my eyes this morning, I knew I had to get out of that room. I have to stop pretending like this is my life. That living off room service and good sex was my lifestyle. I need to be in the rink, in the gym, training and eating good. Instead of going for round who-knows-what with Miles, I got my ass up, showered and got myself down to the beach and tried to salvage some sort of calm.

With the qualifiers and the championships, the last thing I need is to complicate whatever me and Miles have. As much as I tried to push it away, I knew I was attracted to him from the beginning. A large part of me hoped that we could just power through the next few months and push away all our desires to focus on the task at hand. That was until the gala, the game, Christmas – where things started to get real. When it was an intense struggle to fight off the feelings between my legs.

What's worse is that it's not just his looks but it's everything about him. His selflessness, his support, his care and the way he listens to me. Every fucking thing.

Despite my initial rule, and although ambiguous, Miles was the only one to admit how he truly felt. He made that *very* clear since the beginning. I was scared. I still am scared of falling into deep and forgetting everything I have worked so hard on. Every time I'm around him, my self-control shrinks and the little devil and angels on my shoulder disappear, leaving behind a cloud of smoke. Being in a real relationship with someone like him would be consuming, distracting and everything I can't have right now. But everything that a secretly want.

I know I ran off this morning, but I didn't expect Miles to be gone too. He's probably freaking out as well. I finally finish cleaning up the bedroom and packing away our things into our suitcases.

Strangely enough, Miles' suitcase has very little clothes for the week that we've stayed here compared to mine. I'm packing up the last of our things, double checking the bathroom when somebody knocks on the door.

Before I know it, it swings open as I cross the living room in my denim shorts and white tank top. My heart drops through my ribs as I take in the sight in front of me. An elderly black lady with kind eyes in a flower sundress stands in the doorway with a very sad and very drunk Miles on her shoulder.

Oh, no. Miles, what have you done?

This is the first time I've seen him drunk in months. The lady looks around the room before her eyes settle on mine and they soften. I rush over to them, pulling Miles' weight off her. He's sweaty and a lot heavier than I remember. He sinks into me, and I can smell the alcohol. My stomach turns.

"I'm so sorry to bother you. He was wandering around and he said that he was staying here. You're Wren, right?" the lady asks in a thick southern accent. I nod, swallowing the lump in my throat. "Okay, good. He might not look like it right now, but he said some really nice things about you. Take care of him."

"I'm sure he did, and I will," I say, my voice sounding foreign as I look down at him, his face buried into my chest. "Thank you so much."

I try and keep calm as I walk with Miles' arm over my shoulder, which is hard to do when he's a lot heavier and taller than me. He stays quiet as I bring him into the bathroom.

This is why I don't drink a lot. This is why I don't like being around people that drink too much because it brings out the worst in them. It gets out of control when you're not careful and sometimes so out of control that a random person has to bring you back to your hotel room. He has avoided my eyes since he got in here and I don't know how to act around him. What to say. How to make this better. What makes this worse is that he's a sad drunk.

I get some water from the fridge and bring it to the bathroom and rummage for some painkillers in my bag. He stands, leaning against the sink even though I've told him to sit down. He takes a few painkillers and chugs half the bottle of water. Slowly, as if he knows what's going to happen, he bends down to the floor, leaning over the toilet and he throws up. A lot. My stomach flips as I kneel next to him, rubbing his back while he leans his head on his arm on the toilet seat.

"It's okay. Just let it out," I say, rubbing circles on his back. He doesn't say anything, just indistinct mumbles as he sits back up. What happened to him? We have to get to the airport in two hours. He can't be like this right now.

He groans as he sits up, hopefully finished throwing up. I pull his arm around my shoulder and wrap my hand around his middle to help him stand up.

"C'mon, let's get you in the shower."

Like I expected, he doesn't reply, just mumbles something in agreement. When he's able to stand, I stand across from him and part of me wishes I couldn't see his face right now. Tears that are staring to dry, streak his pale cheeks. He catches me staring and his eyes shoot to the floor.

I inch closer, reaching my hand out to pull off his shirt. He helps me to take of his shirt and his trousers. I lean over to turn

334

on the shower as he takes off his boxers and steps into it. He sits down, pulls his knees to his chest, and rests his head on them. He looks so vulnerable that my heart pinches. He's always the one helping me. He's supposed to be the fun one. "I'm sorry. I'm so sorry, Wren," he mumbles as I run the shower over his hair and his back. I place my hand on his cheek, rubbing my thumb under his eye. He melts into my touch. "I'm trying to be good for you, I swear."

"I beleive you. You don't need to be sorry. I shouldn't have run away," I respond quietly.

"I thought…I thought you hated me. That you regretted last night and that you didn't want me — this — anymore. And I saw- I thought I saw Carter."

It feels like someone has taken a pin to my heart and deflated it. He talks about Carter all the time, I'm not surprised that he thought he saw him, especially when he's intoxicated. I should say something. I should tell him that it's not true. To tell him that all I want is to be there for him. To make sure he's okay. "We'll talk about this later, okay? We need to get you feeling better right now." He nods, some of the colour coming back into his face as I run my hand through his hair. "I'm here, Miles. I've got you."

"You've got me?" he mumbles and my heart tears.

"I've got you."

We don't talk much as I help him to feel better. After his shower, Miles gets ready sluggishly and I order him some room service. He takes a few more painkillers and once he's eaten, he starts to look better. We don't talk about what happened. Why he went somewhere to drink or why he thought he saw Carter. I don't push him to tell me, so he doesn't bring it up. I ran away from the problem and so did he. In some ways, we're both to blame.

His humour starts to return on the flight, along with his sobriety. He makes continuous plane jokes which I can't help but laugh at. Even while I'm trying to watch The Lion King, he somehow managed to make terrible puns out of every character that comes onto the screen. The only thing missing, is the way he would make flirty jokes or try and touch me in some way or another. It doesn't feel real that it was less than twenty-four hours ago that we couldn't keep our hands off each other.

When we get back to Salt Lake, the winter air hits us as we run to find an Uber to take us back to our houses. The second my body warms up to the temperature in the Uber, we're already outside Miles' house and I'm struck by another brush of cold air. Miles takes my luggage out of the car, along with his and we walk up to his door.

I almost forgot it was New Year's Day until I take in all the decorations in the house. Gold and silver banners hang from the ceilings and beer cans and Solo cups litter the floor. I take notice of the makeshift photo wall that I saw in Kennedy and Scarlett's pictures from last night.

They were not happy with me missing New Year's with them, but I convinced them to go to Xavier's party and from the way Kennedy was cuddling up to Harry Butler I can tell they had a good night.

"Finally," Xavier exclaims when he sees me and Miles. "Dude, it's been hell without you."

"Can't talk. Head hurts," Miles mumbles, acting worse than he is. He sulks and brings his drama queen ass up the stairs. I laugh and Xavier pulls me into a side hug.

"What's wrong with him?" he asks, looking at me with a funny look.

"He's hungover. Kind of," I reply with a shrug. He laughs and walks in the other direction. I run up the stairs after Miles. He's shuffling around in his bathroom when I walk into his room.

"You're such a drama queen, you know that right?" I shout to him as I fall onto my back on his ridiculously comfortable bed. I've missed this so much.

"I'm not. My head *does* hurt," he whines, walking back out of his room in nothing other than grey joggers. He sits beside me on the bed, his legs crossed next to my head. I gulp, trying not look at his toned stomach. Miles ignores the dismissive look I'm trying to give him as he leans over me. "Are you going to stay here tonight?"

His lips are inches away from mine. I lean up on my elbows and press a quick kiss to his lips and he smiles. I pull away, not ready to go any further but his lips catch mine again in a passionate struggle. It feels so natural to be this close to him after the week we've just had. My mind instantly flashes to last night and the hundreds of other places his lips were.

"I think we both know that's not a smart idea," I breathe when I pull away again. "I don't think my body could take it *and* I miss my girls."

"That's true," he laughs. He moves from over me and rests his back against the windowsill next to his bed. I push myself up next to him. "I'm sorry, Wren. About earlier. I was freaking out and the last place I should have gone to was a bar. Especially after we've spent so much time trying to avoid that. Thank you for taking care of me."

"It's okay. It's my fault too. I shouldn't have just left," I admit. I turn my head to him, but his heavy-lidded eyes are already on

337

me. "I meant what I said, Miles. I am scared. I know you said you're going to be there but what if one day you're not? I can't depend on someone for them to let me down."

My own rambling voice catches me off guard. It's the first time I've said that out loud. To him. Not everyone can understand that overwhelming fear that constantly wells inside me when I'm around him and I'm close to letting go. He pulls my hand into his lap and encloses his hands around mine.

"No. That isn't going to happen. Even if this is for the fake relationship or our real relationship, I'm going to be there. I'm all in. For real," Miles says, turning over my hand in his. He traces the lines in my palm with a long finger.

"I've got qualifiers coming up. Then the competition season begins, and you've got the hockey team counting on you. If we do this and something happens, we're both going to go down. What did you call us? Falling stars? *That's* what's going to happen," I ramble, my voice wavering. "Aren't you worried about that?"

"Oh, I am," he replies cheerfully. "But I know that this is what I want. The good, the bad and the ugly. It'll be worth it."

"What if you change your mind?"

"I'm not going to."

"But what if you do?"

"I'm. Not. Going. To," he snaps, looking at me with fierce eyes. He brushes a strand of hair out of my face. I nod but it's still a hard pill to swallow. It can be easy to say you're not going to stop feeling this way, but it happens. I've seen it happen right in front of me. It can dissipate in an instant.

"Why don't we take it light and breezy? If it makes you feel any better, we can still keep the contract in effect but with some adjustments. If this gets too much we'll tell each other, okay?"

338

Miles suggests. I nod. He holds out his pinkie to me.
"Promise?"
I link my pinkie to his. "Promise." I try and let the idea settle for a second, wanting to believe him so badly.
"I know you're scared Wren and I know you have priorities. I would never ask you to change them for me but I promise you, I'm here. Me and you."
There it is again. Those two words.
I'm here.

CHAPTER 34
WREN

If somebody had told me a year ago that I'd be watching my sort-of-boyfriend play ice hockey - for fun - and not be complaining, I would've laughed in their face. Because that's exactly what I'm doing.

I've always thought ice hockey was a cool sport, I even tried it out a few times in middle school but it was more the boys and the typical culture that threw me off. That was before I met Miles and his friends who are actually the most sweet people I have ever met.

Once I finished practice today, Miles insisted that I come over to watch him practice. He's been having FaceTime calls with my dad, helping him get back into the swing of things which has been great for him. It turns out my dad has a lot more knowledge and experience that he's let on.

The girls and I are sitting behind the players bench; Scarlett on one side, her feet up against the board, Kennedy on the other side of me, her legs crossed, drawing on her Ipad and I'm in the middle, strangely very interested in the game.

Maybe it's just because Miles is playing and I haven't seen him play before. Or maybe I'm just finding an excuse rather than admitting that I could watch him here all day as he shouts at people on the team. He hasn't regained his captain status yet but he's acting like it. He's barking out orders, getting himself riled up as he takes of his hamlet to run his hands through his hair and fuck me if it doesn't turn me on. After knowing what every inch of his body looks like and the thoughts that are constantly circling his brain, it's hard not to find everything he does attractive.

I put my feet up to the board, leaning back as they huddle together as Coach Tucker explains some very confusing tactics to them.

"Are you *actually* enjoying this?" Scarlett asks, completely horrified.

"I think I am," I admit and I can't hide the smile on my face if I wanted to.

"Dick-whipped," Kennedy murmurs, not looking up from the sketchbook she has on her Ipad.

"I'm not," I say back to her, but she shrugs. I turn to Scarlett. "I know Jake is an asshole but didn't you ever feel that way about watching him play? I mean, all hockey players are hot without even trying."

She laughs. "No, jesus. I didn't feel anything for him other than the way he did when he was inside me. I hardly ever went to see him practice. Those weren't a part of the terms and conditions of our arrangement."

"And what exactly was your arrangement?" Kennedy asks.

"The same as it always is," Scarlett starts. "We were just sleeping together but when he started to parade me around because of who my family are, I called it quits. That doesn't mean it didn't hurt when he cheated on me. That fucking sucks no matter who the person is."

"I'm still really sorry about that. He's just an awful person," I say, remembering the way he acted at Sophia's house for the interview. "You don't have to be here if you don't want to. You know? If seeing him is hard."

She sighs, leaning back in the chair, crossing her arms against her chest. "Nah, I like watching your boyfriend shout at him." And at that exact moment, Jake pushes Miles in the chest but he doesn't fall back. Instead, he pushes back, causing Jake to fall into a few other people on the team.

"You better watch it, Callahan," Miles warns. It's empty in here so his loud, deep voice echoes off the walls.

"What are you gonna do?" Jake retorts. I inch closer towards the boards, trying to see them better. "You're girlfriend's watching. You wouldn't want her to see you get beat up, would you?"

Miles steps closer into him, my heartbeat racing but Coach Tucker holds his stick between them, pushing them apart. "You guys better keep it friendly or else you'll *both* be on the bench." I can hardly see their faces but I'm assuming they're glaring at each other as they skate away, getting ready to do the drills Coach Tucker has asked them to do.

"Also," I say, turning to the girls, trying to keep my voice low as I resume our conversation. "He's not my boyfriend. I don't know what he is but we've never actually talked about real labels."

"Maybe you should before your over-active brain starts to think of every possible thing that could go wrong," Scarlett says, digging into a packet of M&M's.

"Believe me, I've already started doing that," I mutter.

"Do you *want* him to be your real boyfriend?" Kennedy asks.

"I want everything that comes with having a boyfriend. I mean, who wouldn't. But we're both so busy. He's got this hockey season coming up and I've got comp season around the corner and then finals are coming up," I ramble. "I just don't think I'm emotionally and physically available for a relationship right now."

"But are you physically and emotionally available for a fake one?" Scar asks.

I sigh. "It's different when it's fake. There are no real feelings at stake and we know we have to make it work if we want to get what we want. When that becomes real, it'll be more dependency and commitment."

"Wren. I'm sick of you saying that your feelings aren't real because they are," Scar groans. "You've slept with him. Correct?" I nod. "And you somehow find his personality charming?" I nod again. "And he looks after you, you look after him and he's not the worst company to be around?" I nod. Again. "So what are you so afraid of?"

"Of it not working out," I blurt out. "Of him realising that I'm not what he wants."

"I hate to sound like a cliche," Ken starts. "But isn't it better to have tried than not to have tried at all?"

"In movies, TV shows and books, yes. But these are my real feelings and there's a very real possibility that if this becomes more serious, he'll realise that this isn't going to work out," I say, feeling the weight drop off me the second the words leave my mouth. "We're just taking it light and breezy."

"Ah yes," Kennedy says in her posh British accent. "The classic 'Light and Breezy.' What are you? Advertising a summer drink at Starbucks? As a romance writer, you couldn't think of anything better to determine your relationship status?"

We all laugh at that.

Honestly, who are Miles and I kidding? We've known each other for five months, we've been fake dating for most of them and we've slept together. We will not be able to take this light and breezy but what is the alternative? I don't know but I'm willing to find out. The last thing I want to do is regret not trying at all.

We watch the team go through their drills, Miles taking the lead once again. I can't tell if he just enjoys telling people what to do or if it's actually part of his role. They start to play a quick game, zipping up and down the ice. It's hard to keep track of who is who with the amount of gear they have on so I'm only guessing. Kennedy has finally put down her Ipad and she's actually seeming interested. Scar is doing the thing where she's pretending that she doesn't care but I can hear her muttering under her breath every time Miles' team misses the shot.

When Miles gains control of the puck on one end of the ice, he hardly looks up as he dodges the opposite team, moving quickly and efficiently. And he looks so hot as he does so. The other team has pretty much given up at this point, not even trying to defend his shot. But right before he has the perfect opportunity to get the puck into the goal, he manoeuvres closer to where we are sitting and he picks up his stick, pointing it right at me and he winks.

He fucking winks at me.

Dimples popping out and all.

And I almost die.

"This one's for you, baby," he says before regaining control of the puck again and hitting it straight into the net. Half of me wants to scream in embarrassment as the rest of the team laugh and the other half of me wants to get down onto the ice and kiss that stupid grin off his face. Instead, I sit there and smile at him, feeling slightly on top of the world at this moment.

When they go back to playing, Scarlett leans into me, whispering, "Whether he did that for show or not, that boy is head over heels for you, babe."

And that is exactly what I'm afraid of.

CHAPTER 35
MILES

Sleeping the night before my first game is the same as trying to go to sleep the night before Christmas. I haven't had this feeling in such a long time. Last season, it was exhilarating but nowhere near as much as this. Maybe it's because I haven't played in so long. Maybe it's also because it's the first time Wren is going to see me play properly.

Since we came back from Palm Springs, I've been training like crazy to get back into shape for this season. The first game of the season is always the most exciting. There's a certain type of rush in the crowd and having the first years' experience it for the first time makes this more thrilling.

We all huddle in the tunnel, psyching ourselves up to play. Most of the team rough each other up a little; bumping their chests together and howling. Others take a moment to pray to their God to guide them through the game. Grey, Harry, Xavier, and I stand in huddle, working out the logistics of the game.

We had a team meeting earlier in the sports classroom to work over tactics, while we looked at past games to plan how to work around it. How to improve.

I'd be lying if I said I wasn't nervous. Of course, I am. If I mess this up, they're going to blame me because they know how far gone I have been. I have to help lead us to victory. I need to earn back some part of my respect around here.

"Don't fuck this up, Davis," Jake mumbles as he walks past our huddle, jabbing his hockey stick into my side. Since the fight, he's gone back to his usual self: annoying me at any chance he can get. I ignore his relentlessness and turn back to the guys.

"As long as we play our best, that's all that matters, right?" Harry asks, looking between us. Xavier bumps him in the shoulder playfully.

"Hilton are an easy beat," Xavier says. "Out hustle, out work, out think, out play and out last."

We all nod, chanting along with him. We've been doing these rituals for as long as I can remember. Just saying encouraging words and affirmations help us get into the get our heads into the game. It works like magic.

"Whatever it takes," Grey shouts at the top of his lungs, this time all the guys join in with the chant.

"Whatever it takes!"

"Good afternoon, hockey fans!" Max Carhart, our student commentator announces. "Welcome to the first game of the 2022 college ice hockey season between the Hilton College Penguins and North University Bears."

Everybody cheers and chant over the commentator as they introduce the line-up for the visitors' team. We start to make our way out of the tunnel as they call out our names while we take our positions on the ice.

I stand in right wing, trying to focus on my breathing as we play the national anthem. I attempt to ignore the tightness in my chest and close my eyes. Big mistake. Flashes of our last game with Carter cross my mind. I can see him skating around the ice in celebration after everyone left. "We fucking did it, Davis!" he shouted, patting me on the back.

I feel the suffocation inside my helmet. I can do this. I have to do this. For Carter. I open my eyes when the national anthem is finished. I look up into the stands and I see her. Wren's sat down, wearing my spare jersey which she stole the other night and looking absolutely devastating. She sees me and smiles wide. Kennedy sits beside her, smiling too but Scarlett frowns, not hiding her distaste for hockey. I tear my focus from them when the whistle blows.

Whatever it takes.

*

"I just can't get over that shot. It was, like, completely legendary," Kennedy exclaims for the hundredth time.

Wren, Scarlett, and Kennedy came over to my place after the game to hang out. Most of the team have gone to a much louder party but I knew that Wren wouldn't want to go to that. Instead, I told Grey, Harry, and Xavier to stay here.

While we were in Palm Springs, it seems like they've all gotten a lot closer without us which is good. Yet, as much as they've hung out, Kennedy is still not over the way hockey works and how my shot wasn't at all 'legendary.'

I was able to get in two goals while Xaiver and Harry got one in each. Grey needs to learn how to chill more on the ice because he was in the penalty box for half of the game. We all helped each other assist along with Tyler and Bryan. It was a really good first game back.

347

"Calm down, Ken. You're going to boost his ego even more," Wren says giving me a small smile. She leans her head into my neck as I wrap my arms around her waist while she sits in my lap, wearing the shirt I got her for Christmas. Across from us, Kennedy and Scarlett give each other knowing glances.

"I don't mind it one bit," I say proudly. I turn to Wren. "It's not like you've even *told* me congrats since the game was over."

Wren's face turns red at my teasing. She *has* said 'well done'. Once with a huge hug and a kiss when she ran up to me when the game ended when I was all sweaty and gross and then again when we got home, on her knees in my bedroom with my hand in her ponytail.

"It was a good game, though. It helped that they couldn't play for shit anyway," Grey laughs. "They looked like they only just learnt how to skate."

Wren snorts. "You spent more time in the sin bin than you did on the ice," she retorts seriously, seeming genuinely disappointed with his performance, and everyone laughs.

I look at her, unable to hide my grin and the raging hard-on. "What did you just say?"

She tilts her head. "What? About the penalties?"

"Nah," I tut, shaking my head. "I want to hear you say it again."

"You want me to say 'sin bin' again? Is this a new kink of yours, Davis?" she asks me innocently batting her eyelashes at me.

"It might be," I admit, having to readjust my jeans. I lower my voice and groan. "Fuck me."

"I can make that happen." She bites softly on my ear, and I press my mouth in a line to suppress my groan. Does this girl enjoy torturing me?

"Uh, please don't," Scarlett cuts in grimacing.

"Yeah, please don't. Can we move on past this? As much as I love hockey, I don't want to talk about it all the time," Harry says, taking a swig of his beer. "Let's play truth or dare."

All the girls look at each other and smile.

"Ugh," Scarlett groans. "Been there and done that. Not the smartest idea with this bunch."

"Why not?" Harry asks, clearly oblivious to the 2021 Christmas Incident.

"Because it brings out a lot of shit that no one needs to know about. Like how, Scarlett had *relations* in the business classroom and how these two can't keep their hands off each other," Kennedy explains with a waft of her hand in our direction.

"That is not true," Wren retorts, sliding off my lap and trying to sit beside me but there isn't much space so half her leg is still on my thigh anyway. She pulls her hands in between her thighs and squeezes them together. "See?"

"See what? That you can last two seconds without making out," Kennedy says back, raising her eyebrows. "It's got a *lot* worse since you came back."

"I second that," Scarlett announces.

"Me too," Xavier and Grey say in unison. Grey stands up and saunters towards the kitchen, no doubt to raid my fridge. He's going to be disappointed when he notices that Wren threw out all of our junk food. He fiddles with the speaker and changes the song to *'Save your tears,'* by the Weeknd.

"Whatever. At Christmas, it was a dare. It's not like we were doing it for no reason," I say looking over to Wren who has got the biggest smile on her face.

"*Exactly*. At least someone agrees with me." She points at me, wiggling her finger in my face. Instinctively, I gently bite at the end of her finger, and she laughs, sliding back into my lap.

"You two are impossible," Scarlett grumbles, slouching back in her seat

"Okay," Harry draws out, looking at me and Wren before turning to Kennedy. "Kennedy, truth or dare?"

"Didn't we just say we're not playing that?" Wren asks, bending over me to look over at Harry.

"Yeah, *we* are but not with you two," Harry replies nonchalantly, returning his attention to Kennedy. Wren nods and snuggles herself deeper into me. "Truth or dare?"

"Truth."

"If you could have three wishes, what would they be?" We all start laughing at how starkly different this question is compared to Evan's ones at Christmas. Kennedy rolls her eyes, pushing her long curly hair over her shoulder.

"I'd wish for endless film in my camera, endless supply of ice cream and… a little person, like an assistant, that can tell me endless conspiracy theories, so I'd never run out." Kennedy lifts her chin up and grins.

"That was a boring answer," Harry says.

"It was a boring question," Kennedy challenges, raising her eyebrow. Harry shakes his head with a light laugh.

"Why are they all endless?" he asks.

"What would be the point of having wishes for them to run out?" Kennedy responds but Harry shrugs. "Greyson! Truth or dare?"

Grey leans in the doorway of the kitchen, giving Kennedy *that* look that he does when he's trying to flirt without really flirting. "Truth."

350

Kennedy pulls her bottom lip between her teeth, thinking for a moment before saying, "What is one thing I don't know about you?"

"How much time I spend thinking about you," Grey drawls. All the girls gag. Hell, I do too. "I'm kidding, Ken, jheez. Anyway, it turns out Evan is not the only child prodigy. I play piano, too."

Scarlett's eyes widen. "Evan plays piano?"

Grey nods. "Yeah, he was born into like me. But, he takes it a lot more seriously. I do it to impress the ladies." Grey winks at Wren and she snorts.

"Thank you, Grey, for that pocket of information about Evan that I can now use against him," Scarlett replies, beaming. I swear those two will kill each other one day.

"My pleasure," Grey replies before shifting his attention to me. "Davis. Truth or dare?"

Wren looks up at me, her green eyes dancing with mischief.

"Dare," I say, turning back to Grey. He quickly chugs the bottle of water that has materialised in his hands.

"Pick a vegetable," he demands.

"What?"

"Just pick one," he retorts.

"Uh, celery?"

"Ooh, bad choice, Davis," Grey tuts. He goes into the fridge, rifling around for said vegetable before he holds up a celery stick. He throws it to me and I catch it with one hand. "Since your beautiful girlfriend, here, threw out all your good food, you can brush your teeth with that and see if she'll kiss you. And if Wren is as-"

"Careful," I warn, "how you finish that sentence, Grey."

351

He shakes his head laughing. "Just brush your damn teeth, Davis."

I do as he says, feeling disgusting as the green stick rubs against my teeth. The girls look at me in horror and Wren laughs, finding joy in my pain.

"You are *not* kissing me with that mouth, Miles," Wren demands, holding her finger in my face at a distance. I make a pouty face at her and she grimaces.

"Baby, you're forgetting that theres a million different ways I can get you off without my mouth. But trust me, you'll be begging to kiss me by the time I'm done with you," I whisper for only her to hear. The second I move my face away from hers, her cheeks inflame.

The game continues around us as Kennedy asks Harry, "Truth or dare?"

"Dare," Harry replies, leaning forward to look at her better.

"Awh, I was kinda hoping you'd say truth," Kennedy sulks, a smirk playing on her lips.

"Why?"

"So, then I could as if you were single or not." Everyone, except those two, exchange glances, smiles creeping up our faces. I knew there was something going on with those two.

"Smooth, Ken," Wen mutters under her breath when Scarlett looks at her with wide eyes. I look over to Harry whose mouth has almost dropped to the floor.

"He's single," I say. "*Very.*"

"This feels like a perfect opportunity to play seven minutes in heaven," Xavier suggests, trying to stifle his laugh. "Should we spin a bottle? I'm not playing, obviously. I'm quite happy with my balls the way they are."

"We don't need a bottle," Kennedy says happily as she stands up. She waltz's over to Harry and grabs his hand, as he blinks up at her, pulling him somewhere that I don't want to know.

"Do you think that's a good idea?" Scarlett asks quietly. "I'm in real protective older sister mode."

"He's a good guy. He's a little much but he's okay," I say, reassuring her.

"You better be right," Scarlett says, pinning me with a Kubrick stare. "Or I'll kill you."

I raise my hands in surrender as Wren smiles and stands up in front of me. She turns around to Scarlett, her ass in my face.

"Leave him alone. Kennedy can handle herself. She completely flamed a guy at Coachella last year without our help."

"I forgot about that," Scarlett laughs.

"What's this Coachella story?" Grey shouts from the kitchen.

"That a story for another time," she shouts back before she pulls me up from my seat. "I want to see if what you said is really true."

Everyone groans as she drags me up the stairs to my bedroom.

CHAPTER 36
WREN

Coming to the rink now feels different. Weird.

It's like I've forgotten what I used to do it for. At the beginning, it was for me to have fun because it seemed cool. Then it was for my mom, because she wanted me to. She wanted me to be a star for her. But today, for one of the first times in a while, I'm skating for myself. For fun. With Miles.

"I don't know how I feel about this. I feel weird," he stutters, turning around on the ice almost falling over. I spin and turn effortlessly just to show off.

"That's because you're used to trying to kill people while you skate," I reply. "Sometimes you just need to relax, y'know?" He glides towards me in his jeans and baggy sweatshirt, as he grabs my hands while he spins me around. He has awful balance. It's like trying watch Bambi on ice: both adorable and ridiculous at the same time. I can't help but laugh when he pulls me in and skates backwards as if we're doing the hokey pokey.

"You're right," he says when he lets go, sliding down the rink seamlessly. "This *is* fun."

"I'm always right," I say with a smug grin, gliding in the opposite direction.

If it wasn't empty in here, I wouldn't have been able to hear him charge up behind me as he wraps his arms around my waist. He pulls me into him until my back is flush against his chest. He kisses me lightly just below my ear where my pulse is hammering. He sends rapid kisses across both sides of my neck.

"What are you doing after this?" he murmurs into my skin; his proximity and warmth makes me shiver. There is something so wildly comforting about being with him like this.

"I'm, uh," I stammer when he bites my earlobe. "I've got to go to my mom's house. She said it's an emergency, but I have to come *exactly* after three."

My mom sent one of her very ambiguous messages this morning. I've slightly been avoiding her since my performance. When we went to Palm Springs, I had an excuse not to talk to her but now after being back for almost a month, I have to turn up to whatever she needs me to. I'd like to request your attendance at my house this afternoon. It's vital that you attend. Do not arrive any earlier than 1500 hours. And because she's the strangest person I've ever met she signed the text message with Yours sincerely, Melanie Hackerly.

"Boo. I was going to coax you into coming over to my house," he groans. "Do you know what the emergency is?"

"No but I'm going to find out. And don't you have practice, like, now?"

"I do."

"Then why aren't you there?" I ask, turning around to see him.

"Because I want to be here instead," he whispers. He kisses me softly on the lips and I mould into him. He moves his lips

355

around mine and I gently bite at his bottom lip. I laugh and pull away.

"You need to go to practice, and I need to get going anyway," I say, skating towards the exit of the rink. "I'll see you tomorrow."

"Wait!" he shouts after me when I sit on the bench outside the rink. He stumbles out of the exit and sits down next to me.

"You told me to remind you about the sports achievement evening this weekend – so this is your reminder."

"Oh shit, yeah," I say, kissing him on the cheek for the reminder. "Thank you, Milesy. I'll order a dress tonight. I wouldn't want to miss you fangirling over NU alumni."

*

I walk into my mom's house and it's eerier that I thought. I half expected her to welcome me with a dramatic monologue in a candlelit room but instead it looks creepier than usual. Creepier than the fantasises I made up on the way here.

I've always felt off being here since the divorce. I know it's never been my home in a sense but something else hangs in the air.

"Mom?" I call out but nobody responds. I walk through the kitchen, and I can't see anybody. I wander through the living room and the den and still, nobody is there until I get to the dining room which leads out to the backyard and pool.

I spot the back of my mom's blonde head first, stood next to one of the lounge chairs, staring out to the pool. When I get closer, I hear another voice, a female voice. I slide open the door, walking carefully out onto the patio.

"Austin?" I ask, my voice suddenly sounding miles away.

Sure enough, my gorgeous brunette older sister turns around. Her heart shaped face is luminous. She's always had flawless and striking features, but this pregnancy has given that a whole new meaning. It's even more jarring when I haven't seen her in person in years. I can hear my heart thumping against my ribs. *Dum, dum. Dum, dum.*

She gives me a side glance before turning back away from me. "What are you doing here?"

"You're late," my mom interrupts, not looking up at me either.

"I'm not. I was trying to find you in the house. You could have told me you were out here."

"Oh, so this is my fault?" she replies. I almost laugh at her absurdity. Why does she always make it difficult to deal with her? She has always been one for the dramatics and to make things seem worse than they are. I make the brave decision to take a seat next to them, while Austin still stands away from me.

"What's going on?" I ask cautiously.

"When were you going to tell me that Austin's pregnant?" My mom's piercing blue eyes stare into mine and my breath catches. I've been avoiding it in hopes that Austin would tell her. I don't know how this has been flipped on me.

"It slipped my mind. I'm so sorry," I say wearily. This is starting to feel like an ambush. My mom gives me a long look without saying anything, just letting her gaze sink into me before walking back into the house.

What the fuck is going on?

I'm left alone with Austin, and I don't know what to say. We haven't spoken since she told me she was pregnant. The same day that she told me *I* had to tell mom. That I had to carry the weight of that secret and accept the repercussions.

357

"I asked you to tell her and you couldn't even do that, Wren. I had to fly out here and tell her myself. I told you that I didn't want to do that," Austin turns to me, showcasing her small bump. Her voice is steady and more dejected than angry.

"I'm confused as to how this is *my* fault. You're a grown fucking woman, Austin. You shouldn't have asked me to tell her in the first place," I say back, sounding more bitter than I intended.

"I was going to figure it out. I told you to just do one thing for me. Do you have any idea how I awful I feel? I could barely stomach the look of disgust on her face," Austin retorts, her sad brown eyes flickering over me. My stomach jolts and I start to feel the nausea kicking in already.

"How do you think I feel after having to keep that a secret on top of everything else? I worked my ass off for the showcase so I could tell her, and she didn't even see the whole thing. She didn't even say that I did good but she somehow managed to let me go away for a week. I don't get it."

"Wren," Austin says thickly as she comes to sit down next to me. The slight anger that was in her face has softened as she takes me in, her shoulders relaxing. "When are you going to realise that that's how she is? She can tell within the first minute of a performance if it's going to go well or not. That's how she's always been."

I don't know when I started crying but I did. Everything is crashing down on me so quickly that I don't have the time to process it. Hot stupid tears rolling down my face. Maybe it was seeing my pregnant sister for the first time. Maybe it was because I feel trapped in a confusing confrontation. Or maybe it's the words that are coming out of my sister's mouth are the kind of thoughts I've spent so long trying to avoid. The ones

358

that creep up at me at night and lay next to me, but I've trained my brain enough to forget them.

"If you know that, why are you still doing ballet? Why do you care so much about what she thinks?" I ask.

"That's the way I've felt my entire life and I can't get rid of that feeling — to constantly crave that validation from her. To make it up to her for not being able to skate like she did. When you're put on that kind of pedestal from so young, it's not easy to just snap out of it. I'm too far in to change my career path now. This is what she's made us believe. To only have this one choice. I thought that you knew that," Austin explains. She reaches out her hand to me, rubbing her thumb over my knuckles. I can feel my hand shaking under her gentle touch.

"I need to go," I whisper. "I can't…"

"I know it's hard to hear, Wren, but you need to be tougher if you want to survive in this world. She's not going to be your harshest critic. There will be people a lot stricter than her. If you want something, if you want to skate, regardless of your reasons for doing so, you need to learn how to hold your head up." Her words sound like daggers straight to the heart, no matter how gently she attempts to say them.

"I want to be able to do things that make me happy without feeling the need to please her. I'm sick of doing it for her and not myself," I admit.

"You'll find out the reason you're doing it soon. If you weren't doing this for yourself, you wouldn't be in this deep. There is a part of you that wants to do this for *you*. And that's the part that you need to hold on to. You're her last chance at hope. Her last chance at a legacy."

Her words weigh on my brain as if I've been watching too much TV. I've known that. Of course, I have. It's all she would talk about when we were kids. Some part of me hoped that if Austin succeeded – which I thought she would – then I wouldn't have to try as hard. I could be good enough for myself and that would be enough.

I made bets with myself. If Austin won her competition, I could come second in mine. If Austin didn't succeed in school, I could be fine too. If Austin could balance her relationship with her work, I could too.

"Why do we have to do this, Austin?"

"Because. She's our mom. She's hard on us but she's given us everything. Even if they're not what we wanted, it's what we have." Austin looks at me with kind eyes, understanding and sympathy laced within them.

"You should have just become a chef," I whisper under my breath. She laughs and the noise almost shocks me hearing her laugh for the first time in years. Her smile reaches her blushed cheeks as she shakes her head lightly.

"Well, since I'll be staying at home when the baby comes, who knows what could happen," she says, rubbing her stomach as she looks down at it. "They say anything happens when you're pregnant."

"You seem calmer than you did on the phone," I murmur.

"I've come to peace with it. I'm happy. Excited, even," she responds.

"Do you know what you're having yet?"

"A boy," she says, turning to me with a grin. My heart doubles in size. "Thank God for that, right?"

"I'm so happy for you, seriously. Dad is going to be over the moon. And I'm going to have a nephew!"

"Yep," she says. "We're thinking of moving back here too. Well, maybe not Salt Lake but closer."

"Really?" I don't bother to hide the excitement in my voice. As much as she can be hard to deal with, I've missed having my sister around. She's the only close family I have here other than my parents even if she's only visiting.

"Yeah. I've missed you, Emmy. I know we weren't the kindest to each other growing up, but this baby has really made me rethink it all. I want to be closer to you."

"I would really like that."

After a much needed catch up with my sister, she stays on the patio when I walk back into the house. For a second, I feel like I'm floating. Hearing what she said about our mom was hard, but it had to be said. There had always been some unspoken rule between us that we could never admit what we were doing our sports for. We pretended to ignore the rants that mom would go on as to how her life was ruined when she first fell in love with dad and got pregnant with Austin.

As kids, it wasn't something we could laugh about. It was a cautionary tale. Something for us to learn from. It wasn't anything we could just joke about because it really was our whole lives. We trained, we preformed and that was it. There was no reason to sit and look into it. By the time I realised what was underneath it all, Austin had already gone to college, and it felt like it was too late. As if bringing it up would start either and argument or a revolution.

When I get to the kitchen to walk out the front door, I'm stopped by my mom.

"I'm disappointed in you Wren," is the only thing I can hear her say. My eyes adjust to the kitchen counter, and I can just about make out my mom's figure. She's sitting with a glass of wine, staring out into the front yard through a sliver in the blind. Yeah, this is how all my nightmares start.

"Oh, really?" I retort sarcastically. She scoffs before taking a large sip of her drink. There is nothing I love more than my mom when she's drunk. Kidding, of course. She is the *worst* when she's drunk.

"Since you've been hanging out with that boy something has changed in you. You would never talk to me like this."

After the day I've had, I don't bother to hold back on my candour. I don't usually like to air out my shit like this, but it needs to happen. There's no use for us to hide this anymore. There's no reason for me to be up her ass 24/7 and let her control every aspect of my life like she has been for the past nineteen years.

"That's because I was afraid of you for so long. I was so scared that you'd stop loving me if I did something wrong. Like you did with dad. But he didn't even have to do anything. You just stopped. No explanation. That was it and you never told us why. I have spent my whole life trying so hard for that not to happen. I thought that if I did my best, if I made you happy in some way, you wouldn't stop loving me."

I take a deep breath. I don't know when I got so close to her; when I could start to smell the wine on her tongue, but I did. She looks at me for a moment, as if contemplating which direction to take. She avoids my eyes when she speaks next.

"You're starting to sound bratty and selfish, Amelia. You seem to be forgetting who paid for all your skating outfits and who pays for half of your rent. Yet you and that boy were so quick to take that vacation, knowing you were lying to me."

"Does that even matter anymore? Austin is happy. Can't that be enough?" I huff. "Listen, we're grateful for the trip but we didn't ask you to do that. You're the one who got us that hotel so you could try to make me forget about how much you hated

362

my performance. Like you do every time. The same thing with the flowers. In some pathetic way for you to apologise and make yourself feel better."

"It *was* abysmal, Amelia. I was not going to lie to you. You needed that sort of feedback for improvement. You need a backbone. If I was hard on you *all* the time, then you would stop skating. I need to find a balance somewhere," she slurs. I've never seen her get this bad before and it's starting to make me feel sick. My heart beats loudly in my ear as I try and keep my cool.

"I can't listen to this anymore."

I turn out of the door as the sun starts to set. The days are short here and the nights are long and dark during the winter. Regardless, I kick my jog up into a sprint as I try to get out of her neighbourhood. I don't know where exactly I'm going. I could have got back in my car, but I don't think I'm able to sit still with all this adrenaline rushing through me. I must have been running for almost an hour by the time I can see my apartment from where I'm stood panting. Instead, I turn left down towards the houses near campus.

I run up into the cul de sac and I see his house. I run up the steps and knock on the door.

CHAPTER 37
MILES

"Wren?" I pull her inside from the February chill and wrap my arms around her cold body. She stands lifelessly in my arms as she cries, breathing heavily. "Wren, what's wrong? What happened? Are you hurt?"

She looks up at me, but she doesn't say anything. My heartbeat triples in pace when I take in her sullen expression. Her face is completely red, and her eyes look tired and dark from crying. I keep my arms around her as I bring her further into the house. I take off her coat for her and she slips it on the hanger, not fully looking at me.

I walk with my arm around her as I take her up into my room, without saying anything. She sits down at the edge of my bed, looking up at me, her mouth twitching into a frown.

"I think I'm going to throw up," she groans before rushing off into my en suite. I run in after her but she's already retching over the toilet. I kneel down next to her and pull back her hair as she finishes throwing up. She coughs and sighs over the toilet.

"I'm sorry. I'm sorry. That was so disgusting," she whispers as she sits down on the floor next to the toilet seat, pulling her knees to her chest. She tries to make a joke but her laugh sounds forced. "How the tables have turned, huh?"

I laugh quietly as I scoop her into my lap while I lean against the bathtub. When I move my hand over her forehead, brushing her hair out of her face, she's quiet as she melts her body into mine.

The slower my hand moves, the softer she starts to cry again with her shoulders shaking. I sit there with her, not sure what to say to make this better. I've always been awkward in these sorts of situations. The pain in her voice makes my chest tighten and I wish there was a way that I could take away all of her hurt. Her cries settle down after a while and her breathing steadies.

"Can I take a shower? I need to brush my teeth too," Wren says between sniffles as she moves from out of my lap to sit next to me. "Can you get my clothes?"

"Of course," I whisper, and I kiss her on the head.

I go into my room and look into my drawer that now has some of her clothes mixed in with mine. You wouldn't guess how many thongs have ended up in my laundry in the last few weeks. I pull out a shirt and some shorts and go back into the bathroom.

She's still on the floor so I reach out my hand and pull her up. Her face is still soaked with tears, but she seems better than she did when she came through the door.

"Are you going to be okay? Do you want me to help you?" I ask, trying to find some way to be of use to her as I shift from one foot to the other.

365

"Miles," she says softly, shaking her head. "I think I can take a shower on my own. Thank you for offering, though. I will definitely take it up another time." She tries to laugh again but it doesn't sound like her own.

I pace my room while she takes one of her long showers. At the rink this morning, I had a feeling that seeing her mom would put her down. She never talks about her like she is her mom. She talks as if she's more like her coach – an inconvenience. After meeting her dad, I couldn't imagine how he was married to Ms Hacks for so long when they seem so different. Mr Hackerly is a kind and a very fun person. Someone who just let her be a kid.

It makes me think that I'm too hard on my mom who has always supported me and never pushed me to do something I don't want to do. She's let me live. No matter how hard I make it for her.

I stop my overthinking and sit down on the bed when the warm air from the bathroom hits me. She comes out of the en suite in shorts and a t-shirt, her hair damp and dripping on her shoulders. I still haven't got used to her in my room like this. Like she belongs here. She sits down on the bed next to me, crossing her legs.

"Do you want to talk about what happened?" I ask, bringing my hand to her back. She doesn't say anything for a while, but she looks fresher.

"Austin came back," she responds quietly, staring at the dresser in front of her. "My mom knows that she's pregnant and even though Austin is happy about it, my mom has found a way to put all the pressure onto me. If Austin doesn't go back to ballet after the baby comes, all of her focus will be on me."

"Jesus, Wren. I'm so sorry." My heart aches for her. If I could take all of her pain, I would do it in an instant. I know how hard she works and sometimes it can't be enough for her. Or her mom.

"You don't need to be sorry. It's just my messed-up family," she replies. "Even now when she's five months pregnant she's still trying to please her. How fucked up is that?"

"That is really messed up but that doesn't mean that you have to. You need to do things for yourself, not for her."

"I know," she says under her breath. "I just don't think it's that easy. I found skating fun when I was a kid, when I was doing it with my friends without the pressure of trying to win a competition. But after doing it competitively, I don't think I could skate anymore without thinking about how to do better. It's, like, wired in me.

"I know it's stupid but I keep constantly trying to do my best, hoping that if I am the very best at everything, then she won't have a reason to stop loving me."

"Wren, you need to be happy. You are not responsible for making somebody else happy. You need to try to find some way to make yourgoals actually *your* goals," I suggest. She turns to me, a small smile on her lips.

"This is me trying, Miles."

She looks at me for a long while as if her eyes are telling me to trust her. Telling me believe that she's able to pick herself back up. As if she needs to let me know that this isn't her first time having this conversation with somebody. I just hope she means it.

"I'm proud of you."

She blinks at me. "You don't need to say that, Miles."

"I do," I say, "you don't *need* me to say it but I want to, okay? I haven't known you long but I don't need to to say that you are the most brilliant person I have ever met. And I-" The words get stuck in my throat and I swallow them. "I think you're spectacular. And I hate that you think that your mom is going to stop loving you for not doing your best. Because you, just existing is enough."

She wraps her arms around me and it feels like it's the first time she's really hugged me. She holds on tight to my shoulders and I squeeze her lower back, pulling her into me as I whisper, *I'm here.*

"You have no idea how much that means to me," she muffles into my neck. *I do,* I want to say, *I do.* She holds onto me tight before pulling back, trying her best at a real smile.

"Enough of this sad shit. Do you want to order food? I'm hungry," she rambles as she flops back onto my bed, clutching her stomach. I don't push her on the sudden change of subject. I pull my phone out of my pocket and open up UberEATS.

"Are you sure? You just threw up," I ask. She nods, pulling her hair out of her face. I try and ignore the streaks of red I can see in her eyes. "What do you want to get?"

"Uh…I don't know," she says, biting her lip.

"You *just* said you were hungry."

"I am," she says defensively. This always happens with her. She complains about how hungry she is but can never make a decision about food.

"Okay, then. Burgers?

"Too many calories."

"What happened to wanting do things for yourself?" I groan as I lean over her. I kiss around her face and her neck rapidly. She tries to escape but I kiss her faster and she laughs, moving up and down the bed.

"I am," she squeals again as I start to kiss her collarbone. "I want to do things for myself but, that doesn't mean I want to mess up my diet right now. I work hard for the body you're so clearly obsessed with."

"That's true but I don't want you to feel like you have to stick to it for me," I say, pulling away from the kiss. Her soft hand moves to my cheek, her thumb stroking beneath my eye the way that I like.

"I don't stick to it for you. I do that for myself."

"Okay, good," I reply as I kiss her again.

*

After completely demolishing our order of ramen, Wren and I lay in my bed, as we let the bloating settle. We put on her favourite movie *'Easy A'* while we waited for the food to arrive, but we hardly watched it while we ate so we're restarting it. In fact, she begged me to restart it because, *apparently*, it's not the same watching something while you're hungry.

Her leg is hooked around mine as I lean on the pillows behind my head to see the TV. For someone who could barely look at me a few months ago, she's hella clingy. It's like we have to be touching at all times. Even after she forced me to restart it, her head is on my chest and she's not even looking at the screen as she stares at the material of my shirt as her nails run up and down my arm.

"What are you thinking about?" I ask, trailing my finger up and down her spine.

"You want the honest answer?" she mumbles into my shirt. "Honesty, always." She shifts in her position and moves to look up at me. Her soft smile turns into a sexy, evil smirk as she climbs onto me. I don't ignore the twitch in my dick when she leans forward, her hands on my chest and her breath falling close to my ear.

"Just thinking about how much watching you eat ramen turns me on," she whispers before kissing my throat. I bring my hands to her ass, squeezing her softly before she gasps quietly in my ear.

"Oh yeah?"

"Mm hmm," she murmurs, her voice sultry and quiet on my ear. "All I could think about was how badly I wanted your mouth on me. On every." She kisses my throat. "Inch." She kisses me again. "Of my body."

I shift beneath her touch as I move my hands from her ass up to her waist under her shirt, my hands spanning her ribs. I can make what she wants to happen happen.

I lean up onto the headboard, her legs on either side of me. Her eyes look greener today as she studies my face before diving into my mouth. I push back with force when her hands come to my hair, pulling, and yanking at my curls. I don't bother to hide the sounds at the back of my throat when she slips her tongue into my mouth. It's warm and welcoming and salty. I break away from the kiss, panting as I move my hands further up her shirt and fuck me. She's got nothing underneath.

The second my hand contacts her breast, she shivers, almost laughing. I run two fingers over her nipple, teasing and rubbing as my mouth explores her neck and her collarbones. She rocks her body into me, her shorts rubbing against my jeans as her tits fall into my hand. She makes a low sound of approval when my hand squeezes her nipple at the same time I bite at her neck. "Take it off," she demands with her eyes closed. I do as she asks and pull up her shirt over her head. I could get drunk just by looking at her before me. She looks down at me, but my eyes are focused on her chest. "Are you going to keep your clothes on or what? This feels like a very unfair game of strip poker."

I laugh as I arch forward to pull my top over my head. Immediately, Wren's hands and mouth are all over my chest and my body as she makes her painful journey towards the part of me that is throbbing. She connects eyes with me as she licks from the top of my chest through the middle of my abs.

God, she could undo me just like this. Her hands reach the button of my jeans, and she unbuttons them without breaking eye contact with me. She moves her hands to my hips as she pulls down my jeans and I help her my lifting up my hips a little. When I've got myself free from them, she places her small hand over me on top of my boxers and I hiss.

"You said you wanted *my* mouth on *your* body, not the other way around," I manage through a shaky exhale.

"It can wait."

"No," I say back as I push myself up from beneath her and instead turn her around until she's under me. Her back lands on the bed with an *umph*. "It can't."

I crawl beneath her legs, and she nudges them open for me as she props herself up onto her elbows. Every time I go down on her, she has to watch. She has to watch the way I work inside her, the way I'm straining and the way she jerks beneath me. I spread kisses below her bellybutton to savour the moment. I know she gets frustrated when I take too long. How she looks

371

at me expectantly, her chest rising and falling with impatience. What she doesn't know is how it turns me on even more.

After a long journey from her breasts back down to the line of her shorts, I finally hook my fingers into the waist band of both materials and slide them down her legs. Just as I expected, she's bare and glistening, waiting for me.

"Do you have to take so long every time?" Wren asks with a groan as I stare at her.

I laugh, nudging her thighs apart even further. "I won't touch you at all if you don't stop with the attitude. Got it?"

She nods her head obediently. I slowly drag my finger between her wetness and instantly she gasps, and her hips move forward. I take my time to run my thumb over her swollen clit while my other hand teases at her entrance, not going in just yet. I can feel my dick jerk when I carefully push two fingers inside of her and she moans. Loud.

I tease her repeatedly without fully pushing in. I push just in and then back out again slowly. I use my other hand to continue rubbing around her sensitive part as my fingers move in and out of her. I take my hand off her clit to make room for my tongue as I circle around her, tasting her.

"Fuck, Miles," she cries, gripping onto the sheets, her heels digging into my back. "Oh my *God*."

I pump in and out of her faster, my tongue moving around her quickly. Her legs open and close around my face as she tries to make some sort of movement between us. Wren starts to roll against my fingers as one of her hands come to my hair, pulling my face further into her. I move my tongue over her faster and her legs tighten around me.

"Miles…" she pants and just by the way my name sounds on her mouth, I slow down what I'm doing to make this last longer, knowing she's close. "Don't stop."

Gingerly, I pull my fingers out of her and she looks down at me, her face red and puffy as she frowns. I bring my fingers to my mouth, and I suck on them slowly, tasting the sweetness of her. She whimpers, her legs still clenching and unclenching around me.

"We're going to finish at the same time, baby," I say as I crawl up the length of her, kissing along her wet thighs. Her face is still in shock, but she reaches to my bedside drawer and fishes a condom out of it, handing it to me. I rip it open with my teeth before standing off the bed to take down my boxers and roll it on.

I climb back onto the bed and her legs are still open, so I kneel between them. I lean over her to kiss across her bare chest and she murmurs. I take my time fitting each of her tits into my mouth and she wiggles beneath me. She feels so perfect. So good. So mine. I make my way down to her pussy again as I line up my dick to her entrance. Even though she's so fucking wet, I take my time to tease the tip at the entrance, sliding up and down without pushing in.

"Miles. I swear to God, if you're not inside me in the next five seconds, I'm…"

Her words turn into loud moan when I push inside of her. I draw back slightly as I feel the way she tightens around me then I go back in. Deeper. Harder. I push myself into her as she screams out expletives.

"Can you be a good girl for me and keep your pretty mouth quiet?" I ask through ragged breaths, remembering that my roommates are probably home, as I place my hand over her mouth.

Each time my name leaves her mouth in that muffled, whiny voice of hers, I push in harder, and her hips meet my every thrust. Fuck trying to savour it. I want the sensation to surge through me right now. I have to move my hand from her mouth to grip onto her waist to keep her from sliding up the bed as I lean down to kiss across her chest and her breasts.

"Why do you feel so good?" I groan into her skin. "I don't understand it. You just feel so fucking perfect, baby."

"I don't know," she laughs through a sigh, the sound rolling off me like a wave. I pull out of her and then go back in slower which only makes her moan again. I push just in and just out, gently teasing each inch as she grips onto my forearms. I look down at her face; her eyebrows pained together with pleasure, and it destroys me. I start to push in again. Faster. She wraps her hand over her mouth to stifle her moans like I told her to.

"Good girl," I pant as I feel the climax ripping through me, while I watch her force herself to be quiet. "I'm going to—"

"Me too."

My thrusts become sloppy as I come while I'm inside her and the feeling is obliterating. The orgasm hits her in waves as she stills beneath me before clenching around me and gripping onto the sheets beside her. She jerks and twitches beneath me when the sensation starts to settle down as she breathes in heavily. I press a kiss to her stomach before disposing of the condom and collapsing beside her.

Instinctively, she hooks her leg around me, pulling us even closer.

CHAPTER 38
MILES

We spend the next few days in one of those heavenly hazes where we're doing nothing and everything, just lost in each other's presence. I don't know we quickly became this. Us. How we so easily fit together like this. We spend the days with our friends, talking shit about whatever's on the rotation for the week. We take millions of photos to post online which are instantly met with comments like, You're my OTP, How do these pics keep getting cuter, and I'm so jealous. And I fucking love it.

"Do you think you'll get an award?" Wren asks, coming up behind me in the mirror while I brush my teeth. She's wearing my shirt and nothing else as she bends over me to pick up her toothbrush. I watch her in the mirror, and it takes all I am to grip onto my toothbrush instead of her.

"Considering how I've been on the bench, and I've only just got back on the team, I'm not expecting to," I say through a foamy smile before spitting and rinsing in the sink. I move behind her as she nods and places her toothbrush in her mouth.

I wrap my hands around her stomach and rest my chin on her shoulder, watching the way her smile creeps up her cheeks while she tries to smother it with her toothbrush. "Do you think you will?"

"Maybe. I don't know-" she mumbles. She takes the toothbrush out of her mouth and pauses, looking at me. "It's not like Darcy has many options."

"You're the best skater on the team, Wren," I say. She pauses the toothbrush at her mouth before shaking her head and finishes brushing her teeth. I move to the side of the sink, leaning against it while she rinses.

We have spent a lot of mornings like this. It makes this whole thing feel even more surreal. I knew that being in a real relationship with her would be fun and exciting, but I didn't expect to feel this overwhelming sense of calm and tranquillity when she's around. She moves to stand between my legs, her hands roaming up and down my shoulder as she studies me with a strange expression.

"You're biased because we're sleeping together," she pouts as if she's just remembered what we were talking about. I bring my hands around the back of her bare thighs, pressing her closer to me.

"Oh, we're just sleeping together? I thought I was your boyfriend," I whine sarcastically as she pushes me in the shoulder. I grip onto her waist as she leans into me, and I inhale her scent.

"Since when?" she asks, kissing along my jaw until she gets to my ear as she whispers, "It's interesting how you're always *begging* to hang out with me, *begging* me to stay over here, *begging* to fuck me, but you've not had the decency to even ask

376

me to be your girlfriend. If anything, I'm still faking it to qualify."

"Is that what you want? You want me to beg you to be my girlfriend?" She pulls away from me and drags her lip between her teeth and nods at me in that sultry way I have spent every night since I've met her thinking about.

In one swift motion, I turn her around until her ass is against the sink. Her green eyes search mine as her eyebrows furrow when I don't say anything. I lift up my shirt on her and run my hands from the back of her knee up to her ass and she gasps when I grab it. Her eyes don't leave mine as I slowly lower to my knees, bunching the shirt in my hands. I leave long kisses on the insides of her thighs as she grabs my hair in her hands, twisting her fingers between each of my curls.

"I want you to be mine, Wren," I whisper into her skin as I inch further up her thighs until I'm almost at where she's waiting for me. "I want you to scream my name when I make you come. I want you in my bed every night. I want you and anything you're willing to give me. I will do anything to get you to be my girlfriend."

The only response I get is a small whimper when my mouth meets her pussy in gentle kiss. I don't do what she's expecting me to do and instead I kiss further up until I'm at her stomach before kissing back down her right thigh. Both of her hands come to each side of my face when I sit back on my heels. A huge grin splits across her mouth as she shakes her head disbelievingly.

"That wasn't so hard. Was it, baby?"

*

Whenever Wren tells me to pick her up at a certain time because she'll 'definitely be ready by then,' I automatically add another fifteen minutes onto the time because she's *never* ready by then. Even now as I'm waiting in my car outside her apartment, it's been thirty minutes since the time she said they would all be ready. Wren is taking Scarlett as her plus-one so I can take Kennedy - for her - as my plus-one.

Sports Achievement Evening is the one night a year where all the sports students – more than half of North U's population – can come together, get awards, get shitfaced and meet alumni that we are definitely not obsessed with. Everyone on the hockey team know the Class of '15 team like the back of their hand. Some of them even got drafted into the NHL when they left NU and our team tries out best to follow in their footsteps. We've watched all of their games on repeat to try and figure out how they were unbeatable for three years.

It's been a tough legacy to uphold but the guys and I are trying everything we can to be as good as them or even better. These events are for the coaches from each team to celebrate a few of their players for different categories. It's a good way to hang out with all the basketball, football, and soccer players – we're all so caught up in our own sports that we rarely get to hang out.

I'm about to start pounding my head on the steering wheel before I see the lights from the main doors of the apartment complex light up. Wren is the first one that I see.

She's dressed in a red satin cowl neck mini dress, her blonde hair curled down past her shoulders as she walks to me in slow motion. *When did that start happening?* My eyes travel from her smug face to her tits to her long golden legs.

I almost forget that Kennedy and Scarlett are walking behind her in equally stunning outfits until they're both pulling on the back doors of my car. I unlock them and they slide into the back while Wren sits in the front, beaming at me.

"You are something else, Wren," I breathe when my voice comes back to me. She pulls on her seatbelt while the girls snicker in the back. I ignore them and wrap my right hand around the back of her neck, inhaling her perfume before kissing her. She tastes like cinnamon and sugar. She pulls back, holding onto the lapels of my blazer before pulling me back in again.

"I see you still haven't figured out how to tie a tie, Milesy," she murmurs when she draws back. She looks down at the tie hanging loose on my neck that I forgot was there. I don't say anything while she works at the tie seamlessly, completely lost in the presence of her. Even when she's finished tying it, she keeps her hands on me, looking at me with hopeful eyes. I open my mouth, hoping that words will come out, but nothing does.

"I'm starting to feel violent just looking at this," Scarlett interrupts with a groan. I turn to her and she's pretending to stab her eyes with her acrylic nails.

Wren blinks up at me, fear slightly crowding her face as if there's something unspoken in the air which she's afraid to address. It's then that I realise that I'm falling for her. Like, really, no sign of the end kind of falling. It's a ridiculous thought and I don't know how I didn't realise it earlier. But I think she feels it too.

The campus gymnasium is filled with black tables and white cloths when we walk in. Name cards are placed on each seat of the table. The sports department take nights like these very seriously as they decorate the gym with gold and black bunting. All the teachers are dressed in their best outfits, wandering around as they pick up punch and snacks.

My leg bounces up and down in excitement as we wait at our table for the guest speakers to arrive. I know I'm acting like a complete fangirl right now, but I can't seem to care when this is one of the best nights NU have to offer. Wren's hand on my knee doesn't help the jittering even though she thinks it does. We're sitting at a table with Kennedy, Scarlett, Xavier, Michelle and Tyler and their partner Beau.

"Dude, you look like you're going to have an aneurysm," Xavier laughs from across me, in his blacked-out tuxedo. Wren's hand tightens on me again as she looks at me with a crooked smile.

"You do know that Josh Raymond is coming tonight, right?" I ask, scanning the room again. As expected, he hasn't arrived in the last three seconds. Xavier shakes his head, letting out an incredulous laugh.

"Don't act like you weren't like that last year, Z," Michelle laughs, taking a sip of her punch. "You practically shit yourself when you met Dean Mayer, and you wouldn't stop talking about it for *weeks*."

"She's got you there," Wren mutters and Xavier shrugs happily. We've all got our particular favourites for the NU Bear's team of '15. Mayer was the left defence for the team and Raymond was the centre and the captain and now they both play for the Utah Grizzlies. "I'm obsessed with your dress Michelle. Where did you get it?"

"I made it myself, actually," Michelle replies with a soft smile, pushing her braids over her shoulder. Michelle, Wren, Scarlett and Kennedy float into a conversation about fashion and a bunch of other girl shit that I don't have a clue about.

Wren keeps her hand on my leg the entire time as she talks to them, constantly reminding me she's still there while I listen to another one of Tyler's boring stories. Don't get me wrong, Tyler is one of the funniest people I know but there is one thing they can't do: tell a good story.

"And that's how I almost got arrested," Tyler ends the rant and Xavier, Beau and I exchange knowing glances.

"So, you went through that entire story – plot twists and all – just to tell us how you *didn't* get arrested?" Xavier asks, running his hands down his face in exhaustion. Tyler nods with a cheesy grin pulling at their cheeks.

"Yeah. Well, you had to know the contexts, obviously," Tyler begins before diving into another deep conversation about how things didn't happen. I float in and out of their chat, checking the door every few seconds before something in Wren's conversation catches my attention and I turn to their half of the table.

"So, how did Miles convince you to date him? I've known him since we were kids and I've never seen him so…." Michelle begins, waving her hands vaguely. I don't say anything as I try to listen but make myself invisible at the same time.

"Whipped?" Kennedy cuts in.

"Obsessed?" Scarlett chirps.

"I was going to say, 'in love' but sure," Michelle laughs softly as every single nerve in my body is set on fire. Wren's hand stills on my thigh as I turn back to the rest of the group, leaning my arm on the table to hide my face from their view while still trying to listen.

In love?

Maybe that is what it was this morning before she left. In the car. Every time I'm around her. But I can't, right? I'm too young to feel that shit. I never felt it with Emily or anything close to it. I've always known there was something deeper underneath it all, but I thought it was just purely a hyper-fixation.

As much as this can be easily labelled as love, I can't love her. She doesn't want that. The sound of her laugh catches me off guard, but I still stay facing away from her.

"That's ridiculous, guys," Wren whisper-laughs. "We have a good time. We talk, we laugh we fuck but he's *not* in lovewith me. We've only just started dating."

"You've been dating since September. I told Z I loved him, like, a month into our relationship," Michelle explains. The girls laugh but Wren's voice is quiet when she speaks next, as if she doesn't want me to hear but I do.

"Whatever. If he was in love with me, I think I'd know and I'd definitely be freaking out."

Finally, saving me from the torture of eavesdropping, the doors open and the entire gym bursts into a loud cheer. NU legends walk through the door – basketball, football, soccer, and ice hockey players dressed as if this is the most important event they've attended. They all take a seat at their designated table under watchful eyes. The screeching sound of mic feedback turns everyone's attention from their seats at the back of the room to the front, where a makeshift stage stands with Billy Carhart, the head of the sports department, behind a podium.

382

"Good evening, everyone," he begins, and we all burst into another fit of cheers. Wren looks over at me now, beaming, completely unaware of what I heard her say. I press a kiss to her forehead, and she turns back to face the front, her back nuzzling into my chest. "As you have noticed, the night has officially begun as we welcome back generations of North's sports stars. But tonight, is not about them. It's about every single student in this room for your dedication to your sport." He goes on a rant about how much he adores our commitment and how he couldn't ask for better people to be playing the sports her loves. I zone out his talk while the excitement wells in me as I itch to get out of this seat and talk to Josh. Carhart hands over to the coaches or the basketball and soccer team while they talk about two students, they're awarding their certificates to.

I pay attention when they announce the skating team's awards and all of the shyness she had this morning about her winning gets thrown at the window as she already walking up to the stage before they announce her name. Of course she knew she would win.

Everyone from our table stands up and claps for her and she throws us an embarassing smile as she receives her certificate from the podium, behind which they play her best moments on a projector.

Kennedy and Scarlett are tearing up like proud parents and I put two fingers in my mouth and whistle. She widens her eyes as she walks back down, loving and hating the attention all at the same time.

"See. I told you you'd win," I whisper to her when she's back at the table, snuggled into my side. "You are brilliant, Wren. Don't ever forget it."

She blinks up at me, tearing lining her eyes but she doesn't let them fall. She opens her mouth but nothing comes out, the same way I was earlier. Instead, she presses a kiss to the corner of my mouth.

After Nash Reading and Wyatt Denton receive their awards Carhart steps in again to give us an interval to walk around and talk to the alumni. This is my chance.

"Are you going to be okay here or do you want to come with me?" I ask Wren, only half meeting her eyes as I scan the room to check if Josh has moved from his corner of the room. My eyes make their way back to her when she places her gentle hands on both sides of my face, shaking it slightly.

"I'll go with you, but you've got to chill. He's not going anywhere," Wren whispers with a laugh, pressing a quick kiss to the side of my mouth. I take in her green eyes and my breathing begins to settle.

"It's just really important that I talk to him, you know. He was Carter's idol," I whisper back, my chest tightening and softening again. My eyes flicker over to Josh and he's standing up out of his seat, pulling at his blazer, flashing a smile to no one in particular.

"I know, Miles. I just don't want you to freak him out with your fangirling," she laughs, pushing out her chair from the table. I ignore her comment and reach for her hand as we start to walk over to his side of the room.

She squeezes my hand and looks up at me, the fairy lights in the room casting a luminous glow into her eyes. I squeeze back and my heartbeat picks up when we're five steps away from him. What do I say? What do I do now that I'm so close to meeting the person that Carter would have sold his left lung for? I inch closer towards him, trying to make this interaction seem accidental. He's dressed in a dark blue suit and tie, his black hair cornrowed down to the nape of his neck. This is what greatness looks like.

Holy shit, I'm totally freaking out.

Maybe I should have let the girls listen to Taylor Swift on the way here for good measure. She's supposed to calm nerves. *"Taylor Swift just gets me, you know?"* Wren said once. He catches my eye and smiles. Instantly, I smooth out my shirt before extending my hand.

"Hi, I'm Miles Davis, current right wing for the hockey team," I say, my voice an octave higher than I intended. Josh looks down at my hand, then to Wren who is beaming at my side, and then he shakes my hand. It's firm and sharp.

"Josh Raymond. It's nice to meet you, Miles," he says, a dimple popping out on his right cheek. Carter would be going insane right now. Honestly, so am I.

"I'm a huge fan of yours, like, truly. You've inspired so much of my team but especially me," I ramble, not knowing whether to look into his eyes or somewhere else.

"Thank you. I really appreciate it," he replies. "How's the season going? I came to see your final last season, it was insane."

"It's off to a good start. Competition is a lot tougher this year. Wait– You came to one of our games?" I ask when the realisation hits me. I'm sure I would have been able to recognise him out of a thousand clones, there's no way he came to our game without me noticing.

"Yeah, me and a few of the guys went. It was a low-key thing. We didn't want to spook you, so we kept it quiet," he explains with a shrug. "If my memory is right, you were really good.

And there was another guy. I think he was number ten. He was, like, a professional level player. Is he here?"

"Carter," I whisper, the smallness of my voice catching me completely off guard. He remembers him. Josh Raymond remembers Carter. I clear my throat as Wren wraps her arm around my bicep, silently reminding me that she's still there. "Yeah, that was Carter. He, uh, he got into an accident a few weeks after that game and he…"

"Oh, I'm sorry, man. Seriously. I only came to that game, but he was truly amazing," Josh says, his eyebrows drawing together with sympathy as shakes his head lightly. I nod in appreciation. "It's not easy to lose a teammate. How is your team doing?"

"We've all dealt with it in different ways but we're getting back into it," I explain, adjusting my collar which has suddenly got too tight. The lights in the room start to dim as the slow jazz music comes into play.

Not only is this an event for the sports students but it's an opportunity for the faculty members to remind us about the old middle school dances we would have. I don't know where this conversation with Josh is going to go but I want to find out. Wren pulls at my arm and my gaze drops down to her expectant eyes.

"We should dance," she whispers into me. I tense at the way she slowly drags her nails from my bicep down to my hand where she interlocks her fingers into mine. She smirks at me, knowing it drives me insane.

"Yeah, in five minutes," I whisper back, and she pouts, turning both of our attentions back to Josh.

"You guys should enjoy your night. I don't want to keep you from having a good time," Josh says uncertainly, tugging at the sleeve of his blazer. Wren looks up at me again, her blonde curls falling into her face before I brush them back.

"No," I say quickly. "I wanted to ask you a few things, if that's okay?"

"Yeah, if you're sure," he responds, looking between us. The music floats into a slow song and Wren squeezes my hand. I squeeze back but shake my head.

"No, it's cool," I say to Josh before dipping my head to Wren. She's got her lip pulled between her teeth the way that makes all the senses heighten. "You should go and dance with your friends."

"Fine," she grits out. I know she's pissed. She tells Josh it was a pleasure to meet him and she drops my hand with a tight smile. She turns around and struts off into the opposite direction, her ass hypnotising me as she walks away. I'm going to have to make up for that later. Josh's voice brings me back to the conversation.

"I'd like to know more about your team and Carter – if you want to," he asks, and I nod.

We float instantly into a light-hearted conversation as if we're old friends. He tells me about his stories while playing for the Bears at NU and how it wasn't easy for him to get to his position as captain. I tell him our game-day rituals. He walks me through his foolproof tactics and how to ensure a win. Talking to him about Carter feels so easy, like he gets him the way I do. It doesn't feel like we talk about him as if he's doesn't exist.

We talk about him as if he's in this room with us right now. I don't know how long we've been talking before I turn back to the crowd when the hundredth slow song plays. I scan the crowd and I spot Wren's red dress.

387

I can only see her from the back, but it only takes a few seconds before I realise that her body is pressed against someone else's.

No.

Nope.

Not happening.

My heartbeat picks up as I excuse myself from the conversation with Josh and storm over to Greyson who has his hands all over her body. There's no real way to describe the anger pulsating through my skin as I get closer to them. Grey's hands are on her hips, her body too close to his as she links her arms around his neck.

"What the fuck are you doing?" I whisper-shout, trying not to cause a scene while I push them apart. Wren looks up at me, her face red, as if she's been caught doing something she shouldn't be. Grey's a good guy. I trust him more than most guys on the team but that doesn't mean I want his hands all of my girlfriend's body.

"We're just dancing, Miles, since *you* blew me off," she says, a wicked grin creeping up her face as she tries to pull Grey close to her again. I push him back with a quick flick and he stumbles on his heels. "You were the one who said I should dance with my *friends.*"

"Just so you don't beat the shit of me, she asked me to, dude. I was planning on trying my luck with one for the netball girls but she totally cockblocked me," Grey chimes in, putting his hands up defensively. I glare at him and he slowly saunters away backwards. I turn back to Wren and she's laughing. She's fucking laughing.

"Do you think this is funny?" I ask, closing the space between us. She holds onto the lapels of my blazer to steady herself as I tower over her.

"A little, yeah," she replies through a giggle. Without saying anything else I pick her up and drop her over my shoulder in a fireman's carry, her ass wiggling in my face as she squeals. "I swear to God, if you don't put me down in the next five seconds, I'm going to call homeland security."

"You're not going to get away with dancing with one of my friends like that."

"Miles," she whisper-groans. "I'm not wearing anything underneath."

"I know," I say through a shaky exhale.

I laugh and smack her on the ass as I walk with her to our table, the crowd watching us but turning back to their dances when they realise, they'd rather not ask any questions. When we get to the table, the girls are there, talking. I grab Wren's purse from the table before turning her around so they can see her face instead of her ass.

"Can you tell him to put me down?" Wren whines. I turn her back around so they can't see her face as she pounds on my back. Michelle shrugs happily, shaking her head.

"Do I even want to ask?" Scarlett asks, shoving her straw into her mouth and taking a sip of punch.

"Wren's been a bad girl tonight, so she's needs to learn a lesson," I say with a smug grin, gripping her thighs tighter with my hand. Wren's tiny fists pound on my back again and I laugh at the amount of effort she's putting into hating this. Scarlett pretends to gag herself with the straw.

"That is the *second* time you've made me feel violent tonight just by looking at you," she groans. "Just don't teach her the lesson in our apartment. My Air Pods can only do so much for noise cancellation."

"Ha-ha," I mock before turning to Ken who has a less distasteful look on her face. "Ask Z to take you guys home, okay?"

*

"Did you really have to carry me the whole way here? I could have walked from the car," she moans when I throw her onto my bed. She scrambles back so she's in the middle of the bed and I climb up to her as she sits crossed legged, the dress only just covering her exposed thighs.

"What would be the fun in that?" I catch her lips with a rough kiss before she starts to fall back onto the bed. I've been dying to touch her like this all night. I run my hands along her thighs, coming dangerously close to her bare heat. "Jesus. Are you always this wet when I'm around?"

"I'm starting to think it's a problem," she rasps, leaning up on her elbows to guide my hand up further up her until my hand reaches where she's soaking. "Especially when you got jealous earlier. That was hot."

I brush my thumb over her clit, and she moans into my ear, arching off the bed. "I don't like the thought of you with anyone else, Wren. Do you understand?"

She nods, her heavy breathing clouding my senses.

"Call me crazy but I think I'm, like, definitely obsessed with you. You drive me insane just by looking at you. *That* is a problem," I groan into her, still keeping my hand over her wet pussy as her legs shift beneath me.

"I kind of like it. Is that bad?" she breathes biting her lip. I shake my head slowly, moving my fingers over her. She starts to sit up off the bed, her hands coming to my face where she kisses me softly. "But, Miles, promise me you won't do that again. Don't push me aside. Because I mean something, okay? And I don't like feeling like I don't."

My heart sinks a little. "I'm sorry. I got caught up and I didn't mean to do hurt you. I don't want to hurt you because you mean *everything*."

"Good. Then, treat me like it," she demands, kissing me deeply. I make the promise to her over and over in my actions and in my brain because there is nothing I wouldn't do for this girl.

CHAPTER 39
WREN

I wake up and my face feels sticky and wet. It's almost as
if I've woken up from a bad dream where I was crying because
even after I've wiped my face, it feels wet again. I wipe my
face *again,* too tired to open my eyes and it becomes covered in
wetness. But then I realise it's because I'm in a relationship
with a damn puppy.

Miles leans over me, shirtless, pressing kisses all over my face
and chest and I can tell it's barely even light outside. It's still
winter so it gets bright later in the day but the fact that I can
hear the faint chirp of birds is not a good sign.

"What do you want from me?" I groan, trying to push him off
me but he continues to kiss my face.

"I want you to get up," he demands between kisses.

"What time is it?"

"Six," he says, smiling.

"And you think that's an acceptable time to wake me up, why?"

"Because I've got a surprise for you," he sing-songs, pulling
me up into a sitting position. He pushes the hair that's stuck to
my forehead out of my face and kisses me deeply. I don't think
I'm ever going to get used to this feeling. The overwhelming
sense of calm that I get whenever he's around.

"Oh that makes this so much better," I say sarcastically when I pull apart from him.

"It's going to be worth it."

It better be.

I drag myself up out of his bed, still wearing his shirt and his boxers. He watches me as I get up and I realise that he's already half dressed. His hoodie hangs on the back of his chair at his desk and his jeans are unbuttoned. What am I missing?

"Why are you already dressed? How long have I been sleeping for?" I quiz and then I gasp dramatically. "How long have you been watching me sleep for?"

"Stop asking questions and get ready, woman," he challenges, throwing a pillow at me.

He follows me into the bathroom, watching as I brush my teeth. My hair is in desperate need for a cut and since I've been borrowing the hair products that he uses and it's making my hair more wavy than usual. Miles leans against the sink, crossing his arms as he watches me apply moisturiser to my face, rubbing it in slow circles.

"In case it isn't obvious, you need to hurry up," he presses. I glare at him and his smile widens. "Please?"

"Why? Where are we going?" I ask through a mouthful of toothpaste. He laughs at me and shakes his head. I spit out the toothpaste and rinse my mouth, turning to him. "You can't rush beauty."

"You're beautiful every day without even trying, baby," he says seriously, wrapping his arm around my waist to pull me into him. He kisses me on the forehead. "Now hurry up. Kennedy and Scarlett are already on their way there."

That gets me excited. Whatever Miles is up to involves my girls so I already know that it's going to be a good day. Even if I've had to wake up at the buttcrack of dawn to see whatever it is he's surprising me with. I finish getting ready, putting on my favourite blue jeans and white sweatshirt, not exactly sure what I'm dressing for.

Miles doesn't really do surprises. I don't either. So I know that this must be special. When I meet his impatient ass downstairs, he's already waiting by the door, my tote bag on his shoulder, ushering me towards him. I pick up my pace and meet him at the door, no idea what I'm walking into.

*

"No way," I say for the fourth time.

"Yes way," Miles says.

"No. Freaking. Way," I say again, punctuating each sentence with a push in his arm.

"Yes way," Kennedy and Scarlett scream in unison. Miles grins at me, rubbing his arm as if I really hurt him.

"I think I'm going to pass out," I say, needing to find something to hold onto. I step back from the curb, careful not to turn myself into roadkill and I inch closer towards the bookstore. It feels like I'm dreaming. I must be because there is no way that I'm standing outside the indie bookstore that I've been dying to go to since I heard it opened. There is also no way that Scarlett got us all tickets to a book signing with Jasmine James.

"Do you think it was worth waking up early for?" Miles asks.

"Yes! If you had told me that this is where we're going I would've got up way earlier," I say truthfully.

Jasmine's first book came out at the same time that I had finally started to get deeper invested in writing. It was a perfect fluffy romcom that she wrote about her and her now husband. It gave me the inspiration to finally pursue my writing more seriously and it gave me the opportunity to find writing communities online and other books like Jasmine's. Since then, I've been following every release she's had and all of the books that are coming up. I even convinced Scar and Ken into reading her books and they have also become obsessed. I didn't think she'd come here for her book tour for her latest release, 'The Stars and You.'

"What do you think she's going to reveal this week?" Scarlett asks, looking down the queue. It turns out we weren't the only ones with the idea of coming here early because there are people in front of us, even some people in tents, probably been here for hours. The store opens in less than an hour and we've been here for almost three.

"Why would she reveal something?" Miles asks, clearly oblivious to the kind of author Jasmine is.

"You know how Taylor Swift releases easter eggs before releasing a song or an album?" I say and he nods. I've been teaching him well. "Jasmine does a similar thing. She has a segment at the end of the book signings where she answers questions and usually, she'll say something that will link to her next release. Sometimes it's just a few words and others it's a whole sentence full of easter eggs."

"And you guys find that entertaining...how?" he asks.

"You just don't get it," Kennedy says, waving him off. "This is our Joker."

"Right..." Miles says, looking between us. He pulls me into him, wrapping his arm around my shoulder. "Why are you so warm? It's freezing."

"It must be all those extra curriculars you put me through before we came," I say, teasing him as he pulls down my beanie further. He smiles at me. One of those real, Miles-type smiles with dimples and crinkled eyes.

"Oh, so that's why you took so long," Scarlett says, nodding. "Makes more sense."

I don't even bother to make a snide comment at that because all I really want is to be sharing my warmth with Miles in this weather. As scary as it was to commit to this relationship, I've started to realise that he has become one of my best friends. He listens to me and does the most insane things just to see me smile. And I would do a thousand insane things to get him to smile too. He's become my favourite person to talk to and the first and last thing I think of each day. As scary as it feels to throw myself into this, I'm glad that we've established a friendship before so it feels less daunting.

I know exactly how Miles felt meeting his idols at the Sports Achievement Evening because that is exactly how I feel walking into the bookstore, knowing that my favourite author is in there. Excited, nervous and a little bit sick. If I had known we were coming here, I would have prepared some questions beforehand. What do you say to someone who basically saved your life without knowing?

The bookshop is small with a deep rustic vibe to it, blue bunting hanging from the ceiling and a huge lifesize cut out of the cover of Jasmine's new book and a stack of signed editions.

It's a weird feeling meeting an author. Often, you forget that they're a real person, putting every single emotion you've ever had into words. And you also forget that they have a real face with real feelings and a very real personality.

We're all anxiously waiting for our turn, Kennedy and Scarlett switch places in the line to have a better look at Jasmine at the front of the queue. Even Miles looks nervous, his arm hung around my shoulder as if it belongs there, tugging me tighter into him as if we aren't close enough already.

"Do you know what you're going to ask her?" Miles asks me.

"I have no clue," I admit. I turn to look up at him, brushing his dark curly hair out of his face. "What do you think I should ask?"

"Well, it's not like she's a genie or something. Or is she?" he asks, raising an eyebrow. I shake my head, laughing. "Then just something you feel like you could use advice on. Since she's older and wiser and all."

"That's true," I say, biting my bottom lip as I nod. We start to move down the queue and I start to feel the nerves in my stomach. *She's just a regular person like you. Don't need to freak out, Wren*, I tell myself. "You guys go first."

Kennedy and Scarlett turn to me, clutching their copies of 'The Stars and You' to their chest. "Are you sure? You're the one that introduced us to her."

"Yeah, I'm sure. I need to mentally prepare myself," I say, taking a deep breath and switching places with them so me and Miles are behind them. "I'm fine. I'm not going to freak out." Miles laughs, rubbing my shoulder. "You keep telling yourself that, baby."

When Scarlett and Kennedy move to the side after their turn, they give me a huge thumbs up, trying to prepare me for one of the best moments of my life. I thought that nothing could top the week that I had with Miles in Palm Springs but this moment is coming in close second. Miles tells me that he's going to stand over at the side with the girls, giving me a moment alone with Jasmine.

I get to her desk and oh my God, she is gorgeous. Of course I've seen pictures of her online but she's not one of those very public authors. As much as she likes to share snippets of her personal life with her husband, it's more pictures of him than it is of her. She has fantastic long ginger hair and unlike her Instagram pictures, she's sporting owl framed glasses, similar to the ones I use when I read. My hands are practically shaking as I place the book down on the table as she smiles up at me.

"Hi. How are you?" she asks, resting her forearms on the book and her whole attention is on me.

"I-I'm great. My boyfriend and my friends surprised me with this so I'm doing great. How are you? How are you finding Utah?" I ask. Great. Word vomit. Exactly what I need right now. I clear my throat.

She laughs quietly, opening up the book to the first page. "It's a lot colder than I thought it would be. Honestly, I don't know what compelled me to pack for a summer trip," she says, shaking her head.

"It can be very deceiving," I say back.

"Who am I signing this for?" she asks, picking up her black marker.

"For Wren," I say, hating how childish I sound. She nods.

"I told myself that I wouldn't ask everyone this but do you have any burning questions? It can be about the book or about life in general. Are you a writer?" she asks, excitedly and I'm taken aback about how chilled out this all feels. All that freaking out I did is borderline embarrassing.

"Sort of," I say with a shrug. She nods understandingly. "I do want to ask something, though. You can totally ignore this if it's stupid but I just want to know if you know how to do something even if it's scary. To put yourself into something that could possibly turn out to be a shitshow." I gasp at myself. "Sorry. I probably shouldn't swear in front of the baby."

She laughs at that, rubbing her stomach. "Trust me, you should hear the amount of curse words Ida's dad uses. It's not going to be any different with this one," she says, pointing at her small bump. "Anyway. What are you worried about turning into a shitshow?"

I sigh. "Everything," I explain. "Mostly a new relationship."

Jasmine smiles faintly, she gestures for me to come closer to the table and I do as if she's about to tell me a secret.

"Sweetheart, I met you…what? Two minutes ago? And I can

already tell that that boy over there is head-over-heels, Blake Lively and Ryan Reynolds kind of in love with you."

I don't mention the fact that we have never said those words to each other. That this is all still new. We're practically still in the honeymoon stage. Instead, I ask, "How do you know that?"

"Because his eyes have not left you since you've been in here," she says flippantly. I turn to him then, catching him standing next to the girls who are gushing to him over their signed copies. Like Jasmine said, his eyes are on me. He's probably listening to their conversation half-heartedly but his eyes don't leave mine. Even when I raise my eyebrows at him, silently asking what he's doing, all he does is grin, knowing that he's got me wrapped right around his little finger. "When I was setting up, I saw you two outside and I just *knew*. I knew because I've been you. I was scared to dive into a relationship with someone I have clearly been in love with my whole life. And it turned out to be the best thing to ever happen to me. I mean, he's put two babies in me for God's sake." She laughs again and I join in. "You are never going to know how it could work out if you don't try."

I stand there, pretty much motionless as I watch her write in my signed copy. I barely register that our conversation has ended by the time I get to the girls and Miles, all of them excited to see what she wrote in there but I don't open it. I tell them that I'll look in it later, not wanting to ruin the sparkle of this morning just yet.

Still, after we've all had lunch together and we've gone back to the apartment, I don't open it. Even after FaceTiming my dad and telling him about the surprise, I can't bring myself to open it. Only because I know that whatever she's written in there is going to be the only thing going through my mind for the next two years. Finally, after I've showered and I'm ready, I pick up the book.

To, Wren.
Firstly, you don't need a man to determine your worth. Gross. You can do that on your own. But when you do have one that looks at you like that and does things for you like he did today,

398

you hold him close and you keep him. Because even on your
worst days, he's going to be there for you if you let him in.
Take care, Jasmine.

I try to take in what she said. How much do you think it would
cost if I asked this woman to be my therapist? I read it over and
over and each time I get chills.
Hold him close and keep him.
I can do that.

CHAPTER 40
MILES

I've been trying to put it into words how it feels when I watch Wren perform. At the showcase it was incredible and liberating but watching her compete? A whole other level. The way she gets pissed when she thinks she's going to be late. The way she takes her hair down after performing a flawless routine. The way she gets annoyed at me when I forget to bring the right water. The way she insults me when I slip up.
It's an addiction.
"Do you ever listen to anything I tell you?" she spits, her foot in my lap as I untie the laces on her skates. We're sitting in the locker room after one of her competitions in LA which I'm sure she's won. I accidentally forgot to pack her phone charger after she told me to get it since she left it in my room. So, she's in a bad mood. Understandable. "Why are you smiling?"
"Because I like it when you shout at me. Is that bad?" I say through a grin, tapping her leg so she changes her foot. She rests her other foot in my lap, allowing me to undo her other lace.

"Yeah, you've got a problem. Get help immediately," she says, trying her hardest not to smile at me. "What are you doing later?"

"You, hopefully," I whisper and she actually laughs at that but she still waits for an answer.

"Miles."

"Wren."

She sticks her tongue in her cheek, again, trying not to laugh as her face turns pink. "I've just competed against one of the most hardcore teams in America. The last thing I'm thinking about is you putting that inside me. My body needs to heal."

"And heal it will," I say, pulling her into my lap so she can straddle me. "After I'm done with you." I kiss across her jaw, down to her neck, across the small exposed skin on her neck and she whimpers.

"We've got one more night in LA. What do you want to do?" she asks between pants.

"I already told you what I want to do," I press again, my dick twitching at the thought. She looks at me seriously. "We can stay in tonight. Your body is sore and I'm exhausted from watching you all day. My eyes can only open for so long."

She laughs and the sound runs through me like honey. "You're so dramatic."

"Only for you."

We do exactly that. We spent our last night here in the hotel room across from Coach Darcy and the other team members, pampering ourselves with facemasks as we watched Brooklyn Nine-Nine reruns. We splash out on room service, filling ourselves with pancakes and waffles until we're so stuffed, we can't even sleep close to each other, needing the space to spread out.

As much as this girl can pretend that she doesn't want me, when we get back to Salt Lake that day, she only orders the Uber to my house instead of hers, meaning she wants to spend the night. I don't mind at all. Being with her sometimes feels like it's the only thing keeping me alive. I know how dramatic that sounds but it's true. Every time I'm around her, I just want more and more and more.

401

"What's your favourite song?" she asks me out of nowhere. We're laying on my bed after one of my games, both tired as hell. Well, I'm laying down and Wren's on top of me, running her hands through my hair.

"Right now?" I ask, trying to think. She nods. "Anything by Taylor Swift...?"

"Good try, Milesy," she says, laughing. "I want to know what your favourite song is."

"Why? So we can do karaoke like we did in Palm Springs?" I ask hopefully, leaning up on my elbows.

"God, no. I'm never doing that again," she groans even though I know she loved it and everything we did afterwards. She looks at me calmly, twisting her fingers through my hair as she whispers, "I might be making a playlist for you."

I gasp dramatically. "Really? For me?" I ask, feigning shock and she rolls her eyes. "Or is it for me but not really for me?"

"Well, you know all about that, don't you?" she challenges.

"You saw it eventually!"

"Yeah, on accident," she retorts. I narrow my eyes at her.

"Where is this conversation going?" I whisper, trying to catch whatever is in her eyes. There's something hidden behind them and I want to know more. There's one last wall that I need to break down. I try and see if I can bring it down and I say, "You know you're my favourite person, right?"

That almost cracks it. Her eyes crinkle as if she's about to cry and I think I've said the wrong thing. What I'm not expecting is for her to hug me. I can count on one hand the amount of times Wren and I have hugged and it's always because the other really needs it. When we were fake dating, it was sort of an unspoken rule that hugging was crossing the line.

"You are so obsessed with me. It's kind of pathetic," she muffles into my skin and I laugh. *You have no idea how right you are,* I want to say. She draws back from me. "I hate to ruin this moment, but my phone needs to charge." I don't get to respond before she's slipped off my bed to plug her phone into my socket.

When she comes back onto the bed, I sit against the headboard, patting my lap and she sits on me, her pink summer dress pooling at both sides of me. I sink my teeth into her collarbone, my hands digging into her sides as her body presses against me. "Where were we?" I ask as I bring my hand underneath her dress, slipping further up her thighs until I get around to her ass.

"You were saying how you're so obsessed with me."

"Right. Of course," I muse, slapping her ass. "I can't get enough of this." I drag my mouth from her collarbone, across her chest to her right side. "Or this." I plant kisses across her neck, and she shivers, a light whimper escaping her mouth when I press a light kiss in the sensitive part beneath her ear. I move my hand from her ass to the other side to touch her wetness. "And this." I rub my thumb over her clit slowly. "Do you like it when I touch you here, baby?"

"Mm hmm," she murmurs, rolling over me. I can feel her wetness on my trousers, and it makes my dick twitch. Her phone chimes with a notification but we drown it out with sloppy kisses and stupid whispers. She wraps her hands around the back of my neck, studying my face before leaving a long kiss on my lips as she rolls over me faster. Her phone chimes again.

"You should get it," I pant as I look down to my bedside table and her phone lights up with tons of messages. "Wren, you have, like, a million miscalls."

"Just leave it," she breathes, still rolling over my fingers as she kisses along my jaw. I can't help but look down to her phone again which hasn't turned off yet.

She finally reaches over, pulling her phone off the wire and balancing it on her shoulder, still moving over my fingers.

"Ken, what is it? I'm kind of…" I press a kiss to her shoulders, gaining a shaky exhale as Kennedy's voice sounds muffled on the phone. They sound like they're taking in code, so I continue moving my fingers around her as she pins me with a blissfully pained look on her face, still mumbling into the phone. God, this might be the hottest thing I've ever seen. "I'll…" she pants into the phone when I brush my thumb over her and she clamps her mouth shut to stifle her moan. "I'll look now. Okay, bye."

"What was all that about?" I ask when she uses both of her hands to type into her phone, not looking up at me. She shrugs

403

before throwing down her phone next to me. She dives into my neck, her hand curling around the nape of my neck as she starts to bite and suck me. "Fuck." I groan when she bites just underneath my jaw but my voice sounds hoarse. "Wren. Stop. That. Shit. You're going to give me a hickey."

She laughs against my throat. "Good."

"You're insane." I still haven't got used to this. This utterly bizarre feeling that shoots through my body when her mouth is on me. Her phone lights up again beside me. She groans as she reaches for it, finally looking at whatever people are spamming her about.

"Fuck me," she breathes, staring down at the phone.

"Okay," I say cheerfully, pulling her even closer to me but she doesn't budge. When her eyes meet mine and I can tell something's wrong. She doesn't look at me like she's about to kiss me again. She doesn't look like she's going to make a witty joke before unbuttoning my jeans. Instead, she looks at me with pain and hurt in her eyes.

"No, literally, Miles. This is so fucked up," she whispers, looking down at her phone then back up at me.

"What happened? Talk to me."

"Do you remember what you were doing in Palm Springs, the day of our flight home?" I shake my head and shrug. I remember getting wasted in the middle of the day and some old lady had to drag my drunk ass to the hotel. "Yeah, I thought not."

"Wren, what's going on?"

She turns her phone to me, turning up the volume but I can already read the subtitles. It takes me a minute to register the video that's playing out loud. Of me. That day in the bar. I start to feel sick. I look up at her and she's not looking at me.

"Shit. Wren, I'm so sorry. I didn't know what I was doing. I was out of my mind."

"I've… I'm…. I've got to go."

What the fuck have I done?

404

CHAPTER 41
WREN

Have you ever wanted to know how many times a nineteen-year-old girl can cry in a week? Apparently, a lot. Since I've met Miles, I've had more emotion breakdowns than I've had my whole life. That's a lot compared to the week of my first skating competition when I was six.

When Kennedy called, I thought she was trying to tell me about more comments on our posts, trying to shield me from the mean ones, like she has been for the past few months. But the softness in her tone told me immediately that was not the case. Naturally, when I started to watch video, I also started to freak out. I knew I couldn't be there and listen to a lame-ass excuse when I was so torn up about it. The constant tightening and anxiety developed into nausea, and I had to leave. When I get home, Kennedy and Scarlett are already there with wide arms, ready to spend the rest of the day trying to help me forget what I saw. What everyone else has seen by now.

"I'm so sorry, babe," Scarlett says, bringing over a cup of hot chocolate with whipped cream and marshmallows. My favourite. I hold the cup between my cold hands and take a generous sip.

"Tell you what it is? He's a Leo. It's the *only* thing that makes sense. Do you know what his rising is?" Kennedy asks, eating dry Cheerio's in her beanbag. I roll my eyes and try and rack my brain to remember it.

"I think he's a Leo rising but I don't see how that's-"

"Hmm," she cuts me off, looking at me thoughtfully. "Double Leo? Not good."

I laugh a little at her adamancy and Scarlett throws her a strange look before moving to turn to me on the couch. She props her leg up and leans against the headrest.

"How are *you* feeling?" Scarlett asks.

"I don't know, honestly."

That day after we slept together for the first time, I knew running away was a bad idea, but I had to clear my head. It was everything I could have wanted but it was also frightening. Taking that step with someone isn't just an easy thing. Especially when you're in a fake relationship. I didn't expect to find him drunk in the middle of the day with an old lady. The last thing I thought is that he would spill all of our private information to a hype-thirsty teenager.

Mason Greer has been trolling the internet for the past two years and everybody across the country knows who he is. He used to post embarrassing videos of kids in a grocery stores and Karen's in malls but then he started to get high off the fame and started humiliating anything and anyone. Any opportunity he got to make a meme and to blast someone online, he went for it. He's exposed many cheating scandals at schools he doesn't even go to because people are stupid enough to talk to him, to confide in him, and not expect him to post about it. There are only a few pictures of him online but he's not very distinguishable.

In the video, Miles is sat in the bar, clearly unaware of who he's talking to and he's babbling. About me. At first, I thought it was fine. Sure, it'll be a little embarrassing but sort of cute. But then he couldn't stop talking and showing pictures and videos of us. Pictures and videos that I thought were only between us. In most of the photos, I have some sort of clothing on but in others I might as well have been naked. It was fine when I heard him speaking about our relationship, how fun it was and then he said that he loved me.

He said that he loved me, but I didn't love him back.

He said that I was incapable of doing it and made it seem like I was this evil monster who didn't love this sweet puppy back. We've been back in Salt Lake for over a month now, but the video only surfaced now because people started to identify him, and it spread around NU. I would have been fine if I didn't look into the comments to see what people were saying about me and about the situation.

MeganDraya45: Who wouldn't love hi? He's so sweet.
BradenMoutbatten99: Who's the girl? The pics are hot.
HSLOT224LIFE: OMG! He's so cute. He needs to dumb his gf ASAP, no Rocky.
TayTay34: She must be insane not to love him. I don't even know him and I'd protect him with my life.
NathanGrey12: I'm starting a petition to get him a new gf.

"If anything, this is more embarrassing for him than it is for you," Scarlett says.

407

"Is it?" I reply, laughing. "This whole thing makes me look like a bitch. The pictures were a little embarrassing but it's not as bad as Miles saying that I'm *incapable* of loving him."

"Well, do you? Love him, I mean," Scarlett asks cautiously.

"I don't know. I like being around him, sure. I like talking to him and the sex is fucking fantastic, but I don't know if love is the right word. Love means dependency, it means commitment and it's something that could tie us together. I don't know if I want that."

"Sounds like love to me," Kennedy sighs in a strange country accent.

"So, what are you saying? Don't you want those things with him?" Scarlett asks sceptically.

"I guess but not now. We work well together as friends, first and foremost. The physical stuff is fun and it's exciting but I'm just afraid that if this merges into one thing it'll fizzle out. We'll burn ourselves out."

"Only way is to try, my love," Scarlett says.

"How can I try after this? No one is going to take me seriously again. I already went down after nationals and qualifiers are coming up," I ramble, talking with my hands.

"Yeah, no distractions for Amelia," she says in a gruff haunting voice. She salutes me and I nod back at her.

"That's right," I say proudly.

"Even if it is with someone you really *really* like," Scarlett murmurs.

"But that *someone* is a double Leo. I, personally, would not put all my eggs in that basket," Kennedy says with a shrug.

"Yeah, and what's Harry?" I challenge while she chews on more Cheerio's.

"How are things going with you two? You've been very secretive about that," Scarlett asks curiously, turning away from me. Kennedy pauses her chewing, making a silly face before continuing.

"Things were doing okay until he gave me the ick," Kennedy shudders.

"What did he do? Is he a double Leo like Miles?" I say hauntingly.

"He's an Aries which makes sense. But the ick is worse than that," she groans, throwing her head back.

"Oh gosh, what could possibly be worse," Scarlett says rolling her eyes. She nudges me with her foot to look at Kennedy who has pulled her wild hair into her face. "What is it?"

She makes a loud groan as she moves the hair from her face before sitting up, looking at us with reddened cheeks and furrowed eyebrows. She crosses her arms, painting on a serious expression.

"So, we were in the den at his house, playing ping pong. Because I'm such an amazing player, I completely caught him off guard and the ball went flying over to his side," she begins before screaming into her hands again. "Then he chased after it. Like, on all fours, scurrying after this tiny ball. It was tragic." Scarlett and I look at each other before we burst out laughing till my stomach hurts. It feels good to laugh like this. The reason why Kennedy has stayed single for so long is because she can be turned off by guys so quickly. The second she seems them do the walk back from bowling or holding their nose when they jump into a pool, she's completely uninterested. To her, once she's got the ick, there is no turning back.

"You're so dramatic," I say when my laughter settles.

"I'm not! He's lucky I didn't get up and leave. It was repulsive," she replies with a shudder.

*

I thought I could see the future. I thought I could see all the bad things happen. I did for a while – I saw the bad things coming but I luxuriated in them regardless because how good it felt. I did it because it was something new, different and an incredibly exhilarating feeling to be with him.

But then it stopped working.

Even when I helped him get better in Palm Springs my worst-case scenario was that he would get caught underage drinking *not* that he would overshare to Mason Greer. I don't care that I was half naked in some of the pictures. I don't care that he slurred about us having sex. I only care that he said that I am incapable of loving him or anyone. Just because I don't believe in something, and I don't want to purposely experience it doesn't make me unable to do it.

That is what upsets me the most when I get into bed that night. When all the lights are off, and the only light is coming from my phone where the video plays on loop as I scroll through the comments. It's then that it all comes crashing down on me.

He is the one who told me that I wasn't insane or crazy for being afraid of love. He made me feel like it was okay and that he could accept that even in our fake relationship. He comforted me and told me I didn't need to be scared and that it was a practical thing.

For as long as I could remember, I've felt that way about love. Since my parents' sudden divorce, love didn't feel like this sacred and out of reach thing to aspire for. It felt like a burden that I didn't want to bear. It felt like a watered-down emotion that people have been holding on to for centuries to make their relationships seem more serious.

I had a feeling in the back of my mind — the sort of feeling I tried to suppress over that week — that he wouldn't be able to accept it. I was more shocked than anything when he acted like it was fine. Augustus made sure that I knew it was a weird thing to feel. That it wasn't natural.

A large part of me hoped that Miles wasn't like that – that he would still care for me in the same way. It was his subconscious talking that day at the bar. It was what he really felt but didn't want to tell me. There is no denying the attraction between us. The constant pull towards each other. But that had always existed within our fake dating plan even when we tried to ignore it. It needed to be acted on and we were both willing to dip our toes in for a second. What I didn't expect to find lingering in there was love which is the last thing either of us need.

He's the kind of distraction my friends encourage but the kind of distraction I can't afford to pursue.

CHAPTER 42
MILES

Have you ever been so completely drunk that you end up talking to the gossipiest person in the world? Because I have. It's just my luck that the morning after I have the best sex of my life that I would run into Mason Greer in Palm Springs while I was out of my mind. After moping about how I thought Wren had hated me, I royally fucked up the last bit of trust that Wren and I had built. I had only just asked her to be my girlfriend – for real – and she's already gone.

When I sobered up later that day, all I remembered was talking to Emily and this guy came up to me. I only remembered his face blurring around the edges. I do remember thinking he was Carter. He had the same soulful eyes as him and deep tanned skin. He looked harmless. Maybe it was all the alcohol I had but I could have sworn he sounded so much like him too. That's why it was so easy to talk to him. It felt like being at the rockery again but with someone to speak back to me. I didn't notice the phone in his hand though.

WHINY GUY COMPLAINS OVER GF WHO DOESN'T LOVE HIM ON NEW YEARS DAY, the caption read on every reposting account. Somehow, someone managed to identify me and spread it around NU. It's one of the first scandals I've ever been involved in, and it doesn't feel good. It was torture when Wren left a few days ago and I went downstairs to Evan and Xavier laughing at me. It got worse when I had to go into class with everyone snickering as if I wasn't there.

If it feels bad for me, it must me a million times worse for Wren. It had to come out at the worst possible time for her and for us. She has all the drama with her family on her back as well as competition season. It's the last thing she needs to deal with right now.

Hearing the video play on repeat and watching myself in a moment that I don't remember is weird. It's like I'm floating outside of my body, out of control of all the stupid things I said. "Dude, this situation sucks but you've got to admit that's it's a little funny," Evan mentions for the hundredth time in the last week. "I mean, you're fucking *crying* in the video."

That's pretty ironic coming from him but I don't say anything. He would kill me if he knew that I know about him and Catherine. We're sitting in the living room, eating Chinese take-out in front of the TV. Xavier and I had a game earlier which we won, luckily. It was a lot tougher than our first game and without Wren there it felt strange. I don't know why a stupid part of me thought she would show up when we haven't spoken since she walked out.

"It's embarrassing is what it is. For the both of us," I say, running my hands down my face.

413

"This sucks, we know it does, but these things blow over. People will find the next thing for them to obsess over. We need to get through playoffs into the finals and we need *you* on our team," Xavier says, patting me on the back. "We only just got you back."

"I know, Z. You're right. I need to speak to her about it," I sigh, stabbing some chicken with my fork.

"What is there to speak about? Just say sorry and move on. It's not like you said you hated her. In fact, you said the opposite," Evan suggests before shoving noodles into his mouth.

"I know but I shouldn't have said it, that's the thing," I explain with a huff, running my hand through my hair.

"Why not? Did you not mean it?" Evan asks curiously, poking around his chicken before looking up at me.

"No, I did. I just don't think me saying that, in that state, is a very smart move for our relationship. Especially when we've just started dating."

"You've been together since the end of September, right?" Xavier looks at me when the words leave Evan's mouth. *Shit.* I almost messed this up even more. I forgot that he doesn't know that it was fake up until a few weeks ago.

"Right, yeah. Regardless, I know how she feels about love. It's still too early to say things like that, y'know," I reply with more confidence.

"Whatever it is, Davis, text her, talk to her, fuck her. Whatever you need to do to get back into the game," Xavier says sternly, pining me with a stare. I roll my eyes and pull out my phone, waving it at him and he drops his smile. I owe it to him and everyone on the team to keep my head on right while we compete this season.

I pull up Wren's number and shoot her a message.

414

Me: Hey. Can we talk?

Wren: Yeah. Florentino's tommorow at 3?

Me: That works. See you then.

*

I thought that waiting until Wren showed up would be the most torment. Though, it felt mostly self-inflicted since the guys forced me to go in early so I could look prepared even though I'm completely shitting myself.

We've never had an argument; we've never had a real reason to ignore each other for days. We have always had this underlying friendship between us even when we started fake dating. It was something undiscussed. We just worked. Even when she pretended to hate me at the beginning, I could tell that underneath it all, she wanted me or to be friends with me, at least.

What I wasn't expecting was Wren to come in, sweaty from working out with an angry look on her face. I also didn't expect it to turn me on so much. Her deep red facial expression is giving angry mom vibes which — come to think of it — I don't hate.

I definitely didn't think she would be completely silent after she slipped into her seat. I don't know where her head's at and I don't know where mine is either. All I want to do is be with her, to have her even with all these complications.

At the same time, I say, "I'm sorry," she asks, "Did you really mean what you said?"

I jerk back in my seat. "What?"

She crosses her arms on her chest, using it more as an embrace as she glares at me.

"Did you mean what you said about me not being capable of loving you — or anyone?" she asks again, her voice weighty with emotion. I watch as her jaw grounds together.

"No, Wren, I didn't. I was drunk and it was my own insecurities and my subconscious speaking," I whisper. I place my hands awkwardly on the table, not sure what to do with them while I link and unlink them. I can't tell if I'm saying the right thing or not.

"I said what I said to you that night out of confidence. You asked me the question and I answered it truthfully. Isn't that what this whole thing has been about? Truth? If it's in your subconscious, then you must have thought about it."

"I'll admit that I was shocked. I've seen the way you read about romance, how you watch rom-coms, I just thought that you would want that eventually. I freaked out when you left in the morning and I thought that going to the bar was a good idea," I say truthfully.

I try and search her eyes. For something. Anything. Something that will tell me that we're going to be okay. But nothing surfaces. It's all darkness and cloudy as if she's shutting me out already.

"I said from the beginning to tell each other when this got too real. When things stopped feeling like pretend. Everything just went to fast."

"You knew I wanted you this whole time, Wren. I never kept that a secret," I say, my voice sounding so far from where we are. "What part of saying that 'I love you' was fake to you?"

416

"Miles." She sighs and looks down at the table before looking back up at me. "You don't love me. You were drunk and we were still pretending."

"Are you being fucking serious right now?" I ask, whisper-shouting. "You think that I risked my spot on the team by getting in a fight for nothing? Do you think that I sat with you and held your hair back when you were going through a tough time because I don't love you? Everything I've done, in and outside of the plan, I did it for *you*. Not for my fake girlfriend but because I wanted to see *you* happy."

"I never asked you to do any of that."

"That's the whole fucking point, Wren. You don't need to ask me to do anything. I will do anything for you. Don't you see that?" I retort, trying my best to cool the angry blood surging through me. "I care about you so much that is scares the shit out of me. So don't you dare tell me that that isn't love."

"I- I don't know what you want me to say, Miles," she whispers. I grab her hand and pull it into mine, curling my huge hand around hers and she stares at them.

"Tell me that you forgive me. Say that you want to make this work because you and me, Wren," I start, tugging on her hands so she looks up at me. Her eyes are dim as she takes me in, swallowing. "We're real."

She stares at me for a long moment, as if everything between us have just been blips in time. As if everything we have shared and been through together don't carry the same weight as they once did. I swear I see in her face the second she makes her decision.

"Remember when we said we'd tell each other if it got too much? Well, it has."

The beating in my chest starts to slow before it picks up its pace again, hammering so hard against my chest that I feel like it's going to burst out. My hearing is solely focused on the beat of my heart as Wren's face in front of me starts to fade away. Is this what it feels like to die? Because it fucking feels like it. I try and take in a few deep breaths to steady my heart rate. I can't lose her. I can't keep going on without her. She is the only reason I got back up. She filled that uncomfortable hole in my chest that was taken away when Carter died.

You.

You.

I just want you, my heart screams.

"What?" I ask thickly.

"I don't this is a good idea anymore. We did what we needed to do for the contract. My team is doing okay with support and you're in the season," she starts with a sigh. "When I'm with you, Miles, I can't focus on anything else. This got too real, too quick for me and you know where my priorities lie."

"Didn't you say you wanted to do things for yourself or was that all bullshit?" I know it's a low blow and it's petty but it's not that easy to not take what she says to heart. How she can try and discard my feelings for her as if they don't mean anything.

"I *am* doing this for myself. We both know why I skate. Whether it was because of my mom or not - I enjoy it and if I have a shot of winning this year's championships, I want to go for it. With everything going on with Austin, I can't fuck this up. Not now. I've worked too hard to give up at the last minute."

"But you can give up on us?"

418

"That's not fair, Miles," she whispers, "you've experienced it first-hand what I'm like when I'm anxious. I'm going to end up pushing you away and I can't do that to you again."

"Wren, I don't care if you'd push me away," I murmur.

"But I do. We worked well when we were pretending because there were high stakes. We *had* to make it work to get what we wanted. Now, I'm sure the whole of NU has seen the video and I can't go through that embarrassment again," she admits, finally meeting my eyes with a sullen expression. Her eyebrows furrow together, and she scrunches her nose.

"Why can't you see yourself the way that I see you? I want you as you are, Wren, no matter how complicated it gets. Can't you see that?" I say, my voice sounding strangled and hoarse. Her face relaxes for a second. "This isn't like last time because I'm here. Let me be there for you, Wren. You are worth it."

"Miles, I can't-," she sighs, closing her eyes for a moment. "You can say this now, but you'll change your mind."

I don't respond. There's nothing left me to say that will get her to trust me. To get her to believe that everything I'm saying is true. To let her know that I am going to feel this way as long as we live.

How could say that knowing Wren is to love her?

I love that she talks about books, and I can't help but listen to her voice that sounds like honey. The way her smile lifts up as she talks about fictional people. The way she catches me staring and tries to tamp down her smile, but she can't resist bursting into a huge grin. *That* - along with her determination and her stubbornness - is why i'm in love with her. Why I can't wake up without thinking about her and why I'm constantly trying to find a new way to make her happy.

419

It would be unfair to say I want to keep her tucked away as my little secret because that would take away other people's ability to know her and love her the way I do.

She keeps her eyes on me for a long time, working over the creases in my face before I drop my gaze from hers.

I can't look at her. Because when I do, I feel like my heart is going to rip right out of my chest.

I keep my eyes on the table when I hear her chair scrape against the floor. I keep my head down when she stands next to the table for a second before walking out of the café.

CHAPTER 43
WREN

Trying to avoid Miles is like trying avoid a test that you know you have to take because no matter how many times I've tried to stop running into him at the rink, he manages to be there every time. It's not as awkward as it was the day after we broke up but it still stings. It hurts the most when I can hear him and his teammates around the corner and he's laughing and when he sees me he just blinks, not saying anything. I don't either. We're always caught in a moment where we're both too afraid to say something. As if it will burst this uncomfortable bubble that we've created around each other.

The last time I saw him still feels like a blur.

I forced Kennedy and Scarlett to watch me practice my routine, needing the last minute tips before the finals. They were both by the boards, watching me intently like I had asked and then Kennedy says what she's thinking, like always.

"Do you miss him?" she shouted into the silence.

"Do you have to ask me that right now?" I said back, trying to control my breathing as I turn and glided down the ice.

"It's just a question," she sing-songed, trying to play coy.

"Yes, I miss him," I admitted, the second the words leave my mouth my stomach turns. "Is that what you want me to say? That I actually miss him so much that it physically hurts that he's not around anymore. That it hurts that he's not waking me up with kisses and his terrible singing. Is that what you want me to say, Ken? Because it fucking *hurts* to even say it out loud."

They both stood there, watching me, waiting for something. Anything. And because my life couldn't get any worse, the sound of the hockey team roared in my ear as they go towards their rink. I turned to look towards the entrance of the rink, waiting for him to walk past, to look back, to have heard what I said and somehow make it better. Is that even what I want? Still, it stung like a bitch when he walked past, did a double-take and continued walking.

Now, it's been a month since then. If I had known that that would be the last time I saw him, would things be different? I don't let myself overthink it. This is good. This is good for us. It's been a month of trying to avoid him at school and my friends trying not to mention him since we saw him at the rink. Part of me wishes that he at least tried to text me. To fight for this in some way but I know he knows that I need space. That's the only way I'll be able to heal. Because this is it, right? We're done.

Unfortunately, Scarlett and Kennedy have really fallen in love with all of Miles' friends. We spent most of our time over there before the breakup and they even became some of my closest friends too. Now, the girls are trying to stay loyal to me by not hanging out with them even though I told them it's fine. It's also been a month of hard work, focusing on myself, and doing things that I want to do.

It's been a month of skating competitions and spending my afternoons busting my ass off at the practice rink on campus. I've had to travel alone to the competitions because they're always at the most inconvenient times for Scarlett and Kennedy to tag along. The first few comps were hell, but I had the girls via FaceTime and Coach Darcy by my side.

422

Darcy wasn't impressed about my latest scandal but she's holding onto hope that people will move on by the time the finals come around. I doubt that's going to happen. I've got used to the sour looks I'm given on my way around campus and the nasty comment every now and then. There's something about people at NU and their need to hold grudges.

I thought that ending things with Miles was the best idea. We were both too attached, and it felt like we were constantly being consumed by each other. It makes sense to break up. I need to focus on skating and my classes, and he needs to do the same. I spent so much time depending on him for happiness. So much time being addicted to his touch, his smell, his voice. I knew that once we slept together it would be another thing tying us together and it would make it harder to turn back. It turns out that not seeing him has made a small hole in my heart that only he could fill with his terrible jokes and even worse singing. I can't say I don't miss him because I do. So much. But this is going to be good for us. It has to be.

Not having to worry about Miles has given me some more free time. I'm still busy with training and competing but when I'm not doing that, I can have time on focus on my writing. As soon as he came into my life, I scrapped one of my dreams to focus on getting back on track. I've managed to write another thirty thousand words of Stolen Kingdom over the last month. Now, I spend lunches in between classes with Kennedy and Scarlett at Florentino's, reading over the latest chapter. I don't know how Kennedy is not sick of being here all the time when she still works here most days. We use half an hour of our one-hour window talking over major plot lines and the other half trying to study.

"You can't end it like that!" Kennedy shouts almost knocking over her coffee. A few people turn their heads and flash us a dirty look. I don't know how we haven't got kicked out yet from the constant destruction we – mainly Kennedy – cause.

"I'm not ending it like that, it's just a draft of the ending," I say, taking a small bite of my scone. "I'm open to suggestions."

"The only logical ending is that Carmen runs away and starts a new empire," Scarlett suggests with a shrug.

"Yes, that sounds better than her *dying*," Kennedy groans dramatically. "Wait, you're making a sequel, right? Please tell me you're making a sequel."

"I'm thinking about it. I need to focus on real work for class instead of this. It's not like I'm going to get it published," I admit.

"You could. I'll design a cover and you can self-publish like Gigi," Kennedy replies, almost falling out of her chair as her eyes widen. "Thirteen-year-olds would eat that shit up."

"It's a possibility but it's also a lot of work."

"Since when are you afraid of hard work?" Scarlett asks with a sceptical look. "Maybe not now but I really think you should in the future. With a bit of editing, it would be perfect. I'm sure G would help you."

"Maybe," I say, trying to mentally add that on my thousand-word long to-do list. "Anyway, I'm thinking of making Carmen fake her death and *then* run away to start a new empire."

"I hate that idea a little less," Kennedy says thoughtfully before her face lights up again. "Will she have a sidekick?"

"I'm thinking that Vita will go with her," I reply.

"Isn't she, like, a million years old?" Kennedy asks, flicking through the printed sheets of my book in front of her.

424

"Yeah, but she's in a middle-aged woman's body. She's basically like a Cullen," I say with a waft on my hand.

"Oh, *that's* cool," Kennedy agrees nodding her head. "I give you permission to end it that way."

"Why, thank you," I reply, nodding my head towards her. Scarlett pulls the paper out of Kennedy's hand and looks over it with a serious expression. They are both my harshest writing critics, but Scarlett looks more at the intricate details more than anything. Kennedy just worried about how hot the protagonist is going to be.

"So, talking about boys…" Kennedy drags out with a whistle.

"We weren't," I say with a bored tone. She ignores it anyway.

"How are things with he-who-shall-not-be-named?"

I roll my eyes at Kennedy and shake my head. They've not managed to go a week without bringing him up and the answer is the same every time, but they can't let it go. They're expecting me to just wake up one day and completely forgive him and move on. To ignore every red flag and let myself get distracted.

"There are no 'things' with him. We've not spoken, and I don't think we will for a while," I respond with a huff.

"Can't you guys at least be civil? It's my birthday soon and I want to invite his friends," Kennedy says, chewing on her bottom lip. "Obviously, if you don't want me to invite them, I won't."

"Do whatever you want to do, Ken. I've got to go meet Austin before practice," I say dismissing her. Scarlett looks up from the papers and flashes a small smile as I get up and walk out of the café.

*

After the heated conversations at my mom's house, Austin and I have been seeing a lot of each other lately while I avoid my mom like the plague. She's planning on moving to Portland with Zion but for the time being they're staying in a hotel in Salt Lake so Austin can visit us, and Zion can see his mom's side of the family.

I've done more baby shopping this past month than I have ever done in my whole life. My mom is an only child – thank God for that – so I don't have any close cousins or relatives from her side of the family. My dad has three older brothers, but they all had kids a long time ago, so I've never got to go baby shopping before and it's so much fun. All the tiny clothes are so adorable that it makes my heart swell but watching the mothers in the stores with their toddlers is just another reminder to take my birth control.

We've also been going to this new restaurant that has opened up called Juno's. It was a phenomenon in Florida, but they've started to franchise, and the food is incredible. Being pregnant has changed Austin a lot. At first, she was a total control freak but now, sat in Juno's with her maternity dungarees and wild hair, she has become more content with having a baby and I couldn't be happier.

"What are you going to get?" Austin asks, skimming over the menu again, biting her lip in concentration.

"The usual: a chicken salad."

"Do you think if I ask for a fry-up with extra tomatoes and extra hash browns, they won't ask any questions?" she asks.

"Considering your belly is the size of a watermelon, I'd dare them to."

"Okay, good." She looks through the menu again before placing it down. Austin smiles wide when the waiter comes over and asks for our orders. When she's floated out of sight, she turns to me. "Have you spoken to mom during comp season?"

"No, I haven't seen her since the first show. We were both pretty catty with each other the last time we spoke," I admit, thinking back to everything that happened that weekend. "Have you?"

She shrugs then shakes her head. "She's doing the thing where she's pretending that I'm not carrying a seven-pound baby thats going to be her grandchild," Austin laughs. "I don't mind. I just hope that she'll come around when he's here."

"I do too," I say, taking a sip of my strawberry lemonade.

"Have you thought of any names yet?"

"Zion is *obsessed* with the name Marley. Which definitely doesn't have anything to do with his undying love for Bob Marley. I kind of love it though." She grins wide when she mentions Zion.

It still baffles me how Zion has made it work with Austin with how stubborn she is. She's like me, in the sense that she trains all the time and has little free time. I remember when they first started dating when they were in high school, and Austin told me that she was going to break it off with him before she left for NU. Then they started to get more serious, and she found it harder to resist him and he was relentless in keeping them together. My mom wasn't happy about it, but she simmered down when she realised that Austin always put her work first. For them, that was never an issue.

"I think you've got your answer. I love that name too," I sigh, leaning back into my chair. I let myself melt into it for a

427

second, as I close my eyes, thinking of all the things that are going to change when the baby is here. Good things. I'll have a nephew, I'll get to see my sister more and Zion too, I'll get to watch this little boy grow up in a happy family.

"You seem sick," Austin comments and my eyes shoot open. I straighten my posture and look over at her.

"I'm not sick. I'm fine."

"No, you're *love*sick. I saw the way your face turned sour when I mentioned Zion. I can tell somethings going on in that weird little brain of yours," she explains, wiggling her finger into my face.

"I'm closer to being actually sick than being *lovesick*," I say with a shudder. She gives me a disbelieving look while she sips her water, her eyebrows raising over the glass. She sets the glass down and sighs.

"Emmy, it's okay if you miss him. This is the first time I've really seen you so happy with someone. When you were with Augustus, it sounded like you guys were bound by a business contract more than anything. Miles sounded fun. He seemed like he was good to you and he was good *for* you," she mentions, leaning back in her chair as she rests her hands on her stomach. I try not to laugh at the irony.

"I do miss him, but I don't have to. The semi-finals are this weekend and if I get in, I'll be going to the finals in two weeks."

"You need to let yourself have fun. You don't *have* to see him as a distraction. That's something you can work on. I thought the same about Zion and now look at us," she begins, gesturing to her stomach. "The only thing I'm waiting on is that engagement ring."

"You and Zion are different," I huff, waving my hands around to give myself an excuse. "Miles and I are at college. We could be going into two different paths at the end of fourth year."

"I think that you're trying to think of any excuse to let yourself be happy. I saw that video, Wren. He *adores* you. Let yourself have that."

She looks at me with tender eyes as I try and let her words marinate. I've always known that Miles felt that way about me but the part of my brain that I can't ignore is telling me that this is only infatuation. Something that can fizzle and burn out. Something that when he spends enough time with me, he'll realise he won't want me anymore.

"But... What if he stops feeling that way." My voice sounds distant and weak. Almost childlike.

"It's like you've listened to nothing I just said," Austin concedes with a frustrated grunt. "You're never going to know unless you try. Even if he does, which I'm sure he won't, at least you can have some memories together."

"I don't know, Austin. This month has been hard, but it's been productive."

"Okay, how about this? When you get into the finals, because I know you will, go and talk to him. If there's a part of you that wants him, see where his head is at and give him a chance," Austin suggests.

"A chance?" I groan.

"Yes, a chance. You need to rest and have fun."

"I'll rest when I'm dead," I mumble. With wicked timing, the food arrives, and Austin's thoughts become clouded by the smell of her meal instead of me.

429

CHAPTER 44
MILES

"**Y**ou're lucky that I haven't cracked your head open yet, Davis." Jake shouts another threat to me from the showers while I finish getting ready in the locker room. Some of the team shout a 'Yeah' in agreement and the howling begins. Again. We've just finished our quarter final game which we almost lost. It was a close tie until the last few minutes of the third period, and we managed to pull through. On top of all this unnecessary shit from the team, I've got to go to my mom's 50th birthday party later which I've been dreading all week.

*"*God, can everyone chill out? We didn't lose, in fact we did the exact opposite," Tyler says with a sigh. They nod at me before dapping me up and walking past me.

"We *almost* lost because you acted like you were out of your fucking mind," Jake spits, walking around from the showers.

"But we *didn't,* that's the whole point. Give him a break," Xavier retorts, drying himself off. Jake inches towards me, a nasty look on his face.

"I'm sick of giving poor Miles Davis a break. He needs to man up and get his head in the game," Jake shouts, squaring up to me. I'm sick of his shit. I tower over him and glare. "What you gonna do, Davis?"

"You know exactly what happened last time we did this, Callahan," I bite out. "Step the *fuck* back."

He stares at me for a minute, resisting to back down. Most of the team are now gathered around us, ready for a fight to break out. Luckily for him, he steps back out of my face and turns back.

"Listen, we've got one more game before the finals," Coach begins, standing at the door of the locker room. "There's no point trying to blame each other. All you need to do is work together on doing better. Understood?"

"Yes, Coach," we all say in unison.

A few more sly comments are thrown my way before I leave to go back home. Each game day with the team has become another opportunity for them to berate me. I've become an easy target after losing Carter. After he died, the whole team was disappointed in me but with Wren's help I was able to turn that around. For the most part, other than Jake, everyone was fine with the way I was playing. We've played well through playoffs, and I was able to get a few goals in but then Wren and I broke up. I didn't think it would affect my performance, but my mind has been so distant. It's just become another thing that I can't move on from. Another thing that I can't stop thinking about.

I knew that if I tried to stop her from leaving, she would still go. I'm a distraction for her and the last thing I want is her future being jeopardised because of me. Even when she acted like she didn't like me at the beginning, we were still hanging

431

out nearly every day as part of the contract. We were tied together in a strange way that neither of us could pull away from as much as we tried to deny it. It was an instant connection for me but for her, she could pull away just as easily. She's denying the part of herself that wants this. Us. And that is what hurts the most. Even when I try to not let her get into my head, she manages to weave her way in there and I can't focus on the game.

*

Knowing what Mrs Hackerly is like, I try and be on best behaviour with my mom. I should be lucky that my mom isn't controlling over what I eat and that she almost doesn't care much about what I do. My parent's main priority, my whole life, was making sure that I was happy. They busted their asses for me and Clara to pursue what we wanted to do. Whatever I was doing, they just wanted to make sure that *I* wanted to do it and not for any other reason. Part of the reason I started to play hockey was because I enjoyed it, but I also wanted to do it because it's what made Carter and I grow closer.

Growing up, we both discovered our love for hockey early on. As soon as we got into a junior league it was all we could talk about. Our families supported us, but Carter's older brother, Ethan wasn't happy with the attention we were getting. He was bitter and let us know that every time we were on our way to the rink. Their parents always brushed it off as sibling rivalry but there were things going on in private that Carter asked me never to tell his parents.

I stayed on the hockey route my entire life and my parents have never told me I couldn't do it or that I *have* to do it. That's why

I feel for Wren so much because even when she tries to act like she wants to do it, it's really her mom's dreams that she's trying to pursue.

As much as I'm grateful for my parents, the one thing I do not like is birthdays in the Davis family. Every year, no matter whose birthday it is, we have to have some sort of a celebration. For as long as I can remember, birthdays have always been a sacred tradition within our family. There's something about bad music and shitty birthday cake that turns my family upside down. We have stupid rituals like the cake flip where the birthday person has to flip their cake and catch it the right way around. We always do speeches and when the party has died down and it goes from neighbours to close family, we each have to say one thing that we love about the birthday person.

As a kid, *that* was always my favourite part. Maybe it was an ego thing, but it was the part I remember the most when I go to sleep that night. Every year before I moved out, my mom would tuck me in and ask what the best part of the day was. "*I liked the most when Carter said I was like his brother,*" I would say before falling asleep. It was those little things that made me appreciate my family even more. This year, for one of the first times, I have no idea what to say about my mom. I feel like a stranger.

When I get to my parents' house, as expected, the lawn is littered with neighbours and distant family, half naked kids running up and down and babies passed out in strollers. One of my older cousins work the barbecue even though we're powering through the last few weeks of winter. Kids run and scream on the front lawn, chasing each other with sticks. Old R&B songs blast from speakers through the windows as I walk

433

through lawn, stupidly carrying a bouquet of flowers and a card. The first person to spot me is my mom's sister, Whitney. She's a few years younger than my mom but she has almost a hundred kids and has not aged a day since I was born. She's a short, tanned woman with a sleeve of tattoos on her right arm, making her by far my coolest relative.

"Ay, Miles, you're almost as tall as the doorframe," she exclaims, squeezing me into a suffocating hug around my middle.

"It's good to see you too, Auntie," I say when I'm free. She squeezes my cheek with her thumb and forefinger, turning my face at ridiculous angles. "Do you know where my parents are?"

"Yes, they're through there," she sighs, pointing down towards the living room. "They're speaking to an older couple; it looks kind of private."

"An older couple?" I ask.

"Yes, I've seen them around here a few times. Your parents are speaking in Spanish if that rings a bell," she explains before rushing past me to save one of her boys from burning themselves on the barbecue.

I don't have to ask anything else because I know who they are. Carter's parents are here. Before I was born, my parents became close friends with Elena and Mateo Reyes since they lived next door and Ethan is around the same age as Clara. Growing up around them, they taught me and my family how to speak Spanish and it's become useful in so much of my everyday life. Even though they're both fluent in English, Carter's parents wouldn't let me into their house unless I greeted them in Spanish.

434

Both of our families have been standoffish with each other since the accident. At first, my parents were over at their house nearly every day bringing food the same way all of Carter's family was. It was hard in the beginning to talk about him but over time, they've become more open to talking about him and the memories that we made. My dad told me to give them a little time before I go over to see them because of how close me and Carter were so I've only recently been to see them on my own. I went a few weeks ago but the visit was short. Mr Reyes told me that it was too hard for them to see me even though it's almost been nine months without Carter.

I move into the kitchen, a little away from the living room to keep my distance while they talk. What *are* they talking about? My parents have been checking up on them regularly but why would they choose today to have a private conversation? I take a scan through the fridge to find something to eat but naturally it's filled with uncooked seasoned chicken and cold mac and cheese stocked in containers. I look through the cupboards and grab a packet of Cheeto's to snack on while I wait. I could go out and greet my thousands of cousins but they're too chaotic for me right now. I already checked that Bryan, my favourite cousin who's my age, couldn't make it from LA today so there's no point talking to all the little kids.

"Miles?" I hear a quiet voice breathe from behind me. I turn around to see Mrs Reyes, a tall woman with dark set eyes, and although she's getting older, her skin is aging well. I try and swallow my chip as she looks at me, scanning my black jeans and hoodie. She inches closer towards me, her hands shaking a little as they come to rest on my arms.

"*Es bueno verte, Tía,*" I say, my Spanish sounding so strange on my tongue.

435

"*Tú también*. Ay, you've got so big," she tries to smile but it doesn't quite reach her eyes. "How are you, *amor*?"

"I'm doing okay."

"Good. That's good," she replies, her eyes drifting away from me. "Are you still playing hockey?"

"*Si*. I've got another game until the championship," I say softly.

"That's good," she says again. "That's good." I wiggle out of her grip a little to place my hands on her arms, trying to steady her.

"*¿Estás bien, tía?*" I ask softly. She nods slowly and she opens and closes her mouth. As she takes a sharp inhale, Mr Reyes comes around the corner and he connects eyes with me. He notices what's happening and he shakes his head softly. "It's good to you see you, *tío*."

"You too, Miles," he says walking towards us. He puts an arm around Tía Elena and mumbles something in Spanish to her. Her eyes don't move as if she hasn't even registered whatever he just whispered to her. "We better get going. It's getting late."

Mr Reyes nods at me and they walk out of the kitchen, leaving me confused. It isn't getting late, the sun is still up, but I don't say anything to stop them. I haven't known how to act around them since Carter died and I don't know when it's going to get better for them. I can't imagine what it must be like to lose your child.

My parents walk around the corner into the kitchen and when they see me, they act as if I've not seen them in years. I haven't been around here since Christmas Eve, but we've spoken on the phone. Although the conversations were short, the communication has been better than it was a few months ago.

436

They both embrace me in a hug at the same time, my dad practically crushing me.

"Happy birthday mom," I declare, reaching over to pick up the flowers I got her. She looks down at them and then at me with a grateful smile.

"Aw, thank you, Miles," she responds. My dad winks at me from behind her before sauntering off to contain the raging party behind us.

"It's no problem. Are you having a good day so far?" I ask, shifting from one foot to the other.

"Oh, it's been wonderful. I wasn't expecting this many people to show up though," she says with a huff. "It's a lot better now that you're here. I'm really glad you came."

"I wouldn't miss it," I grit out. Clattering sounds behind us and my mom's head shoots back on instinct. "You better go take care of that. I'll be around if you need me."

She holds the flowers up to me and mouths, 'thank you' before following the sounds that come from behind her. I stand in the kitchen for a while trying to psych myself up to engage with the rest of the party. I quickly down a glass of punch before setting off into the depths of the house.

*

It's not until after 1 AM when the party is finally over. The only people left to clean up is me, my parents and Clara. Even though I was dreading it, the party didn't turn out to be as bad as I thought. I got to see tons of my family that came from up and down the globe for my mom's birthday.

She was constantly showered with compliments and given hundreds of presents which were mostly wine and flowers. The cake flip went well after years of practice and the speeches automatically made my mom cry. We all said something nice about her too – even me. I cheated a little and just said that I'm grateful to have her as a mom. Because I am. As much as what she did is still going to take time to heal, I'm ready to give myself that time and the space for healing.

Clara has taken the backyard to clean up and dad's taken the front. I don't know what mom has done but the living room is spotless again. I've been trying to clean up the hallways, picking up paper plates and Solo cups until I walk down the left corridor where the master bedroom is. The door to my parents' door is cracked open a few inches and I spot my mom in there. She's sat on the bed, still wearing her birthdays sash and crown as she looks through photos on the bed. I try and look without being seen, ready to walk past this private moment.

"Can you believe you were this small?" she says quietly, not looking up from the photo in her hand. "I can tell you're there, Miles."

God, I must actually breathe really loud. This is not the first time someone has been able to tell who I was without looking at me. I push down the memories of Wren and her ridiculous talent as I walk into the bedroom cautiously. I sit down on the king-sized bed, and I'm instantly reminded of waking up in here on Christmas morning.

The bedroom is filled with large boxes as if they've just moved in. It's really just a lot of childhood memories like our baby clothes, birthday cards and some of our old toys. They're both too afraid to keep them in the basement and they said it makes them feel closer to us when we're away from home. I take up one of the photos and it's of me and my dad, riding my first bike down our neighbourhood street. The memories look brighter and even better than I remembered them.

"I remember this day," I murmur holding up a picture of the first hockey game I went to. I'm in a jersey five sizes too big for me, sat on my mom's knee with hockey cap on her head.

"I do too. You couldn't keep still the whole time but *every time* I tried to pass you to your dad, you didn't want to go to him. You were such a mommy's boy," she says ruefully.

"Yeah." A wave of comfortable silence settles over us as we look through the pictures. The memories seem so close yet so far away from where I am now. I'm turning twenty in a few months and a huge part of me still feels like a kid. A huge part of me still *acts* like a kid.

"I'm sorry Miles," my mom says, snapping me out of my trance. She's still looking down at the pictures, running her finger across one of them. "I ruined this bond between us last year because I couldn't keep it a secret from you for any longer."

"I know, mom but I didn't make it easy for you either. I just thought you guys loved each other," I whisper. She looks up at me and I can see the tears lining her eyes. It's hard thinking you know someone your whole life o then realise some of it was a lie.

"I do love your dad and I love you and Clara more than anything. I made a mistake, but your dad and I found each other again. The most important thing is that we're happy now."

"Are you though? Happy, I mean?"

"More than anything. Thats all that matters."

"Yeah, I guess you're right."

"I'm always right, my love," she says and squeezes my face between her hands. "Did your team get into the finals?"

439

"Just about. The game is next weekend if you want to come?"

"I would love to," she beams. "What about that girlfriend of yours? Will she be there?"

"Probably not. She's not really my girlfriend anymore," I say, a sharp pang jolting through my chest.

"Why not?" mom asks, her hand coming to rest over mine. "I know I was a little weird that day, but you guys seemed lovely together. She was really kind."

"Yeah, she is. I just... I made a mistake, and I don't think she's ready to forgive me," I admit.

"Well, what was the mistake?" I explain to her what happened at Palm Springs and to my surprise, she doesn't judge me. Or us. "Well, take it from me, it's not easy to be forgiven. Those kinds of things take time but all you can do is prove to her that you deserve another chance."

Another chance.

CHAPTER 45
WREN

International Kennedy Day is April 20th. Mark it in your calendars because I have been forced to tell every single person that I breathe next to that this is her day. And her day only.

I don't think Kennedy has stopped talking about her birthday since the second March was over. She has always loved her birthday more than Scarlett and I ever have. Our birthdays are at such weird times. My birthday is in the midst of summer on June 16th and Scarlett's is August 19th, just before school starts. Kennedy has always had the perfect birthday. I have spent countless April 20th's with Kennedy to know that the day can always fluctuate depending on the weather. Some years it's scorching hot and others the winter chill still manages to make an appearance.

We are in for a rainy day this year so we're planning a party at our apartment. Kennedy wanted it to be a surprise, but she's been helping us decorate and organise regardless. There is something biological within her that although she loves the idea of a surprise party, she also needs to be in complete control of what happens on her day. She chose the theme, the food, the decorations, and the music. Me and Scarlett are merely the ones who have to put up the balloon arches and cover the house in silver decorations. The only part that we've managed to keep a secret are our costumes. She wanted to have a celebrity themed party where everyone has to dress up as their favourite.

Helping with the party has been a good distraction from my final competition later and everything Miles-related. I just about made it into the soloist finals against Grace Reed from Tipton College. I've had an idea for my final routine engraved in my memory since before competition season began. I always knew that I wanted to end with one of my favourite sequences where I can pay homage to multiple different figure skaters. Even now, just past eight am, I'm cutting it a little close to be at home instead of at the rink.

"Happy birthday, Kenny," Scarlett yawns when she finally wakes up.

Kennedy and I have been up for almost an hour, sifting through a photo album from high school where we took Polaroids together and a ton of baby pictures that Kennedy printed out. We're planning on hanging them up somewhere for tonight because there is no better way to yell 'today is all about me' than with millions of baby photos of the birthday girl.

"Thank you *but* my birthday wish is for you to stop calling me Kenny," she frowns as Scarlett takes a seat next to her at the breakfast bar. Scarlett sticks her tongue out her.

"Well, it can't come true if you say it out loud," Scarlett retorts, rubbing the sleep out of her eyes. "Do you always have to wake up so early on your birthday?"

442

"You only turn twenty once," Kennedy says with a grin.

"Okay, which picture says, 'I was funny and cute as a kid, but I *still* am in a *different* way?"

She holds up four pictures, but they all look the same in some way. In one of the photos, she's sat at her birthday party table at a play centre at the head of the table with a sad face. In another picture, she's sat between me and Scarlett in McDonald's in high school where she is sulking again. In the last two, she's got the same miserable expression but one at a beach in South Carolina and the other in her childhood bedroom. As much as she loves to take pictures, all the ones that I have of her, she's sulking in some way or giving me a death stare.

"I say the first one. You're the centre of attention yet you're still sad. It's so you," Scarlett says.

"You're so right," Kennedy agrees, sorting it into another pile.

"Are you two still not telling me what you're dressing up as?"

"Nope," I say, shaking my head. "You need to have at least *one* surprise."

"Okay, fine. Will I be able to recognise you though? You can't dress up as some famous figure skater because they all look the same to me," Kennedy sulks.

"I'm not telling you *anything*," I retort, my arms akimbo, trying to sound as serious as possible.

"Give me *one* clue," she pleads, flashing her brown doe eyes at me. She turns to Scarlett flashing the same expression and of course, she folds.

"Okay, just one," Scarlett begins, holding up her index finger to her as if she's a baby. "One of us is going to be one of your favourite singers and one of us is going to be one of your favourite actresses."

443

"Oh, wow, that really narrows it down," Kennedy groans sarcastically. The theme makes so much sense for her because she spends so much of her time within celebrities' lives. If I didn't know how much she genuinely adored her favourite celebrities, it would be seen as creepy.

"Let's just put these pictures up because I need to go soon," I say, stepping away from the table full of pictures.

"You're just trying to avoid telling me what your costume is," Kennedy says, squinting her eyes at me.

"It's going to be a surprise. A good one."

"I might not be the only one getting surprised tonight," Kennedy mumbles, flashing Scarlett a glance. Something unknown dances between them and I just push it off as I try to focus on what my day holds. Compete then party. I can do that.

"You guys are still coming to the show, right?" I ask, grabbing a water from the fridge.

"I get to watch you perform in the finals on my birthday that's, like, the *best* birthday gift ever. I wouldn't miss it for the world," Kennedy beams.

"Okay but if you need to leave early to come back here, that's fine too," I ramble. As much as she can say she's excited, I know some part of her is disappointed that my final competition has to land on her day.

"We're going to be there, Wren," Kennedy says, trapping me in one of her infamous hugs. "Now, go and practice."

*

I know this routine like the back of my hand. It's something I've been working on and adding to over time for as long as I can remember. Coach Darcy told me to save it for last in case I get into the finals and now, I'll finally be able to perform it in front of an audience.

The last few shows had a decent turn out although it was mainly the other teams' supporters that came. We've been up and down the state competing. Nonetheless, coach and the dean are thinking about changing the curriculum format a little to adjust to the way that people perceive skating now rather than how it used to be. It just sucks that I wasted so much time trying to boost my image for them to change their minds at the last minute. The remaining five people on my team are trying hard to work on drumming up support but it's too little too late. With Miles and I's relationship going up and down, when we were together people were more interested but then after the video came out, everyone has gone back to how it was before. I'm counting on the rest of the team to get the support back up to its standard.

As I glide on the ice, it finally sinks deep into me that this is what everything has been leading up to. All the days where I would get nauseous with anxiety and bust my ass all day, has finally paid off and I'm only doing it for one person only. Myself. If my mom wants to live vicariously through me, she can do that in the by-lines but I'm not letting her control me anymore. I've found something liberating and brilliant about skating for myself. I listened to what Austin said and I held onto the part of me that knows I'm doing it for me. It doesn't feel like I *need* to do it anymore. I simply just want to.

The rink has stopped being a prison for me to work like a hamster in a cage and it's become my sanctuary. My home. I feel most alive when I'm skating, when I'm able to let the music take me across the ice as if it's second nature. I've started skating with the girls and our friends at the public rink in town and I can just enjoy myself. I can just live. And when it stops feeling like that, I'm going to stop. I'm not going to force myself into doing it to find what I once had. When it's not fun anymore, I'll find something else. I'll have to.

After hours of practice, I go into the locker room and pull out my phone to talk to Gigi. I had to schedule an appointment to talk to my friend. She's suddenly so busy with her series and doing her online classes that I've hardly had time to talk to her. At exactly three forty-four my phone lights up with a call.

"Hi, Emmy," she says, followed by a long sigh.

"Hey, G, what's the big news?" I ask, readjusting my socks on my ankle. "If it's something to do with Mr Dixie's immune system, I don't want to know."

"It isn't," she begins with a long dramatic pause. "I got a deal with Tiger Publishing Agency."

My heart almost breaks in half – part joy and part jealousy. She has already made it so big as a semi-famous author through self-publishing, but this is different. *This* is her big break. My best friend the author. What is this life? As much as I am proud of her, I wish I could do the same.

"Oh my God, Gianna! I'm so happy for you. This is insane," I exclaim. She's quiet over the phone for a second.

"It's not insane. You were the one who told me you were sure that it would get picked up," she replies.

"Either way, it's great. I am so proud of you, Gigi," I say. "You should come to Kennedy's party tonight. It's not going to be too crazy, and we can celebrate your deal."

"That's exactly what my mom said but I'm going to stay home. We could go out for lunch soon though?" she asks quietly. I don't push her anymore on it. Growing up with her, I've always known that she would take a little longer than the rest of us to adjust to extreme social situations.

"That sounds good. I'll text you later," I say, standing up from the bench. "Wish me luck for my competition."

"You don't need my luck, Wren," Gigi says before ending the call. I push down all the jealous feelings and try to be happy for my best friend. This is it for her.

I grab my duffle bag from my locker and walk down to Coach Darcy's office. Her office is a large classroom that's been converted into an office. Even though she doesn't need all the space, she somehow managed to snag one of the coolest offices in the whole University. There was a rumour that she used to live in here because the room was so big, yet she didn't need to use up all the space for the shrinking ice-skating team.

"Hey, coach. Are you ready to go?" I ask, walking through the open door. Coach is looking at her cabinet full of trophies for the school, zipping up her coat. I've spent way too much time in here to know a story about every single trophy in the cabinet. A lot of which were won by my mom.

"Yes," she replies without looking back at me. "Are you ready? This is a big competition, Wren."

"I'm ready. I'm excited, even," I say, only half lying. The fact that I don't feel sick to my stomach is a good sign. She turns to me, her short brown her swishing over her shoulder.

"You sure?" she asks, walking towards me. She places her hands on my shoulders, squinting her eyes at me as if to study me. "All eyes are going to be on you."

"If you're trying to scare me, it's not working. I'm ready, Coach," I say bravely.

"If you say so, *chèrie*," she whispers.

*

447

I thought I would be nervous when we drove half an hour away from Salt Lake. I thought I would feel that sick feeling in my stomach as I put on my silver figure skating dress. I also thought I'd feel a little queasy when I put on my lucky skates. I thought I'd feel worse when I saw the girls in the crowd with a very pregnant Austin next to them. But for some reason I'm not. I've spent the last two months preparing for this. I've put the work in. I've had no distractions. Even when they call out my name and *'Flying'* starts to play, I feel settled. Even when I'm ready in my position on the ice, I feel fine.

I'm ready.

CHAPTER 46
MILES

I knew it was a good idea to come here. After Kennedy practically forced me to, I had no choice. Whether or not she sees me and shouts at me to get out, it was worth coming to see her preform. Every time I've been to see her, she's completely mesmerised me. I tried my best to stay as hidden as possible so if she saw me, she wouldn't freak out and I think it worked. She won. She fucking won. It wasn't a close call. It wasn't a 'she just made it.' She won with flying colours. My Wren. With a complicated ass routine to *'Flying*,' by Cody Fry. The last minute of the routine had every one of the edges of their seats as she turned and glided up and down the ice. She received a two minute standing ovation from the hundreds of people in the room when her routine finished. When they called out her name, she stood on the ice as they hung heavy medals around her neck and handed her a huge trophy. I could see Kennedy and Scarlett basically crying with happiness across from me as they hugged each other when she won. I think it was one of the first times I've *truly* seen Wren smile. Not a fake sarcastic one that she likes to throw me at my bad jokes but a real one. A real, toothy, red faced, Wren-type smile.

I just want, so desperately, for her to smile at me like *that*.

The second she walked off the ice, a huge grin still on her face, I sprinted down the steps to catch up with her. A part of me is telling me to wait but another part of me pushes forward. Maybe I should turn up to Kennedy's party and say something then, but after seeing that performance, I don't think I can wait any longer.

I get to the changing room door and without thinking properly, I push it open, the flowers I brought with me almost getting ruined in the process. Half of me was expecting her to have gone already. To have run out, leaving behind a cloud of smoke but she hasn't. Instead, Wren is sitting on the bench staring at the trophy in her hands. I don't need her to tell me I'm breathing loud when I inch closer to her. She turns around, and her face is red and slightly sweaty, her blonde hair sticking to her forehead.

"What are you doing? You can't be in here," Wren says without missing a beat as her smile drops. She stands up, placing the trophy on the bench and closing the space between us.

"You were fucking incredible, Wren. Like… So good. Congratulations." Words fall out of my mouth at a stupid pace as I try and breathe properly. This is the first time we've been this close in weeks. Long and hard weeks. I hold up the flowers. "And I- I got you these 'cause I knew you'd win."

She looks down at the pink and white tulips and a smile tugs at her mouth as she takes them. "Thank you, Miles. But seriously you can't be in here." She tilts her head up to me as I tower over her. Her eyes flicker from each of mine until they land on my mouth for a second and her breath hitches.

450

"Why not? There's no one else in here." It takes her a while to register what I said but when she has, she looks around for a second.

"That's true," she says quietly as if debating her next move. She stares at me, her eyes dropping to my chest. Her mouth twitches. "You're wearing the shirt."

"What?" I ask before looking down at the shirt I got as a joke which says, 'I heart my girlfriend.' Was it risky to wear this? Probably? But it's making her smile, so I'd do it again if in a heartbeat.

I barely register it myself as I crash my mouth into hers and she gasps, dropping the flowers to the ground. I don't know what part of my brain told me to do that, but I let myself fall into her for a second. Wren's mouth feels so welcoming, like both of ours belong together. It feels like coming home. Her hands reach around my middle, lightly gripping onto my shirt. I let my mouth explore hers quickly before pulling away.

"Shit. I wasn't thinking. I've just missed you so much. I had to see you and I'm so sorry about everything. I want you so much, Wren, and I haven't been able to stop thinking about this – us," I stutter, taking a step away from her, not knowing what she wants. So, I continue speaking. "And I know you said you needed space but I feel like I don't exist when you're not around. I'm nothing without you. And maybe I should have grovelled more or tried harder but all I can give you is me for now."

She looks at me for a moment, her eyes searching around my face as I ramble. She steps closer towards me, closing the distance I created, and she shakes her head lightly at the shirt I'm wearing before she pulls the neckline of it, drawing me in even closer. She kisses me softly once, tenderly, as if she's still thinking about it before she comes back with more force. A strangled sound comes out from the back of my throat when her tongue sneaks into my mouth without warning. I don't know how I've gone months without this. Months without feeling so complete. So, at home. When I notice my hands have been hanging at my sides, I reach up to her waist and I squeeze her tight. She gasps.

"Did I hurt you?" I mumble into her mouth.

She shakes her head passionately. "I'm just sore from practice." She walks backwards into the lockers until her back is flush against it. I use the opportunity to kiss down her bare collarbone and chest, taking my time to savour this moment again. The moment I got her back. Sort of. She whimpers softly when I bite at her shoulder.

"Miles," she pants.

"Mm." I bring my hand up to her thigh until it reaches her ass and I squeeze it softly.

"Miles, someone can come in here, like, any second," she says more clearly. I press another kiss on her collarbone and her jaw before moving off her and taking a step back. When I look at her, her lips are parted, and her chest rises and falls quickly.

"You're right," I say. I open my mouth to speak again but it falls shut when I hear the door behind us open. Gingerly, I turn around and Kennedy and Scarlett are both stood in the doorway, staring at the space between us.

"Hey, we just wanted to say congratulations, but we've got to go back home to set the rest of the things up. You're still going with coach, right?" Scarlett asks, her gaze shifting between as she speaks.

"Okay," Wren gulps. I turn back to her, and her face is still red. "Thank you and I'll see you there."

452

"Okay," Kennedy draws out before giving me an evil grin. "Miles, are you coming to the party?"

"I, uh, I don't know if that's-" I stammer, suddenly forgetting how to speak.

"Yeah, he's coming and he's also taking me home," Wren interrupts nonchalantly as if we've already discussed this. I turn to her, and I can feel my own face heating up. "You can wait, right?"

I nod until my head goes dizzy. She smiles gently as she shoo's us with her hands and we all walk out of the changing room. After Kennedy and Scarlett leave, I stand outside the door, running my hands down my face, laughing at myself at the absurdity of it all.

That's when I realise that I really want this.

I want her and her shyness. I want her and the way she blushes. I want her when she's sweaty from working out or when she's stressed, tapping a highlighter in her mouth. I want her friends to catch us making out like high-schooler and we pull apart, knowing that all we want is to be touching at all times.

I want *everything*.

Anything she's willing to give me.

*

After realising that she's going to take more than fifteen minutes to change, I stand outside of my truck for Wren to finish getting ready. I don't know what to do with myself. How am I supposed to go about this situation? I think this is her giving me that chance that my mom talked about. Even though I spent more time kissing her than asking for that chance. I had hoped that she would want to speak to me but that's as far as I planned.

Finally, she comes out of the main doors, wearing pink shorts and a loose shirt, her hair tied back into messy bun as the flowers hang out of her sports bag. She rolls her eyes playfully when I open the door for her to get in. This is the Wren that I've missed. *Who am I kidding?* I've missed every part of her. Once she's in the car, I go back around to my side.

"You didn't have to do that," she says, fiddling with the hem of her shirt, looking at the near empty car park.

"I wanted to."

We're quiet for most of the drive, not sure how to approach the elephant in the room. We've not spoken in almost two months after she wanted to end the contract and we just kissed in the changing room. I don't know if she just wants to pretend that never happened or if she wants it to happen again. With the weird side glances she's giving me, it's hard to tell. I know I have to say something when we're parked outside of her apartment and she's not making an attempt to get out of the car. I angle my body to turn to her but she's still facing straight ahead.

"Wren. I'm really sorry about the video and about what I said. I shouldn't have gone to the bar that day and I especially shouldn't have talked to a random stranger about our business," I say in one go, barely breathing.

It's better to get it all out now than pretend that we've been fine for the last two months. She looks at me now, the darkness making it harder to distinguish what colour her eyes are.

"It's okay. I shouldn't have pushed you away either," she replies finally. "I've thought about it a lot over the last few

454

weeks and I forgive you. I didn't make it easy for you when I left that morning and I've never been good at communicating how I feel. It turns out that you weren't the only one who was hyper-fixating." She laughs a little and it's the kind of laugh that could melt into my hands.

"I understand, though. You had a lot going on."

"I think…I think I was just so afraid of what *could* happen that I never gave it the chance to actually happen, y'know?" she explains, her eyes suddenly glistening.

"I get that." We're quiet for a while. Lost between a moment of quiet and comfortable silence. "Are we going to be okay?"

"I want to give this a chance, Miles," she begins.

"But…"

"But I'm still scared. I have, like, a gazillion things going on in my brain at all times and I don't know how to handle it. If I can't control it, how will this work?"

"Let me *help* you, Wren. You're so used to doing things on your own that you're pretty fucking stubborn. I want to experience life with you, no matter how bad it gets."

"I want that. I want to let you in." She places her hand on mine, holding it tight without breaking eye contact with me. I feel so at home in her hands. Like nothing else matters other than us in this moment right now. "Thank you for coming today."

"Thanks for not shouting at me," I say. She laughs and pushes me in the shoulder. Then something takes over her face. The lines in her face crease slightly as it becomes hard and worried. "Shit, Miles. What about your games? Did you get into the finals? When is your last game?" she asks frantically.

"The seasons over, Wren," I mutter solemnly. The memory of our last game runs through my mind on a loop. I'm surprised

I've not thought of a reason to bring it up until now. "My parents even came to the game."

"What? That's great but I can't believe it's finished already."

"Yeah, it finished last week," I explain. She looks at me as if there's more to say, her eyes looking into me with an expectant glare. A wide grin splits on my face before I lean into her and whisper in her ear. "'We won."

She pushes me away from her, pounding on my chest with her little hands. "You almost gave me a fucking heart attack. I'm so happy for you. I'm sorry I couldn't be there, though."

"It definitely wasn't the same without you but you're here now."

"You're right. I'm here now," she says, biting on her lip and looking at me the way that makes my dick jerk. Her eyes soften, a dreamy look in her eyes.

"*But,*" I drag out, placing my hand on her inner thigh. I drag my hand further up her leg until my hands are under her shorts, just reaching the line of panties. "I know how you can make it up to me though."

"Oh, you do?"

I don't have to make any more subtle comments until she's straddling me in the driver's seat. Her hands rub from my shoulders till they cup my face as she runs her thumbs just under my eyes in the gentle way that I like.

Cautiously, I pull back the seat so it can lie flat against the backseat. Wren places her hands on my chest, looking over at my face between each line - as if she's trying to memorise me - before her mouth meets mine. It's not frantic and desperate like our last kiss – it's gentle and calming. Her body falls softly against mine in a sigh when my hands travel from her outer thigh up to her ass under her shorts. Her hands roam underneath

456

my shirt as her mouth explores across my jaw and my neck at a painfully slow pace.

"I missed you so much," she whispers into my skin. I swear I feel every hair on my body stand up when the words leave her mouth.

"I've missed you too," I say back when I'm able to manage. She starts to shift down my legs, pulling up my shirt so she can kiss from my neck and down to my happy trail. An unknown sound leaves my mouth when she nips and kisses at my lower stomach. She starts to work at my jeans, and I take in a deep breath, ready for her to absolutely devour me.

A loud knock pierces through the heavy breathing. Her wide eyes lock with mine as she tries to sit up. We stay still for a few beats, breathing in each other's faces, acting as if we didn't just hear it. I sit up on my elbows with her and the knock sounds again at the window. It's too steamy in here to see but I hear a familiar voice outside.

"Miles, stop trying to get your dick wet and just tell me which apartment it is," Grey shouts, knocking rapidly on the window again. I wind it down slowly and when he catches Wren's eye, instead of stepping away like a normal person, he leans his forearms on the window. "Hey, Wren."

"Hi, Grey," she says quietly, her words coming out more of a question. She tries to climb off me, but I keep her there, her back resting again the steering wheel.

"Dude, you could have texted me," I say rolling my eyes.

"Yeah, I tried. It must have been hard to hear over all the moaning," he retorts, tilting his head to the side. He looks at Wren. "Not you. It was mainly him."

"Well, that makes me feel less embarrassed," Wren says cheerfully. She flashes me a mischievous grin before turning to him. "It's 407."

CHAPTER 47
WREN

"What if everyone starts asking us questions when we go in together," Miles asks. We're outside of my apartment door but as I tried to open the door, he blocked it with his body. The muffled music coming from inside reverberates off the door as loud voices shout over it.

"Do you really think we're that important, Davis" I ask, raising an eyebrow. He shrugs. "Besides, it's Kennedy's Day, no one is going to care that we're together."

"Maybe we shouldn't have stayed in the car for so long," he looks back to the elevator and then to me. I don't know why he's acting so skittish, like we need to sneak around. I don't hate it though. I liked the idea of us getting caught in the locker room or in the car.

"Don't tell me you're regretting it because just five minutes ago you said it was the best head of your life," I whisper in his ear, standing on my tiptoes. He tenses beneath me and swallows hard as I open the door behind him.

As I expected, our apartment is full of drunk teenagers dressed in hilarious costumes. The balloon arch that took us all morning to fix has toppled over into a heap of popped balloons in the corner. People walk back and forth from the corridors to the living room where we tried to push back our furniture to make more room. I finally installed a lock on my bedroom door to avoid the odd partygoer landing in a drunken mess in my room. I'm trying my hardest to find it within myself to enjoy tonight and attempt to conquer my fear of parties. We decided to keep the party fairly small so our landlord doesn't attack us and so we can actually fit people into the space.

Miles and I scan the area, trying to find a way to keep ourselves hidden until I've got into my costume. Yet Kennedy finds some way to stop us on our way to my room. When her eyes connect with mine across the corridor, she sprints up to us.

"Miles. Fancy seeing you here." Kennedy winks at him, dressed how she dresses every day in a blue denim dungarees and white tee. She said that she doesn't need to dress up because she already knows she'll be famous someday. Miles looks down to me and he blushes when his eyes connect with her wild ones.

"Happy birthday, Ken. I got you something," he says, riffling through his pocket. He lets out a frustrated groan when he reaches into his wrong pocket and of course, a condom accidentally drops out.

"Oh, wow, Miles. For me? You shouldn't have," she teases as she picks it up from the ground. He snatches it back off her and shoves it back into his pocket, glaring at her.

"Ha-ha," he retorts sarcastically before he pulls out her real gift. I watch from beside him as he rambles. "It's a Canon gift voucher so you can get that endless film for your camera like you wished for. My sister is a filmmaker, so she got me a good deal. She added her number on the back if you ever want to-" Before he can finish his sentence, she pulls him into a deep hug, nearly suffocating him. Kennedy has these kinds of hugs that even though you kind of want to pull away, she makes them so comforting that all you want to do is melt into her. "Thank you. Thank you. That's so thoughtful," she exclaims. While Miles' back is to me and her blushed face is turned to me, she points at him silently behind his back. *Keep him,* she mouths to me. *I'm trying to,* I mouth back.

"Okay, let him go," I say out loud, pulling Miles off her. "I need to change into my costume."

"I'm *so* excited," Kennedy squeals. "Scarlett has refused to get ready until you have so she's aggressively playing beer pong with Evan."

"That's not concerning at all... Anyway, you're going to love it," I beam, pulling on Miles' arm down the corridor and into my bedroom.

Touching him feels like such second nature that I don't think twice before kissing him again on the mouth before he backs up into my bed. We might have already made up for lost time in the car but when I'm around him, I can't keep my hands off him. It feels like we've spent so much time apart yet at the same time, it feels like we've been together this whole time. He sits down at the side of my bed as I slowly back away from him. It's no use trying to fight the ridiculous grin that has spread across my face. After my championship win and having his mouth on my body again, I feel like I've reached a new high. A high that I'm not going to worry about falling down from.

"Did you not bring a costume?" I ask as I pull out my outfit from my closet. I lay it down next to him and he looks at it and then at me.

"No. I was half expecting you to scream at me and tell me to leave," he says with a shrug, pushing himself further back on my bed so his legs swing forward. "Why didn't you?"

"What do you mean?" I draw my face into a puzzled expression, pushing off my shorts to the ground and stepping out of them. I can tell his eyes are on me as I wander around my room for my last bits of my outfit in nothing but a thin top.

"How come you didn't push me away again?"

If I hadn't spent the last few months, thinking over that question, I would have been more caught off guard. After spending so much time with Austin telling me straight up how much I could have ruined something good, I've come to realise the underlying fears I've had about committing to a relationship. It turns out that my sister is a perfect relationship guru.

"I'm sick of pushing people away. I just want to exist, y'know? Fear and guilt have controlled my life for so long but having you in my life makes me really fucking happy and I don't want to jeopardise that again," I explain. My body feels lighter the second the words leave my mouth.

He just nods at me with a little smile, not knowing what to say. Secretly, I don't want him to say anything. I just want him to understand.

"Can I tell you something?" he asks.

"Of course," I reply. He sighs, throwing his head back dramatically, like always.

"I didn't want to do all the romance grovelling shit because I knew it wouldn't help," he begins. "I know you, Wren. And as much as you love to read about that kind of stuff, sometimes, the reality is, space is better. Time is better. If I was constantly showing up, making a fool of myself just to get you to talk to me, it would have given you more of a reason to push me away. So, I'm not sorry that I didn't grovel. Believe me, I was pining after you in secret. That's always hotter, right?"

I shake my head at him, laughing. I'm glad he did that for me because he's right. The only thing that can help people heal is time and the ability to find yourself on your own.

He's something else. Something so completely different and I can't enough of it.

"You're insane, Milsey," I whisper and he grins at me.

I start to pull my top over my head, turned away from him in my mirror but he creeps up behind me and finishes pulling it over me. He presses featherlight kisses onto my bare back where and I can see myself slowly dissolving into him.

I try and wiggle out of his grip when I realise he's seeing more than he should. It's not that dark in my room so he can definitely make out the faint scars and bruises on my back from hundreds of childhood accidents and training mistakes.

"Do these hurt?" his voice sounds strangled as he speaks into my skin.

"No." I swallow. "Most of them are old."

"How come I didn't notice them before?"

I don't know when we got to the point where every touch from him feels like fire, but it did. Hot molten lava each time he so much as brushes past me. Now, it's at full intensity as he kisses across my shoulderblades.

"Because I didn't let you," I reply.

"You don't have to hide from me, Wren," he says. This is why being with him feels like too much. Because he says things like that to me, healing my inner-child as I want to fall apart in his arms.

"I'm not. I just hate how they look," I admit. I watch him in the mirror as his face is entirely concentrated on my back, his forefinger tracing a pattern across my skin. "What are you doing?"

"Telling you how beautiful you are by drawing hearts on your back," he whispers seriously, continuing to do so.

"Taylor really got to you, didn't she?" I joke but he doesn't laugh. He turns me around and I don't think I've ever seen him this serious before. He holds onto my shoulders, almost shaking them as he looks me directly in the eyes.

"You do realise that your body is made for one thing, don't you? It's meant to keep you alive. That's it. It's not going to be perfect all the time," he tells me.

"I know that. I just...I just don't like how it looks. That's all."

He swallows, his eyes softening, almost frustrated. "I love how it looks. You look like a warrrior, Wren. Hardcore."

Hardcore

That word.

Again.

The words get stuck in my throat. I would scream them if I was brave enough but I don't. Instead, I kiss him on the cheek and I break away from him, but he keeps his hands on my bare stomach when I reach over to get my outfit.

"Who are you dressing up as?" he asks as I unpin my bra and start to step into the sparkly dress beneath me.

"I'm disappointed that you are asking me such a question," I say dramatically. He shrugs at me with an adorably innocent expression. "I'm assuming you know who Taylor Swift is."

464

I tease him on purpose because I know how he tries to hide his obsession with her. "Doesn't ring a bell," he replies sarcastically, and I flip him off.

"Anyway, the jumpsuit that she wore on her 1989 tour is one of her most iconic outfits to exist. It's an inside joke. Kennedy will get it," I explain, swaying the sparkly skirt in the mirror. I apply red lipstick to complete the look.

"I have no idea what any of that means but you look hot," Miles says, wrapping his hands around my waist. "I'm dresses as the doting boyfriend, obviously."

"Perfect. Your hot is really popping out now," I reply, laughing. He pulls my back further into him, his chin resting on my shoulder. "Don't you think we work better apart? You won the college cup, and I won the championships. Isn't it weird that we did that without each other?"

I don't know what made me continue speaking but it's all that is on loop in my mind. I want to move on, and I want to let myself be happy with him but there's large warning signs in my brain that are telling me that I was more productive when we were apart.

"But we didn't do it without each other. Not really, anyway," Miles murmurs into my skin.

"What do you mean?" He lifts his head up. His face softens and his eyes connect with mine.

"We worked on our training together to get us where we are. We never had the chance to see how it would work between us while we had our big competitions. I know you get stressed and so do I, but we never had the opportunity to stress out *together*," he explains.

"That's why I pushed you away," I say quietly, my eyes tearing away from his for a second as I stare at his hands on my waist.

"I'm still trying to learn how to let people in, even if it completely messes up my schedule."

"Where would we be without that insane schedule of yours?" Miles retorts before spinning me around to face him. "C'mon the party is going to be over if you don't hurry."

*

By the time we've ventured out of my bedroom, the party was very much *not* over. I've seen more Kardashian's in the last thirty minutes than I have seen binging the show with the girls. I texted Scarlett to get ready too, so we don't have to leave Kennedy in anticipation any longer.

I'm still waiting for her to change so we're hiding away from Ken in the kitchen while she tells someone a dramatic story across the room. Watching Kennedy talk without being able to hear what she's saying, is one of my favourite things. She always speaks animatedly with her hands and makes every story she tells into a blockbuster.

"Can you just guess who I am?" Grey asks for the millionth time. Miles' body comes even closer time as if we're not already attached at the hip as we lean against the kitchen island. "I'm an actor."

"Yeah, you've said that but it's not making it any easier, dude," Miles sighs with an eye roll. Greyson looks at Harry who is dressed as Harry Styles which was easy enough for him to do since they have similar styles. He's wearing dark brown leather flared trousers and a sweater vest, and he painted his nails purple.

"I don't know either," Harry shrugs, trying his best at a British accent but he still sounds Australian. Grey comes over to me again, his tanned face close to me, his dark brown eyes staring into me. I can't hide the smile that's creeping up my face as Miles' expression turns hard with jealousy just like it did at Sports Achievement Evening when I danced with Grey to piss him off.

"Wren, I *know* you know who I am," Greyson says sternly. I try and hold in my laugh as I slowly bring my shoulders up and then dropping them.

"You look like how you look every day," I say quietly, gesturing to his outfit. He shakes his head and inhales, taking a step back from me. Miles comes closer to me again, wrapping his arm tightly around my waist, as if we can't be apart for longer than a few seconds.

"I'm Charles Melton, you dicks," Grey sighs after taking a shot. We all stare in confusion and the realisation washes over us almost at the same time. "I wanted to do someone who was also Korean, y'know? I don't watch enough TV to even know who else is out there that you'd recognise."

"Well, at least now we know," Harry says, patting him on the back as Grey sulks away into the living room.

"Anyone want to take a stab in the dark and guess who we are?" Michelle asks, leaning into Xavier who, for one of the first times, isn't wearing sweats.

Instead, he's wearing a black suit that matches Michelle's long black gown. They are by far my favourite outfits that I've seen today. There's something so elegant about them. I only just got to know Michelle before Miles and I broke up and I'm so ready to hang out with her again.

"Obviously, you're Beyoncé and Jay Z," I say. Michelle shoves her face into her hands, laughing and throwing her head back.

"It was very limited for black couples to find a celebrity that everyone would know," Xavier explains. He raises his Solo cup. "Here's to diversity."

"Hear hear," Miles says, raising his cup too and everyone agrees with light chuckles.

"You are both very drunk and very right, Xavier," I say, and he clinks his cup to mine.

Without really known how, they break out into a conversation about the Hollywood industry and the controversy it upholds. Being friends with them, you never know which direction a conversation can take but that's what makes them all so interesting. One minute we can be talking about a TikTok audio and the other we'll be talking about oblivion.

"Oh my fucking God!"

I hear a scream that can only belong to one person.

The birthday girl.

Kennedy pushes through the crowd of people in the kitchen and when she reaches me, she holds me out to her at arm's length. She takes a prolonged look at me up and down. Miles backs away from me, giving Ken the room to look at me properly.

"Her 1989 tour outfit?! How?" Her words come out in a breathless hurry. I raise my eyebrows at Miles as if it to say *I told you so.* He sticks his tongue at me and smiles wide.

"I have my ways," I say coyly with a shrug. Her mouth hangs open as she inspects my outfit again. She takes her time to feel over the sequins.

"We were meant to show her together!" Scarlett screams as she runs around the corner in her costume. Kennedy repeats her same over dramatic reaction over Scarlett's outfit.

We tried to each go for an outfit that not only reflects Kennedy's taste and personality but two of the things that have

468

cemented the bond we have. *Jennifer's Body* was our favourite movie growing up and we were all obsessed with Megan Fox as Jennifer. It was the kind of movie we shouldn't have watched so young, but it became a comfort movie for us. We also grew up in love with Taylor Swift and every single song she's released in her discography. Believe me, since Taylor's Version of '*Red*' came out, we've listened to it nonstop. It just made sense. We just make sense.

I'm not surprised when more of our friends turn up and gush over our outfits for most of the night. It was a hassle for us both to get such good replicas of the real outfits but it's definitely worth it. Scarlett, Kennedy, and I huddled in my car to get away from the noise so we could FaceTime Gigi who was dressed in her Kristen Stewart themed outfit. Because she has one of the greatest minds, I've ever interacted with, she pulled parts of all of Kristen's famous roles into one outfit. After enough socialising with Sophia as Haley Kiyoko, Miles and I lock ourselves back into my room to have a break before my social battery completely runs out.

"I missed you, Milesy. Like, a crazy amount," I murmur as we lay on our backs on my bed after getting to know each other's bodies again. My body aches from the competition but from the insane positions Miles just put my body in, I feel like I could melt like butter in his hands. He rolls over and presses a kiss onto my bare shoulder.

"You said that already," he whispers into me.

"I know. I just really mean it, and this is probably the only time you're going to hear me say it again," I say, playing off the aching in my chest as a laugh. "I'm not used to saying all this sappy shit out loud."

"I've missed you too."

CHAPTER 48
WREN

I've been trying to think of some way to make it up to Miles for missing his last game. If I wasn't so stuck in my head, I would have been able to focus on something other than my competitions. I would have been able to be there for him, cheer him on and congratulate him right after his game. The girls said that they didn't want to tell me because they thought it was best that I didn't know.

I didn't expect us to fall back into our old routine so quickly. Its barley been a week since Kennedy's party, and we've been to the gym together every day like we used to. We're still firing out random question even though I feel like I know him like the back of my hand. And to think that a few months ago, I was so determined to get him out of my life as soon as this fake dating plan worked. Then somehow, I started to fall for him. Hard. He still makes me want to rip my hair out but all of the other positive aspects of him outweigh the bad. I don't know how I feel about how easy this all feels. How easily I could slip back into this routine and find it so normal. He feels so safe. Comforting.

So, I'm letting myself have that.

We've been so caught up within each other since the party that we've been avoiding our upcoming spring exams. Kennedy's birthday is usually a physical marker to sort out my exam timetable but this year I've been thrown of course. For some reason, I'm not as frightened as I was. I'm happy with just existing, no matter how looming the future feels.

After hearing about Miles' childhood stories about when he used to come here as a kid, I knew that choosing to come to one of Salt Lake's ski resorts would be the best idea.

I didn't really think that through.

Although there are remains of the sun still shining through, it's cold as hell even under my hundreds of layers. It's worth it to see the sheer joy on Miles' face when we get out the snowboards. It looked a lot easier in the movies. We struggled and waddled down small hills and bumps, trying our hardest not to fall face first into the snow.

We spend most of the morning on the ski lift to take in the glorious sight beneath us. I've not been to one of these places since I was a kid. Getting to see the whole of my city almost covered in snow is one of the rare things that I don't appreciate enough. Even though my nipples are rock hard under both of my sweaters, I'm still grateful. I push away all the worries that I should be feeling about my exams and instead try and let myself luxuriate in this moment.

After going on the ski lift for the last time, we rush into the insanely cosy café in the resort. It's a small rustic cottage style building with delicious smelling coffee and pastries. After stiffly walking towards a table, we return to our question game.

472

In the time we were apart this is what I've missed the most. Not the sex. Not his face or his body. Not his house or his extremely comfortable bed but this schoolyard game that we play where we can ask each other anything. Almost nothing is off limits as we fire out more questions.

"This is a fun one," I exclaim, shoving more strands of hair into my beanie. I slide over his phone back to him as I keep on one pair of my gloves. "Are you a gambling kind of person or do you like to take things slow and steady?"

"I took a gamble with you, so yes," Miles answers, smirking as he takes a sip of his hot chocolate. I frown. "What? I did. You were being difficult with me at the start, and I still went for it."

"That's not true," I say quietly. "I always liked you, kind of, I just chose not to show it."

"You were really bad at hiding it," he laughs, throwing his head back. I nudge him under the table. "Maybe if you could control the way you whimpered every time I touched you, I wouldn't have been able to notice."

"Whatever," I say, feeling the heat creep up my cheeks. "I don't think I gamble enough. I always take the easy road. I want to be more spontaneous, though. Instead of sticking to strict schedules."

"I think you should," he suggests before picking up his phone. "I can't believe I've never asked you this. Where do you see yourself in ten years?"

The question catches me a little off guard. Like Austin, I always had a very simple plan for my life: skating. It's always been that and it probably always will. Being high up on that ski lift made me realise how insanely insignificant we all are. Merely salts of the earth. But I want to see more of that. I need to see more places that aren't confided in the states.

473

"I don't want to stay here, that's for sure. In ten years, I want to have moved out of Salt Lake, seeing new places, experiencing new things. I can skate and write anywhere," I say. "I see myself somewhere hot. Tropical."

"With anyone in particular…" he drawls, leaning forwards into me so I can see deep into his green eyes.

"Maybe," I smirk, biting my lip. I shrug and he nudges me under the table. "How about you?"

"Honestly? I want to play in the NHL until my bones don't work anymore and I'm an old grandad with a saggy dick," he says matter-of-factly. I laugh at his analogy. "But I don't want to be doing that alone."

"What do you mean? Xavier has explained his ten-step plan to me, like, a million times."

"What if I completely loose motivation or if they do?It's so easy to fall in and out of love with sports. If I stop enjoying it, I won't be able to play anymore and I won't be able to do it for Carter," he says quietly, not fully meeting my eyes.

"Then you can stop. The only person you owe it to to continue playing is yourself. He would be so proud of you, Miles," I say. I reach my hand out and hold his through his thick gloves.

"You love hockey *now*, right?"

"More than anything."

"Then that's all that matters. You don't need to worry about if you fall out of love with it eventually. When it happens, you'll know and you'll find a way to move on," I explain, my words not fully reaching the impact I was aiming for. "I don't think you should worry until it happens. Take it from me."

"Are we still talking about hockey, Wren?" He chuckles softly, his smile not completely reaching his eyes like the usually do.

"I don't know anymore."

474

We're caught within another one of those silent moments where it feels like nothing else exists except the substances of our souls. They are the kind of moments where even in an overcrowded café, we're able to see right through each other. Every time I'm with him, I feel like I'm laying another part of my bare to him and he accepts it with welcoming arms.

"You remind me so much of him." Miles' voice snaps me out of the daydream I almost fell into. He is concentrated on the mug in front of him, not braving to meet my eyes.

"Carter?"

"Yeah," he says, looking up at me with a soft expression. "I think he would have really liked you."

*

We finally make it back to Miles' house after freezing our asses off in the cold. His house has become a second home for me. I have way too many clothes here and his bed has started to feel like my own. Waking up here, in his bed, doesn't make me want to freak out and run for the hills. It makes me want to turn my head into his pillow, breathe in his scent, and scream with happiness. Everything here is starting to feel like home. *He* is starting to feel like home.

"Can we order food? I'm still hungry," I sigh, as I grip onto him like a koala while he plays on his PlayStation, his controller resting on my ass.

"You say this every time and then you *never* choose anything," Miles groans. I push myself up on my forearms when he throws the controller onto the bed. I roll onto my back, and he immediately comes over me, trapping me in with both his arms at the side of my head.

"I know what I want," I demand. He tilts his head to the side, an evil smirk playing on his lips. "I want to get Chinese but first…"

I drag out my sentence purposefully as I watch his dark green eyes focus in on my mouth. I drag my tongue across my bottom lip before slowly pulling into my mouth the way he likes it. He lets out a shaky exhale as his face inches dangerously close to mine. His hair almost falls into my face when his lips barley brushes mine as the air around us thickens. His hot breath hovers over me without completely crossing the remaining space between us.

"I want you," I whisper. The three tiny words barely leave my mouth before his mouth is covering mine in a hectic rush. On instinct, I reach for the back of his curly hair, pulling him deeper into me. I don't know what comes over me whenever I'm around him but suddenly I'm so hungry. Insatiable. My vision starts to blur when his tongue coaxes my mouth open, and the warmth hits my throat. I whimper into his mouth as his weight drops onto me. He leans up off me as if he hurt me and quickly wraps his strong arms around my waist and flips us over until I'm straddling him. Miles bites on my lip gently as he pulls away, looking up at me with glossy eyes as he positions himself against the headboard. Both of his hands come around my face, searching me.

"You're so fucking beautiful, Wren. Just… devastating," he breathes, shaking his head in disbelief. My face instantly heats up and I smile into the next kiss, letting my mouth explore his for a second. He starts to pull at the first of my many layers and my sweater doesn't budge.

"This is very unsexy, huh?" I pout, trying to pull my sweater over my head as well. It gets caught with my other one and Miles yanks on it until I'm free.

"Never." He starts to pull off his own layers, his clothes getting tangled like mine. I laugh as I try and work his jumpers over his head. His wild hair falls free from the neck of his jumper, and he sighs deeply.

"Why does it have to take so long to get naked?!" I huff, rolling onto my back to work down my jeans and leggings.

"I'm sure a relationship guru somewhere would have a field day with this," Miles laughs, sitting at the edge of the bed to undo himself of his layers. I look over at his red face and I don't hide the ridiculous grin that's spreading on my face.

"I guess we're peeling back the layers of our relationship," I beam when he's in nothing other than his boxers. I climb over to him on the edge of the bed and sit in his lap. I hook my arms around his neck as his hands journey up and down my bare back.

"Your puns are worse than mine," Miles chuckles, pressing a kiss in between my breasts. I snake my fingers into his hair when an involuntary moan leaves my mouth as he starts to make his way down my chest.

"Yeah, but you love me for it."

I don't let time stop when I say it. I don't overthink every single syllable that just left my mouth. He doesn't either. He just looks up at me, his mouth on my rib cage, his eyes set in mine.

"Yeah, I do."

*

477

After exploring each other's bodies and eating our food, we shower together before slipping into bed in our underwear. Since we got back together, we've spent a lot of time in these moments. The ones where we just look at each other. Like, *really* look at each other. It would frighten me if I didn't enjoy it so much. Just looking at him, enjoying him, knowing I have him.

His hands lie comfortably on my waist while I run my hands down his broad shoulders to his back, not saying anything, just completely lost within his comforting presence.

"Has anyone ever told you that you have a perfect body?" he whispers out of the silence, and I start to laugh. He brings his face even closer to mine so I can look straight into his eyes.

"What?" He pushes my hair out of my face softly and lets out a laugh of his own.

"I just mean that you fit so perfectly with me. Here," he explains.

"Oh, so *that's* what you like about me. So, you don't like my personality?" I mock. He hums shaking his head lightly.

"Not really. I like this more," he whispers carefully. He takes his hand from my waist and runs it down my stomach until he touches me between my legs, lightly brushing the inside of my thigh close to my heat. "Especially the noise you make when I touch you there."

"What isn't there to like?" I whisper, my breath getting caught in my throat at the contact of his hand. "About my personality, I mean."

"You're so stubborn and you act like you hate me most of the time." He shrugs, a cheeky grin spreading across his face,

"Well, you know I don't. Not really, anyway." I run my hands down his back, pulling him closer into me. "I'm basically naked in your bed. What more do you need?"

"I want you to tell me what you like about me." He doesn't miss a beat when he speaks. His eyes suddenly fiery and expectant. I swallow. I try and laugh but it comes out strangled as he keeps his gaze on me.

"Oh, you're serious."

Dead serious.

"Would it kill you to say one thing you like about me? Just one," he pleads.

"Your hair," I say quickly. He almost jerks back at the sudden quickness in my tone. It was the first thing that came to mind, and it truly is my favourite thing about him. His hair is chestnut brown and wavy. It always smells like coconuts, and it almost melts in my hands anytime I run my hands through it.

"Really? Why?"

"Because I can run my fingers through it. I like it when I can slip my hands between each of your waves, and it feels like you're melting into me. I like it when it's the only thing that I can see when you're between my legs," I admit, doing exactly that with my hands as he blinks at me. "I like feeling you. Touching you. Sometimes, I feel like I'm so desperate to have you. Everywhere. On me."

He sucks in a breath at my omission, his cheeks becoming hot with heat. God, what is happening to me? He looks beautiful like this, all flustered. "I would let you do anything to me, Wren. Absolutely anything."

"I know you would and that scares me a little," I say laughing. He doesn't say anything, and it gives me the confidence to continue complimenting him.

"And this," I say, holding his face within one of my hands. His dark green eyes stare into mine as I trace the space between them down his nose. His Adam's apple bobs as he swallows. I rub my thumb just beneath his eyes as they flutter closed for a second before I run my finger gently over his full lips, studying him. "I like your mouth but I like what comes out of it more. I like it when you talk. When you tell me stories as if it's the first time you're telling them How you're constantly giving me little pieces of yourself. I like how easily your face fits into my hands. Like you were made for me."

He watches me carefully, almost afraid to speak. I don't know why I said what I just said. I never say things like this. I love to read about it but saying it out loud always cringes me out. Something has changed within me, but I can't find the effort to care about it right now. Instead, I press my lips to his cautiously, drawing back at the last second as I catch his bottom lip between my teeth. He smiles softly.

"Is that one nice thing good enough?" I ask against his lips.

"More than enough," he whispers. "Now I know you don't hate me."

"I could never hate you, Miles. Even if I tried to. You are insufferably addictive."

The rest of the night, we stay mostly quiet. I don't know what that whole thing was. Something about it felt determining. As if it's marked a shift in our relationship. Everything I said was so true that it worries me.

It's well into the night when I feel Miles' thumb stroking my cheek and my eyes flutter open, heavy with sleep.

"What is it?" I ask sleepily. He waits a beat, opening and closing his mouth. I have to squint a little to make out the faint smile on his lips in the darkness.

"You're my best friend," he says certainly. It comes out so quickly that it almost passes as a question. My heart expands like a balloon, and I exhale slowly to let it deflate.

"I don't know how Kennedy and Scarlett will feel about it, but you're slowly becoming my favourite person," I admit. "But don't read into it," I add sharply before my eyes shut again, almost letting the sleep pull me under.

"Oh, I already have, Wrenny."

CHAPTER 49
MILES

I've never been good at school. I've especially never been good at exams. There's something about the complete pressure and unwavering nausea that I feel whenever I'm in the exam room. Maybe it's my young optimistic brain talking, but I think they are a way to prove how shitty my memory is and how hard I find it to retain all the pieces of information that I've learned in class. I'm thanking all my lucky stars for managing to get through this second year at NU doing my fitness and well-being course. For most of the course, it's all practical assessments which I can usually do fine on until the spring exam season comes around and I actually have to get my head down to do work.

It's been even more difficult trying to focus on anything other than Wren fucking Hackerly. She has utterly consumed my every thought at the worst possible times. If I'm driving to pick up food, it's Wren. If I'm sat in class, the only thing on my mind is when I get to see her. When I'm training, all I can think is to count down the minutes until I can walk the distance to her rink and skate with her for fun.

Above all, I'm struggling the most right now as she lies at the end of my bed on her stomach, a paperback in her hands and a highlighter in her mouth. She taps the pen on her bottom teeth repeatedly. The sound has been driving me equal parts insane and horny. I've been sat here for an hour, not able to even look at my textbook. I shouldn't even feel this much desire for her, considering we've been fucking like bunnies for the last few weeks.

All I can think about is how badly I want my mouth on her. How I can see a sliver of her toned stomach poking out of her shorts and crop top. How I know that if I put my hand up her shirt, I will be pleasantly surprised to find that she's not wearing anything underneath. I'm almost giving myself paper cuts as I latch onto the book to avoid touching her.

"Stop staring at me, you perv," she murmurs without looking up. I still don't know how she does it. Since the day I met her, she's managed to sniff me out without even batting an eye.

"How do you do it? Just tell me. Is it a superpower or some shit?" I ask, finally shoving my textbook aside and coming down to lay next to her. I was never going to get any work done anyway. I prop my arm up and rest my head in it, watching her read.

"It's not a superpower. Plus, I've already told you. You just breathe really loud," she shrugs. She looks at me, her brown eyes dancing with delight. Her eyes scan my body before she returns back to her book. "*Especially* when you're turned on." I don't have the energy to fight her on it. And I don't have to look down either so see how hard I am. You would think that

I'm a pubescent teenager who's never seen a woman's body before but there is something so mesmerising about her.

"So, you've known this whole time, but you don't want to do anything about it?" I tease.

"Miles, I need to study," she sighs her face still set on whatever novel she's reading.

I can't resist any more, so I move my hand slowly to her waist, my hand grazing the bare skin underneath her shirt. I can feel her shiver under my touch, but she doesn't break eye contact with the pages in front of her. I lean over to press a kiss to her shoulder, and she squirms. She still doesn't tear her eyes away when I bite at her collarbone gently.

"Just take a break," I whisper, placing a kiss in the spot below her ear. Heat starts to creep up on her face, but she still doesn't move. "Just five minutes."

"You said that last time and then you went down on me," Wren whines as if she hated it. I asked her to take a break and she obliged. In fact, she was the one who started making love eyes at me and she practically begged me to go down on her. Okay, maybe 'begged' is a bit of a stretch but she was pretty enthusiastic by the way she was screaming my name and shoving my face further between her thighs.

"Yeah, but that doesn't count," I argue, murmuring into her skin, before pulling away to look at her clearly. Her cheeks have returned to their famous red colour.

"I came. Twice. Doesn't that count?" She looks at me now and I can see how badly she's trying to fight it. How badly she's trying to resist me.

"Well, if we're going by that logic then I guess I have you beat." She's quiet for a minute, opening and then closing her mouth, trying to make sense of what I meant.

"That's why you were in the bathroom for so long," she gasps, pushing me in the shoulder until I'm flat on my back. She leans over me, loose strands of her hair dangling in my face. The second her eyes connect with mine, she forgets everything she just said and climbs on top of me. Both of her knees fall onto the bed beside me, her hands brushing the hair out of my face. "Just five minutes," she repeats with a shrug before diving into my mouth. Our mouths meet and I swear I can feel myself floating outside of time. These are the kind of absorbing moments which I live and breathe for. They're needed a lot more during this exam season.

The kiss deepens and becomes more frantic as she moves across my jaw and down to my neck. The initial sensation makes me want to laugh but it quickly turns into a satisfied groan when she starts to suck and bite me gently.

I tell my brain to move my hands and I travel up her shirt, just reaching underneath her tits. I didn't know how cold my hands were until she shuddered, naturally rocking her body into mine. I brush my thumb over her nipple before slipping my hands out and pushing her down until her body is flush against me.

Wren's hands dive into the back of my head as she plants more kisses down my chest. My hands slip between the material of her shorts and her panties, but she shakes her head and rolls of me, leaving me panting and hard. She scrambles away from me, sitting crossed legged on the other side of the bed.

"What's wrong?" I ask, kneeling up on my elbows.

"Miles, we're never going to get anything done."

"I don't know if you've noticed but it's really fucking hard to get anything done when we're in the same room," I groan. She nods her head as if this is as equally to upsetting her as it is to me. I crawl over to her and rest my hands on her thighs. "Can't I just touch myself while you work, or would that be weird?"

"No," she gulps. "I would just want to touch myself too."

Her soft eyes connect with mine as her cheeks burn red. It doesn't take anymore silent glances before she moves from next to the window and lies down at the top of the bed, propping her back up with some cushions. She starts to pull down her shorts until she's in nothing but dark panties and a loose shirt. On instinct, I pull down my jeans along with my boxers as I kneel between her legs, holding onto my throbbing cock.

"This doesn't count, right? We can just do work after," she whispers as she starts to trail her hand from her stomach down to where she's soaking. She pulls her shirt over her head and throws it on the ground. I have to swallow in a breath before nodding. "I would rather have you inside me, Miles."

"I know but if we do it that way, we're never going to stop," I admit, the words both paining and calming me. I watch as she runs her hands from her tits to her stomach and then back up, her eyes completely locked with mine. "Do you touch yourself when I'm not here?"

She nods, pulling her bottom lip between her teeth. I shift on the bed as I start to move my hands slowly up and down my length. Her breathing starts to pick up faster as she runs two fingers over where she's dripping on her panties. I force myself to slow down so I can savour the moment. Before I know it, she's already pulled off her panties completely so she's bare in front of me. I loll my head back and close my eyes to take a deep breath.

"What do you think about?" I ask hoarsely. She teases herself by dragging her fingers down her pussy and back up, collecting her wetness. Her eyes flutter closed. "Look at me when you're talking to me, baby."

She lets out a soft moan that almost undoes me before her eyes open slowly. She immediately focuses in on my dick, and she swallows before her eyes make a slow journey up my body to my face. She licks her lips as her eyes zone in on me as she starts to rub circles around her core.

"I think about this…" she pants. "You. I think about you touching yourself while I watch."

"That turns you on?" She nods and her pace starts to quicken as she shifts and moves up from the bed. I use one of my hands to press her stomach down to stop her squirming. "What else do you think about?"

"I think about your hands on me. Everywhere," she whispers, using one of her hands to cup her tits and circle around her nipple. I start to move faster around my shaft. "I think about the things you say about my body when you're inside me."

"Like what?"

"About how good I feel around your cock. How our bodies fit perfectly together. How you always take your time because you know it annoys me." Her words are broken up by pants and moans as she slips two fingers into herself. "How you love the noise that I make when I come."

That's what undoes me. The breathiness and whine in her voice, mixed with the complete bliss on her face while she touches herself is what destroys me. Her eyes open and close as she moves her fingers in and out on her as I do the same around my dick. It's a lot different when I do this in the bathroom when I can't see her. But now, with her straining in front of me, I know the orgasm is going to hit me soon. I move over to straddle her stomach, my dick just inches away from her face and her breasts.

"Fuck, Miles," she moans loud, ripping through the heavy breathing in the air. I bend over her to kiss her on the lips, but her mouth is hanging open between pants that she barley gets to reciprocate it. "I'm close. I need you to touch me."

"I'm not going to touch you. I want to watch you fall apart. Can you do that for me?"

She starts to squirm and shift beneath me as her pace increases. The sounds of her hands moving in and out of her make me move faster around myself. She lets out a strangled cry as the orgasm rips through her. Wren shakes and twitches beneath me as the high settles over her. Her eyes fall closed for a second before she looks up at me and I lose it. My hand pumps my dick a few more times as the sensation washes over me.

I groan as I come over her chest and her tits. Another constricted moan falls from her mouth as I collapse beside her, careful not to crush her with my weight. When our heavy breathing subsides, I peel myself off her to go into the bathroom and get a warm cloth to clean her up. When I get back into the room, she's still lying down, her hand thrown over her eyes.

"See, that was better than doing work, wasn't it?" I say as I climb over her, pressing the cloth to her chest. She hums when the warmth hits her and moves her hands from her eyes to look up at me.

"I guess," she says sarcastically, an evil smile playing on her lips. I fold over the cloth to the clean side and move it slowly over her breasts as she watches me. "We really do need to get something done. You know what we need to do."

"I don't think I do," I groan. She slides out from beneath me and pulls her shirt over her head. I fall backwards on the bed. She stands behind me, leaning over me upside down. Her hair falls to cover us like a curtain when she bends down and sets a tender kiss onto my lips but pulling back at the last moment. "Just text them."

*

The only way we've managed to get any studying done is when we have everyone at my house. I usually hate large study sessions, but we all have a subject in common that we can help each other with. We're not always the most productive bunch but this close to exams, we're all stressing out, so we know we have to work hard.

Xavier, and I sit at one end of the dining table, working together on our course, with spreadsheets and diagrams. Evan and Scarlett are trying to work together but they're doing more shouting than revising. Scarlett wheeled over The Whiteboard 2 from their apartment to do some work on and strangely enough, Evan has the same one but they're arguing over who has the correct equations. And Kennedy is the only one without an exam. Out of all of us, she's the most chaotic but somehow has her life together more than the rest of us. She was able to finish her final piece early so she's helping Wren with her creative writing exam. They're sat as far away from us in the living room, so Wren and I don't make an excuse to take a five-minute break.

It was going well until Scarlett suggested that we order food, and all concentration was lost. We've been trying to convince ourselves that it's a good idea to get some rest food. Really, we're all sitting around the table, stealing fries and chicken wings from each other as we take our very well-deserved break, listening to *'Ivy'* by Frank Ocean.

Perfection.

"I swear to God, if you try and take the same piece as me *again*, I'm going to saw your hand off," Scarlett warns Evan in a steady but deathly tone. He raises his hands in surrender and sulks in his seat across from her.

"No weapons at the dinner table, kids," Kennedy coos. Scarlett throws her a sarcastic smile before sulking, mirroring Evan's position. Xavier throws me a knowing glance and I make the mistake of looking at Wren across from me.

If there were more seats at this table and if everyone didn't rush to sit down as soon as the food came, I would have made sure that Wren and I were further away than we are. Instead, she's sat across from me, staring right at me as she licks off ketchup from three of her fingers. Fuck me. She has got to be doing this on purpose.

"What are everyone's summer plans?" Kennedy asks from beside me, looking around at everyone expectantly. Obviously, the first one to jump on the opportunity to brag is Evan.

"As soon as the semesters over, I'm off to Bali for a few weeks. Then, my family have business in Tokyo and London so, of course, I'll be going with them," Evan answers with a sigh, as if he's actually upset about it. We all look at him and try to hide our jealousy and disgust. Except Scarlett make no effort to hide it.

"Ugh, gag me with a spoon," she says, rolling her eyes.

"Happily," Evan replies. Scarlett actually gags this time. "Is someone upset because the Voss empire is slowly crumbling?" Everyone watches between them like a ping pong game.

"Don't project onto me, Branson. It's not my fault your buyers are not getting any younger. Isn't the CEO of your largest investor in adult diapers?" she mocks coolly. He opens his mouth and then slams it shut. "Yeah, I thought so."

"Anyway," Wren says, dragging her gaze from Scarlett to Xavier. "What about you? Are you doing anything fancy?"

"If you're wondering if I'm not going to be here so you guys can do what you do *every* night, the answer is yes. I'm going to spend some time with Michelle's family in LA," Xavier explains, looking between us both suspiciously.

"Calm down, Z, you're acting like that's all we do," I say when I notice Wren slowly retreating back into her chair.

"It *is* kind of all you do," Evan mutters. I throw a bone at him, and he stares at it in disgust. He looks between me and Wren. "Are those your plans then? For the summer?"

"Pretty much," Wren shrugs, beaming at me with a toothy grin. "I'll probably be going up to Oregon a lot when my nephew comes, though."

"Ah, I forgot his due date. When is it again?" Xavier asks. Out of all the guys, he's been the most enthusiastic about Wren's nephew. I love kids too. They are just tiny drunk adults and I find them hilarious. But Xaiver has always loved kids. He has three younger siblings, so it's always been in his nature. He has this innate desire to be a dad. If he wasn't in NU, he and Michelle would have at least five kids by now, I'm sure of it.

"In a few days hopefully," she replies. Xavier nods and we all dig back into our food before it gets cold.

Spending more and more time with these guys has made life a little more bearable. We get a live action comedy show by watching Scarlett and Evan interact. We have some rational thoughts from our very own peacekeeper, Xavier. Wren and I are often the butts of the jokes that Kennedy makes. We work well together. Somehow. Finding friends like these isn't easy to come by and I thank my lucky stars every night that I'm stuck with them.

"How much are you betting that we'll all get back to work after this?" Xavier asks when we are all stuffed and bloated from too many wings and pizza.

"I'm betting my life savings that we'll all get back to work but less than ten minutes in, these two," Scarlett starts, gesturing between Wren and me. "Will think of some lame excuse to go to the bathroom together."

"Can we stop with the sex jokes?" Wren says laughing.

"You're all acting like you've never been around two people that have regular sex. It's concerning."

"*I* was just asking a genuine question," Xavier says with a shrug, but I can see the smile creeping up on his face.

"I know you were, Z," Wren replies calmly before her voice climbs up. "I'm on about everyone else. Miles and I fuck. So what? Matter of fact, that's exactly what we were doing before you guys came."

I look at her in amazement shaking my head and everyone starts to laugh. She's been trying to hide how annoyed she gets when they make those kinds of jokes, but I didn't think she would actually say something about it. I don't mind the jokes. Not at all. As long as they're always concerning us and that she's no sleeping with anyone other than me. She scrapes her chair out from the table and walks over to me. Everyone's laughter is still dying down, so they don't notice when we slip out of the room.

"I think we should do it now, just to piss them off," Wren smirks as she runs up the stairs.

492

"You're insane."

"Am I? Or am I just practical?"

CHAPTER 50
WREN

Exam week was hell. As expected.

It only dawned on all of us the week before that we've spent so much time doing everything *but* revising. Every time we met up for a study session, we'd all be ready and prepared to do two solid hours of studying. In reality, we spent a good hour with our heads down before one of us, usually Ken, had yet another story to tell that we needed to listen to. Immediately, our focus is broken and all we want to do is talk. We managed to pull through at the last minute and we all did pretty okay. Now it's just the waiting game until we get our real results back.

The only thing that got me through last week was knowing that I'd be meeting my baby nephew very soon. Austin and Zion are finally settled in Oregon, and they've been waiting for baby Marley to show up. He took his time but ten days after his due date, he came out a healthy light skinned baby with the most hair in the world. I haven't had time to see him yet, but I finally get to meet him today.

The flight was lonely without Miles' awful singing, but it was sort of refreshing. Since Kennedy's birthday party, we have not left each other side for any more than twenty-four hours. I didn't know how badly I had separation anxiety from him but since we got back together, I've been latched on him like a koala. I can't help it sometimes. Being with Miles is like taking a warm shower. It's like having the first bite of a chocolate chip cookie when it's all gooey in the middle. He is every good thing about this world, and he makes me feel like the best version of myself whenever he's around. We thought it was best for him to stay in Salt Lake while I visit the baby, just to make sure that we're both healthy enough when I meet him.

A weird rush runs through me when I land in Redmond. It's strange to travel on my own but it's even stranger to be travelling to see my nephew for the first time. I don't get to be around many babies but the second I am, I'm hit with instant baby fever. There's something so magical about pregnancy and birth but because I know it's not all sunshine and rainbows, I will be steering clear from that for a while. Even when I'm in Zion's truck, on our way to their new house, my knee can't stop bouncing up and down.

"You okay, Emmy?" he asks, glancing at me, using the nickname he convinced Austin to start calling me. Zion has always been kind to me, even when I treated Austin like a bitch most of the time. He's always had this calming energy about him. It helps that he loves books as much as I do too.

"I'm just excited," I admit, unable to fight off the smile on my face.

"Austin is too. I am as well. You're going to be the first Auntie to meet him," he replies, looking over at me again before turning his attention to the road.

"Really? I thought Austin said your sisters were coming down."

"Nah, they're coming in a few weeks when the weathers a bit warmer for them. It's not easy trying to adjust from the Jamaican heat to whatever you call this," he laughs.

It's a miserable day in Portland. I kind of hoped that the sun would come out so I could spend some time outside here, exploring. I've only been through Portland on my way to competitions so, I've not been able to just see the sights as they are.

I also hoped I'd get to meet Zion's sisters. When the girls and I were in high school and Austin and Zion were dating, we were strange kids and got really invested in their lives. It fascinated all of us because we had never seen my uptight sister become such a chilled-out person. After our mini deep dive, we found that Zion has three older sisters all living where he grew up in Jamaica. They're all Kumina dancers and as tween girls, we got obsessed quick. I never told Austin about my little obsession, but I was secretly hoping of gushing over them in person.

"Aw, that sucks," I say. The car starts to pull into a cul de sac which I've recognised from the pictures I begged Austin to send me. When we're parked, I turn back to Zion as I go to unclip my seatbelt, *his* leg is bouncing up and down. "Is everything okay?"

"I, uh, wanted to ask you something," he begins. He looks up at me, his dark eyes searching around my face. "I've already asked your parents and they said it's fine, but I wanted to ask you, now that you and Austin have got closer."

"Ask me what?" I can hear my heartbeat thumping against my chest rapidly as I try to exhale.

"I want to ask your sister to marry me."

Every thought I had in my mind shatters into oblivion. My sister. A married woman. With a baby. And though the baby was unexpected, this might be the best thing to ever happen to her. I'm surprised my veins don't pop out of my forehead as I stare at Zion for what feels like an eternity, blinking at him.

"You know you didn't have to ask me, right? But the answer is yes. I think you should ask her to marry you right now," I ramble. "Oh, my God. This is insane."

"I know," he grins. "I just wanted to ask you, just in case."

"You guys are perfect for each other."

What's even more perfect, is their son. Holding this tiny baby in my hands, I suddenly feel complete and he's not even *my* baby. There is an overwhelming sensation that occurs when babies are around. This baby is going to grow up, he's going to laugh, he's going to cry, he's going to make mistakes and he's going to achieve great things. What makes the feelings all that more empowering is that he has two loving parents who are going to love him. What more will he need?

*

After spending a few days with Austin and her new little family, coming back home was bound to be chaotic. I was on edge, waiting for Zion to get down on one knee. But when I realised he wasn't going to do it with his future wife's little sister around, I kept my distance. I tried to time my trip perfectly so I could be back in Salt Lake when our grades are put in the system.

The girls and I all sat around the kitchen island, loading and reloading our grades while on FaceTime to Miles, Xavier, and

Evan. After a few refreshes and crossing our fingers, the page loaded up with our grades.

We all passed. I don't know how we managed to get through it, but we did. We found any excuse to have a group study session without actually studying. But somehow, those days when we actually put our heads down, paid off.

To celebrate, we got a table for the six of us at Juno's. After hyping it up for so long, they finally agreed to eat here with me. It feels more hectic than just going here with a pregnant lady during the lunch hour. Instead, we're crammed in a back booth, trying to shout at each other over the noise coming from the bar. I'm practically sitting on Miles' lap as he sits on the outside of the booth. Across from him, Evan sits as far away from Scarlett as possible while she scooches up next to me. In between them, Kennedy and Xavier are squeezed in together.

"I just don't understand how we all passed," Miles says, taking a sip of his Coke.

"It's because I manifested it," Kennedy says as if it's the most normal thing in the world, tapping onto her temples. "We didn't chase. We attracted."

"I'm just going to pretend that I know what that means," Miles mumbles. He brings his hand under the table, squeezing my thigh and pulling us even closer together. His touch on my body has started to feel so natural. As if this was always meant to happen.

"Manifestation isn't real," Evan guffaws. Scarlett shoots him an evil look, but he misses it.

"I wouldn't say that if I was you," she singsongs. Kennedy pins him with an angry expression, and he slowly slouches in his chair. I've had countless conversations about astrology with her, so I'm not surprised when I zone in and out of the conversation.

My gaze automatically shifts to Miles. He's watching between the four of them as they argue, not saying anything. Just observing. Something has changed in him, and I can't figure out what. There's still the sarcasm and the wit that I fell for, but he's become more relaxed. Smoothed out. He doesn't feel the need to prove anything, and he just exists. With me.

I have too. I don't hate the idea of saying cheesy things every now and then to the people I care about. What I didn't expect was for my life to turn into one of the rom com's that I love. The ones that always feel so out of reach. But I fucking love every part of it.

It feels like that song, '*golden hour*' that Miles always plays. The lyrics go through my head on repeat.

We were just two lovers, feet up on the dash, drivin' nowhere fast. Burnin' through the summer, radio on blast, make the moment last.

"Stop staring at me, you weirdo," Miles murmurs, still watching the argument unfold in front of us.

"I see you've learnt my trick," I laugh, nudging him with my shoulder.

"I don't think I have. It was a fifty-fifty chance you were either asleep or looking at me," he laughs, turning towards me and he adds sounding like Schmidt from *New Girl*, "Because who can resist this face, right?"

I shake my head at that gorgeous face of is, sticking my tongue in my cheek so I don't laugh. My breath hitches when his hand moves even further up my thigh, but his face remains focused, as if he isn't about to make this meal much more interesting. Instead of trying to ruin the night with my libido, I squeeze his hand between my thighs and his journey stops. I hook my right leg over his left one and his thumb starts to rub small circles on the inside of my thigh.

"Do you not think we're close enough already?" I ask, trying to keep my voice low as the voices around us die down. I can feel their eyes on me, but I keep mine locked with Miles' green ones.

"At every table, I'll save you a seat," Miles whispers.

If I couldn't hear the way my heart started pounding in my chest, I'm sure it would have fell straight though my ribs. When the unsettling thrumming noise stops, a smile creeps up on my face before it turns into an ugly laugh. A real, shoulder shaking, laugh of disbelief. Miles' face drops.

"Are you seriously quoting Taylor Swift to me right now?" I ask, barely able to let my laugh settle.

"Yeah, well, you already know how much I love you. I've said it when I was drunk, and I said it out of anger, and I knew you wouldn't let me say it again on its own. That's boring."

"You just did."

My words sound so far away from us. As if I'm floating outside my body, watching and letting myself slip into this moment where I never thought I would end up. Here, in a bar restaurant with five of my best friends, and my boyfriend telling me that he loves me for the first time. He loves me and I believe him.

"Oh, yeah. I did," Miles murmurs.

I put my hand on his cheek tenderly, turning his face closer to mine. I act as if we're the only people in the room. As if nothing else exists other than us, right here, in this moment. I press my lips to his and I kiss him softly. It's the kind of kiss that could spiral out of control if you let it. The kind of one that leads to many more, but I don't let that happen. Instead, I pull away until we're centimetres apart.

"I'd save you a seat too."

The second I let us slip away, we're met with groans and gags from the rest of them. The only person who's smiling is Xavier. Sometimes, I feel like he's the only one out of all of us that actually understands what it feels like to be this in love. No matter how scary it is.

More music comes to mind. This time, it's the first-dance remix of 'Lover' by Taylor Swift. When did I start doing this?

"Can you believe we've only got two more years of this?" Scarlet asks, nostalgia drowning in her eyes. Everyone turns to her and suddenly, the mood has shifted into a calming silence. "Like, we're going to be doing real people shit soon."

"I don't think I'm ready for adulting yet," Kennedy groans, shoving her face into her hands. "Do you think we'll still be friends in five years from now?"

"If Scarlett and Evan don't kill each other before then, sure," Xaiver replies and we laugh. "You guys believe in different universes and shit, right?"

"Of course," Kennedy beams. I nod and so does Miles, Scarlett and Evan.

"Well, I think that in another universe we would still be friends. I think we'd make it to each other somehow. I mean, if it wasn't for Wren and Miles, we wouldn't be sitting here right now. Maybe you girls would be on one side of this resturant and us on the other, celebrating our grades, not even knowing that we're existing in the same time frame. Do you ever think about that?"

"Shit, man," Evan murmurs. "I think about that all the time. But actually hearing someone say it is crazy."

"I definitely think we'd still be friends in a different universe," Scarlett mentions and we all agree.

"I didn't mean for this to go all existentialist, I just wanted to say that in a few years, I want to be living by the beach."

"No one is stopping you, Ken," I say with a shrug. "I'm getting out of here as soon as I can."

"Me too," Xavier sighs. "I want my own family."

"Is that what Michelle wants?" Miles asks from beside me, his hand still on my thigh but I feel him everywhere.

"She'll do anything I want to do. The same way you'd do anything Wren asks you to," Xavier laughs but Miles isn't. He looks down at me, a quiet smile playing on his lips.

"You are extremely whipped, my friend," Evan says, shaking his head at us. I don't have the energy to fight him on it and neither can Miles. He just looks down at me like we're the only people truly existing now.

"I am," Miles says proudly. "I will follow you around Barnes and Noble and hold your books for you for the rest of my life."

"Are you sure? I get a lot of books," I murmur, raising my eyebrows.

"And I'll hold every single one for you."

*

The rest of the meal goes by in a haze. We talk about the same four topics on rotate, somehow managing to put a spin on the same topic we've been discussing for weeks. The only constant I could focus on was Miles' hand on my body. The way he needs to rest it on me as if I'm going to slip away. Even on the drive on the way home, his hand grips onto my thigh as he drives me and the girls to our apartment. When we're standing in the doorway once Kennedy and Scarlett have gone inside, his hand rests comfortably on my waist as my back hits the door.

"I meant what I said earlier, Wren," Miles says, breaking the comfortable silence.

"I know."

"I'm going to say it again. I'm warning you before you freak out on me," he says, raising his eyebrows. I pull him in closer from the hem of his shirt.

"I want to hear you say it again."

The darkness of the hallway has given me more confidence than it should. I've been testing the waters, barley dipping my toes in, trying to feel how it would be. I want to jump straight in. I want to fall and never come back up for air so long as I get to spend it with him. I knew from the beginning that as much as I tried to avoid it, I was bound to fall for him. He's my person.

"I love you, Wren. You're my best friend and I love being around you. I love being there for you and protecting you even when you don't want me to and I'm *in* love with you. So desperately. I don't think I would ever be able to stop loving you. If you try to push me away again, I won't let you. Because I'm in this, okay? Me and you."

"Well, how am I supposed to compare to that?" I laugh.

I don't know why I joke. I don't know why I can't just say it right off the bat. Just tell him how I knew that I felt this way about him since we talked in the diner after Sophia's party.

"I love you, too. You're what's good for me, Miles. In every universe, it's me and you."

"Me and you," he repeats, smiling. It's the kind of smile that makes my heart double in size. The kind of smile that makes this whole thing a little less daunting. When I think he's going

503

to lean down and kiss me, he pulls me into a tight hug instead and my arms wrap around his middle, holding him close so I can hear his heartbeat. "Are you still scared?"

"A little."

"We'll be alright."

EPILOGUE
THE SUMMER MILES

"Are you nervous?"

I run my hands from her shoulders down to her waist as I stand behind her in the mirror, losing my mind over how good she looks in her dress. I'm sure we're breaking every wedding ritual right now, but I can't bring myself to care. I know Kennedy would have my head if she saw that I was with Wren in her dress already. I rest my chin on her shoulder and she beams in the mirror.

"No, I'm just excited. One, I've never been here before and two, I've never been a maid of honour before," Wren says.

We've been in Jamaica for the last few days, trying to catch up on sleep as well as helping Wren do her bridal duties to her sister. Austin and Zion wanted to get married as soon as possible but they also wanted to do it somewhere hot. I don't think I could deal with another wedding in Salt Lake after going to hundreds of my cousin's weddings. It made the most sense to come to Zion's hometown to have his wedding where his family are.

As soon as we came off the plane, the humidity hit us worse than it was in Palm Springs. We were greeted by Zion's large family and Austin and Marley who flew out a week before. Mrs Hacks is still not open to the idea of Austin's new life, but their dad has shown up. We spent the first day after we got on our feet with Wren's dad in the bar below the hotel we're staying at. Every time we meet with him, he's got a new story to tell us about baby Wren and it makes me heart implode.

"I'm mostly excited for the food," I sigh. Wren turns around, her light green eyes boring into mine. "Do you know how long the service is going to take?"

"I hope you're joking. This is a very special and romantic day," she protests.

"I know but can't it be special and romantic *and* short?"

*

The ceremony is special and it's overly romantic, but it is not short. Wren had to stand in her light blue maid of honour dress at the front of the wedding isle in the patch of green grass at the wedding venue. I had to sit in the line of chairs in the blistering sunlight as we waited for more guests to arrive.

We exchanged private moments between us as we couldn't speak while Wren and the other bridesmaids waited for the ceremony to begin. Even when Austin came down the aisle in a luminous white wedding dress, all I could focus on was Wren, beaming, with fresh happy tears welling up in her eyes. Even when Marley started crying on Zion's mom's knee, I still couldn't tear my eyes away from her. Being here in the sun, her freckles have appeared on her face and down her arms. It felt like we were out there for hours as the wedding ceremony moved on around us, our eyes locked most of the time.

When we finally get out of the heat, we're entered into a large room with the AC on – *thank God* – where all the food and drinks are served. Jamaican food is absolutely insane. I could live here for the rest of my life.

I follow Wren around like a lost puppy, holding her bag as she greets all of Zion's family and some of her family too. She gives an emotional and funny maid of honour speech which has almost the entire room in tears. I keep my hands on her most of the night. When Zion and Austin have their first dance to *'Is This Love'* by Bob Marley, we dance from a distance, her head resting on my shoulder as I rest my hand on her hip, swaying us to the music.

"They look so happy," Wren whispers into me. I brush her shoulder with my hand reassuringly before she starts to cry for the hundredth time today.

"They do. But for the love of God, stop crying."

"I can't help it," she sobs into me. *This woman.* I rub circles on her back and change the subject.

"I like that they have a song just for them. Do we have one?"

She looks up at me as if I offended her. I can't help but laugh at her sudden change of expression from sadness to near anger as she sniffles.

"Of course, we have a song, Miles, and you know which one it is," she says matter-of-factly. I shrug, trying to rack my brain for an answer. "Do you think I'd be still dating you if we didn't have a song?"

"I'll try not to take that personally," I murmur, and she pushes me in the shoulder.

"Come on."

She pulls at my arm as she starts to walk through the crowds of people in the room and leads us through the door. She drags us down the corridor of this fancy hotel until we get to a dark corridor, where the lights only turn on the further, we walk down. She looks into some of the rooms as if she knows her way around perfectly. When we get to the end of the corridor, she jingles the door handle to the right and opens the door which lead to a flight of stairs.

"Where are we going?" I ask as she starts to sprint up the stairs.

"I know a shortcut," she pants, her ass swaying in my face.

"How? We've literally been here a week." She ignores this with a laugh until we reach the top of the first flight of stairs to another door which she opens with ease. We're in darkness for a few beats before a light turns on and we're somehow back into our suite.

"How?" I ask breathlessly as I cross the bedroom into the open living room and kitchen area, looking back to the door where we came out of.

"I have my ways," she shrugs, looking through her bag from under the couch. She pulls out her speaker and holds down the button to connect it to her phone.

"You're insane," I say, walking over to her. Her blonde hair that she curled especially for today falls down across her face and I brush out a strand from her eyes before pulling her further into me. She blinks up at me smiling as if we're the only people in the world.

"I know," she says cheerfully as she sets the speaker on the kitchen island. "Come and help me move this out of the way." We take a while to move the couch out of the way along with the few chairs that scatter the room and the coffee table until there's a large space in the middle only holding the carpet. Now we're both sweatier than ever in the heat as I huff and stare at her. She has a daring look on her face as she grabs her phone from the kitchen before returning to stand in front of me.

"You can have one guess to what our song is," she demands, her green eyes staring up at me, as she tugs on my tie and pulls me into her.

"I'm guessing it's a Taylor Swift song based on your excitement." She nods waving her phone between us suggestively. "I don't know, Wren. I'm sorry."

"Don't be sorry. Just be grateful you have a super cool girlfriend with impeccable music taste," she says with a flourish, as she hits play to the song she's chosen. My heart expands as soon as the instrumental begins and the moment that she played this to me for the first time hits me. "See."

She throws her phone on the couch as she snakes her hands around my neck as the first verse to *'You Are in Love'* by Taylor Swift plays over the speakers. I wrap my arms around her waist as she brings her body closer to mine and we fit together perfectly.

"Do you remember what happened when I played this for you?" she asks as she sinks into my chest, her arms falling loose around my neck.

"I was driving us back from the gym and you insisted on putting a song on. You put this on, and I said it was good, but it felt like you were trying to subconsciously convince me to fall in love with you. Like you were trying to manifest it or something. You then told me that that's never going to happen, but you thought it was one of the best love songs," I explain, as we sway back and forth to the music.

509

"And then what happened?" She starts to laugh into me, knowing what I'm going to say. I press a kiss to her head, and I chuckle into her.

"Then *you* fell in love with me."

"I did," she laughs softly before breaking away from me to look up at me. "I really did and hard too."

We stay close to each other as the song plays on a loop, letting the words settle around us. *You can hear it in the silence. You can feel it on the way home. You can see it with the lights out. You are in love. True love.*

That's exactly what it feels like being so desperately in love with Wren. I can feel her everywhere. It feels like no matter where I go, where we are, there's always something tying us together. There's always that true, consuming kind of love that lingers between us whenever we're around each other. If a pink heart was a person, it would be Wren. She makes me so happy that it almost makes me queasy when I think about it too much. I don't get time to think before her phone starts to ring through the speakers. She groans into my chest as we waddle towards the phone, her arms tightly around my waist, not baring to look at it.

"It's Scarlett," I say when I catch a glimpse of her phone. She groans even louder. "Maybe something's wrong. You should answer it."

"Fine," she moans pulling out of my grasp to answer the FaceTime. She falls into the couch which is now at the far end of our suite, and I sit next to her, sweeping her into my lap. The phone lights up with a puffy faced Scarlett as her phone balances on the kitchen island of their apartment while she stands across from it, leaning against the sink with her arms crossed.

"Hi, Scar, what's up?" Wren asks, smiling into the camera. I lean my face into the frame and wave. Scarlett rolls her eyes at me. We've developed a very strong love-hate relationship which I don't mind. Wren has been trying to convince me that she doesn't actually hate me but it's hard to know sometimes.

"Hi," she says sharply. "I have a question to ask."

"Shoot," Wren replies, pushing her hair out of her face.

I notice her necklace in the camera screen and the clasp has fallen to the front. I move my hands gently over her and pull it around the right way. She presses a kiss to my cheek as a thank you before turning her attention to Scarlett.

"You guys are disgusting," Scarlett huffs. "Anyway, have you seen The Whiteboard anywhere? I don't know how I can't find it. I only have the one that I use for school not *our* one."

"How could you lose The Whiteboard? It's huge," Wren replies, and Scarlett shakes her head with a short laugh. "I haven't seen it in a while. Our lives have been pretty put together recently so we haven't needed it."

She's right. Since we finished our exams, we settled into a comfortable rhythm with our friends where we can actually get work done as well as hanging out. Kennedy is always working on a new project for class and giving us free drinks from Florentino's. Xavier and I have been training like crazy and going on double dates with Michelle and Wren. Evan and Scarlett are still constantly arguing about whatever assignments they need to do for business class, finding new ways to insult each other. Wren is working the hardest out of all of us; still working on her writing and skating while trying to juggle the relationship with her mom.

"Huh," Scarlett says disbelievingly. "What about you, Miles? Have you seen it? At your house, perhaps."

"Uh, no... Why would it be at my house?" I ask with a sceptical look. Wren looks up at me and widens her eyes and I realise what she meant. She probably thinks Evan has taken it. Typical. "Have you asked, Ken?"

"No, Miles, I haven't asked the one person currently living with me right now," she retorts sarcastically. "I have a feeling someone has taken it, but they won't own up to it."

Something catches her eye above the screen as she glares as if she's talking to someone indirectly. Wren and I give each other a suspicious look before we turn back to Scarlett whose face has suddenly turned a deep red colour. I can't tell if she's blushing or if she's pissed.

"What? Do you think Evan took it?" Wren asks. Scarlett waits a beat before turning her attention back to the screen.

"I know he took it," she bites out.

"Scar..." Wren says slowly. "Please don't tell me he's with you right now and you're holding him hostage."

"I'm not holding him hostage," Scarlett says rolling her eyes. "I asked him to come over and he was stupid enough to agree."

She slowly pans the camera around to face the other way and that's when we both see him. Evan is sat in a dark blue suit in their apartment with his arms crossed against his chest. He doesn't look like he's being held hostage. He looks too comfortable. Like he's enjoying it. He smiles at the camera before blowing air up to push his blonde hair out of his face.

"Hey, guys. I hope you're having a good time," Evan begins with a smile. "Jamaica is beautiful. I've been a few times-"

"Shut up," Scarlett demands, pulling the phone around to face her again but this time she holds it closer to her face.

"Scarlett, you're insane," Wren says, laughing. I can't help but laugh too at the fact that she seems so used to this. As if this is a completely normal Scarlett thing to do.

"Whatever. I need to get it back, like, now." She pulls the phone closer to her face so we can straight into her green eyes as she lowers her voice. "I'm having a crisis, Wren."

"I'm sorry, Scar. I'm sure Kennedy can help you out. I'm coming home in a few days; can you hang on until then?" Wren asks, scrunching her nose up. Scarlett opens her mouth about to speak but Evan butts in.

"What's the crisis?" Evan asks loudly. "I'll help."

"I would rather gauge my eyes out than ask you for help," Scarlett replies with a disgusted glare, shuddering, before ending the call.

THE END.

1. nobody can know this is fake
   ↳ only 2 survive + Ken!!

2. family?? ← to be determined
   ↳ dad is going to freak!

3. appropriate displays of affection in private only? bruh...
   ← anti-PDA zone

4. PDA only when necessary

5. go out twice a week and always leave
   (Jarod) → sleepovers ts

ACKNOWLEDGEMENTS

First things first, thank you, reader, for choosing this book and allowing me to take you on this journey. Thank you for allowing Wren and Miles' story into your heart and I hope you can take something away from this. Whether that be how in love I am with the idea of love, or it be the lessons learned by the characters.

Thank you to every single person who pushed me on this book and let me know that it was okay to write while I had other priorities. This is only my second novel and I know there is still a lot of work to be done for future projects, but I am so thankful that I have had the time and space to let my creativity flow.

The idea for this series was simple: write a three-part book series, centering around three best friends, based off me and my friends. At first, I thought this idea was stupid, something that could be written a million different ways but the second I thought of a decent plot line, it all came to me.

Maybe it was an ego thing, or maybe it was complete self-awareness, but I realised that my friends and I are pretty funny. We're funny in the way that we'll make a quick snide comment and get everyone in hysterics, laughing until our stomach hurts. But we're also funny in the way that is absolutely appalling to others – meaning we'll make a terrible with the complete lack of awareness of how bad it is until nobody laughs. Then, once the silence washes of us, everyone is laughing.

Over the past seven years, I've grown a lot with the same friends that I have now. We've been through many phases, and we've turned into the successfully immature women we are today. We might not take a lot of things seriously but that is kind of what inspired this book. After writing my first novel, I wanted something else. Something that I could hold on to and say 'Look, I made this.' This book gave me the opportunity to reflect reality in a different way. It gave me the chance to pull apart parts of my friends' personalities and weave them into the characters that I create in a similar way to how we act in real life. This is truly, a silly little book because life is silly sometimes.

My first book was derived from parts of myself but not to the full extent. Writing as a seventeen-year-old about a twenty-seven-year-old was hard. Writing about Jasmine's life felt out of reach. Only just tangible. But writing this book and planning my other two, I have been able to strive for something achievable and realistic. Okay, maybe I won't be able to fall in love with a hockey player but something close to it.

This book is for the 'this is me trying' girlies especially. As you read through these pages, I hope you take something from Wren and Miles as it serves as a subtle reminder to take a break and know your limits.

BOOKS IN THIS SERIES
NORTH UNIVERSITY SERIES

In this steamy, heartwarming and hilarious series, three college students navigate the truths of what their future careers may hold and the love and hate that comes along with it.

The series is set in Salt Lake City, Utah and the first novel focalises on Wren Hackerly, star figure skater at North University in her fake dating plot with hockey team captain Miles Davis. Wren has always been independent and she sticks to a strict routine. There is no way in hell that she'd change that. Especially not for a man. But when fake dating Miles becomes her only hope at staying on the team and keeping Miles off the bench, she can convince herself that it's all for a good cause. Right?

In the electrifying sequel, readers follow fashion and business student Scarlett Voss in a mission to uncover the truths of her family but when Rich Boy of the Year Evan Branson can't keep his nose out of her business and the two are paired up for an end of year project, can the they put their family feud and general hatred for each other to the side while compete for a grade? Scarlett might get under his skin but can he keep his feelings at bay when she opens up to him about her family's history or will he blow his cover of knowing more than he lets on?

Kennedy Wynter, an eccentric socialite and artist, has been hit with the worst creators block of her life before her final year at North University. She makes the decision to go back to her home town of South Carolina in hopes of the familiar town to leading her to creative release. Not only is she reunited with her family, she also has to confront some of her demons: one of them being a gorgeous six-four surfer named Luca who broke her heart. With their families so close together, there is no way she'll be able to avoid him all summer so she does the best thing she can think of and instead invites him on the trips she takes around the town to spark up inspiration. If she's going to bump into him, she might as well make it purposeful, right? But as they spend more time together in sweltering summer heat and it starts to feel exactly how it used to be, inspiration isn't the only reason why sparks flying between the pair.

<u>Fake Dates & Ice Skates</u>

STAY IN TOUCH!

Instagram - @janboswellauthor
Tiktok - @janboswellauthor
Sign up to my email list to be the first to hear about
bookish news -
https://substack.com/profile/99039411-janisha-
boswell?utm_source=substack_profile

Printed in Great Britain
by Amazon